VOICES OF THE

Xiled

VOICES OF THE

Xiled

a generation speaks
for itself

edited by Michael Wexler and John Hulme

A Main Street Book
New York   London   Toronto   Sydney   Auckland

A Main Street Book
PUBLISHED BY DOUBLEDAY
a division of Bantam Doubleday Dell Publishing Group, Inc.
1540 Broadway, New York, New York 10036

Main Street Books, Doubleday, and the portrayal of a building with a
tree are trademarks of Doubleday, a division of
Bantam Doubleday Dell Publishing Group, Inc.

Book design by Gretchen Achilles

Library of Congress Cataloging-in-Publication Data

Voices of the xiled : a generation speaks for itself / edited by
    Michael Wexler and John Hulme. — 1st ed.
        p.   cm.
    ''A Main Street book.''
    1. Young adults—United States—Fiction.   2. American fiction—20th
century.   3. Short stories, American.   4. Generation X—Fiction.
I. Wexler, Michael.   II. Hulme, John, 1970-
PS648.Y48V65   1994
813'.0108054—dc20   94-19672
                                                            CIP

ISBN 0-385-47449-0

3   5   7   9   10   8   6   4

CONTENTS

Contents

INTRODUCTION

A few months ago it became clear to us that we weren't connecting with any of the images that the new, self-appointed
"twentysomething" authorities had been creating. We're not in
Seattle, not in the corporate world, not "slackers," not going to
law school, not skiing in Colorado, not anything specific. It's dis-
concerting when you realize that Douglas Coupland's *Generation
X* has no connection to your life, *13th Gen* was written by two guys
in their forties, and all the movies and TV shows about people our
age are just soap operas in disguise.

One night we began thinking: Does anyone out there identify
with all this crap or is it just us who can't seem to get it? Well,
maybe they weren't being honest, but after a pretty thorough
search we couldn't find five souls who actually related to any of it.
And it's not just the writers, artists, and cynics of the world who
are still looking for an articulation of their voice. It's Bob Marcus,
the consultant; Bryan Largay, selling marine supplies over the
phone in Santa Cruz; Emily Muschinske, at school in New Jersey;
Steve Chudnick, living at home and supposedly working at a
rental-car place; Matt Ryen, at law school in D.C.; and Rob
Schwartz, the production assistant in L.A.

Anyway, it doesn't take a genius to figure out the problem:
None of the people we're talking about has ever had his or her
own public voice. In fact, this generation hasn't had a chance to
say anything at all. We just sit back and watch various critics try
their hands at explaining to us who we are and why. Everybody

and his brother are experts on the subject, but nobody has bothered to ask the people in question what they're all about.

After looking high and low for some mainstream voice that even closely approximated what we were thinking, after looking for any expression of a world that even resembled the one we or anyone we knew lived in, we decided: Fuck it, we'd write our own book. This flash of brilliance lasted about two days. While we wanted to say *something* real (if there is such a thing), we didn't want to deliver yet another enlightened sermon on the enigmatic nature of young folk. We're all sick of labels and code names and pop sociology insights about this "mysterious" group of "twentysomethings."

So we took the flip side instead. Why not avoid the analysis train and let the people in question speak for themselves? It's really a simple concept: We'd collect the best short stories by up-and-coming writers and allow them to express what's happening in their own lives. Throw the reader right in there with the sharks— no shampoo planet, no bullshit generational handbooks, no stilted sitcom scenarios. Why not let people say what's on their own minds, in their own words. That's what we wanted to hear and people we know wanted to read.

John was heading out to Illinois on an emergency mission to repair things with his girlfriend, so we decided to put a tiny ad in the *Chicago Reader* displaying Mike's home phone number and address in New Jersey; we figured if anyone ever called, John could meet up with them out there. The first day it ran, the ad was next to a blurb from some kid trying to sell his bicycle:

> Attention Young Writers!!! Short Story submissions now being accepted for *Voices of the Xiled*—an anthology documenting the thoughts, experiences, emotions of today's "twentysomething" generation. Unpublished writers welcome and encouraged. Send Manuscripts to *The Outpost*, Highland Park, NJ. Call for more info.

"The Outpost" was really Mike's mother's house. Figuratively, though, it was a gathering point for travelers and ideas, a place for

anyone who had something to express or communicate. One guy who sent in a story from Chicago was a graphics designer and whipped us up a logo for free. Mike told his brother Ari not to answer the phone like an idiot. We were ready.

No one called. Not even John. On the third day, though, the phone rang. By the end of the week forty-two people had phoned. The mail started to roll in. John was ranting on and on about these "incredible" meetings. People he had never seen before were connecting with the idea—clearly they had something to say that had not yet been heard by the culture at large. In ten days, three hundred manuscripts were stacked in Mike's room. The concept was clicking. *Voices of the Xiled* was for real.

When John came home from Chicago, we took our two favorite stories and a few letters, wrapped up the clunky proposal, and shipped it off expectantly to Warren Bratter, an editor John's mother knew. He loved the idea, and although he was fifty, Warren really had a feel for what we were trying to do. Unfortunately, his company published only educational books in foreign languages and in foreign countries. Nonetheless, he joined the project.

About two weeks later Mike came home from work and found a letter from one of the publishers Warren had contacted. It looked thin. Finally, after examining the envelope under a light, he tore it open and read the news: They wanted to see the four chapters we had sketched out in the proposal.

We had manuscripts but they were all from the same area, and many overlapped in theme. How could we get an accurate national cross section of what people were thinking and writing? Frantically, the search began. We posted flyers in bookstores and coffee shops, nailed placards onto bulletin boards, and filled newspaper dispensers on the street with our flyers. We contacted grad schools, talked to literary journals, called up old friends from English classes. Ads (bought with credit cards) went out in *The Village Voice, The Madison Isthmus, The Louisiana Gambit,* and *The San Francisco Bay Guardian.*

People started calling in from all over—not only for information but just to touch base and voice their encouragement for the project. Three of these callers offered to help out in Chicago, San Francisco, and Iowa. They were volunteering to collect stories and represent *Voices* in their respective areas of the country. The word was beginning to spread.

One day the mailman appeared at Mike's door with about forty manuscripts. Austin, Texas; Burlington, Vermont; New York; Michigan; Canada. How did someone from Canada get wind of this? We opened the package and read the cover letter. This one explained that the sender, Ron Krakower, had heard about our project from Marty Friedman in Washington D.C., and that Marty sends his regards and best wishes. Neither of us had any idea who Marty Friedman was.

The project had taken on a life well beyond the classified ads and had somehow found its way onto the word-of-mouth network. Not only were people sending in their own work, but they were actually recommending the idea to friends. To this day, we have no idea how half of these submissions found their way to our door. Everyone was represented, from award-winning writers to office temps, from investment bankers to fishermen to guys who worked in video stores (a category of its own). From experienced, published authors to first-time writers who had "been waiting for something like this" as a place to send their tentative and often fascinating creations. We lived on the phone, talking to writers all over the map; people from every social scene and every imaginable background and place.

The submissions process had become both overwhelming and inspiring. Three thousand envelopes filled Mike's basement, each containing not only stories but detailed, often personal letters addressed to the *"Voices* Editor"—little pieces of various lives and experiences sealed up in paper bags.

One weekend we went out to Warren Bratter's place on Long Island, sifted through the manuscripts, and began narrowing the field. We had no real credentials save our membership in the generation at hand and a desire to let people speak for themselves. First, we relied on instinct, choosing stories and themes that clicked in some intangible way. As the process evolved, however, we found ourselves falling into the trap we sought to avoid, self-selecting yet another analysis of the generation. In choosing the stories by instinct, we were expressing *our* agenda, failing to present accurate, unbiased voices, failing to avoid the hypocritical generalizations that *Voices* was a reaction against.

Everything went back in the pile and the process started from scratch. The second time through certain recurring themes began to present themselves. Searches for identity, disillusionment, altered states of consciousness, instability, and life on the road emerged over and over again. Balancing these themes, then, became a part of the decision-making process, providing all the numerous voices more accurate representation.

In effect, all the stories, included or not, became instrumental in establishing the direction of the text. From three thousand entrants to twenty finalists, the whole project and all its ups, downs, moments, and incarnations eventually filtered down to one manila folder.

We had our collection. Unfortunately, though, no one wanted it. Publishers and agents had all passed—"Personally, I really think you're on to something but it's just not right for us." Mike's brother suggested scrapping the original idea and assembling a collection of rejection letters instead. We even got a no thanks from an editor who didn't exist. We called her up to ask why, but it turned out Lucille Schulman was a phantom, a made-up name of an editor who chose to blow us off altogether.

We'd given up on the normal channels and were preparing to publish it ourselves through one of Warren's connections in Costa Rica. The plan was to print it cheap, import back into the States, load up the car with copies, and drive cross-country trying to sell it ourselves. It sounded like a decent idea.

In the end, though, we managed to publish *Voices* in the more conventional form in which you're reading it. After nearly a year of limbo we could finally notify the writers who'd submitted. The rejections were hard, having been rejected all the way through ourselves. But calling the accepted contributors was a worthwhile reward—a host of conversations blending excitement and disbelief.

One of the great ironies of the whole experience is that neither of our own stories made it into the book. We submitted them under pseudonyms and both cut each other's unintentionally. In a way, though, it makes sense. *Voices of the Xiled* was never about two guys appointing themselves spokesmen for a generation. As we said before, it's just some young people and what's happening in their worlds.

—Michael Wexler and John Hulme
October 5, 1993
Highland Park, New Jersey

VOICES OF THE

Xiled

Mr. Wexler,
Fred Leebron told me awhile ago
that you were looking for work for
an "outside" anthology. We've just
moved and everything is very
mixed up here. Are you still
interested in seeing some of my
work for your anthology? What
is this anthology to be like?
Let me know at the below
address.
George Angel

Santa Cruz CA

From Miller, *Famous Ocean Liners Photo Postcards*, a Dover publication

Mike Wexler
c/o The Outpost

Highland Park NJ

The *Homeric*. British-American, White Star Line, built
1922. © 1988 by William H. Miller, Jr.

Thanks,

Mitch Berman

Mitch Berman is the author of the novel *Time Capsule* (G. P. Putnam's Sons). His work has appeared in *The Antioch Review*, *Omni*, *The Nation*, the *Los Angeles Times Magazine*, *Boulevard*, *The Gettysburg Review*, and *The Village Voice*. Based on what he has seen living in New York for the past fourteen years, he can now confidently predict that the city will soon become a vast squatters' settlement, with cardboard shacks choking the streets, suspicious-looking meats being roasted on wire hangers over open fires, subsistence farmers keeping armed guard over patches of tiny green tomatoes in Central Park, weeds cracking through the broad sidewalks of Fifth Avenue, and bands of children heaving these chunks of cement through the lifeless windows of Sony Plaza and Trump Tower.

In Portland, Oregon, where it doesn't rain several dozen days a year, people know the odds and leave their windshield wipers on when they park their cars, and deep puddles rarely form on streets planned and planed for wetness, and the rain, as if in deference to engineering and expectation, never falls in sheets and torrents, but takes the form of a constant drizzle barely thicker than a mist, a drizzle that, falling through the air, pastelizes the colors of the buildings, and that, having fallen, grays out and darkens those colors; in Portland, landlocked Portland, connected by a river to the sky, a very thin young man with an electric guitar in a hard-shell case walked in the gutter of Yamhill Street to even out his height advantage over the young woman beside him.

A voice so high it was more a whistle than a voice came faintly through the drizzle: "Bass-tarss!"

Billy and Melissa turned the corner and the source of the

sound opened up to them: three bald male figures, one of them with an arm extended toward an old black man who was falling away from the arm, toppling lock-kneed as stiffly as a Douglas fir. The upturned hand of the old black man, falling, and the down-turned hand of the young white man, felling him, were almost touching, suspended in a release that seemed a caress or a caress that seemed a release, each lingering on the moment of contact before giving the other back to the other's world.

It was a long block, and sight and sound were very slightly out of sync: Billy and Melissa saw the old man fall against a metal trash can a split second before they heard the clatter, saw him open his mouth, like a clown in a silent movie, before his voice rang out thinly: ". . . young . . . bastards!"

"Skinheads," said Melissa. Bottom-heavy in spit-polished military boots and baggy camouflage pants, they wore khaki jackets with swastika shoulder patches. One had WHITE & PROUD stenciled across his back like the name of an athletic team.

"Watch the Strat?" said Billy, setting the guitar case at Melissa's feet.

To Melissa, who had never lost the thick-limbed, bowlegged swagger of the child athlete, Billy had always looked twiggish, kite-like; but now, as he ran away from her toward the skinheads, toward the unknown, toward the future, his orange nylon shell flew open, and the slivers of his legs beneath it seemed no more substantial than a butterfly's body between its giant wings, tiny, careening, willy-nilly, buffeted by chance. Billy's shout came back at her inarticulately down the long block.

The white and proud skinhead was kneeling before the old man, who was on his hands and knees and whose long jaw, lengthened by a scraggly white beard, opened longer. The youth tilted his stubbly head and parted his lips as if to give the old man a kiss or a bite on the face.

Melissa saw Billy grab the skinhead's collar from behind and yank him backward, heard herself murmur Billy's name, and heard in her murmur a warning, inaudible as all such warnings always are; heard in her own voice, it seemed to her later, a voice that was not her voice and an awareness of all that would happen next.

The skinhead, seated on the sidewalk where Billy had pulled him, drawled in a tone that did not seem entirely unfriendly, "You don't know what side you're on." He embraced Billy's legs, and Billy folded down.

Melissa got herself in the middle without knowing how. A fist among all those fists caught her on the jaw, and she staggered under the impact of the punch and of the fact that it was the first time since her tomboy days that anyone had punched her, and when, in the months to come, she would remember what happened next, she would remember that it had happened at a great distance from the place where she stood, too much in shock even to rub her jaw: at that distance, an old man crabbed off sideways on all fours and a young man she knew was standing up, waving his arms to fend off blows from three others, then falling, falling slowly, his arms moving closer to him until they covered his head, until he was down and rolling, until he stopped rolling and there were boots, only boots now, that kicked him. The asphalt heaved up against Billy's chest; the asphalt, which had been expecting rain, drank down Billy's tears. He could not remember the last time physical pain had made him cry.

Melissa found herself at a phone booth saying "Ambulance" until a voice answered, "ambulance" when asked what service she needed, "ambulance" when asked where she was. The ambulance that swept up silently—there wasn't enough traffic to need a siren —to the phone booth on Fifth Street and Yamhill was running its wipers.

"Poor kid," said a paramedic.

"No," said Melissa, because it was what she could say.

"Lay down," urged the paramedic, bearing down on her shoulders with his hands. "Your eggs are a little scrambled, that's all. Everything's gonna be all right."

Melissa lay on the stretcher, and the stretcher started moving across the rain-darkened concrete, and there was a bump, and the ambulance started moving across the rain-darkened asphalt. She ran two fingers over the guitar case that lay beside her, leaving tire tracks on its wet black pebbled skin. She wished she could throw it into reverse, reel it all back, back past the ambulance and the voice in the phone, past the old man and the skinheads, past the run and past the rain; she wished the band had played another encore and she had closed up the club a few minutes later. She'd kept Billy's guitar for him. Melissa sat up and said, *"It isn't me!"*

Melissa was treated for cuts and bruises and discharged from James G. Blaine Memorial Hospital after a night of observation. Billy remained in a coma for the rest of that weekend and the entire month of April. Prisoners and municipal employees X'd days off their calendars, praying for vacation or release; Melissa sat beside Billy's bed in a molded purple plastic chair and read to him until she grew inured to Muzak and cherry-scented antiseptic; nurses took Billy's pulse on day shift, night shift, graveyard shift; Billy's mother appeared, asked her son a battery of questions, then rehearsed, over his inert form, her farewell speech to Billy's father, which speech treated in some detail her twin discoveries of yeast sensitivity and crystal technology, as well as certain imperfections in her relationship with Billy's father, among them the lack of "normal sex" for six years and three months, and she summed up these imperfections with the Japanese word *wabi,* explaining that in Zen Buddhism the key to understanding life's true perfection lay in such apparent imperfections, in such *wabi,* and after saying all this, Billy's mother came no more; Billy's father, struggling with several mighty confusions that the delivery by Billy's mother of her farewell speech did nothing to alleviate, did not come at all; the coarse red hair on Billy's head, oblivious to mother and father and even to the life or death of Billy himself, continued growing out from a crew cut, and in growing, simply and without comment, marked the passage of time, the way a metronome will click indifferently for music or for mayhem; technicians dollied in an electroencephalograph and razored patches out of Billy's hair and fixed electrodes to his glossy bluish scalp and tweaked his pale facial skin to make the stylus twitch and jag across tractor-fed computer paper, and the skin stayed pink long after the technicians had gone; Melissa put headphones over Billy's ears and played him tapes of Hendrix and Santana; Billy began to dream, and the doctors wrote REMS on the chart that hung at the foot of his bed, wrote it without knowing whether Billy was dreaming of rain or shine, whether he was hearing Hendrix or Muzak or nothing at all, whether his windshield wipers were on or off; and an intravenous unit dispensed clear foodstuff into Billy's bloodstream, dripped, and dripped, and dripped, like a metronome, like a rain.

Melissa was getting to the end of *Alice's Adventures in Wonderland* when Billy interrupted her. "What did you say?" he asked, quite distinctly.

"Billy?" Melissa leaned over him and took his hand.

"Yes?" Billy frowned, his eyes still closed. "What did you say?"

"When I was reading to you?"

"No," Billy said slowly. "Before that. You said, 'Skinheads.' You were afraid. But I want to tell you something." His eyes came open, resting on Melissa. "Don't worry. They're cowards." He closed his eyes again. "That was what I wanted to tell you."

When Billy awoke Melissa discovered that he did not know her name. The doctors shined lights in Billy's eyes, CAT-scanned and EEG'd him and beat on his joints with red rubber hammers, and wrote on the chart, "Organic damage to L hemisphere. Aphasia & amnesia, mod.–severe—prognosis unclear. Reflexes & sensorium intact."

Billy's father, of whom Melissa had heard only rumor, carried insurance that paid for Billy's private room. Each morning he sent a floral arrangement so perfect it did not look real. The handwriting on the florist's card was not a man's.

Melissa tried to teach Billy the difference between gladioli, chrysanthemums, and daffodils. When Billy called them "those plants," Melissa bought him *The Little Golden Book of Flowers*. Billy had not forgotten how to read, but he stopped every few lines to jab a word with his thumb.

Melissa would lean in beside him and say, "Sound it out."

A psychologist gave Billy the Minnesota Multiphasic Personality Inventory and Sternberg's Memory-Scanning Procedure and told him, "Your *retrograde* amnesia is wearing off—you'll begin to recall more and more from before the accident—but your *anterograde* amnesia will make it hard to retain anything that happens from now on. So I'm going to ask you to write down everything that happens to you. Will you do that for me?"

"Yes," said Billy.

"Otherwise," the psychologist said with a grin, "you might forget where you parked your car."

"Do I have a car?" said Billy.

Billy would sit erect, the back of his bed cranked as far forward as it would go, playing on his unamplified Stratocaster solos that wandered from song to song, key to key, era to era; solos that climbed toward crescendos only to find their ladders pulled out from under them, solos like stories written in disappearing ink, solos like columns of figures that did not add up but that continued adding, adding. Sitting so straight, with some of his hair still spiky and some of it starting to lie down over the shaven patches, Billy looked wet and quizzical, like a newborn chick.

Each afternoon he was wheelchaired upstairs to play with blocks and walk up and back between two rails that looked like a gymnastic apparatus. Every evening, before her shift at the club, Melissa spoiled Billy's appetite for the hospital dinner with smuggled foods: most, like raisins and pistachios, Billy could now recognize immediately; some he still seemed to taste for the first time.

A Hershey's bar made him close his eyes and frown slightly as he ate.

"This one is my favorite," he announced, as he had several times before. "What's it called?"

"Sound it out," Melissa told him.

"Choc-o-late." He said it with a long *a*.

Billy logged every new flavor, every new idea, every doctor, nurse, and visitor in red, yellow, and blue five-by-eight spiral note-pads, each of which he'd titled BILLY'S BRAIN. For Melissa, guiding him through his discoveries was something like raising an outsized child. It had occurred to her—first as an abstraction, then colorized by altruistic overtones, and finally with plain desire—that whatever Billy's experience with women before the injury, he had now recovered his virginity. She liked to wipe him down with a wet washcloth and smell his skin.

Billy's father came after dinner on the eve of Billy's release from Blaine Memorial. He stood beside the bed in high-heeled pumps, a long floral cotton dress, and subdued quantities of lipstick, eye shadow, and blush. Billy's father had breasts.

"Dad?" said Billy.

"I realize this comes as a shock," said Billy's father in the same deep, assured voice-over voice that used to say, "Customer Service," when Billy had telephoned the Oregon Mutual Savings Bank, the same voice that had always called Billy "son" and Billy's mother "your mother," the same voice that had, long before, explained sex to Billy in clinical and terrifying detail.

"Where's Mom?" Billy asked.

"Your mother's gone to Idaho," Billy's father told him. "She left me and went to Idaho."

Billy reached to the nightstand for his blue notepad and set it on the tongue-shaped table that had been wheeled over his midsection for dinner. "Mom's in . . ." he murmured as he wrote.

"I-D-A-H-O," said his father.

Billy looked up. "That's bad."

"Your mother wouldn't say so." Billy's father half smiled. "Your mother would call it *wabi*. May I sit down?"

"Uh-huh." Billy's face was in his notepad.

"Thank you, son," said his father, pulling up the purple chair. "Isn't your girlfriend here tonight?"

"Melissa," said Billy. Marking his place with a thumb, he flipped pages until he came to the heading M, and ran his finger down the side. "Melissa," he said again.

"Melissa," his father agreed.

"What day is it?" Billy asked.

"Wednesday," said his father.

"Every night except Monday," Billy read slowly, "Melissa works at Club 666, where they have live rock music and serve alco —alcoholic bev—bever—"

"Beverages," said his father.

"You've been there?" Billy asked.

"Billy . . ." said his father. "I would have come sooner, but I had to go to Colorado for the operation. And afterward I didn't want to upset you with the way I look. How are you feeling?"

"I'm not sure," said Billy. "They say my memory is messed up, but I can't tell—I can't remember anything to compare it with."

"I wish somebody would wipe out *my* memory," Billy's father said quietly. "Then I'd know myself only as a woman."

"That's how *I* look at you," said Billy.

Billy's father rose halfway out of his chair and kissed Billy on the cheek and forehead. "Thank you. God! Thank you for that." He was clenching Billy so tightly that the bed creaked with his sobs.

"You're crying, Dad," said Billy.

"That's nothing new for me," said his father, subsiding into the chair and dabbing at his eyes with the napkin from Billy's dinner. "I just used to hide it from you."

"Your chest feels kind of funny," Billy said.

"Saline implants," said Billy's father. "They make an incision beneath the armpit"—he traced it with a French-manicured fingernail—"and then they slip a kind of water balloon into the subcutaneous envelope over the pectoralis muscle."

Billy was looking at the remains of his dinner, the picture that fluttered silently across the television screen, the painting of a sad clown on the wall. Finally he reached over to the nightstand and lifted the lid from the box of See's chocolates. "Do you want a—? Would you like one of these?"

"Oh, no thank you, son," said his father.

Billy picked up the remote control and turned the television off. "What about your job?"

"I quit," said his father. "I'm temping."

Billy pushed the heels of his hands against the edge of the table and his fingers groped the air. "What did they—what did they do with—"

"The surgeon didn't cut my penis off," his father said in an equanimous tone, as if describing something that had been done to someone else. "He re-formed the penile tissue into a vaginal tunnel. It's like turning a finger of a glove inside out. I still have sexual sensitivity, though not the reproductive capacity. He also gave me a cervix with an os. I'll be able to fool the gynecologist." He leaned over Billy. "You're taking notes again?"

"I have to." Billy read over what he'd written. "Did it hurt?"

"Not the operation itself," said his father. "I was under a general anesthetic. But I'm still tender."

The sad clown looked at Billy for a while. "When did you get it done?"

"On April twelfth," said his father.

Billy stared back opaquely.

"Today is the ninth of May," said his father.

Billy flipped back a page in his notepad. "What's *wabi?*"

His father took a deep breath and crossed his legs with the soft sigh of panty hose. "According to your mother, the seemingly flawed thing can be perfect—if it has the perfect flaw. *Wabi* is this state of true perfection." He watched the eraser on Billy's pencil doodle figure eights in the air. "Your mother told me a story—"

"A true story?" Billy asked.

"If it's not," said his father, "that would only give the story its own *wabi*. Are you sure you want to write it all down?"

"Yes," said Billy. "Should I put it under W for *wabi* or M for *Mom?*"

"M," said Billy's father.

In capital letters neatly centered on the page, Billy wrote, MOM'S STORY.

"A Japanese nobleman wanted to impress a wise old sage," his father began, "so he went out and purchased the rarest and most beautiful tea service money could buy. He had the sage over for tea, but the sage said nothing about his tea service. The nobleman smashed the expensive tea service to bits and thought no more about it. A ragpicker found the pieces in the nobleman's garbage. Every night, by the light of a candle, he sifted through the fragments and glued the tea service together again. In six weeks the ragpicker was finished, and he invited the sage for tea. After the tea ceremony, the sage told the ragpicker, 'I have seen this tea service before. Only now has it truly attained the quality of *wabi*.' "

Billy stacked the empty dishes in front of him, then unstacked them. "Is that why Mom's gone?"

"I don't know," said Billy's father. "But I was forced to think about a lot of things when your mother left me. I made many decisions in just a few days. Maybe too many."

"Yeah," said Billy.

"Be that as it may," said his father, "there are some decisions you can't go back on. Like one very important decision your mother and I made twenty-three years ago."

"C'mon, Dad." Billy's legs were squirming under the sheet.

"Twenty-three years ago," his father rolled on, "your mother and I decided to have a child. God blessed us with a wonderful baby boy." He seized Billy's hand and began kissing it. "And I *thank* God, because despite everything that happened between your mother and me in the next twenty-three years, and despite all her talk of *wabi*, and despite the fact that she's left me—"

He was sobbing, and Billy cried too, perhaps for his father, perhaps for himself, perhaps because he cried easily now, or perhaps simply because human beings have a tendency to mirror the facial expressions of others near them. A nurse came into the doorway, saw them, and left.

"May I have a tissue?" Billy's father asked.

Billy passed him the box from the nightstand, and his father blew his nose with a resounding honk. Billy remembered that noise, and another, *aSHAsha!*, which was his father's sneeze. It always surprised Billy to stumble across something he remembered.

"I want you to come home and live with me," his father told him. "Your mother kept your room just the way you left it. The house is too big now that she's gone." He watched Billy for a time. "Well?"

"I don't know," said Billy. He had just noticed that his father had left lipstick all over the back of his left hand. Billy didn't want to wipe it off in front of him, and his hand began to tingle, then to itch, then to crawl with itches like a hundred bugs were on it. He couldn't wait for his father to leave the room.

When Melissa came in, Billy was flipping through the pages of his blue notepad. Slowly, reading, he told her, "My father was here to see me."

"I know," said Melissa.

There was a silence, and Billy said into it, "My father is a woman."

"I know," Melissa said again, sitting at the edge of the bed and stroking his forehead. "Dr. Hansen told me about him."

"Her," Billy corrected. "Because, y'know, any man with a vagina and breasts out to here *deserves* to be called a woman."

Melissa smiled. "That's true."

"My father is my mother," said Billy.

It was raining, but the drops were so fine that from across the room Billy and Melissa could not hear them hit the window, could not even see them, knew it was raining only because the mist beaded up occasionally and ran down the glass. In most places rain is an event, noticed and remarked, but in Portland it is, like time or gravity, a thing assumed. Time and gravity and rain cut canyons in the earth, change the shape of a mountain as easily as a thumb smudges a newspaper's text. They are the agencies of erosion, and their operation is as gradual, as inevitable, as gentle and as brutal as forgetting.

"You know something?" said Billy. "If I want to know what happened to me, I have to pick up my notes and *read* about it." Billy closed his notepad. "At the end of the day, I feel like I haven't done anything."

Melissa arose, drew the gauzy curtains around the bed, came inside them, and kissed Billy on the lips. Billy raised neither a protest nor a hand of assistance as Melissa stripped the bedding and hospital gown from him, stepped out of her Levi's and her underpants: passive and pliable, he simply allowed her to do as she wished. He knew she meant him no harm.

Billy told Melissa his dream: "I'm swimming in salt water, warm and pale and so clear I can see all the way to the bottom. Something's shiny down there, so I dive, and the water presses in on my face, cooler and cooler. It's coins, ancient gold coins, each one with a different face that I know from long ago. If I can take them with me I'll never forget anything again.

"I grab two handfuls of coins and push off from the bottom, but now I'm losing my breath and I can't swim with my hands full, and I start sinking down.

"So I have to let go, and the gold coins drift back across my face and I start to rise through the water. I'm deeper than I thought. I don't know if I'll reach the air before I drown, but I can see a light spilling across the surface, and it gets smaller and stronger as I rise. It's the sun, brighter than any coin."

He took Melissa's hand, pressed it between his chin and collarbone, and forgot about it. "The ocean will always be there," Billy said. "I can always go back down and touch anything I want, I can know it, I can have it. I just can't keep it."

He reached for the buzzer.

After a minute the nurse's voice came from the intercom. "Yes, Billy?"

"Is it too late to get some ice cream?" Billy asked.

The nurse laughed. "What flavor do you want?"

Billy asked Melissa, "What's that one I like?"

E. J. Graff

"I've wanted to be a writer since I was eight. But until I went to an artists' colony, Yaddo, and spent a month among fiction writers, I wrote only poetry. Listening to their nightly talks, I began to see that plot and character helped tackle moral questions—my obsession. So I set out to write a story that looked at a basic female moral dilemma: making a choice, taking control of your own life, and accepting the consequences.

"I grew up an outsider—Jewish, bookish, queer—in Beavercreek, Ohio, and fled east as soon as I could. Now I live in greater Boston with my lover/partner, another Ohio expatriate I met here. My essays and stories are in publications ranging from *The New York Times Magazine* to *The Kenyon Review;* I stay afloat writing marketing for firms with a social and environmental heart."

"Like a Normal Human Being" was initially published in *Iowa Review.*

LIKE A NORMAL HUMAN BEING

Friday afternoon I'm lying on the open sofabed flipping through *National Geographic,* looking at the exotic snakes of India—the hooded Indian python, the king cobra, with diagrams of their bizarre insides—one lung way up here, another down there, all their organs squeezed and twisted to fit in.

Ed's pickup just pulled out of the driveway—he's on his way to the evening shift at the video store, so he's gone till at least ten-thirty. And my mind is made up: this girl is going to *be* here when he gets home. After all, it isn't fair, me dragging in like a tomcat Saturday or Sunday mornings, or afternoons. He only agreed to me going out to the bar sometimes; he didn't agree to me getting a girlfriend and disappearing every weekend. Which is pretty much what's happening.

Then the phone rings.

"Expecting anyone?" she says.

"I was just waiting for some good-looking woman to call," I say. I lean against the kitchen wall, pushing my dishwater hair back over my shoulder, the red cord twisting around me.

"Well, don't let me keep you," she says.

"Oh, you'll do," I say. While we talk, I run my finger along the cord spiraling across my hip. Cath's got that deep voice, half-flirting, but so serious in the center. You hear a voice like that and it's all over. Everything inside you dissolves.

By the time I get off the phone, I'm meeting her in an hour and a half at Park Street, so we can walk to where they have the Concerts on the Common. She wants to sit outside and listen to Whitney Houston. Cath says everyone knows Whitney's gay, or at least bi, Cath has some friend who supposedly knows Whitney's ex-girlfriend. Yeah, right.

It's past four in the afternoon, so there's not much light in the apartment—it's a small studio, one little window in the kitchen, so most of the time it's like the twilight zone. I don't know how Ed spends so much time here zombied out in front of the VCR. I'm pulling out my denim jacket when I catch a whiff of the gerbil cage. I put their wriggling brown bodies into the Rubbermaid bucket we use to wash the floor. Their claws scrabble and slide against the sides, desperate to escape.

So I head out to see Cath, what's the worst that could happen? Ed's basically supported me for three years, since I left home. And he took care of me during that disgusting time in the fall. So what's he going to do, kick me out? Or beat up on me? In five years he's never hit me, just threw me around a couple times when he was drunk. Nothing serious.

It's not like I have him on a leash. It's not my fault he never goes out for a beer with his buddies after work. Anyway, I'll come home on the first train in the morning. He won't even have time to miss me.

I fill the tray with clean shavings and lift the gerbils back in. One nips my finger. I drop it into the cage and slam the top with a clang. Those things *hurt.*

Cath and I wind up at the bar after the concert. We couldn't really hear Whitney, they build those fences so high almost no sound escapes. It was a scene, these kids trying to leap up the wood fence while the cops are looking away, guys hawking balloons and T-shirts, Cath and me holding hands, sort of hidden by the way we're leaning back on the damp spring grass, giving each other these little smiles if anyone looks at us funny. To hold hands with her, outside! I keep looking around, feeling light-headed, my hand giddy where it touches hers. Yeah, yeah, two girls, I want to yell to this one guy who keeps looking over at us, over and over, like he can't believe it. Yeah, queer girls. Believe it.

At the bar you don't have to deal with these jerkoffs. You walk up into the steamy half-dark, the smoke stinging your nostrils, the excited lights flashing all over women's bodies, women in tight black jeans and chinos and Reeboks, cool in T-shirts and muscle shirts and jackets rolled up to the elbow—the first time I went, I was so terrified to be near all these women squeezing past me to get onto the dance floor, I just stood there frozen to a post, my fingers practically breaking my empty beer bottle, too nervous to shove through the crowd to get another. You better believe I stared. I practically took notes on their clothes.

But it's not just the clothes. It's the way they hold themselves, hands in their pockets or slung over each other's shoulders, eyes roaming over the floor. It's the way they laugh, heads back, the way they lean against the pillars as if they owned the room. You feel like you've died and gone to heaven. You want to grow up to be just like them.

One thing surprised me—the way they all hung in groups, twos, threes, fives, dancing with their buddies all night. Half the time you couldn't tell which ones were lovers. Seemed like no one was there to meet anyone, seemed like they all had their friends already.

But it just seems that way. After a while, the music takes over your heartbeat, pounding down the thoughts in your head, you get dizzy breathing the smell of the hair of the woman in front of you —it was the third time I went, she was standing by herself, this tall woman with amused eyebrows that sliced you in half as you passed her, her breasts just crescents poking up from the purple T-shirt tucked into her jeans, her upper arm muscular and tight inside her rolled-up sleeves—I managed to smile before I had to look away, and then her hand was on my shoulder, asking me to dance. By the end of the night her thigh was rubbing against my pants while we danced, she leaned down to brush my throat with her mouth, and off we waltzed to her house.

Oh my God, and I used to think sex with Ed could be good. I was grinning myself silly on the train home the next morning, I just couldn't believe it.

But I was good, I didn't give out my number, I didn't ask for hers, I got home before Ed was even out of bed, I poured frosted flakes and orange juice and brought it to him practically before he turned over to say hello. Big old Ed, ruddy face crumpled from the pillow. Oh sure, he sulked a little bit, but we watched cartoons in bed all morning, and shot down aliens at the arcade all afternoon, teasing each other mercilessly, me tugging his flyaway orange ponytail, him winning extra games at invaders and me at caterpillar, like we used to.

I did, I really used to like sex with him. Or I thought I did. God, I practically had to tie him down the first time. We were at his house, his mother out shopping, both of us virgins—me fourteen, him eighteen. He said he was afraid of hurting me, he was afraid I was too young. But not too afraid. He knew exactly where the condoms were in his father's top drawer.

Back then I used to grab the wheel and steer us toward the far reaches of mall parking lots when we went to the movies, I was always on the lookout for likely fields and empty farmhouses when we were out driving. One rainy night in March we parked his mother's station wagon in a field shaded from the road by a stand of cedars. Afterward we untangled our clothes, racing to beat my curfew—but we were stuck in the muddy ruts. Ed got me home long past midnight, my guts in knots, tensed against my mother's fists.

She really did a job on me, Ed was pretty upset when he saw me the next day. Pretty soon after that, he got his own apartment, and I stopped even pretending to live at home, just moved right in with him.

I'd been practically living with his family anyhow. His family was great. They had these finches, Eenie and Meenie, that whirred around the living-room bookshelves and tugged thread out of your shirt. And at dinnertime, his family always set the table and ate all together, sitting down—or mostly they did. Anyway, it was a *house,* not the back of a goddamn motel, where dinner meant somebody shouting an order to whoever was working the grill, usually me, my brothers squeezing past, fighting over the last packet of ketchup. So Ed's father harassed him about his grades, so he wanted Ed to be an engineer, so big deal—Ed's too smart to be a goof-off, somebody had to rag him to shape up. After dinner I kind of liked helping his mother clean up—they had this great kitchen, copper-bottom pots, butcher-block everything, matching tea-towels for drying the plates. She always asked about school and stuff—not just asking, she really listened. I even liked it when his sister practiced the clarinet—Mozart and stuff like that—even if Ed called it "Louisa's bump-and-whine routine."

Then I'd go home and there'd be my dad, listening to Springsteen sing "Born in the USA" on the jukebox over and over, long after the last customers took off, hunkering over his beer as the Budweiser globe went round and round, blue in the dark.

That first moment you walk into the bar, everyone turns around to check you out. You pretend not to notice, but for a minute you can barely breathe, you feel like the latest model on display, exhilarated, your heart going a mile a minute in your throat, sick to your stomach, certain you're wearing the wrong shoes.

But not Cath. Cath doesn't even give them a cool glance. She just takes off her jacket and you see her muscled upper arms and that bit of strong shoulder under her sleeveless shirt. That stops a few hearts.

So I kiss her neck to let them all know I'm with her, I tease her till that amused smile squeezes out of her cool brown eyes. Of course, at the coat check we run into three of her friends. They kiss and hug like they haven't seen each other in years, and then they all start talking about some meeting the night before about Central America and the CIA, and I can't follow a thing, I must have "Dumb" written all over my forehead.

So I check out their clothes to see if I look okay in my black jeans and Reeboks and white V-neck T-shirt. The one wearing the leather bomber jacket checks me out pretty thoroughly, so I must be all right, even if I am the only one with long hair—the rest of them have it angled so short their necks go right up to their cowlicks. I start talking to her, maybe playing with her jacket a little bit, just goofing around. Cath looks over at me with her eyebrows, as if to say, well, I'm glad you're making yourself at home, and takes my arm and introduces me all around.

This guitar duo starts up and we can't hear anymore, so they all go upstairs to dance. It hits me again, that smoky half-dark, red lights bouncing everywhere. I want to touch every one of them, I can hardly believe this is real and I'm allowed to be here, I'm half dancing toward the dance floor, bomber jacket leans toward me and asks if anyone wants to dance, so she and me and the one in the Hawaiian-print pants head onto the floor, and Cath goes off to the bar with our beer orders, and everything's perfect.

I mean it, perfect. There's a bunch of college girls in Bermuda shorts and enormous T-shirts dancing wildly in a circle, showing off, and there's this older couple, must be forty, in their little pumps and pressed trousers and froufy hairdos waltzing to the disco beat—one of them keeps bumping into me, and I don't even mind. And when Cath comes on the floor, I nudge her to look at these two black women dancing so steamy, one behind the other, hands on hips—and Cath pulls me over to her and we close-dance for a minute, and I bite her ear, and she spins me out so we're mock-jitterbugging, and I'm so happy I could die.

There's the little beep-beep-beep of an alarm clock. It takes me a minute. I hate waking up lost in limbo. When the nuns taught us about limbo, I used to think that floating in gray nothingness must be worse than burning in hell. In hell at least something would be happening, you could *do* something.

Then she says, "Oh God, is it Monday already?" And I smell Cath's warm brown smell, and roll against her, reaching around to her chest to pull myself up into life. I kiss the small knobs of her spine up to the tender spot at the base of her brain.

"Today's the perfect day to go to the zoo," I say into her ear. "I want to show you the bongo antelopes, the ones you remind me of, with their royal antlers." They stand there staring down at you, too proud to scamper toward you trying to be friends like the zebras, too confident to shy away like the sika deer.

"Bongos," she says. "I swear you make these animals up." She stretches herself against me for a minute, and I roll on top of her, pinning her down with kisses. "No, no, I've got to get up," she says. "Move, sweetie. Seriously, I have to go to work."

"I'm at work," I say, kissing her wrists.

"Oh, you always have a line, don't you," she says, pushing me away. "Listen, get up. No kidding. You made me late last week."

While her shower rushes, rectangles of light slip across her posters for political rallies and museum openings. Her life is so *alive,* I'm going to learn so much with her—I'll start reading newspapers, I'll go to museums, I'll join one of her groups, I'll *do* something with my life.

"Does your brother know you're gay?" Cath says when she comes back into the room, beads of water dripping down her back.

"Hmm?"

"What does he think when you disappear for the weekend?"

I curl on my side, hugging the pillow to my belly. All weekend I kept meaning to call Ed, but mostly I forgot. And besides, I'd think, maybe just then wasn't the best time, really—maybe it'd be better to wait till I saw him, then explain.

"Hey. Up." Cath steps into her blue underwear. "I have to leave. That means you have to leave."

"You could always give me a key," I say, "so I can sleep in like a normal human being."

"Oh, I could, could I. A normal human being, let me inform you, doesn't live your life of leisure. A normal human being goes to work Monday mornings." Cath snatches the comforter away. When she starts to pull on her maroon sweater, I hop up and wipe off the water still on her back.

"I don't see how you can live off social security," she says. "Don't you have to be in school to get that after you're eighteen?"

"I am in school," I say, pulling my underwear and jeans out from under the bed.

"I thought you said you weren't."

It's too early for me to remember what I said and what I didn't. "The government doesn't know that," I say. Actually, it was a kid I met at Salem State who got social security after his father died. But I haven't seen him since I dropped out of school in October.

Cath throws me my denim jacket and holds open the front door. "I've got to get going. Really. I'll give you a call later, okay?"

"No, no, I'll call you." I kiss her neck. She gives me a funny look before she picks the *Globe* up from beside the forsythia. "Trouble with my brother," I say. "He'll get over it."

Ed opens the store at ten on Mondays, so before I take the train to Salem I hang for a while in a coffee shop near North Station, making patterns on the Formica with the sugar and salt. The bums drift in, the businessmen scan the paper and flirt with the waitresses, not like they're interested but like it's a habit they can't stop. When someone leaves behind a newspaper I flip through Monday's Sci-Tech section until the nine-fifty train—Chet Raymo's nature column can be great, once he wrote about actually watching a copperhead squeeze off its skin.

A muffled cheering is roaring up from the TV when I walk in. Ed leaves it on sometimes so he doesn't have to hear the silence behind him when he leaves. He hates being alone in the apartment, even for a minute.

He can be grumpy and sullen after a weekend alone, but he gets really pleasant once he starts talking to customers, so I figure I can call him at work, maybe meet him for lunch at Papa Gino's at the mall. He made assistant manager almost right away, he'll make manager soon—he likes finding out about people and helping them pick something out. He really is a good guy.

Two women dressed up like bees are squealing down the aisle for a chance to win major appliances. I flip off the TV and lie down on the sofabed, falling into his stale smell crumpled in the sheets.

Worse than waking up lost is waking up groggy in the afternoon. It's like that awful time in the fall, when I couldn't get out of bed for maybe days at a time, except to pee or grab something from the refrigerator.

At first I just wanted to stay in the blankets and not think about anything. Ed kept trying to get me up, tugging on my toes or my ears when he went by. Once he started tickling me. I about killed him for that, I yelled at him if he ever did that again, bastard, he'd really regret it. After that he let me sleep.

But sleeping wasn't so great for long. Maybe the worst part was the nightmares, using a broken beer bottle to beat off creepy little monsters trying to crawl up my legs till their blood got muddy and I stuck in it like quicksand. Or I had one of those machine guns my dad had in Vietnam and I was shooting heads off people, bam bam bam, but they grew back in these huge animal shapes, their enormous jaws chasing after me, and I was frozen to the asphalt.

Waking up was just as bad: like I said, there's no light in here, limbo. Lying there awake, alone, feeling a little nauseous and greasy from the dirty sheets, the bam bam bam noise starts going in your head, telling you what a shit you are, a useless worthless shit who can't even get up to brush her teeth, and you just roll over and try to go back to sleep so it will all shut off. When Ed was there I was actually glad. It wasn't as bad, curled up against his muscular legs. Sometimes he spoonfed me cartons of Chinese food or ice cream, and I listened to the TV hum above the blanket's fuzzy horizon before drifting down to an easier sleep.

Once I woke in the dark to the click of the door, no idea whether it was morning or evening, what month, what year. I struggled to shake off the numbness. The red numbers on the clock glowed six fifty-five.

Objects were swimming up in pools of thinning blue. On the bookcase was the big maroon "S" of Ed's varsity football letter that he never got around to sewing onto his jacket; my *Time/Life* science books and college biology book; seashells from York, Maine, where I spent summers with Ed's family, and from Orleans down the Cape, where I went with Margie's; and a little stuffed Santa.

A Santa. Christmas songs had been jingling on the radio, and a day ago—or two?—Ed said on the phone, "I don't know if we'll come this year." He must've been talking to his mother about Christmas.

I'd been in bed for two months.

The blue veil thinned completely, leaving the room a watery white. I shucked the blankets and stumbled into the bathroom, splashed my face with water, and went to the dresser for jeans and a sweatshirt. As I zipped up, I heard the door click shut again. Ed was panting from his run, sweat beads on his temples. As he looked at me, his shy, closemouthed grin spread across his face.

"Want eggs?" he said.

I spent that day flipping through my nature books or standing at the little window watching the clouds shift. At first he was reluctant to go to work, like he was afraid I might go back to bed again if he left. I shooed him out. But when he came home that night he scooped me into the truck and drove us to Singing Beach. I couldn't believe how fresh the air was on my skin, so wild and alive, the ocean's foamy tumble and roar making me want to plunge in. I kept butting up against Ed, goofy from the salt air and the sharp stars.

At home I took a hot shower, just to feel it alive on my skin. My head filled with the minty smell of Ed's soap, and I started thinking of everything that ever made me happy. Sandpipers running along the lip of the tide on Crane's beach. My ankles chilled numb as I stalked crayfish in the creek with the neighborhood kids. Lying on Grandma Mae's braided rugs in a mess of Sunday comics, listening to Joni Mitchell and Janis Ian. Sneaking out to the night roar of high school football games with Margie. Fingering through Woolworth's plastic squirtguns and Groucho noses and silver fright wigs with Margie in eighth grade. Making out with Margie in the breathy dark under the summer covers. Margie's father catching us necking the week before we started high school, cursing me to hell and back, threatening me with jail if I ever came near her again. Margie's scribbled letters from her aunt's in New Hampshire dribbling away. Weeks of loneliness surrounded by a thousand lockers slamming at Salem High.

Until I met Ed.

Next day I borrowed Ed's truck, drove to Doktor Pet, and bought the gerbils. It was scary to drive again, the onrushing lights and sights and split-second decisions too much after two months of silence. But it was worth it when I picked up their warm bodies, running my palm over the tiny ears and tails. I was so proud, picking out the gerbil food and water bottle and everything they needed to be happy. So there, so there! This is *my* fucking life.

When I pulled up to the parking lot behind the store, the gerbils scrabbling in their cage on the mats on the passenger's side, Ed waved at me from behind the plate glass. He ran out to meet me, his face smeared with delight, and offered to drive home. I slid over to the passenger seat and turned back to peer for a strong minute at his face, searching it to see how he'd react to what I had to say. I looked so hard I got that eerie feeling I was looking into a mirror, that his face was mine, that how he felt was how I'd feel. I had to look away.

It took me a week to say it, even though every morning on the walks he made us take around the block it ran in my head like a cassette, this little rap about how it didn't have anything to do with him, I wasn't going to hurt him or leave him or anything, blah blah blah. But I kept watching for the right time. Once a little shiver of disgust ran through me when I watched him lean over to put on his running shoes, a little blubber spilling over the frayed band of his jockeys sticking up above his gray sweats. I pushed my hair back over my shoulder and sat down to talk—but then he stuck a finger through the gerbil cage and started goofing around with them, calling them little names, and I just couldn't. Another time I sat next to him, the sofa cushions sagging beneath me—of course he was folding up the bed as soon as I got up each morning—and I smelled his beery breath, his elbows on his hairy thighs as he hunched over, staring at the VCR—and it was like the whole room was tilting toward him, like I was falling toward him, and I curled away, repulsed.

"What is it?" he said, not looking at me.

"Nothing."

"Some kind of nothing. You've been looking like that all week."

Okay, I thought, this is it. I took a couple of practice breaths.

"Chill out," he said, still looking at the TV, but really kind, not like he was scolding at all. He picked up my hand and kissed it. "You're so intense. Everything's going to be okay. You'll get back on your feet, you'll figure out what you want to do."

Just when you write him off as a dumb lug, he comes out with something like that.

"I want to make an agreement with you," I blurted out.

He got really still. He clicked the pause button on the VCR, and these two oversize faces stopped, one of the mouths half-open, frozen in the middle of saying something.

"I want to go to the bar sometimes," I said.

He knew exactly what I meant. He knew about Margie. He knew about every girl I'd ever had a crush on since I was fourteen.

"Nothing serious, Bear. I don't want to get away from you or anything. I just—I just have to, sometimes." I felt retarded, trying to explain my thoughts after not having any for so long.

He sat there facing the TV, a beer and the remote control between his knees. "Nothing serious?" he said, his voice sagging.

"I swear, I swear to God." I tried not to, but I was pleading, I wanted to run my hands over the orange hair that ran over his ears into the flimsy ponytail, to soothe him and make him smile.

"Nothing serious," he said, like a contract, popped the top of the beer, and took a long drink. It wasn't until he turned to me sharply that I realized I'd taken an ecstatic breath.

"Don't worry, old Bear," I said, hugging him to me, rocking him, rocking him with happiness. "Don't worry, Bear, everything will be fine."

Squeak, squeak, squeak goes the gerbil wheel, and I sit up in the dimness, wondering whether he remembered to put water in their bottle over the weekend. The clothes I've been wearing for three days stick to me, so I peel them off and pull on some clean ones. Sure enough, the water bottle is empty. I take it into the bathroom, and while I'm running the tap I glance up at the mirror.

It's a shock, seeing my stupid brown eyes and sideways nose in front of all that foggy thought, the dirty blond hair spilling every which way over my shoulders.

And then I hear the door. Shit.

What's worse, the phone rings. I know right away who it is.

"Hello," he says. I sit down on the toilet.

"No, she's not here right now." He gives a short laugh. "No, I'm not her brother. Yes, I'll tell her."

In front of me is the creeping black line of mold in the shower's cracks, and the yellowed tile he tried again and again to scour white. Not like Cath's bathroom with its clean white free-standing tub, surrounded by shower curtains decorated with a crayon-bright map of the world.

He has a beer when I come out.

"Your girlfriend called," he says, looking out the window at his parked truck.

"I heard," I say. Then I realize what I just admitted.

He snorts and tosses back some beer. "You going to call her or what?"

"I thought maybe you and I could watch a movie. I could go out and get some Chinese for dinner. My treat, ha ha."

"Ha ha," he says, dead flat. Shame flushes through me. I head over to the gerbil cage and slide the water bottle in. I want to bite free of him so bad my teeth ache.

"Well, I'm starved," I say. "Don't you want to eat?"

He takes another long swig from his beer and tosses it in the sink. It clatters to a stop. The hollowness in my stomach swirls with it.

"Why don't we just order a pizza," he says, resigned, and pulls another can from the refrigerator. "I brought home a couple of movies."

Relief breathes out of me, leaving behind a narrow thread of excitement. Everything will be fine.

The phone rings again. I sprint into the kitchen to pick it up. "Hello?"

"Oh. You *are* there," Cath says.

"I just walked in." Hearing her voice, I go damp.

"I forgot to tell—whoever—why I called," she says.

"One of my brother's friends."

Ed snorts again and walks into the other room.

"Right. Listen, you left your backpack here. I just found it when I walked in. I didn't know if you keep anything important in it."

"Nothing much. I have my wallet in my jacket." Watching Ed out of the side of my eyes, I try to keep my voice from flirting. I reach over to the refrigerator and grab an apple.

"Well. Sounds like this isn't a good time. Talk to you later," she says.

"Yeah, thanks," I say, and hang up. I bite into the apple, hard. I want to cry.

Ed's pulling videos out of his backpack. I lean over his shoulder. "Looks like action/adventure flicks for a change," I say. "Cops conquer evil. Boys conquer jungle. Me Tarzan, you Jane, unnggh."

Ed drops the pack on the bed and stands up. "You pick one out, I'll call for the pizza."

"Hey, this one's a romance comedy!" I call to him. He nods, turning his back to me as he speaks into the phone.

When he comes back, he puts his arm around me and draws me close. The acrid smell of sweat under his arm is familiar, almost tender. I close my eyes. The pressure in my chest is terrible.

To my surprise, he strokes me all the way down my body, his hand slow across my thighs. Something inside me quickens, and my breath spins. I try not to let him see me cringe—I'm so relieved that he still wants me, that I still have him. I bite into his shoulder, a little harder than I mean to. He flinches just a little and grabs my hips and pulls me on top of him.

Trying not to let him see how stiff I am, I shove myself up against him, grabbing for his zipper. I think of Cath—running my face over the ripple of her appendix scar, the incredible curve of her ass, the sudden rise of plum-brown hair between her jutting hips. When Ed's tongue strikes my mouth I jerk back. He puts his hand on my hip and holds me still. We lie close together, his slow wet breath on my face. I turn my face down into the pillow.

I *want* to want him. Why can't that be enough?

The doorbell rings. I start to giggle. I don't know why, I get a little hysterical, the kind of laughing that leaves you bruised, almost like you're crying. The bell rings again. "Coming!" I yell, dragging on my jeans and T-shirt and scrambling for the door. I plop the steaming pizza box down on the bed and eat with a vengeance, strings of cheese trailing from my teeth.

After we're stuffed, leaning back on the pillows, Ed tosses the box on the floor and reaches over to touch my cheek.

"Leenie?" he says, his eyes closed, curled on his side like a child. Leenie, that lost name.

"Leenie, let's get married." I put my face back in the pillow.

"Let's get married. *Married.* We could have babies. My parents would be happy. Everything would be great."

I know what he wants. He wants me to hide out with him forever, trapped and unhappy on the leash of his paycheck. He wants to pretend we're still kids together. Like I'm not turning into a woman all by myself.

"Think about it, at least. Will you think about it?" His voice lingers. I bite the pillow and fight the hot tears starting to rise.

I lie there, stark awake. A headlight scrapes the gray walls and escapes. I keep seeing Cath floating past me, Cath's skinny arms moving in a smooth jerk as she dances, her eyes gleaming as she looks someone over with a quick flick, her smile and eyebrows razor-sharp.

The little red numbers glow two oh-seven. I get up and prowl the room, finally taking one of my *Time/Life* books into the bathroom where the light won't bother Ed. But I keep staring blindly at this page of twisted cocoons and migrating monarchs. Panic hits me when I think I might not hear her voice till tomorrow.

In half a breath, I'm on the highway in Ed's pickup.

It's weird on the highway. The few headlights stream by like extraterrestrials. The DJ's hey-guy voice echoes in the car and out into the gigantic night, I'm bebopping in my seat to the Shirelles and the Supremes, tapping the horn until it lets out an excited yelp.

I zoom into Boston doing seventy-five, eighty, barely slowing down to toss a fistful of coins in the tolls, speeding around midnight delivery trucks, accelerating through the red lights that glow eerie and alone at deserted crossroads, barreling around the Jamaica Way so fast I'm tossed from one lane to another as the road throws up surprising curves.

When Ed's truck shudders to a stop, you hear it echoing all down the side street. I tap on her window. The yellow smell of the forsythia floods my head. "Cath?" I whisper, loud. "It's me, Arlene."

The shade moves slightly and drops again. I'm hopping back and forth a little, hoping I'm not crushing the hyacinth, the chill of the spring mud making my toes and soles ache in my Reeboks.

"Hurry up, come on in." She chains the door behind me, putting her hand on my elbow. "Are you okay? Is anyone after you? Should I call the police?"

I look down at her feet. Her second toe is longer than her big toe. I never noticed before.

"I'll make you some tea."

Her kitchen clock, a funky black plastic cat with rhinestone numbers, makes enormous clicking sounds, wide-awake eyes sweeping from side to side. She quizzes me. Am I hurt? Is anyone else hurt? Is there anyone she should call? Her voice slows to a suspicious halt.

"Did you have a fight with your—ah—brother?"

I want to crawl under the table.

"Arlene, *say* something. Christ!" she says.

"I just had to get away."

"From?"

"He makes me sick. I can't live with him anymore." I'm surprised how violently it comes out.

"Him," she says, waiting for me to go on.

I stare down at the honeypot.

"Your boyfriend."

I nod. She gives a little snort of disgust. Just like Ed's when he found out about her.

"And you want me to take you in?"

"Just till I find a job," I say hesitantly.

"Thanks for letting me in on the plan." The kettle's sputtering before it really starts to whistle. Cath gets up and stands by the stove, her arms folded.

"You scared me half to death, you know, when you tapped on my window," she says. "You're lucky I didn't call the cops on you." Just as the whistle starts to pierce the room, she turns off the gas and the sound dies into a sigh. She pours the steaming water into two mugs, and puts one in front of me. The mouthwashy smell of peppermint slaps my face.

"When I figured it out, about your boyfriend, I decided I had to stop seeing you."

I sit there gripping the honeypot. I want to slam her against the wall. "You don't mean that," I say, not sure whether it makes it out of my mouth.

"Why did you lie to me?" she says.

And then she's off and running, quizzing me like I was a juvenile delinquent. Does he know I'm seeing her. How long have I been with him. When I tell her his family kind of took me in because mine wasn't so hot, she wants to know was my family violent. How can you answer that? And then she puts her hand over mine, right, like she knows anything about it.

More third degree. Does he support me. Am I in school. I actually tell her about the day I thought I saw Margie between classes and practically knocked over half the campus running to catch her. But when she turned around, it was some strange girl in a perm and makeup. Next thing I knew it was Christmas.

I'm hunching over my mug like it was a private campfire. When I look up, her head's tiny and terribly distant.

"You can stay tonight, Arlene," she says, her words dragging toward me over the miles, sad and slow, "but you have to leave in the morning."

Sitting in traffic in Ed's pickup, I look over at the sullen morning huddle waiting for the bus. Secretaries in heels and lipstick twitter about their weekends with their boyfriends. A black guy in a leather jacket and a backpack is probably off to engineering classes at UMass; he wants to get the hell out of Mission Hill. And there's a woman dragging on a cigarette, someone I've seen at the bar, maybe a short order cook heading for the midday shift.

What the hell, I could do that. There's worse things than working a grill—like cleaning motel bathrooms, you wouldn't believe what people leave behind when someone else is going to clean up the mess.

I drive way north, past Salem, past Marblehead, up to Plum Island. Ed'll kill me, but he'll get to work somehow. I take off my Reeboks, tie the laces together, and throw them over my shoulder as I walk up the beach. The sand's damp and cold, so cold it shoots up my back and hits the base of my head. But the cold feels good, the gritty sand grinding into my bare soles. It's too late in the morning to see many birds, but I sit down anyway—not on the beachy part of the beach, the part the tourists like, but up in the dunes, near the brush, where you can hear the waves slap the sand and the tall grass rustling around your ears, like somebody sighing.

This kid comes by. He must live in that row of houses that's right before you get on the island, because he's pedaling like crazy, butt in the air, on his mountain bike, the kind that does okay in sand because of the fat tires. I guess he doesn't see me because he hops off, letting the bike drop on its side in front of this mess of brush, and scrunches down to peer between the branches.

And I get it: he's found a nest. When I was nine, down by the creek I found a deep-basketed nest holding three speckled eggs no bigger than my thumb. I got a lot of crap for coming home with my clothes all muddy and scratched up. Not that I cared, I used to run down there nearly every day anyway, before or after school, or both.

Still, the day I went down there and found these skinny rags of birds, damp bits of egg sticking to them, screeching like hell, I was so surprised I froze. Their beaks were sharp and nasty, stretching so wide you'd think they'd snap their twiggy bones into bits. Those huge mouths were scary—like all that hunger scraping open their gullets was just too big to fit inside.

Sam Hurwitt

Sam Hurwitt grew up in Berkeley, California, and is now in Budapest, living on film reviews and a sack of potatoes. He has a B.A. in philosophy and religion from San Francisco State University, and he never thought for a moment that it would help him get a job.

His publishing history consists chiefly of book reviews for the *Express* in Berkeley, arts reviews for *The Budapest Sun,* and poetry for *Howl,* a San Francisco literary journal. He also spent two years as a poetry editor at *Ink* magazine in San Francisco.

Due to the modern obsession with specialization, Sam spent his college years reading very few books very closely, and graduated without ever reading Aristotle or Thomas Hardy. He is now obsessively making up for lost time, but he still hasn't read Aristotle. Western philosophers, he says, construct elaborate systems to describe how people as a whole experience reality, completely ignoring the fact that people never experience reality en masse. Most great philosophers could benefit greatly from a few dancing lessons.

Sam has seen thirty-two of Shakespeare's plays and knows only that he knows nothing. He has begun to suspect, however, that the world is good.

JONAH 2:5

Thales said the world is water, and I believe it. I can feel it pressing down on my shoulders and stinging in my eyes. When I inhale, the air is thick with water vapor. And I'm drinking it, I'm drinking it down deep into my lungs where it nestles in pockets like red-hot dewdrops. My sweat is pouring out of me as if some little god inside turned on a faucet wedged in my spine. Ninety-nine percent of my body is water, and I can feel it all welling up in briny slime on my skin until the warm river washes it away. Out with the bad water, in with the good.

It has become my custom to shower every morning. Lora's

habit, really, not mine. I've always hated showers. I used to be able to go a couple of days without bathing, and no one seemed to mind. I'd just wash my pits and run out the door. Lora changed all that. If I did that now, my arms would feel as if they'd been dipped in wax. I wouldn't be able to tell the bristles on my brush from the ones on my head. I've got to get clean. But I wish to God I didn't have to bathe.

I don't like bathwater heat. It's not the honest stinging heat of morning tea or the quick, pounding heat of an open fire. It's a subtle, insidious heat that sings madrigals to you as it sucks your life out through your pores. I don't like the way the stream makes me feel, as dense as a water balloon, like Godzilla being pelted by tiny bullets. And I don't like the fear. I don't want to slip and break my neck or go blind when the shampoo gets in my eyes. I figure it's only a matter of time before something awful happens to me in the shower.

From the shower stall I can see the open attic door, and I'm afraid of that too. It's just beyond the reach of any ladder that could fit through the bathroom door, so we've never seen the attic. But I suspect a martian lives up there, and my housemates seem to have become its lovers. I knew all three of them before we got the place, and they were all fairly rational. But now they've changed. One of them brought four goldfish home to be our pets. Now I ask you, what kind of goddamned pod-person pet is a goldfish? Might as well get a banana slug—it's got the same personality, and you don't have to listen to the tank bubbling all night. I picked a big ugly orange and white one with fin rot. My housemate wants to flush it down the toilet because it ate her goldfish. She should have expected that when she named her fish Schopenhauer. Mine's named Mothra. It's a matter of role models, basically. But all of my housemates have become strange to me. They shower with a macabre spore thing that looks like a macrame brick with potato-eye tendrils reaching out. I wouldn't want that thing touching me, but I guess the martian demands hygiene from its lovers. I know Lora does.

It's over. The shower, I mean. The relationship, too, but I'm not thinking about that. You must understand that I don't care about the strange silence, the three eggs instead of five, my unbalanced weight in the bed. What matters is that I can see now. There's no one standing in front of me.

In Japan, crises are simple. Giant monsters with names like French artists—Rodan, creature from the outer deep, or Go-gan, friend of Rodan—terrorize the city, and Godzilla rises from his nap on the ocean floor to restore the status quo. He slams the foreign invaders through a couple of buildings and then returns to the water. It's like King Arthur in a green rubber suit, only with more frequency and three million dollars more in property damages.

Here, it's not so simple. We have Elvis, Jesus, Disney, L. Ron Hubbard, but we don't know when they'll come back. It may be when we need them least. Meanwhile, we have to deal with our own problems as best we can.

I have the light turned up all the way. The dimmer was a compromise. My housemates don't like any bright lights. I suppose their alien lover has sensitive eyes. I can't stand poorly lit bathrooms. They make the mirror useless. You can't see what you've got caught in your eye in manufactured twilight. Lora's bathroom was always poorly lit. She was probably fucking the martian too.

I don't know why I told her that I drank blood. It was New Year's and I was drunk and I was at Greyhaven, a place that had shaped me, so any newcomers had to conform to my chosen reality. And I do like the taste of blood. I had just never opened someone up to get it.

Later that night she asked me if I had any razor-sharp knives around. I was glad I didn't. Eventually—weeks later—we did it. Lora had brought a razor blade and she cut me too deep on my thumb. I still have a scar. It wouldn't stop bleeding. She was drunk when she did it. It just kept coming and coming and it was so thick and I don't even remember cutting her. But we opened each other up and drank the thick salty choking red stuff. We smeared it all over each other, ruining my best blue sheets, and we tore into each other like wolves until all we were was a scarred and rutting mass. I hated it. It hurt. And I kept thinking of that line from *Macbeth:* "By the pricking of my thumbs, something wicked this way comes."

My clock radio is blaring. The snooze time always runs out while I'm in the shower. I suppose it would be the doorbell if I lived in a friendlier neighborhood. If Lora were here, she'd glare at me. She has a problem with sounds. The neighbor's dogs used to keep her up at night, and she made me promise that if I ever got her pregnant I'd kill them.

All my piles of paper get speckled with water as I run to turn the radio off. It's playing a particularly pretentious Sisters of Mercy song. Lora and I liked the same music—death rock, old blues tunes, rap, punk, Irish folk songs, and loud oppressive classical music. At first, she didn't believe that we had as much in common as we did. I did. I had faith from the start. I held her head when she convulsed on the carpet, and I knew I was really in love for the first time in my life. She played me a tape of her first aura reading, and I showed her the book my father drew for me when I was six. She cried when the balloon I had given her slipped from my fingers while she had been tying her shoes. She had to see my failure as a betrayal. She had been raped twice. Never fool yourself into thinking that pain is useful. Pain's just there. And after nine months I'm not there. Neither of us had seen that coming. Deep down, we had both assumed that everything would be all right.

I told you I'm not thinking about that. It's true. That kind of story demands a moral, and I don't have one handy. I must have left it in my other pants. Were I to fictionalize my life, I'd make it a Russian novel, only without all the sermons. Here's a helpful hint. When you read a Russian novel and the anguished moralizing becomes too cumbersome, scribble "Insert Godzilla" in the margin. The inner turmoil of any petty government functionary would be put into perspective instantly by a rampaging sixty-foot reptile. There are no theses in life, only examples. And my failed love life is the furthest thing from my mind. That's not why I have to get clean.

I don't want to tell you this.

I had a burrito last night. I had to go across town to get it, because there are no restaurants in my neighborhood. I wanted a burrito, and I wanted it with black beans, not pinto. And I wanted avocado. They call it guacamole, but I couldn't taste anything but avocado in it. I wonder at what stage an avocado becomes guacamole.

When I was four, my family was split along very specific lines. My mother and my sister were fond of avocado, and my father and I preferred papaya. I'm not sure why those two fruits are connected, except that you cut them in half and remove the center before you eat them. I later grew to appreciate avocado, but it was too late. My parents had long since split up, and my sister and I followed suit. I like every fruit now, except pears.

It was late when I came home. The BART station was closing, and I had to leave through the back door. I don't know if you noticed how cold it was last night. I've always loved the crisp taste of winter air, but last night I couldn't taste it at all. It just made my tongue feel clammy.

A woman rose out of the bushes, pulling her shirt down to cover herself. I didn't know why she had her shirt up, or why she was lying down in the bushes. I didn't want to know. She was very large and very dark, and she was staggering toward me, telling me not to run. I wasn't running, I told her, not exactly. But I stopped walking and stood there, exactly like Tokyo waiting for giant rubber monsters. She was large. Her face was masculine and streaked with dirt and tear tracks. Little beads of perspiration dotted her forehead like shimmery zits, and her breath stank of wine. The rest of her smelled bad too, of sweat and smoke and unwholesome things, but it was a fresh kind of bad. It wasn't the twelve-day-old bad of the man who knocks on our door looking for old bottles. She had started the day clean.

"Please. I need three forty-four to buy canned milk for my baby. He's three months old. He's home right now with my thirteen-year-old. I'm real sorry to bother you, but I need the money."

"I can't. I'm sorry."

"Please. I swear I just need it for my baby. I'm drunk. Damn right I'm drunk. But I'm not going to buy any more. Just some milk for my baby."

"I really can't afford it. I'm not doing so hot myself."

"I need the money. Please. I don't want to have to shoot you. I've got a little gun, but I don't want to use it. I just want to feed my baby. Please."

I don't know if she had a gun or not. It didn't look like it, but she was fat enough that I couldn't really see the other side of her. I looked in my wallet. There was only a ten, a one, and some coupons. I gave her the ten.

"Thank you," she said, and she started to cry. "I'm sorry. I just need the money. Why can't black people stick together? Why? I asked some of my so-called friends, but they wouldn't give me no money for milk. They paid to get me drunk, but they wouldn't buy no milk for my baby. Why aren't they good? Why aren't they good like you? Let me suck your dick."

"No."

"I'm sorry. Why do people have to act like that? And they say they're my friends. I can't take all this money from you. I just need three forty-four for the milk. I swear that's all I'm buying. Walk with me. Walk with me to the store, and I'll give you your change back."

"I really should be getting home."

"Walk with me."

I walked with her for a while. Her name is Mandy. She graduated from Fremont High School at seventeen, and had her first child eight months later. She started using and dealing then too, but she says that's over. You've got to be clean or Jesus won't take you, she says. Her father died while she was in high school, leaving her a house. Welfare covered the rest, except when she was drinking. She has five children.

"There's Andre. He's thirteen years old. And Nicole, she's eight. Natalie's two. And Leroy. No, wait—I forgot about Victor. He's five. And Leroy's only three months old. Pierre's thirteen, Victor's five. . . . Hold on a minute."

"It's all right. You don't have to . . ."

"They're my children. We've had forty-two presidents, there are fifty states in the union, there were twelve apostles, and I have five children. I know who they are. Andre's thirteen. Nicole's eight. Victor's . . ."

"Five."

"Five. I got to start over. Andre's thirteen . . ."

"Thirteen. Nicole's . . ."

"Eight."

"Then Victor."

"Victor's five."

"Natalie . . ."

"She's two."

"Natalie's two. And?"

"And Leroy . . ."

"Three months old."

We never made it to the store. The nearest one was closed, and I wasn't going to go any farther. We talked for about an hour. Then I told her I needed to go home. She started to cry again. I gave her a hug. I usually don't notice it, but when I'm hugging someone, I make a little sound, halfway between humming and growling. Because that's all I have, really. Because I have damn little to give in this world, and all I see is need. But for a moment there is hug—and all I am is this giving.

"Ooo," she said, "take me home and fuck me or I'm gonna shoot you."

"No."

"You have a girlfriend?"

Yes, I said, I do.

Stewart David Ikeda

Stewart David Ikeda earned his MFA in writing from the University of Michigan, Ann Arbor, where he was awarded a Merit Fellowship and two Avery & Jule Hopwood Awards for a novel-in-progress and a story collection. His poetry and prose have appeared in *Ploughshares*, *Glimmer Train Stories*, and the *Minetta Review*, among other publications, and have received awards from New York University, the Kentucky State Poetry Society, and *A Different Drummer* magazine. Born and raised in Philadelphia, Ikeda now lives in Madison, where he teaches writing and Asian American literature at the University of Wisconsin.

ROUGHIE

It's a TV voice replaying in your mind, saying a life don't matter, as you watch Little Man hiding from a service revolver. And what's one more or less dog's life anyway?

Little Man bent over behind a reeking Dumpster, crying. Just home from school—still wearing his knapsack, his Turtles bag, still holding the clay candlestick he made in pottery—to find his father in the pen out back with Roughie, pistol in one hand, other trying to lock the gate behind with an old, tied-up electric cord. And Little Man's stepsisters crying too, faces pressed up against the storm fence like at the zoo.

Sound of backfire on the street. His father usually says, That's just a car backfiring, Little Man. Maybe firecrackers. Just take the girls down in the basement and finish your homework. But now, Little Man hears the boom and jumps anyway.

Get back! his father tells the girls, in his big bullhorn cop's voice. GET BACK NOW!

They just go on. He slaps the fence, knocks them on their butts. Tama staying down, holding her head, but crying on and on, not missing a beat. Singing out, Don't do it, don't do it—and Maddy as usual saying nothing.

Little Man collects himself, breathing trash, old chicken from the Dumpster, mourning Roughie. 'Til he can't stand it. 'Til best thing's to get it done, fast, clean, over and out. Makes him leave his cave to watch, maybe help—but swearing aloud he won't shoot her himself.

Roughie looking electrocuted, shaking like an old dying woman. Growling, like she knows a Magnum got a bead on her. Glazey-eyed, drooling like Little Man seen on that old junkie booting on the stoop yesterday. Only, old junkie felt no pain. Roughie, she'd beg for it herself if she could speak. She'd be brave, say, Right between the eyes, and hold her breath to make an easier target. But here she's not in her right mind, hurting with rat fever.

Do it, Daddy, Little Man says, hopping the fence. He's a rare boy that way—so sharp and stubborn—just views a situation and, right off, knows what time it is, makes the decision, sticks to it like Krazy Glue. 'S why he's in that school gifted program—got that hardheaded sticking power, like now, with his little heart breaking, he sticks solid with his father. Says, I'll get the gate—she won't get out. Make the pain stop, Daddy.

Little Man's father eyeballs the boy. Red-eyed, clear as day he's been chugging a few hard ones. Feeling painless himself, or anyway won't remember it. Stink-breath and wobbly, his gun hand waves up and down in slo-mo like a palm tree on "Hawaii Five-O." Tells Little Man, Fuck off outta here now, boy. Take your sisters in the house.

I gotta stay with Roughie. She'll be scared if I ain't with her.

When his father whops him, Little Man's nose starts spilling over his white shirt, but he don't back off one milli-inch. Just standing, not even crying. In this miserable, man-sized voice too big for his small body, he says, You heard Daddy, you girls get in the house now, quick. Roughie won't stop hurting 'til you go. Please.

Like she's been possessed all sudden, Tama stops bawling, blinks her big eyes, and gets up off the ground, still holding her head. Maddy follows—scared to be two feet away from Tama. Door slams behind, and you hear Tama shout inside. He ain't *our* daddy. And Little Man's father, dark as a storm, shout, You just wait, you little bitch! You're in my goddammed house now!

But Little Man digs in next to his father and waits, just waiting like Buddha. Soft as a park pigeon, he says, Roughie—Daddy, please.

His father looks at the gun stupidly, then raises it at Roughie, zombielike, like since he don't know what to do he decides better just shoot something. But then, Daddy's all shaky, got the quivers, and there's a click, then a pop, just like that. Flame from around the barrel, just like when you first stick a match in the oven pilot that's been off for a while. Shot's not so loud itself, but keeps going and going on, bouncing like a Super Ball up and down the backs of the yards and houses.

You wait for it to stop and all to quiet down, but then hear a terrible, terrible whine, like a sick baby crying at night, but it's Roughie. See her caved down in front, ass hung high in the air, shivering like she's in Alaska without an igloo. The most beautiful dog ever. Makes you wanna cry yourself, seeing her chest, all sexy and hairy white and gold, with a big red chunk out of it, and she down begging on her front paws with the side of her face and nose in the dirt. That son of a bitch . . . old, drunk, shaky son of a bitch missed from no feet, only took a fat piece outta her heart, but didn't finish the job. You wonder how this sorry shot, always strutting around big Mister John Wayne policeman, ever killed a man before.

Little Man and his father froze stiff, locked up, like before they wasn't scared of no rabid dog, but a half-dead, miserable pile of bloody hair scared them into mummies. Hear Tama just inside the screen door, wailing louder than ever. Look around and notice heads popping out of neighbors' houses, the two Johnson boys opening and closing the blinds at their rear window, ducking back. See that giant, Octavius, bolt out into his yard, shirtless, rippling like Arnold Schwarzenegger, carrying his own piece and looking dizzy and blinded like he just woke up.

Oh shit, shit, he shot her. Devil shot Roughie. Po-lice bru-tal-i-ty!

Everybody buzzing and hushing each other and clucking their tongues, even weeping, because near everyone loved Roughie. They knew her, remember her hounding the grocer, stalking the subway, trucking after the Good Humor van, summertime, playing with kids in the sprinkler. Lotta folks think more of her than Little Man's father. Now he's scanning around looking trapped, shouting, Mind your own nosy businesses; there's nothing for you to see here. He starts swinging 'round with the pistol, pointed down a little, and you see the heads pop back into their houses like squirrels in a tree, except for Octavius. He just spits and yells, Yessir, Officer, and starts back in, slow. But even Octavius loved that Roughie. Yells, She worth twenty of you, before disappearing.

Roughie's ass comes down, finally, crumples over into the dirt in a heap. If anything on this earth worse than readying yourself to die, then getting only *half* killed, only Jesus can tell you what that is.

Little Man's the first one of them to snap to. All four foot something of him jerks awake, and with those tiny brown hands he tries to take the pistol from his daddy. That wakes up Senior. Says, Get back, damn you; you'll get hurt, don't . . .

And Little Man: We can't leave her like that, Daddy. It's okay, I'll do it, I know you don't want to do it. I can do it.

See, a special boy—Little Man's no coward. He adjusts. He floats.

There's a blur and scuffle, and old Roughie lifts up her eyes like she'll pull the trigger herself with just willpower, then POP! and this time you wait for the bouncing to stop. Pop, pop, down the block, and it's all quiet and you hold your breath and pray for Roughie. 'Til she starts whimpering again.

Then you see Little Man. His expression all squirming brown pain; looking old, used, in his white button shirt and leather belt that wraps near twice around his skinny body, *strangling* that pistol. Got that bulging knapsack, half as big as he is, piled on him, like a midget soldier in a Vietnam movie. And camouflage eyes to match —frosty, into the North Pole, gone. You see his fingers start squeezing again.

It's the voice in your mind and on the TV that says a life don't matter. But a life's not nothin'. You're pissed. But you're outta there, fast as feet will take you. And you don't know how things ended up for Roughie.

May 3, 1993

to whom it may concern:

I dont know if this is what you really
are looking for but I know it doesn't hurt + try
These are just my own personal feelings and experiances
growing up in this generation. Please let me know
where I may get a copy of your book when
published.

Sincerely,

Michèle Joley

San Francisco, CA

Fred G. Leebron

Fred G. Leebron grew up in Narberth, Pennsylvania, and attended a Quaker school in Germantown. He has been a program vendor for the Philadelphia Phillies and Eagles, and for six months he worked on the locked unit of the Philadelphia Psychiatric Center. He has traveled extensively in Peru, Thailand, China, Guatemala, Mexico, Denmark, and Indonesia. Currently he lives with his wife and two-year-old daughter in San Francisco, where he works for a nonprofit organization providing housing to the homeless. He has published eighteen stories, in magazines such as *Ploughshares*, *The North American Review*, and *Iowa Review*, and is working on a novel.

LOVELOCK

The billboards into Lovelock, Nevada, promised dinner and drink coupons, a roll of quarters, hot showers, cable television, king-sized beds, breakfast coupons, twenty-four-hour free coffee, air conditioning, and a swimming pool, all for only thirty-nine ninety-nine, and Benjamin West, after three nights dozing in rest stops by the side of the interstate, could not help but be swayed. Lovelock came up on the left-hand side in the middle of the Nevada flats, a one-street town with a skyline of gas stations, hotel-motel-casinos, fast-food restaurants, auto dealers, insurance brokers, a combined elementary–junior high–high school, a chamber of commerce. West took the Chevy down Main Street, keeping his eye out for a name that rang true from one of the highway advertisements. The Lickety Split, The Bell Weather, It's Your Night, On the House, Holiday Inn, Motel 6—their signs lighting up in the dusk like struck pinball targets. West pulled into the lot of Lucky Andy's Roadside Hotel-Motel-Casino. That was the one with the five dollars in quarters and twenty dollars' worth of coupons. He parked between a pickup truck with Wyoming plates and a small Winnebago motor home out of Florida. He had one hundred and eleven dollars left. He got out of the car, slammed the door locked, and crossed the lot through the stolid heat of dusk to the lobby entrance. Through smoked windows, he could see a small casino, with thirty or so one-arm bandits, four card tables, and a horseshoe-shaped bar. In the refrigerated lobby, a slot machine stood to either side of the registration desk. West peeled off two twenty-dollar bills and laid them before a woman with tall blond hair and platinum-painted fingernails. He was too tired to be subtle. "Will that do?" he said.

"Sure will." She smiled at him. "Do you want an upper rack or a lower rack?"

He looked at her in numb confusion.

"First floor or second floor," she said.

"Second."

She gave him a key, a roll of quarters, and a wad of coupons, her fingertips grazing his knuckles. He glanced at her quickly, but she was already occupied with something else.

He walked stiff-legged back out to the car, walked as if he'd been riding a horse for the last four days instead of a car. His right groin muscle ached, so that he almost walked bowlegged. Over the course of the past twenty-seven hundred miles, he had given up trying to get some circulation going throughout his system by stopping every hundred miles, and just drove until he couldn't take the pain and the cramping and the stiffness anymore. When he slept at the rest stops, he slept folded into the front seat, as if afraid that one of the unsavory types who populated these urine-soaked places late at night, all night, would try to steal the car out from under him. He was a tired motherfucker, and he found himself assimilating the personality he projected of every state he passed through. In Iowa, he had been bland and unassuming, slumped low in the car as he drove, like an old man. But by North Platte, Nebraska, where the all-night roar of motorcycles cut into his sleep, he'd begun to swagger and curse, and bought a six-pack for a last two-hour dash down the interstate before sleep overcame him. When he dipped into the tip of Colorado, he felt unaccountably swank, wealthy, a Denver Carrington let loose on Fort Collins, and he tucked in his shirt and nodded gravely at gas station attendants, and touched two fingers to his forehead even though there was no hat there. Now Nevada, where whorehouses and casinos stood as wide-open and brazen as McDonald's and Motel 6. West was ready for it.

He sauntered over to the car, recognizing his own ridiculousness and enjoying his ability to recognize it, reveling in the no small accomplishment of traversing the bulk of the country without a driver's license. From the trunk within the trunk of the Malibu, he pulled out clean underwear, fresh jeans, and a white T-shirt, and hobbled up the fire escape–style stairway to his second-floor room.

In the airless mush of humidity and disinfectant, he undressed and got in the shower. Almost four days without a shower, and he was so ripe with the odor that it seemed to coat him like a second skin, the smell of Iowa corn and pigsties, Nebraska wheat and truck exhaust, Wyoming slag, Utah salt. When he'd driven past the Great Salt Lake, he'd pulled over and gotten out and taken a few steps across to the hills shimmering like quartz in the heat. He felt as if he were walking on the moon, the thick bed of shifting, sucking salt suspending rules of gravity and air. He could barely breathe. He got back in the car and gingerly drove through Utah, the road lined with scallops of tires burst open and shredded by heat and traffic.

Now, in the shower, he held his mouth up to the gush of water and rinsed his teeth first, the four-day grit of fast-food hamburgers and funny sandwiches snatched from the glass refrigerators of gas station convenience stores, the thick, sugary film of two dozen caffeine soft drinks, the occasional chocolate bar for energy and digestion, the odd six-pack of beer drunk on the sly over the last bit of midnight road before fatigue closed in and shut him down at a desolate roadstop in Iowa City, Ogallala, Rock Springs. He enjoyed the taste of the water, its chemical pureness of chlorine and fluoride and Nevada minerals, as if it were actually all chemical and not water at all, but some post-nuclear solution that could cleanse you in and out, above and beyond. He drenched his hair with it, then diligently applied soap to his crotch, lathering the testicles, drowning the pubic hair with foam. He ran the soap down each leg, picked up one foot at a time and worked a coat of white between each toe, soaped up his chest and back, then began in earnest on his underarms. It took a long time to take the smell away, and even then he knew that it would come back. Over drinks later, he would begin to smell it working its way from his pores. His smell, which was now the smell of the country and the car and the interstate and a conglomeration of rest stops.

He changed into the fresh set of clothes and descended the metal staircase, each step pinging under his tired weight, to the parking lot. The place was packed with RVs, station wagons, convertibles, minivans, four-door sedans, two-door economy cars. It was America on vacation, caught in the only town for two hundred miles, the oasis of Lovelock. He passed the outside of the casino again, not at all curious. West had been eighteen when Atlantic City had opened up its massive hotels to gambling, and at first he'd been hooked, driving out every weekend during his senior year in high school with slick-talking friends who convinced him that he only had to *know* he could win, and then he *would* win. After five hundred dollars over a month and a half of weekends, he recognized the myth of it. Now he fingered the roll of quarters in his pocket and counted up how many drinks it would buy.

The restaurant was on the far side of the lobby, a curtain-draped wood-paneled spectacle done up like a Spanish galleon, with waitresses and waiters swashbuckling along in sashes and eye patches and mock swords strapped to their thighs. According to his coupons, he could have the fifteen-dollar salmon steak for five dollars, or the twelve-dollar T-bone for seven. Obviously the T-bone was fresh and the salmon was not. West stood patiently at the entrance, waiting for one of the pirates to seat him. He shivered in the cold of the arctic air conditioning and wished he'd brought his jeans jacket with him.

One of the pirate waitresses finally beckoned, and he walked his athletic, groin-pulled walk to a little two-person booth with a table the size of two plates. He sat and smiled gratefully at the waitress. The seat backs were so high he could see nobody, and he was spared the embarrassment of others observing his solitary eating. He waved off the offer of the menu.

"I'll have the T-bone and a pitcher of Bud," he said, showing his coupons.

She nodded and left to fill his order.

Above the booth backs and all around him swirled the idle but passionate chatter of families and couples eating and drinking after a day of driving across desert and plain. West patted down his damp hair and leaned back in the booth. He wondered if he were allowed to fall asleep. Automatically his legs pumped for the brake, the gas, and he shot awake, his eyes swimming with images of late-night driving, when cars appeared to miraculously jump guardrails and swerve in his path and animals created by headlights and road reflectors and angles of perception crouched in the middle of the lane. Only five hundred miles farther and he'd reach San Francisco. He rubbed his eyes and waited for his dinner.

When it came, he ate slowly. The steak was charred on the outside, rare at each cut. The baked potato looked like and was as hard as an egg laid by some prehistoric bird. He dabbled with the iceberg lettuce, Pollock-dripping an array of dressings but unable to get it to taste like anything. He drank. The meal would be twelve dollars plus tax and tip. He would have fifty-nine dollars left. The drama of money. He would need two full tanks of gas—twenty-eight dollars—and a ten-dollar reserve for tolls. That left about fifteen dollars to have a few drinks at the casino bar, to the accompaniment of the clatter and jangle of the one-arm bandits and the clacking of the roulette wheel. He made himself finish the meal.

He was tired and a little woozy, but this was Nevada and he had to drink. He crossed through the lobby to the casino. He sat at the horseshoe-shaped bar and ordered a bourbon on the rocks. An inlaid video poker game stared up at him from the bar. EASY MONEY! EASY MONEY! He moved down a seat to be away from it. At the slot machines, fifty- and sixty-year-old ladies in blue jeans and neckerchiefs loaded coins in, five at a time, accompanied by the whoops of yet older men in cowboy hats and Levi's. Everybody was from someplace else.

He sipped at his drink. Two seventy-five. He had to go slow. His clean clothes made him sleepy. Twenty-seven hundred miles and he was not even there yet. He just wanted to be there. When he'd finally gotten hold of Bob Fields, he'd felt reassured. "You just take as much time as you need," Bob had said. "The job's waiting for you, it isn't going anywhere. Seven days, eight days. I'd say nine maximum. Can you make it in nine?" West had counted his money. "Would it be a problem if I got there a little ahead of schedule?" "No problem at all," Bob said. "We're on a day-to-day contract with the security company. But nine days maximum. Okay?" The guy was utterly reasonable. He had not even tried to hide his breathing on the phone—a low rattle that occasionally rose to a wheezing. West trusted him instantly.

The job paid room, board, and benefits, plus five hundred dollars a month—a pretty good deal, West thought. It would give him a chance to put some distance between himself and prison, and he could figure out what the next step was. He held up his empty glass and waited to catch the bartender's eye. After a pitcher of beer and a shot of bourbon, he was not really so drunk as he thought he should be. Perhaps Lucky Andy's watered their drinks. What had intoxicated West most about the Atlantic City casinos was that, when he was gambling, they gave him drinks *free*.

But that had not helped him in the quixotic struggle to convince himself that he *knew* he would win. Now he was convinced that he had lost five hundred dollars not because the theory was wrong, but because he had failed, ultimately, in *knowing* he would win. He looked at the video poker game and reached into his pocket for the quarters.

"Hey, buddy."

The damn thing apparently talked. He glared at it.

"Hey, buddy. Over here." Someone was knocking on his shoulder as if it were a door. "On your right."

West swirled the bar stool around. His interlocutor, his rescuer, was a man of thirty-odd years and six and a half feet, a white cowboy hat cocked on his head like a second grin, a strong jaw, five o'clock face. An open-lipped toothy smile, waiting for the go-ahead to continue talking. West was delighted to discover that he was drunk, after all, and at the back of his mind he was frightened by it, too, he could feel it coming on like a train through a tunnel, and he was trapped by it. There would be nothing he could do but get up after it had run him over. He wondered if he would have to throw up.

"What," he said uneasily.

The smile drew shut in a line of gratitude, at having been recognized by the chair. The chair nodded for him to go on.

"I've got my hands full, buddy, if you know what I mean," the smile said. "Two ladies." The hat wagged in a direction West could not follow. "I was wondering if you might help me out." He clapped West familiarly on the shoulder. "How about it?"

West looked at him, trying to discern the motivation for such a gift. It was some kind of scam, belied by the easy smile, the white teeth, the open face.

"What the hell," West said. He slouched off the bar stool. "Where are they?"

The smile steered him around the curve of the bar. "Name's Jack," he said.

"Scott," West lied. It was his favorite of fake names.

"Well, Scott, by the end of the night you'll be thanking me. I just know it."

They pulled up at the far end of the bar, underneath a cold shaft of air conditioning, where two women in their twenties sat stirring their drinks. One of the women looked up. She had long dirty-blond hair waved around a thin face. A smirk spread, which she did not attempt to hide. West had to admit that she was beautiful. "You found somebody," she said.

"This is Scott," Jack said.

"I'm Lisa." The woman frowned at West and gave a sideways nod of her head. "This is my sister, Ana. Don't fuck with her."

Ana looked up at West frankly, with uncautious eyes. Her short brown hair was parted incidentally in the middle, and faint freckles rose with a blush in her face. "Be nice," she said to Lisa. She took West's hand and shook it. Her wrist seemed as thin as his thumb. "I'm pleased to meet you," she said.

"He's a jerk," Lisa said. She jabbed West in the shoulder with her index finger. "I'll repeat myself. Don't fuck with her."

"I'm out of here," West said. He turned to go. Somebody caught his arm and he assumed it was Jack, but when he looked down, it was Ana.

Jack laughed. "Okay, babe. I did my end." He offered the crook of his elbow to Lisa, and she took it and rose off the stool. She was wearing a tank top and very tight jeans, and she undulated in such a way that West instinctively checked to see if his mouth was open.

"You two be good." She smiled fakely at both of them, while Jack began to lead her away. "Honestly," she said. "I don't care what you do."

West watched them go, two tapered backs. Ana still held on to him, and he could not bring himself to move. He shut his eyes and then opened them, expecting to find himself staring down at the video poker game. She let go and patted the empty seat beside her.

"Join me," she said.

Obediently he sat on the stool.

She touched his hair lightly. "I like your hair," she said. "It's clean." He tensed, liking her touch, wanting her to go further. She selected a lock and stretched it unpainfully between two fingers. "Don't you worry about Lisa. She's my younger sister but I frustrate her terribly." She said it in an even way, without irony.

"The way she was"—West felt for each word—"I thought she was older."

"It's because I'm a little slow," Ana said. She let go of the hair and turned his head to face her. "Retarded. Would you mind kissing a retarded girl?"

"No," West said. It was a weird joke, but he'd play along. "I wouldn't."

She pulled his head to her and kissed him, long and tight-lipped, as if she had learned by watching television, her face moving instead of her mouth. It was still a nice kiss. He drew back.

"Did you like it?" she said. Her finger traced his face.

"Sure." West glanced around the casino to see if anyone had noticed. They hadn't. He rubbed the back of his neck. He liked her bangs and how small her nose was. He felt as if the back of his head had been shot off and all the air was rushing in. He reached for the back of his head. It was still there. He wondered if this were the train of his drunk finally coming, to knock him out.

"Can I buy you a drink?" she said. "I have ten dollars." She took out a purse from a little red pocketbook and showed him the money. She handed him a personal identification card that said TENNESSEE in a hologram across her face. She pointed at the birthdate. "I'm twenty-five," she said. "See." Effortlessly she flagged down the bartender. "What are you drinking?"

West shook his head and swallowed to see how close the drink was to overpowering him. It was not close enough. "Bourbon," he said hoarsely.

"Bourbon," she said. The bartender nodded and went off to make the drink. "Bourbon," she said again, drawing out the *r,* tasting the *n* on the roof of her mouth. He could see her that clearly. "What's it like?"

He'd never thought much about it. "It's like," he began. He swallowed. Soon the alcohol would overwhelm him, and he'd be saved. "It's like water mixed with the skin of red apples. Like the very sweet bitterness of apple skin."

"It doesn't sound very good," she said.

"It isn't," he agreed. But it was sure as hell going to stop him, which was lucky.

The bartender returned with the drink. It was straight up, no ice. West nodded at Ana and forced a sip. He hated warm bourbon. He made himself take a gulp. Bile rose halfway up his throat and he was pleased. "Thank you," he said.

"Do you have a room here?" Ana said. She touched his hair again and he froze. "Jack has a room. Lisa and I share a room. I think I'd like to see your room." Her hand fell lightly to the back of his neck, and she squeezed it tenderly between her thumb and index finger. He shivered. He looked at her. The air conditioning fluttered her bangs. She took in his look with what appeared to be mild interest. "Are you ready?"

She was behind the curve but she was not that far behind. But she was far enough behind as to be behind the curve. She was capable of complex thought the way a twelve-year-old was capable of complex thought—serendipitously. It was a long word and he took a dip with it into the bourbon. He wished he did not have a room. He wished he were back at his old seat at the other end of the horseshoe. He wished—almost—that he were back in prison.

"How, exactly," he said. "How exactly did we get into this?" He leaned his head into his hands, her fingers falling down his back, and shut his eyes, saw explosions of light, and opened them again.

"I think you're nice," she said.

"Oh, I'm nice." He sighed. "I'm very nice." He drained his drink. He could feel his train of drunkenness coming through and it was not going to knock him down, it was going to take him with it. He reared off the stool. "Let's go."

She stood, reached for his hand, and caught it. They walked out of the casino, hand in hand, she holding on tight enough so that he knew not to break loose, but loose enough to seem as if she understood he would not think of leaving her. The bright light of the lobby hit him suddenly, and he reeled at it. She guided them to the door and opened it for them, still holding on to his hand.

They were outside, in the night. He hoped the air would help, but it was flat, dry desert air, ineffectual. She led him toward the parking lot, to where the cars sat caged in their heat and grease.

"Where's your car?" she said.

"Don't know." He could see it quite easily, the black vinyl hood, the wide brown body. The Pennsylvania license plate peeking out between the Winnebago and the pickup.

"Ours is over there."

He looked at her arm as she pointed, the way it extended out of her short-sleeved dress in a stunning, naked pureness, the subtle looseness of flesh around the upper arm, the taut forearm with a hint of muscle, the impossible narrow wrist, the fingers long and slender. He wanted to eat them. Their car was a four-door, dull silver Toyota that looked almost blue in the sparsely lighted parking lot.

"We're going to visit our aunt and uncle in San Diego," she said. "Where are you going?"

"Los Angeles," West said.

"Maybe I could see you on our way back. That would be in two weeks." She pressed his hand.

"Sure." He touched her arm, followed it up toward the shoulder, just to see if he could. He certainly could. His fingertips felt for the sleeve opening and he was in and feeling the very light titillating growth of hair at her underarm. And then past and lightly pressing the swell of her breast, touching it at the very base of the bra before the nylon consumed it, measuring its potential size. Already he was hard. He wanted to bring around her hand that so persistently was locked in his and make her touch it. He was aghast to discover that that was just what he was doing.

"Not in the parking lot," she said.

They led each other through the rows of cars and vans and pickups and campers to the metal staircase.

"The second rack," she said.

Up the stairs, the loud pinging like coins dropping down a well, and along the thinly carpeted porch of a hallway to his room. He fought with the key for a moment, wanting it to take long enough to allow her to escape. Instead, she moved out of his light, to give him a better chance to open the door. She strode in without invitation, and he followed, turning on the light and at first hesitating but then shutting the door firmly and flicking on the air conditioning.

"It's just like ours," she said. "I knew it would be."

He started for the television, to get some more noise in the room, but she intercepted him. She caught him and hugged him tightly, her cheek against his, as if they were saying goodbye. He looked forlornly beyond her to the television, which he now realized he had considered his last hope. Against his chest, her breasts seemed to be throbbing, demanding his attention.

The buttons down the back of her dress came easily to him, and he unhooked each of the four discs while her hands slipped down to his buttocks and pressed and then got a grip and squeezed, each hand to its own buttock. Her dress fell from her shoulders to her forearms. In the honeycomb of light—for the overhead lamp had a straw basket shade that released thin sheaves of illumination—he saw the creamy part of her neck, the soft cups of her bra. Without waiting for her to step from her dress, he unhooked the bra. She was undressed in such a way that it looked as if perhaps she were trying to dress. He hesitated, and she came out of her pumps and her dress and her bra all at once.

He fell onto the bed with her and bucked against her, squirming to kick out of his sneakers and jeans and trying to get her panties down her legs. She sighed. He could not tell whether it was a sigh of resignation or enjoyment, and again he stopped. It struck him, taking her in—the incautious eyes, the incidental part in her bangs, the minute nose dotted minutely with freckles, the calm breasts with the inerect nipples—it struck him that it was a sigh of indifference. The bourbon rose in his throat and he shut it down, willed it back to a place he had yet to discover. He was atop her.

"What's that?" she said.

She was fingering a pimple on his right buttock.

"It's a pimple," he said. "I've got a pimple there." He forced his tongue inside her mouth.

"Oh," she said around it. "A pimple." She giggled, it was another word whose sound she seemed to like.

He slid his hand along the inside of her thigh, and at the same time moved her under him so soon her free hand would be where he wanted it to be. He felt the hair between her legs and then probed inside. She was a little wet, not quite wet enough. He was terribly hard. She grazed him, then gripped him. He massaged her wetness.

"I have to ask you something," she said. She was slightly out of breath, holding on to him. "Should you be doing this?"

"Yes." From his perspective, it was just too late, the train had come through and he was on it and he just had to ride it. He just had to follow this through. He pulled against her grip, trying to get loose.

"It's a strange hotel," she said, her face turned to the side so that she appeared to be examining the loud air conditioner and the green curtains that quivered against it.

"You're not kidding." He was finally where he wanted to be. He started.

"You sure you should be doing this?" she asked again.

"Yes." Now retreat was impossible. He had no choice.

"How does it feel?"

He didn't answer her, he kept at it. She clung to him.

"Do you like it?" she asked.

"Yes." He did.

She squirmed. "I think we should stop."

"Soon."

"Are we going to stop?"

"Yes."

She touched his face. "When are we going to stop?"

"Soon." If she would just be quiet, he was almost ready.

"I don't like it."

"I know." He stopped. Through the sheaves of light he could see her eyes, wide open and indifferent. She had certainly had experience in masturbation, but it had not prepared her to understand. He was sure she would be all right. He pulled out.

"Los Angeles," she said.

He came against the bedspread, unable and unwilling to rein it in. It seemed to him that he came for a long time, but he could not be sure. He tried to hide it from her. She was already pulling on her panties.

"Can I use your bathroom?"

He clutched a swath of bedspread around him, began to dry himself off while he still came. "Of course," he managed.

She moved to the bathroom, picking up pieces of clothing as she went. She shut the door behind her, then laughed, and opened it. He turned his back to the sound of her, felt the light of the bathroom on his shoulders. She hummed and made water at the same time, like a song with instrumentals. He finished drying himself off and began to get into his clothes. She got off the toilet and flushed and washed her hands in the sink. She was fully dressed and he was trying to shimmy into his jeans.

"We leave at seven tomorrow for our aunt and uncle's," she said, touching his back with her clean hand. "Will you come see us off?"

"Sure." He finally had his jeans on. Where was his shirt? Frantically he scanned the room.

"I have to go."

He nodded his agreement. He spied the shirt under the corner of the bed and bent to pick it up. Behind him, she started for the door.

"Won't you kiss me good night?" she said.

Relieved, he stood. They kissed each other on the cheek. She opened the door and was through and shut it quickly behind her. He listened. She did not walk immediately away. She stood at the door and called in, softly, "Don't forget tomorrow morning. Seven A.M." He nodded at the door, even though he couldn't see her, even though he had no intention of making the engagement. Finally, he heard her leave.

He went to the sink in the bathroom and splashed water on his face. In the yellow light, his hands looked green. He felt a little green. He located the toilet, lifted the seat, got down on his knees, and stuck his finger down his throat to help things along. He gagged around his finger. At last, it came, so much liquid, as if he'd not eaten anything in a long time. He let it come, he tried to encourage it to come, he tried to be patient. Sweat broke out on his back. His throat was raw. He stood, went back to the sink, and drank tap water from the cup of his palm. He put his mouth to the tap, rinsed. He considered taking another shower, but concluded he could not spare the time.

He took a last look around the room, gathered up his dirty clothes, and shut off all the lights. He stood at the door. It was past midnight. He opened the door and slipped through and shut it softly. Lightly he made his way down the metal stairs to the parking lot, the steps almost silent, making only the faintest jangle.

He navigated the rows of vehicles to his car. He unlocked the door, got in, shut the door, and started the engine. He waited a few seconds to make sure it was ready, then backed out of the space and crept to the exit. Only after he had turned right out of the lot and was on Main Street did he switch on his headlights. The road was lined with twenty-four-hour convenience stores, and he was terribly thirsty. Straight ahead and beyond the town, in the blackness of the flats, was the interstate, occasional lights of solitary traffic scudding across the overpass. He did not think he could afford to stop. In his mouth was the taste of tap water and vomit. The still-sunbaked car smelled of it and of his new sweat and of the old sweat that he'd been unable to air out. Once he got on the interstate, he would allow himself to roll down the windows. He would stick his head out the window as he drove, taking in the air like a dog. He laughed at the comparison—it was appropriate.

Now he was up on the interstate, over Lovelock and past it. He could not quite risk rolling down the windows yet. He was terribly paranoid. He deserved paranoia. Almost suffocating with the smell of himself, he drove through the flats.

At 3 A.M., West pulled into a gas station on the outskirts of Reno, Nevada, with nothing more on his mind than filling up the tank, picking up a couple cans of soda, and getting the hell out of Nevada. By his calculations, it was quite possible to arrive and be already settled in San Francisco before the Tennessee sisters even woke in Lovelock.

West climbed from the car and stretched. His legs and arms felt numb and shaky from lack of sleep and a hangover of indeterminate magnitude. The air smelled of gasoline and money, the dry, papery, handworn, printed odor of stacks of bills lying on a counter somewhere up the boulevard, where in the distance the city glowed like a red hole sunk in the middle of the desert.

West limped his way over to the glassed-in window where an attendant sat hunkered down under a green baseball cap and a rack of cigarettes that appeared to extend from his head all the way up into the ceiling.

"You can't come in," he said via a microphone to a speaker that came out above West's left ear.

"I know it." West took out a twenty and laid it in the projected pocket pushing out from the window. "Can you give me a tank of unleaded and a couple of Cokes?"

The attendant slid the pocket back inside the window, took out the bill, held it up to the light, and sighed. "I'll push in your gas order now, but fetching the drinks will take a few." He pointed behind him at the brightly colored mini-mart that lined the walls—green and orange and red bags of assorted potato chips, pretzels, cookies; a row of glass refrigerators stocked with beer, soda, and fruit drinks; two stunted aisles piled with toilet paper, detergent, dog food. The attendant punched in the unlimited dollar amount for West's pump, and stood up. He nodded down at his hands. They were clutching a walker. He began to maneuver his way out from the cashier's post like a car doing a three-point turn.

"No hurry," West said. He wiped his mouth with his hand and came away with crushed flecks of dead skin. His voice sounded like a rasp. He went back to the car and started pumping.

Across the boulevard was a huddled, shady outline of a trailer park. His hand felt hot and oily around the handle of the pump, and it kept slipping. He had to concentrate to keep the mechanism pressed in, and even then it slipped. He tried to relax. A drop of sweat worked its way from his underarm down the side of his chest. With his free hand, he patted his T-shirt to soak up the perspiration. As soon as he had finished, he felt another drop emerge. The boulevard seemed slick beneath the watery street-light. He touched his hand to his forehead and it came back damp. At seventeen-fifty, the gas pump clicked off.

He screwed on the cap to the tank, replaced the nozzle, and was squeezing back into the car when he realized he had forgotten his change and the Cokes. He righted himself and crossed back to the cashier's window.

"I thought I had me some free Cokes." The cashier grinned from under his cap. He couldn't have been older than thirty. "Or a big tip. Whatever." He stuck the Cokes and West's change into a glass box to West's left, and shut the little door. "Now you can open it."

West reached in and got his sodas and money. He considered

leaving the eighty cents as a tip, but decided that would be both weak and self-serving. He clenched the two Cokes in the fist of one hand and returned to the car.

He sat in the Chevy, staring out the smeared windshield. In the hotel room at Lucky Andy's, thin sheaves of light had illuminated aspects of Ana's body, her small breasts, the creamy part of her neck. He'd tasted her nipples, a salty sweetness. He started the car and drove out from the pump. At the end of the gas station, he looked right, studying the boulevard into Reno. The cars on the road appeared to be from a different era, wide bodies with tail fins and brake lights that slanted like eyebrows. He turned left. Within half a block, the interstate arrived, a minor conflagration of on-ramps and overpasses. He stretched against the seat, only to discover that a pool of almost gelatinous sweat had formed at the small of his back. He wiped his mouth, and then cracked open one of the Cokes. Without further consideration, he guided the Chevy up the on-ramp heading east, heading back toward Lovelock.

On his way across the desert, he searched the landscape for signs that he had not been this way before, that he'd only imagined it. The moon lit the bed of rock and sand into shades of blue, and the night sky met the land with walls of depthless black. He couldn't tell anymore what had happened, what she'd said, what he'd said. What they'd done. He took a long swallow of Coke and waited. He could feel it coming. He pulled over onto the shoulder of the road and quickly got out of the car. He walked around the back of it, and descended a soft slope into the flats. The ground was hard under his feet. The crumbles of land that had broken loose felt like marbles against the thin soles of his sneakers. Rocks jutted out across the desert, their points glinting like wrecks in a sea. He could still feel it coming. It bent him at the waist, and the seat of his jeans was suddenly damp with his sweat. He vomited.

Was it what he had done, or what he had drunk? His eyes filled with tears from the effort and pain of puking. Around him, he could feel the dry earth soaking him up. He was careful not to fall. When he had finished, he tiptoed out of the semicircle of it, walked a good distance away, and peed.

Afterward, he climbed the soft slope to the road and walked out onto the middle of the pavement. He could still feel the heat of the sun rising from it. Above and around him, the night was turning, fading, draining into day. Blue crept into the sky. He would still reach San Francisco by the end of this one, provided the sister didn't have him arrested. She did not seem the type. She would dismiss him instead. He could live with that. He did not mind being dismissed. In the distance, he heard something coming, and he turned and saw, about a mile back down the interstate, a truck making its way toward him, the lights atop its cab standing out like a hairline. The truck honked two times, as if it could see him. He crossed back to the side of the road and got into his Chevy. What was left of the first Coke had spilled over onto the floor mat, and the car smelled of sugar and caffeine. In a day, he would sell it. He cracked the second can of Coke and took a sip. He swished it around in his mouth like mouthwash, and spit it out the open window. He tried another sip. It tasted better. Up ahead, the truck was still coming, lumbering across the flats toward him. He started the Chevy. He would miss it, when he sold it, but he'd be relieved as well. It was a damned good car.

It moved weightily over the road, through the flats, as if it knew it had been this way before and resented having to repeat it. He laughed and gulped at the Coke. The truck came up from the other direction and shot past him in a clatter of wind and metal and tire flaps. He finished his Coke and tried to lick the film of it from his teeth. Clouds approached in the gradual blueing of dawn. He would arrive in Lovelock on time. A paper bag caromed across the flats. From a great distance, he spied another oncoming truck. It was just him and the truck and the paper bag. He wondered what he would say to her, if her sister knew, what either of them would say to him. He wondered why he was doing this to himself.

To leave nothing undone, nothing to chance. To save himself from his conscience. To extend a trip that was bound to end in the hollow disappointment of a crummy job. To stall the onset of the rest of his life. But California, he was going to California! That was *someplace,* by God. He tried the radio. Nothing, not even static. Sparks ought to have had a radio station, but he was too far past it, closing in on Lovelock. The sky around him filled with the flat whiteness of heat and haze. He had somehow missed the actual sunrise, and now the sun had slipped out of view. It was already above the car somewhere. He could feel it through the vinyl roof, but it wasn't even six yet. Yes, it was. It was exactly six. Lovelock in thirty miles. He ought to slow down. He didn't want to get there early, just in case what awaited him proved unpleasant or unfair. He ought to be stretching this out, the passing rockscape, the dry, cracked barrenness, the hot wind coming into the car. This feat of motion. He turned the steering wheel slightly, to see if the car would obey it. He drifted into the right lane, then back to the left and over toward the double yellow line. He could still do whatever he wanted. It was almost mid-June, the steady, relentless, ripening, approaching summer, the sweat of the car mixing with the sweat of the road. Soon he would be in San Francisco, with a job, an apartment, resigning himself to routine, a city, the deadening haul of daily work. He jiggled the steering wheel again, it was still with him, it made the car respond. He adjusted his rearview mirror to see if anyone was coming. There was no one. When he turned his attention back to the road in front of him, the second truck was upon him. He jerked awake, jerking the car with him to the right, then correcting himself. The truck was already fifty feet past, curving toward Sparks. It had not even been close.

He had not slept since the rest stop in Rock Springs, twenty-four hours ago. It was affecting his driving. He shouldered up over the wheel, willing himself to concentrate. The first billboard approached, a blaze of red and orange rising out of the white rock of the flats. He squinted at it. It was not Lucky Andy's. Lucky Andy's colors, he recalled, were the red and black of the pirate sashes and eye patches and pantaloons, with some gold thrown in for the treasure hunters. He thought of the horseshoe-shaped bar and his stomach seemed to stand up and spin against his skin. His chest still felt tender from the rawness of the vomiting.

Within ten miles of Lovelock, the car appeared to catch a tail wind that made it go faster than he thought it should. He could feel the wide trunk buffeting in the swirl of air. His hands on the steering wheel were greasy with sweat. He braked just to see if he could. The car slowed, but not as much as he had hoped. The billboards were coming fast and furious, as if they'd been held in check for the last hundred miles and were suddenly let free. They gave the flats color and a skyline. Just as he thought that perhaps Lovelock had passed him by, the road opened to his right and the car skated down the off-ramp and he was calmly turning onto Main Street and facing down its procession of gas stations, hotels, motels, casinos, and convenience stores. It was six-thirty. He pulled into the parking lot of a Denny's and turned off the car and got out and stretched his legs and looked up at the sky and kicked at the loose gravel in the lot, to see if he had changed his mind about this. He went into Denny's and bought an iced tea and drank it standing up in the men's room. He urinated, splashed water on his face, and ran his fingers through his hair like a comb.

Outside, at the car, he hesitated about whether to drive the few blocks to Lucky Andy's or walk. He got in and started the car, pulled from the lot, and drove the three and a half blocks. He parked at the curb, got out, and crossed the street to Lucky Andy's. It was six-fifty. The parking lot of Lucky Andy's was still packed with America on Vacation. He found the four-door Toyota with the Tennessee plates and waited next to it, as if expecting a ride.

Lisa came out first, from a door near the ice machine, shouldering a blue-striped beach bag and lugging a tan suitcase. He resisted the impulse to help her. Her face was flushed by the time she reached the car.

"What do you want?" she said, pushing past him to the trunk of the car and dumping the two pieces of luggage on the asphalt.

"I came to see Ana off," West said.

"Well, how about that." She opened the trunk and began to lever the heavy suitcase in, using her knee and shoulder. "Are you going to help me, or what?"

West pitched in with the suitcase, and it thunked onto the floor of the trunk. The car jounced on its shocks. She threw the shoulder bag in, and looked up at him.

"You look awfully guilty," she said. Her tan line showed at the white straps of her tank top. She was wearing shorts, and her legs stretched out of them like swords. He shrugged. "I don't want to hear about it," she said.

"I slept with her," West said. "Last night. In my room."

"In your room," she said, mouthing the words as if they were part of a foreign language. Evidently, Ana hadn't told her. The heat hurtled at his forehead. He'd been up too long. The parking lot glinted with mica chips and car hoods and radio antennas.

"Scott!" Ana yelled. "Scott." In shorts and a pink button-down shirt, she came loping across the sparkling space toward him. She hugged him, her bare legs against his jeans. Even in daylight, she was still nice, her cream skin, the uncautious eyes. "You came."

"I bet he did," Lisa said. She slammed the trunk shut. "What the hell do you want with us?" She stood up straight. She was still not tall enough. "Too bad Jack isn't here."

"Are you all right?" West said to Ana.

"I'm fine." She nodded vigorously. "I know I wanted you to, even if I didn't like it. It's easier by myself. I guess it's the one thing I can do best by myself. Not like I can't do things by myself. I shop for Lisa, you know. I can count change." She held out her hand to him. "Give me some change and I'll show you. I'll count it."

"Jesus," Lisa said.

West stood wavering beside her. He felt very odd.

"You were inside me," Ana said. "I remember that. I remember how it felt. It felt like nothing new. It felt like I could have had my arm inside me. Well, not that big. It didn't do what I needed it to do. Are you going to give me some change so I can count it?"

"I have to sit down," West said. He sat in the parking lot. The heat sealed his mouth. It was awfully hot. He could feel a sunburn coming on, spreading along the back of his neck. Maybe a stroke. He wouldn't mind a stroke. He could feel the dampness of his jeans wedding itself to the stickiness of the lot. He was going to be stuck there. He looked up at the faces of the sisters, blurred by their height and the haze. They were going to need some sort of forklift to get him up. He looked up at them for a long time, his mouth half-open. Their heads bent to listen. The sun was a shoulder above them. It had popped out of the white sky.

"Get up." He could hear Lisa's voice. She pulled at his elbow. "Come on, up with you."

Gradually, he stood up. The parking lot felt like the deck of a great boat, tilting toward the hotel, the street, the hotel again. He righted himself. Now Ana was holding on to his arm. Morning traffic began to flow past on the street.

"Do you know what you've done," Lisa said. It wasn't a question. West nodded anyway, through the thick heat, his neck a lever for the unwieldy emptiness in his head.

"I'm sorry," he said.

"Sorry doesn't do a whole hell of a lot for her," Lisa said. The sun on her face hid her expression. He listened to her, waiting for what she decided. "You think just by showing up you can somehow save yourself from your conscience." She shook her head, the sun holding her eyes. "A jerk like you." She chewed on her lip. "What if," she said, "what if I just left the two of you together like this in the parking lot, stuck here like two posts in cement. What if I did that? What would you do then, Scott?"

"Are we going to call the police?" Ana said.

Lisa turned back to the car, stepping away from the sun, and hitched up her shorts. West saw her clearly, the thinness, the suppleness. "I never wanted to know," she said. "Let's just get out of here." She walked around and unlocked the driver's door and got in and shut it. She started the car.

Ana still held on to West, silently, without expression.

"Ana," he said. "I'm sorry for what I did."

"I wanted you to." She kissed him as the car exhaust rose around them. "And you're coming to see me off. Don't mind what Lisa says."

"Ana," Lisa called from the car. She wouldn't look at them. "Goddamn it."

"Okay." Ana kissed him again, goodbye. Suddenly, but without any kind of accompaniment, she was crying. He could feel her tears on his face. "It's been a wonderful day."

Lisa leaned over and opened the door for her. Ana backed away from West and stepped into the car. Her foot caught and she fell against the seat, her legs sticking out. She curled them up to her chest, those bare legs, and her sister reached around her and pulled the door shut. She stared at West through the window, Lisa did, as if she had something to say to him but she couldn't remember what it was. It could have been *I'm sorry for you,* it could have been *I hate you,* it could have been *I knew.* Instead, she just shook her head and turned back to face the windshield.

West watched them leave, the car rolling out to the street and then turning right and pulling through Lovelock, the bland faces of the always-open convenience stores, to the interstate, where they climbed through the heat onto the road west, the car a silver blur as it raced away from the town. It was seven-thirty. He would have to drive for four hours through the heat, until he reached the Sierra and the temporary relief of the mountains before the sun-boiled stretch of the California central valley. He crossed the street and got into his car, the vinyl hot through his jeans, sweat seared to him. He watched his foot work the gas, felt his hand pop the emergency brake. The car hummed when he turned the key. He looked out the windshield, particles of air shimmering in waves off the pavement, rippling the storefronts of Main Street, the flats beyond it a colorless smear. He pulled a U-turn and headed out toward the interstate. He got on it gingerly, and kept the car to a moderate speed. He would have to be careful for a long time, so as not to overtake the Toyota from Tennessee.

Amanda Filipacchi

Amanda Filipacchi lives in Manhattan and writes in her messy apartment. She keeps her blinds closed at all times so no one can see her while she lives.

Born in France in 1967, she moved to America when she was seventeen, and wrote *Nude Men* while enrolled in Columbia's graduate creative writing program. It has been translated into eight languages.

She is now fervently working on her new novel.

"Nude Men" is an excerpt of a novel of the same name from Viking/Penguin.

I am a man without many pleasures in life, a man whose few pleasures are small, but a man whose small pleasures are very important to him. One of them is eating. One reading. Another reading while eating.

I work at *Screen,* a magazine on movies and celebrities, here in Manhattan. For lunch I go to a little coffee shop that is farther away than the other standard lunch places. It is also more expensive, less good, and less exciting, but it has one tremendous advantage. No one I know goes there.

Recently I discovered another coffee shop. It is even farther away, but the lighting is better for my reading. And no one I know goes there even less. Or more. Or whatever. You know what I mean.

This morning was exhausting at work. I sense that I will get one of my headaches this afternoon. I am hungry for food and literature. As I leave the office building for lunch, I try to decide if I have the strength to walk the extra distance to my new, well-lit coffee shop or if I will settle for the closer one with inferior lighting. I opt for light. After such a morning, I deserve to have a perfect, intensely pleasurable meal. On top of it, I want to see very clearly what will happen to Lily Bart in *The House of Mirth.*

The restaurant is called Grandma Julie's, and it's as cozy as its name. I'm sure everyone feels a little embarrassed walking into a place called Grandma anything, but once you're inside . . . the warmth, the neatness, the sheer professionalism, make you forget your shame.

Today the place is full. I ask the waitress how long it will take to get a table. She says two minutes. I wait, thinking my lunch might not be ruined if I truly get a table in two minutes. A woman enters the coffee shop and waits in line behind me. She's in her late thirties and looks perfectly nice, normal. Two minutes later, the waitress tells me there's a table.

The woman behind me touches me and asks, "Are you alone?"

"Yes," I say.

"Would you mind if we shared the table?"

I visualize my lunch spent sitting in front of a stranger. It would be hell. Her eyes would be resting on me while I read. She might even want to talk: "What are you reading? Do you work around here? It's unusually cold today, but they say it'll get warmer by evening. There's so much noise in this place. I asked for tuna salad, not egg salad. I can't eat this, I have high choles-terol."

My first impulse is to mumble, "It doesn't matter," and rush out the door to my old coffee shop.

What I do answer, very distinctly, but with a slight grimace to soften the blow, is "I'd rather not."

The woman and the waitress stare at me with more surprise than I expected. I try to think of a justification for my response and come up with "I . . . *have* to eat alone. But you go ahead if you want." I gesture toward the empty table.

"No, no, you go ahead," she says, touching my arm with more familiarity than I like.

I sit down, making sure my back is turned to the woman I have just rejected so that she won't be able to observe me. She has ruined my lunch. Even though I'm alone, I won't be able to concentrate on my novel because I feel like a villain. I have never done anything like this before in my life. I eat my grilled cheese sandwich, unable to read, furious, not making eye contact with anyone. How dare the woman do that! I order Jell-O to cheer me up.

I glance furtively at the customers around the room. I'm curious to know where the woman ended up. I look at the people seated at the counter. They all have their backs to me except for one, at the end. She is turned in my direction, her legs are crossed, her elbow is resting on the counter, and she is looking at me fixedly, with a slight smile. At first I think she is my rejected woman, but when I look again I see that she clearly is not. This woman is beautiful, sexy, late twenties. She has a very thick upper lip, which gives her a pouting, capricious look, an air I simply adore in women. Like the actress Isabelle Adjani, my fantasy woman.

She seems like the feminine type, the romantic type, the Sleeping Beauty type, blond hair, the type my girlfriend would perversely say looks jaded because she happens to have a charming face and laugh lines on either side of her mouth.

I am not absolutely certain that she is looking at me. I don't have terrifically good eyesight, so although I was able to notice her plump upper lip, I might be mistaken as to where her pupils are directed. She could be staring out the window next to which I am sitting. Or she could be looking at the businessman at the table in front of me, or at the secretary behind me.

I decide to take a risk anyway. I don't know why. It's not like me. Perhaps because after having bluntly rejected a woman for the first time in my life, I need to bluntly accept one too. I gather every ounce of courage in my body and smile at her, sort of unconsciously sticking out my upper lip so we have something in common.

She pays her bill and walks over to me. Her stomach softly hits the edge of my table as she slides into the opposite seat, making my three cubes of green Jell-O jiggle.

I am racking my brain for something to say, when she says, "I like your mouth."

"The feeling is mutual," I answer with a James Bond tone. I am amazed at the good fortune that made her mention my mouth, giving me the opportunity to come up with this ultimately seductive answer, which surpasses any I have ever heard in movies.

To my great chagrin, she seems annoyed by my response. "I didn't mean it that way," she says. "I study people's features, and your mouth is simply aesthetically satisfactory."

"The feeling is mutual," I want to repeat, but don't dare. "Thank you," I say instead.

With my spoon I scoop up a big green cube of Jell-O, but it jiggles so much from the shaking of my hand that, halfway to my mouth, it plops back down into the dish.

"You should have cut it in two," says the woman. "It's too big."

I try to figure out if there's an erotic insinuation in that comment, but I'm not sure.

"Yes, I should have," I say, and put down my spoon.

For the first time since she sat down, she smiles. She points to the book lying next to my elbow and asks, "What are you reading?"

"The House of Mirth."

"Is it good?"

"Yes, it's great. Have you read it?"

She shakes her head and asks, "Do you work around here?"

"Yes, not too far away. Do you?"

"Sort of. What work do you do?" she asks.

"I'm afraid it's not very interesting. I work at *Screen* magazine. I'm a fact checker."

"I know *Screen*. I've bought it a few times. It's a lot of fun."

"Thank you. I guess that's what I should say. What work do you do?"

"I'm a painter."

"Ah! How nice. Is your work exhibited anywhere right now?"

"Yes." She pauses. "I work at home."

"That must be the best place for a painter to work," I say, feeling a little confused by her sudden switch of subject. "What type of painting do you do?"

"People. I paint people."

"I love people. I mean, paintings of people. Are they abstract?"

"No. Well, everything is abstract in a way, isn't it? But no, my people are not strictly abstract."

"So, you paint people. That's why you said you study people's features. It's because you paint them."

"Yes, that's why," she says.

"What types of people do you paint?"

"I don't really paint 'types,' unless you call men a type. I paint men."

"What types of men?"

"I don't really paint 'types' of men, unless being naked is a type. Is a naked man a type of man? Some types of men are almost never naked. Then there are the others, who are also a type, the type who are *not* almost never naked. Which type are you?"

I stare at the transparent greenness swaying almost imperceptibly between us. I wonder if there's an erotic insinuation in her question.

"Such a thing is hard to know," I answer. "I never figured it out myself. Is your work exhibited anywhere, or did I ask you that already?"

"My work is exhibited in *Playgirl* magazine. Toward the back of the magazine. I get two pieces shown. Sometimes only one, spread over two pages. My work has been appearing for six years."

I plunge my spoon into a cubical section of my green gelatin dessert and lift it to my mouth. "So, you paint nude men," I say, squishing the sweet greenness between my tongue and palate.

"Yes. And I like your mouth, so I was wondering if . . . you'd like to pose for me."

I grin at her, hoping there's no gelatin stuck between my teeth. "I'm flattered, but one's mouth is not a very good representation of one's naked body."

"A mouth is a very good representation. There are clues and signs in a mouth. Will you do it?"

She gives me that pouting, capricious look, making her upper lip flare out more than ever. Her resemblance to Isabelle Adjani in *The Story of Adele H.* is striking. I melt. There is nothing I would not do for the owner of that upper lip at this point. I'm usually very shy, but this woman seems like such a good catch for me, and I'm so attracted to her, that I think I will agree to pose for her. At least I can get into her apartment, and then, at the last minute, if I become chicken, I can always change my mind about posing.

"You want me to pose nude for you?" I ask.

"Yes I do. I spotted you from all the way over there, remember?" She points to the counter. "I'll pay you thirty dollars an hour, if it's okay with you. That's the standard price. But if you want more, we can discuss it."

I cringe at her words. I don't want to have a professional relationship with her, just a romantic one. I should have accepted right away, before she brought up money.

"I would love to pose for you," I say.

"I know. I'm glad," she answers. Her voice is soft, and her face delicate and serene. Her hands reach inside her bag.

"When are you available?" she asks, handing me her card.

"Anytime. When are you?"

"How about Saturday at 6 P.M.?"

"Perfect," I say, delighted at the late hour she chose.

"Could I have your card?"

I jump up in my seat, tap my pockets, and say, "I don't have one with me right now, but here, this'll do just as well, if you don't mind." I write my name, address, and phone number on the paper napkin under my Jell-O dish. I hand her the napkin, which she takes between her thumb and forefinger, pinkie lifted. I think I detect slight snobbery, but I'm not sure.

She reads it aloud: "Mister Jeremy Acidophilus." She added the "mister." She keeps staring at my name on the napkin, looking puzzled, and I know what's coming next. She says, "Acidophilus, as in the yogurt culture?"

Here we go. One of the big dramas of my life. "Yes, the yogurt culture," I reply.

"Is there a story behind that?"

Although the truthful answer would be "None that I know of," I decide instead, perhaps because I'm slightly masochistic, to say: "When my father was a young man, he saw the word on a yogurt container and thought it sounded very intelligent and interesting. He made it his name." This is a lie I made up a few years ago but never had the guts to use on anyone. The most daring thing I ever do, sometimes, when people ask me my name, is to adopt a James Bond tone and reply "Acidophilus. Jeremy Acidophilus." The truth about my name is that there is no anecdote about it, not even a rumor. Some people are named Bazooka, others are named Fender; why should some not be named Acidophilus?

She folds the napkin in four, looking at me with a tiny smile. Mocking? Perhaps. Playful? More likely. She slips the napkin in her purse and gets up, hitting the edge of the table with her stomach again, a little harder this time. The two and a half cubes of gelatin dessert dance in unison.

"Well, Mister Active Yogurt Culture, Mister Friendly Bacteria, it's been a pleasure meeting you," she says, shaking my hand with small, hard fingers that are nevertheless not rough.

She walks toward the door. I don't turn around to watch her go out. I'm not the type to stare at a woman's backside; not that I don't want to, but I'm afraid someone might see me do it. At the last minute, however, I do look back and I see it, just before it disappears behind the door. It's nice, small but not too, with a clearly defined pit, or slit, or whatever you call it, that I can see through the fabric of her skirt. I heard recently that some women undergo cosmetic surgery to have the cheeks of their backside spread farther apart. Supposedly it makes a nicer outline, nicer definition. I can imagine how that might be, though it seems a little too finicky. Anyway, I'm glad to report that my new woman will never need that surgery.

I stare at my two and a half cubes of green with satisfaction. I do not eat them.

That was a very pleasant encounter indeed. I look around the room very bluntly. No meek sweeps of the head, no furtiveness. Large, broad sweeps of the head. Where is my rejected woman? I feel eternally grateful to her. If it hadn't been for her, I would never have felt the need, nor had the courage, to return my new woman's smile. I would have accused my eyesight of fooling me. I would have buried my nose in my book, even held up my book as a shield against the charm of the plump upper lip.

I pay my bill, get up, and look at all the faces as I walk toward the door. I would like to find her, smile and nod my head as I pass her. She is not there. I leave Grandma Julie's. I think I will walk the extra distance in the future. Who knows, I might even share my table with a stranger.

Bryan Malessa

Bryan Malessa is largely self-educated. He was expelled from the Georgia public school system in his early teens because of drug abuse and "antisocial" behavior. He spent his fifteenth year in Alchemy—an experimental rehabilitation program funded by the state. After many years of working various menial jobs and a stint competing with the U.S. Cycling Team, he retreated to the mountains of far northern California to concentrate on writing. At twenty-five he reentered school, first attending the College of the Redwoods and then moving on to UC—Berkeley.

"Looking Out for Hope" was initially published in *ZYZZYVA*.

in memory of Raymond Carver

Dear Raymond: Would have called but they disconnected the phone. It doesn't matter. If it was connected, I probably wouldn't have called anyway. Seems like the only time I get in touch these days is when melancholy finds its way home. But what the hell, it's payback. I know I'll be hearing from you again at not the pleasantest of times. I didn't want to hit the bottle, so I figured I'd better start writing. I can't remember when we last spoke. Everything was going smooth there for a while, until last summer. We couldn't make rent, so I had to head Alaska way to work the fish canneries. Hitched two thousand miles in five days. Saw the Yukon from a flatbed Ford driven by an Indian. Things weren't much better up there. I sent the few dollars I made to the homestead, then traded off stealing food with Lenny on the rebound through British Columbia. It was crazy, sneaking coffee creamers off tables between the restaurant's front door and the restroom, but we got it down to a science; you would've loved it. Jeanne stayed busy waitressing at the Humboldt Diner until they filed bankruptcy. The pennies she saved kept us fed for a week or two. Frankly, this recession's kicking our ass; when are they going to start calling it a depression? After a two-month search, I found a couple weeks' work running firebreaks along the ridges near home. But state budget cuts axed that job. Now I'm working as a baker's assistant making minimum wage. How the hell can I work my forty hours a week and still keep losing ground? I don't even have a credit card, and they quit bothering me about those alimony payments long ago. Just rent, food, and utilities are putting us under! I was sure this wouldn't happen again, things were going too smooth. I've already asked every friend I have for money too many times, and they've all been good to me. But a man's got respect. I can't keep on and on asking. I've got to give. And do give, when I can. But now something else is about to give, I can feel it, and it don't feel good. The bills never stop. What do you do about these damn things? I've got ten bucks to my name. I already owe the landlord a hundred dollars and next month is coming fast. Jim did me good for last month's electric bill, but now I have another and still haven't paid him for the last. The crab season is about to open. Good money on the docks, if you can score a job and make it through the month without sleep. Last year they were pulling twenty-hour days. I go to the boatyard every day after work hoping for my lucky break, but so far, no cigar. The wife is taking it OK. We take it out on each other every now and again; we know this can't go on forever. I mean, we're good people. We do our part. You know this, Ray. Hell, I practically did the running for the both of us when we used to go hunting. I don't know. I honestly don't know, Ray. Sometimes I just want to pull the plug. I think you did the right thing getting out of here and all. Work has really slowed at the lumber mills since you left. They've got skilled labor pulling green chain these days. College graduates. Can you imagine that? All those years of school to pull green chain. It doesn't rain as much here now, either. Really slowed down the last few years. The deer are thinning a bit, too. And the government hunters killed three mountain lions last month. It just seems like everything's changing. Remember fishing down at the river's mouth? Why can't things be as simple as they were when we were kids? You remember Old Man Parker? You probably wish you didn't. I'll never forget the color of your face. I thought you were going to die. And then you telling me that was the first and the last time you'd get drunk. I knew better. Anyway, he died a couple weeks back. They've already started bulldozing his place—the house and barn. Putting in a new supermarket or something. That was the last piece of stomping ground left of ours near town. They're even building out where your bullet grazed that doe we chased all night through the woods. I used to dream of buying Parker's place and keeping it forever. I was going to throw a big party and invite all the cronies for old times' sake. Now it's gone and I can't even keep up on rent. I know I'm rambling. I just needed to get some of this off my mind. It's not all bad. I found a crisp, clean dollar bill near the coffee shop this morning. That's got to mean something. At least it bought me a fresh cup of coffee. Just sitting in the window with my steaming cup, reading a newspaper someone had left, and smoking butts from the ashtray was enough to make me feel like I was on my way back up. Of course, when I got back home, there were more bills in the mailbox. I don't care! What can they do? I can handle spending some time sleeping in the car on the south jetty while I get my feet back on the ground. The wind coming off the ocean will probably do me some good. In fact, I know it will. I'll try to keep the loose ends from fraying too badly. Tell the pretty lady hi. You keep looking out now. We're going to find it out there, somewhere.

Chris Hallman

"I was born in 1967 in Grosse Pointe, Michigan, but grew up in a suburb north of San Diego. Although the fact should not change a reader's view of the story at all, I think it's interesting and a little funny that Utopia Road is the actual name of a street I lived on from when I was five to about ten. To compound matters, there was another Utopia Road in the next town over, from which we occasionally received stray pieces of mail."

"Utopia Road" was initially published in *Other Voices*.

UTOPIA ROAD

They came to Utopia Road when there were no olive trees, no lawns, no ice plant hillsides; they came when it was a blacktop street and tiered lots the color of grocery bags, when the sidewalks were white and even the sewers were new. They came more often when the foundations had been laid, driveways cut into the curb, addresses assigned. Up and down the street, similar families stood on the concrete slabs of their living rooms, waving to one another as if to attract the attention of someone in a plane. From station wagons and rented cars they watched muscled men erect spindly sculptures from piles of two-by-fours. Soon, it was possible to discern the style of one house from another. Spanish, ranch, colonial, Victorian. The more curious crept around the houses on lots adjacent to their own, peering up flights of winding plywood stairs, invading the Sheetrock rooms into which they would eventually be invited. Sod, stacked like jelly rolls, arrived on trucks with high metal walls. Trees, eucalyptus and acacia and palm, appeared overnight in the ground near the street. Pleased with the progress, they watched from a distance as tiles and shingles were set delicately in place.

Water rushed through underground pipelines, passing through filters and sieves in distant windowless buildings. Electricity was generated in automated power plants, crossing deserts on suspended cables. Both moved in swift currents. In a week, the toilets flushed, the spigots ran, and the garage doors opened automatically. The tall cement streetlights tinged the air yellow when dusk was perceived by an electronic eye set on a black metal utilities box at the top of the street. The construction workers cleaned the houses of bent nails and tar paper, swept plaster chips and sawdust, and then rode away on the beds of aging pickup trucks.

They moved to Utopia Road on a three-day weekend. Arriving in a caravan of family-sized vehicles and brightly colored moving vans, they carried into the houses upright pianos, overstuffed chairs, and boxes marked fragile in stenciled letters. They formed lines and passed along shadeless lamps, garbage bags stuffed with winter clothes, garden hoses, and milk crates filled with kitchen appliances. They worked through the night, replacing darkness with the trained headlights of a dozen minivans, the streetlights adding a dim yellow sheen from a distance. When it was over, they collapsed on quilts and afghans and carpets that had yet to be stained by their timid pets. Immediate families slept together, their limbs overlapping in a recuperative hibernation. They barely breathed and no one snored. The Gibbs family came out of it first, rising together in the late afternoon and stumbling to their driveway. They pulled plastic outdoor furniture from the garage to the sod lawn and sat, sore and stunned from sleep. Awakened by the movement, the Springers next door came outside as well, absently following the sound. The families introduced themselves and listened to their stomachs growling. The fathers left to find food and came back with chicken in red and white paper buckets. Others woke now to the smell of the meat and walked up the street slowly, as if strolling or merely exploring, and joined the group on the sod lawn. The Shalladays, the Haysletts, the Dautremonts. Two more men took directions from Mr. Gibbs and made a second trip for food. The new neighbors ate and talked and laughed. They exchanged phone numbers, made plans for dinners and card games, and did not notice when the streetlights flickered on all around them.

The men spreads shards of bark where there were no plants to hide the natural light brown dirt, and neglected the timed sprinkler systems they'd paid extra for. Their wives planted gardens and fed tropical fish papery multicolored flakes. The children stood together at the bus stop in the morning, dew wrinkling the pages of their schoolbooks; the boys drove go-carts made from particle board, the girls talked to themselves and their dolls.

Water ran through the houses like blood, the slim plastic pipes a system of veins and arteries. It sat in freezer trays in crescent shapes and hung loose in the air on chilly mornings. Electricity was channeled to the houses, spinning through fisted mats of wires in the black utilities box. The neighbors tapped into it through wall sockets resembling small excited faces. The electricity sang, blended, cooked, compacted, and spoke. When it was used up it seemed to vanish entirely.

For several months, static ran through the air and gave the neighbors sharp shocks when they touched metal or each other. Small weeds that grew in the seams of the sidewalk somehow gave Utopia Road a lived-in look.

The Royces, the family in the corner house, became the subject of hushed discussions. Mr. Royce, a hulking crew-cut man, failed to return the casual waves of the other men, and Mrs. Royce became infamous for her ability to throw the dead bolt of their front door so it made a whiplike crack. On Utopia Road's first Halloween, the Royces posted a sign on their stoop that said "Do Not Ring

Bell." Rumors spread that Mr. Royce was partially retarded and a veteran of the Bay of Pigs and that Mrs. Royce was a bankrupt fortune-teller and a terminal agoraphobe. Their only child, a boy named Tom, was the sole teenager on Utopia Road, and though he was not as reticent as his parents (he used the street as a runway for his fleet of remote-controlled airplanes, the children following him in packs), he was quietly discussed along with them. Fathers told tales of being anonymously strafed by miniature Cessnas, and mothers claimed to have seen him standing over injured boys in the street. Tom denied the aerial attacks, said he no longer owned a plane like the one described, and the bruised sons always took the blame for their wounds on themselves. He was a dark boy, even his eyelids and armpits were tan, and he was thin, efficiently built, his muscles like ropes under stretched skin. Most of the mothers were secretly attracted to him, considered him handsome and manly even at sixteen, and several, under the strained hum of a vacuum cleaner, played with the idea of seducing him for an afternoon. Sleek as a skink, Tom wandered up and down Utopia Road cocky and bare-chested. He took up smoking shortly after Easter and learned to exhale in large white puffs that could be seen from a distance.

The mailboxes of Utopia Road were small-scale replicas of the houses that loomed behind them. The carrier was a kindly, gray-haired man named Mr. Rapp. While delivering Mother's Day cards and Get Well notes to the small model homes set on posts at the end of the driveways, Mr. Rapp beamed at finlike palm fronds shifting in the breeze. He walked carefully across layers of red pumice, pausing frequently to feel the bark of a nonindigenous tree or pity a blue-belly lizard flattened on the asphalt. Since the beginning, Utopia Road had been his favorite part of the route. One day, while he was delivering a small brown box that smelled faintly of yeast, Mr. Rapp was struck by an extremely odd thought. He looked around himself, saw sheets of tiny purple ice plant flowers, frail heads of birds of paradise, a sinister ivy clinging to a salmon-colored stucco wall, and realized that everything he saw had origins in other parts. Everything had been brought here from somewhere else. Cement, seed, metal, plastic. None of it was natural. Mr. Rapp was thrilled and saddened by being abruptly witness to the capacity of man. He let the package that smelled of yeast fall to the ground and looked up and down, focusing on nothing. He opened his lips slightly and touched himself in several places as if he had misplaced a pair of glasses.

Someone put a cherry bomb inside the mailbox in front of the Gibbs house. Shards of plywood scattered in the air when it blew, and the burnt husk of the model home fell in the street. Though they couldn't prove it, the neighbors privately held Tom Royce responsible for the explosion.

On the Fourth of July, they barricaded the end of the street with red, white, and blue painted sawhorses and decorated trees and fire hydrants with crepe paper streamers. They brought outside long simulated-wood tables and sun-faded beach umbrellas. They ate food they had carefully prepared and wrapped in plastic. They held events for the children—a bike race, a water balloon toss, a mini-parade with a patriotic theme—awarding construction paper ribbons to the most talented or best dressed. The men were pleased when Tom Royce, who had watched from a distance for most of the day, asked to sign up for their afternoon Ping-Pong tournament. Unfolding three Ping-Pong tables on a level part of the street, the men nudged each other and whispered words of confidence, pleased to have this opportunity to put the boy in his place. Tom drew the only bye in the first round. After ten minutes of stretching, he won his second-round match easily, forcing Mr. Holderness's shots into the nylon net with a clumsy-looking combination of English and slice. In his next two matches, he made the ball skirt off the table at gross angles by incorporating an odd high-toss serve; distracted by their wives teasingly rooting for Tom,

Mr. Springer and Mr. Bohnenkamp couldn't keep the spastic ball in play. Tom helped himself to plates of lasagna and potato salad as the men huddled in a group and discussed strategy for the finals. Mr. Gibbs received advice and warnings. To return a pair of smashes, Mr. Holderness swore that Tom had appeared in two places at once. When the final match was played, Tom switched playing styles altogether and wedged his paddle between his index and middle fingers like the Olympians. He beat Mr. Gibbs quickly with a wicked tight-arched backhand.

Dejected, the men shrugged it off, awarded Tom the stiff blue ribbon, and completed several unwatched consolation matches in the quirky glow from the streetlights. Tom affixed the ribbon to his belt, sat on the electronic eye on the black box at the top of the street, and watched the neighbors gather their belongings and ornaments. Later, under a sky full of colorful, flowery explosions, the men complained to their wives about the sudden animation in a boy normally withdrawn and laconic.

Mr. Gibbs is working near the free-form carp pond he'd had installed in May, pulling tall weeds that have the pond under siege. On the weeds' stalks are curving clawlike spines which inflict wounds that swell and ache. He has pricked himself several times. He stands above the weeds and pulls with the muscles in his back. The roots make muffled popping sounds and come up in his hands. The carp, red and white and tan, avoid the activity, swimming in tight circles on the other side of the pond. After removing each weed, Mr. Gibbs takes a breath and surveys his yard, sweating into the waistband of his work pants.

At first, he thinks the sound is an insect, a housefly or honeybee. From a distance, from the ground, it has that kind of report. He grunts and swats behind his head, concentrating on the careful placement of his hands. It approaches until it makes the sound of an alarm clock, an oven timer. Then it becomes the sound of frying bacon. Mr. Gibbs pulls another weed and wonders who is running a lawn mower in his yard. He lifts his head and holds his breath. Hydraulic fan, he thinks, chain saw. He is struck on the back of the neck and the force throws him. He hits the ground with half his face. When he opens his eyes he sees the small wrecked plane on the other side of the pond. Wings broken, grids of wood exposed along the fuselage, a softer electric razor sound coming from the gas engine, he can make out the windbreaker and the sunglasses of the small painted pilot in the cockpit. The carp nip at bits of cloth and balsa wood floating on the surface of the pond. Delirious, Mr. Gibbs tries to purse his lips like the calm fish. There is his neck, his face, sharp points of pain in his hands and forearms, and a tiny click as power to the plane is cut from somewhere nearby.

They woke to find the rain gutters torn from their houses. Some of the metal lengths hung precariously from the roofs, their joints hyper-extended, others had been stripped completely and bent into Z-shapes. They felt the smooth crimps in the aluminum with silent amazement, and then searched their yards for footprints or animal tracks.

"It's Tom Royce," Mr. Gibbs explained when they discovered their similar predicament. He reached back to the base of his skull and touched a row of metal staples that ran like a zipper down his neck. "It's him, I swear to God."

When night fell, the men gathered in front of the Royce house. Several brought long-handled garden tools which they held like weapons. They shined concentrated flashlight beams in the windows and called for Tom to come outside. After ten minutes, they spotted the distorted neon glow of a cigarette dodging behind a pane of clouded glass near the front door. When Mr. Gibbs threw a rock onto the roof, Tom appeared and faced them from the upward slope of the driveway. They shined their lights in his face.

"I didn't do it," Tom said. "The rain gutters. It wasn't me."

"No?" Mr. Gibbs said. He stepped forward, turned, and

parted his hair to show his shaved neck and the row of metal staples. "Well, how about this?"

Tom tried to speak but stuttered. He looked left and right as if to appraise his chance for survival, then broke for the door. Mr. Gibbs caught him by the foot, and Tom fell on a brick path. Leaping on top of him, Mr. Gibbs pounded his fists into the boy's body and threw elbows into his face. Tom fought back meekly; the rest of the men watched silently. When they heard a bone pop, Mr. Shalladay and Mr. Oberholser pulled the combatants apart. The boy collapsed and lay motionless. Mr. Gibbs paced excitedly and peeked around the shoulders of the men who held him at bay. After several seconds, Tom reached up and covered his right eye with both hands. He stood slowly, careful of his balance, and shuffled toward the house. When he'd disappeared, Mr. Gibbs gave a primitive laugh and cleaned a brush wound with saliva.

A yellow For Sale sign materialized in the Royces' front yard the next morning. It stood solidly, boldly presented, as though marking a grave. The neighbors called the number printed on the placard, and gawked and marveled at the low asking price—Mr. Springer suggested there might be unseen structural damage. The ranch house with an intercom system and a flat ceramic cooktop sold in a week and a half to a family named Moore.

The Royces moved immediately. The neighbors watched from the shade of the Springers' screen-enclosed porch, drinking iced tea and commenting on the three figures hefting a grandfather clock into the back of a moving van. The Royces loaded a rifle case, two pool tables, a basket from a hot-air balloon. A computer, three antique metal mannequins, four identical televisions. When the van left they filled their car with potted cacti and Styrofoam wig heads. Before driving off, the Royces took a moment to stand at the base of Utopia Road and stare up the street. Reclined in their seats, the neighbors made conscious efforts not to move under the stiff gaze.

When the Royces' car rounded the corner, Mr. Gibbs sipped from his glass and looked at the faces gathered around him. The staples on his neck had been removed, leaving a squiggly pink scar and a dusty layer of stubble. He gestured to the street and said, "Good. Now things can get back to normal."

In the morning they found their pets dead. Legs rigid as tree branches, the animal faces tight and strangled, some were found floating in swimming pools, others huddled in the dark corners of garages.

"Poison," Mr. Gibbs told his wife. "He poisoned them some-how."

They buried the animals in shallow graves, under trees that had been losing leaves. They marked the spots with crosses made from lumber, the pets' names written quickly in pencil against the grain of the wood. The children pressed their palms against the mounds of disturbed earth and worded goodbyes in their minds.

Light bulbs burst in their sockets. Bits of roofing fell to the ground like rotted fruit. Small geysers appeared periodically where sprinkler heads had been broken off, and they found windows shattered mysteriously. One afternoon, the cathode-ray tube of the Bohnenkamps' television spontaneously exploded, spraying the family with small bits of glass.

A week after the Royces left, a rumor spread that Tom had been sighted behind a row of split-leaf philodendron. He had a wrench, the story went, and was doing something to a fire hydrant. His bare skin seemed slightly gaseous, not quite solid, and he didn't bob his head or make a sound when he moved away.

They lost power. The cutoff came one night at dusk, preceded by three staccato electrical surges. Their first instinct was to jostle the wall switches, play with the on-off mechanisms of their machines. They went to the fuse boxes and found them rusted but unchanged. When it was fully dark, they visited each other and were comforted by a sense of mutual crisis. Only the streetlights seemed to be unaffected, the yellow light casting a bleary pall over Utopia Road. The neighbors lit candles as thick as baseball bats, spacing them evenly through the dark houses. Families congregated and watched the colored wax melt away. The power outage seemed to come with a special sort of silence, a subtle primal challenge. They found they could distinguish the smells of inanimate objects and hear whispering through walls they thought were sound-tight.

In the morning, the men gathered around the black box at the top of the street. They searched the metallic surface for whatever damage Tom Royce had caused, touching it gently as if moving it might inflict further injury. Crouching, several men placed fingers on the box and peered into the electronic eye as if it were a microscope. Opaque, the size of a sand dollar, they saw only the eye looking back at them. Staring up at the streetlights, still lit in the daytime, the men hypothesized about the problem and guessed at who to call to fix it. They considered taking the box apart, but could find on it no screws or clamps or bolt heads. A few of them lined up on one side of the box and tried to tip the thing, but it was no good. They stood there confused. When it became awkward they retreated to their respective homes.

The faucets went dry—they cut into water lines and found chalk dust in the pipes. Rafters made splintering sounds at night and carpet curled on itself like sun-beaten paint. Plaster peeled off the walls in soggy strips. The Haysletts' house shifted on its foundation: they could see it tilting slightly to the right when they stood in front of the mailbox and compared the house to its tiny replica.

Mr. Springer dug a pair of shallow trenches from his pool to the independent Jacuzzi near his house. Using two trash cans outfitted with wooden fins, he rigged a waterwheel system, powered partially by three solar panels on the roof. The water ran down the trenches, spinning the trash cans and a long dowel rod connecting them. A rubber belt was attached to the rod and the shaft of a small turbine generator. The water gathered in the drained Jacuzzi and was sucked back up to the pool, using power from the solar panels. The system provided enough energy for a few low-watt bulbs in the Springers' house.

Late one night, they held a formal meeting to discuss their alternatives. Some wanted to have Tom Royce arrested, others thought they should take the law into their own hands. When Mr. Gibbs suggested they find the Royces and firebomb their new house several neighbors shouted approval and stomped their feet on the floor. "That won't do any good," one wife hollered over the ruckus. She claimed to have just that night seen Tom flying down the street—with arms spread and toes pointed, he swooped past her like a prehistoric avian. The neighbors voted to call in a specialist.

Mrs. Bohnenkamp remembered seeing an exorcism ad in the classifieds of a national women's magazine. She dug the slick out of a pile in the garage and called the long-distance number listed there. The exorcist was an American Indian named Laughing Coyote. Mrs. Bohnenkamp thought she heard the click of wooden beads through the phone. The neighbors gathered money for the Indian's fee and sent for him.

A week later, a small delegation met Laughing Coyote at the airport. The group stood pressed together at the gate as if posing for a picture. Coming down the jetway, Laughing Coyote was not hard to spot. He had stiff gray hair that hung to his shoulders and skin the color of a house brick. He wore faded blue jeans and a large silver belt buckle. Unprompted, he walked to the group from Utopia Road.

On the way home, the neighbors explained that their ghost, their apparition, their whatever, was not a dead person—he was still alive and presumably living nearby. To give Laughing Coyote the flavor of Tom's tactics, they related some of the boy's antics.

They told him stars could be seen through Tom's liquid form. The old Indian watched the land wash by and said good words. He gestured in ways that made their problems seem typical and easily solved. The neighbors glanced at one another and smiled, congratulating their wisdom.

Laughing Coyote told them to park at the base of Utopia Road. When the car stopped, the Indian got out and moved quietly across the asphalt. The neighbors followed. Laughing Coyote stopped on a manhole cover and squared himself with the road. Appearing to glance from a scrub oak that had fallen across the sidewalk to round holes where stucco had come off the houses, he stared at Utopia Road as if he were thinking of buying it. He looked at twisted garage doors and patches of tan dirt where sod grass had shriveled and disappeared. His eyes lingered on a mass of witchweed attacking a privet hedge and the yellow light from the streetlights. He sniffed the air and cocked his head as if to listen to the water rushing beneath him.

Finally, the old Indian stepped off the manhole cover and approached the neighbors. He gave Mr. Gibbs their money in a business-sized envelope and got back in the car.

The Detweilers moved within a week. It took them eight hours to load their belongings into a silver U-Haul. The others stood by and watched, kicking lava rocks loose on the uneven sidewalk. Mr. Gibbs grabbed Mrs. Detweiler's arm as she hurried by with a drawer full of utensils.

"What are you doing?" he said.

"What are we doing? We're leaving. We're jumping ship."

"But this is our home."

Mrs. Detweiler gestured to the place in the street where Laughing Coyote had stood. "That was a sign," she said. "I know a sign when I see one."

"Come on. That guy was a fake. Cowboy boots, string tie. He was a fraud."

"We're getting out while we still can."

Ceiling material flaked away in chips, revealing cottony pink insulation. Dry rotted walls broke apart like clods of dirt. Sidewalk sewer openings crumbled away until there were gaping holes in the street.

The Oberholsers left at night, said goodbye to no one; the Holderness family abandoned everything they could not fit into their station wagon and hatchback. Some boarded their windows and made plans to collect their belongings when they'd settled elsewhere, others moved formally, sweating it out until the scheduled dates. The remaining families stayed inside. For heat and light they burned wooden hangers, bits of furniture, cardboard, and family files. They sat in groups and spoke infrequently. They stopped sleeping in their beds.

The Springers got lucky. A single man whose job was bringing him west agreed to buy their house sight unseen. The Springers told him about the house's problems over the phone, but the man said it was more an investment for him than an actual living space—he had seen the neighborhood during a visit six months before and thought everything would be fine. The Springers took the man's first offer and agreed to pay three points.

On the morning of their move, the Springers sat quietly on their front step. The air was still and thick. After a long wait, a yellow moving van turned onto Utopia Road. It executed a complex U-turn at the top of the street and stopped in front of the house with squealing noises from the air brakes and bursts of cola-colored exhaust that tinged the sky.

The Gibbs family crossed the street slowly, a shuffling group.

The two families and the movers loaded the belly of the van. Sheet-wrapped furniture, knee-high stacks of framed pictures, boxes that had once been Christmas presents. A toolbox, a toaster oven, various pieces of electronic equipment. The Springers left behind mattresses that tore and fell apart when they tried to disassemble them. The movers bolted the doors of the van and left for the new house.

The two families stood around the Springers' station wagon. The children looked at each other strangely, twisting their bodies on rooted feet. The women hugged and wished one another good luck, and the men shook hands solemnly. The Springers climbed in their car and idled down the street, waving until they vanished.

Late in the afternoon, Mr. Gibbs waded knee deep into the pond in his backyard and tried for half an hour to grab the slick dodging carp with his bare hands. It was nearly dark when he got a metal-headed rake from the toolshed and gaffed the cream-colored fish from the shoreline. Beached on the wilted grass, the carp wiggled back and forth slowly, quietly suffocating. Mr. Gibbs cut the plastic handles off a jumprope, ran the frayed cord through the fish's gills, and carried them into the house swinging from the makeshift stringer. Mrs. Gibbs laid the fish out on a cutting board. She cut off the heads and tails, boned and gutted them, and set the fillets in a frying pan. She took them back outside to where Mr. Gibbs was starting a fire, using paper towels, some dry twigs, and flint stones from his youngest son's rock collection. When he got a spark they both blew on it until a flame caught a dry leaf. They got the fire going and took turns holding the pan over the flames.

"It's going to rain later," Mr. Gibbs said over the sound of the fish. He jerked the pan so the fillets shifted position.

"Yes," Mrs. Gibbs said. She took a deep breath and looked up. "Look at the moon."

They ate inside, dividing the fish into five equal portions. Alone on the plates, the carp looked barren, slightly unhealthy. The family sat on the floor in a circle and ate with their fingers. When they finished, they wiped their mouths with the backs of their hands and plucked small rubbery bones from between their teeth. The children cleaned the dishes with pond water and re-placed them in the cupboard.

They bedded down in the living room, putting on jackets and scarves. They wrapped themselves in blankets and pressed their bodies together. They unrolled thermal sleeping bags and hid in the diffuse glow underneath.

They had no clocks, no watches that worked. They had no pendulums or sundials. They did not know what time it was when it started to rain. The sound woke them and they rose, groggy and disoriented. The air was warm and moist from their breath. They listened to the rain pelting the roof. It was dull-sounding, a rumbling, the first perception of a distant stampede.

Mr. Gibbs retrieved a large rubber mallet from behind the sofa. He stood, resting the mallet on his shoulder, and looked at his wife.

"I'll check the windows."

She nodded and tended to the children.

Mr. Gibbs went upstairs first. He had boarded all the windows that had shattered or collapsed and on these he rechecked his work, feeling around the edges of the planks for moisture. He inspected the nails. When they weren't tight he choked up on the mallet and tapped them into place. The rain made a different sound against the wood. It was deeper and muffled, like knocks on a hollow box. The wind howled from an indiscernible place outside. Mr. Gibbs stopped his work and listened to it. When it faded he could hear one of his children, the youngest probably, sobbing downstairs. His wife was saying, "It's only the wind. Don't be afraid. The wind can make noise sometimes . . ."

Mr. Gibbs tightened a screw with his fingernail and finished the upstairs rooms. He came back down and went into the kitchen, pulling the curtains across the sliding glass door. He rehammered a few nails in the boards over the sink. In the family room, he shut the flue of the fireplace and examined one of the few remaining intact windows. After jostling the panes with his fingertips to see that they were secure, he looked out at Utopia Road. The scene was dark and wet; because of the sheets of rain he saw it all as if it had been shoddily drawn in the off-speed pages of a flip book. The street, near the curb, was a river. There was white water near the gutters. Lit by the flickering streetlights, a section of wooden fencing floated downstream like a raft until it caught on an abandoned car. Mr. Gibbs moved closer to the window and set his hands on the sill. He felt a dizzying coolness. He thought, *I'm thirsty,* and the raindrops came horizontally, splattering themselves against the glass as if they were trying to get at him.

John Schaidler

Minneapolis, MN

May 18, 1993

Voices of the Xiled
The Outpost

Highland Park, NJ

Dear Xiles,

Please consider the enclosed story for publication. I saw your ad in the **Voice Literary Supplement** (May 1993) and hope it will be appropriate for your anthology.

I turned twenty-nine two months ago and realized, much to my dismay, that I have only a year left to celebrate the joy of Generation X, twenty-something slackerdom disenfranchisement that has shaped my existence to this point. Soon I will be thirty and my life will be over. I'll do nothing but watch ESPN and drink clear beer 'til I shrivel up and die.

Still, an anthology of writers in their twenties is a cause for celebration not lament. So let me say that I, like most of my friends, have never had the same job for more than a couple of years, grew up on Space Food Sticks and t.v. dinners, never bought a Beatles album in my life and know Gilligan and Mr. Ed far better than I know my own parents. I have done everything from selling VCRs to driving a forklift, stuffing envelopes to mowing lawns and painting houses to directing t.v. commercials. In the last ten years I've quit, been fired and been laid off in pursuit of a no-such-thing-as-a-career.

I spend my copious free time spinning frighteningly realistic modern day yarns of what life is like for those of us trapped beneath the monumental weight of financially corpulent, culturally vacant aging Baby Boomers.

I hope you enjoy the story.

Thanks for your time.

Sincerely,

John Schaidler
John Schaidler

Melanie Sumner

"My name is Melanie Sumner. I was born in Middletown, Ohio, but I usually lie and say that I was born in Georgia. I love the South like people love an ugly baby. I really did grow up in Rome, Georgia. I went to college at the University of North Carolina at Chapel Hill, where I majored in religious studies. I used to stay up all night trying to finish a story; when I showed it to my teacher, Max Steele, I would sweat. If he didn't like the story, I got mad. Later, I took myself seriously, and that was a pain.

"When I received my M.A. in creative writing from Boston University, my parents suggested that I had been in school long enough to get a job, so I went to Atlanta and looked through the want ads. Maybe I didn't try that hard. After a year, I decided to leave the country, mostly to make people appreciate me. The Peace Corps took me on, and I lived in Senegal, West Africa, for two years, sporadically teaching English. When I came back to the United States, I moved to Wilmington, North Carolina, where I did odd jobs and some teaching at Cape Fear Community College.

"The late Seymour Lawrence bought my first novel, *Polite Society,* which will come out with Houghton Mifflin on February 11, 1995 (this would have been Sam's sixty-ninth birthday). I've published stories in *The New Yorker, Story, Story Quarterly,* and *Boulevard.* Right now, I'm a fellow at the Fine Arts Work Center in Provincetown, Massachusetts. (Two of the other writers in this anthology, Fred and Dean, have turned up here too. We have a lot of potlucks.) I love to write, even when I hate to write. I read compulsively, but I'm always discouraged by the short supply of interesting female characters in American literature. I throw books at walls. In my work, I'd like to discover the fourth-person point of view."

1.

When I was little I worried that one of my arms or legs might come off, or that my head would roll away, and then nobody would recognize me. In the family portraits that I supplied for the refrigerator door, in which I loomed out from the center of the page with a tiny parent on each side of me, none of us had all of our parts. I liked to walk up to people with my arms pulled up inside of my shirtsleeves and say, "Shake my hand."

My father let himself be horrified. "Is that my girl?" he'd ask. "Is that Rickie?"

"No!" I roared. "It's the Monster!"

Sometimes we played the game too long. Then I would pull my arms out of the shirt and wave them to show that I was normal.

"Oh no," he'd say then. "Don't try to pull the wool over my eyes. You're that mean old Monster. Where is my sweet girl?" He'd call out for me in a lonesome voice, and I answered until my throat was sore.

"Why, it is Rickie!" he'd say at last, folding me up in his arms to press my face against his rough cheek.

2.

He was killed when I was fourteen, and until then I didn't really believe that people died. If asked, I would have said that people die and go to heaven, or turn into butterflies, or rot in the dirt, according to whatever I was reading that month, but I didn't really believe any of it until I saw my father lowered into the ground. He had just been crossing the street and was hit by a green Chevrolet.

That year I wore hats and talked out of the side of my mouth. "Oh God," I said. I practiced saying it in the bathroom mirror, or in the reflection of the oven door; I practiced looking bored, derisive, and inwardly amused. On a high-school form, in the space marked FATHER'S OCCUPATION, I wrote, GHOST. School failed to offer me anything I needed to know. One day I tore all the class notes out of my ringed notebook and divided it into new sections, labeling the first one RULES TO LIVE BY. Rule Number One was: *Do not cry.*

I began listening to my Uncle Carl's radio show because he sounded so much like my father. I would fall asleep with the radio turned down too low to hear the words, imagining that my father was just in the next room, talking to my mother. "Now this time I believe he has found his niche," my father had said when Carl took that job. It was the same thing he'd said when Carl had become a preacher, when he'd been a used-car salesman, and for the two weeks he tried his hand at marriage. My mother thought Carl was immature. When she told me she didn't like his radio show I started listening to the words.

On the show, broadcast from Nashville, he called himself Dr. Foxx. He claimed to have crawled inside of the radio to escape his ex-wife, who he called Wickedness. "Hello out there," he said at the beginning of the hour. "This is Dr. Foxx, the little man inside your radio. That's F-O-X-X at WXYT, playing what you want to hear. Wickedness, honey, are you out there?"

I wrote Rule Number 15: *Be sardonic.*

My mother sent me to a psychiatrist. At first I liked the idea, because I was reading *The Bell Jar,* but I dropped out of psycho-therapy in much the same way I had dropped out of ballet and tap and piano. "What happened?" my mother asked.

"He's retarded," I told her. "He plays with blocks."

"People want to help you, Rickie!" she cried, going on in this dramatic voice about my personal life, but I didn't listen. Since the funeral she wore house shoes all the time and just sat around the house, circling the want ads in the back of the newspaper. Some-times when I woke up early I found her sitting at the kitchen table with a cup of coffee, her head down in her hands. She said I was shutting her out, and I was, but I couldn't make myself act any other way. The balance was gone in the family, and I had to be careful. She and the shrink inspired Rule Number 18: *Nobody but you will ever come inside of your mind. If they try, then just make fun of everything and confuse them, or just be cold.*

My only friend was the little man inside the radio, and on a dare to myself I wrote Carl inviting him to visit me. The letter was addressed to Dr. Foxx and signed Wickedness; I didn't think he would come.

3.

"My how you've grown," he said at the airport. In the last year I'd gained twenty pounds and gotten braces on my teeth. I wore one of my father's undershirts and kept my hands shoved down into the pockets of a pair of camouflage army pants.

When I saw him I waved my hat. For the occasion I had stuck a cardinal's feather in the band. He wore a suit with country and western stitching and carried a briefcase. On his hand he wore the ring my father had left him in the will. He talked to my mother about the flight, weather, and old relatives. None of the sardonic things I had planned to say came out right, so I just followed behind them. If one of them turned around and said something to me I acted surprised.

That first night he sat in my father's La-Z-Boy recliner in the den and talked to my mother about his new plans. "I'm thirty-nine years old," he said, "and I think this is my last chance to do what I really want to do in life." He had decided to leave WXYT and take some correspondence courses that would enable him to become a certified psychological counselor. He was talking about a Ph.D.

"That's all fine," my mother said, "but whatever you do you have to stick with it this time. You run from one thing to the next. You were gung ho about the ministry too, when you got into that." She paused for a moment and then launched into her next topic. "I never understood how anybody could get a divorce after being married for just two weeks. I never heard of such a thing."

Carl lit a cigarette. Nobody smoked in our house because my

mother didn't put out ashtrays, so I was waiting to see if she was going to get him an ashtray, or if he would have to ask.

"Adela, let's not bicker," he said. "Everybody makes mistakes."

"We learn from our mistakes."

He sighed and looked over at me. "What grade are you in now?"

"I'll be in the tenth."

"I bet you have to beat the boys off with a stick." He was holding the cigarette very still now, so the ash wouldn't drop. She gave a little cough.

"Would you like me to put the cigarette out, Adela?"

"No, smoke if you have to," she said, getting up to look for an ashtray.

I picked up a *Better Homes and Gardens* magazine from the coffee table, sucking my cheeks in to make myself look thinner.

The next day I drove Carl to the country club to have a golf lesson. He said the first thing a doctor had to do was learn to play golf, and I needed a licensed driver in the front seat. My mother often cried when I drove. She would walk to the car with a determined step, her face carefully fixed in a blank expression. When she had fastened her seat belt, locked the door, checked it, and gotten a good grip on the door handle she said, "I'm not going to say a word this time, not a word." Throughout the trip she repeated, "I'm not saying a word." When I made a mistake she screamed, "Oh Lord God, help us!" That's not why she cried though. She cried because when we were in the car together I said things to make her cry. Afterward I felt sick about it, but I couldn't help myself.

Now she followed us out to the driveway, calling out, "Carl, you make sure she sits on those cushions!" She claimed I was too short to see over the dash. "Watch her, Carl—she doesn't yield!"

As I pulled out onto the street I took the cigarette he offered, driving perfectly straight while he leaned over and lit it in my mouth. By now I was confident of my ability to smoke in any position. "Adela is a very controlling woman," he said. "She still treats you like a child, and that's not the impression I have of you at all. I hope you don't mind me saying that." He was not even watching me drive. In his Dr. Foxx voice he read aloud the church signs: GET RIGHT WITH GOD, JESUS IS COMING—ARE YOU READY?, HELL IS REAL.

At the club when he pulled my father's golf carts to the green, I wondered if anyone thought he was my father, just at a glance. I settled myself at an umbrella table by the pool, wearing a caftan that covered my body from head to toe. I thumbed through my notebook, which now had several sections. My notebook contained all of the important information about me, and I was always afraid someone was going to steal it. On the denim cover, I had printed in fat letters, I WOULD NOT DO THIS TO YOU. At home, I kept a tiny pile of powder on the cover, so that I would know if it had been disturbed, but usually I carried it with me. Sipping diet Coke from a straw, I propped my feet up on the edge of a chair and waited for a new rule to come to me.

Across the low stone wall that encircled the patio, the bright green grass of the golf course looked as flat as paper, dotted with carts and the thin, arching lines of golfers. The balls popped and cut through the air. From the pool I heard screams of Shark! and turned to watch the slippery brown bodies dive into the deep end. The girls in my class didn't get in the water until they began to perspire, and then they only waded in the baby pool. They lay in lounge chairs, oiling their skin and combing out their hair, alternately whispering and shrieking. This summer they all wore big sunglasses that made their heads look small. I had grown up with most of them; we dug tunnels to China with flatware, went through attics, and slept side by side in rooms glowing with nightlights, but although I could identify each voice with my back turned, I didn't know any of the girls anymore. I lit a cigarette. One of them stared at me, whispered something, and then they all turned and stared. I wrote Rule Forty-five: *No matter what you are doing, act like it is the normal thing to do and people will believe that.*

After his golf lesson Carl came over and ordered two Bloody Marys. When the waiter gave me a second glance I put on my sunglasses and tried a smoke ring. I had never had a Bloody Mary before and didn't know if I was supposed to take the celery stick out or leave it in the glass. "If you say Bloody Mary one hundred times you will die," I said, watching him stir with his celery stick. "It's a game I used to play on long car trips, when I was a kid."

"Did you ever say it one hundred times?"

"No."

"I'm glad." He looked at his watch, then removed two amber plastic vials from his pocket, taking one pill from each, washing them down with his drink. When he removed the celery stick and began to eat it, I did the same, although I normally didn't eat celery because it sticks in my braces.

If you want people to find you interesting, ask them about themselves, I had read in a book called *How to Make Friends and Influence People.*

"Who are you now?" I asked. "Dr. Foxx or Carl?" He lit a cigarette and blew a perfect smoke ring.

"You strike me as a perceptive person," he said. For the rest of the afternoon I tried to keep a perceptive look on my face.

He was telling me about women. "My ex-wife was completely crazy," he said, leaning forward. "I didn't know that when I married her. I just thought it was time for me to get married. Your father thought it was a good idea, although he had never met Nancy. She was attractive enough, and intelligent, quite a bit older than the women I usually date. 'My biological time clock is running out,' she told me. Can you believe that?"

I shook my head.

"As soon as I married her I realized it was a mistake. I slept on the couch. She tried all kinds of things to get me to come into the bedroom, but I had absolutely no desire for her."

"Oh," I said. I tried to imagine him having sex. Then I didn't know where to look.

He smiled. "I shouldn't talk about this to you. Are you uncomfortable?"

I removed a rubber band from my braces and shot it into the bushes. "Forget about it," I offered. "It was just two weeks, like camp."

"Camp," he said. "I like that."

As we walked to the car he put his arm around me. "I like you," he said. "I feel like I'm entering a brand-new world." I imagined us driving up onto the ball of a new world.

In my room I leaned out the window to smoke a cigarette. I was directing a movie. Then I was wearing a long black coat, pushing past photographers on a busy street in New York City; Carl was standing on the corner, hailing us a cab.

"Rickie! Supper!" my mother yelled. During the meal he talked to my mother about how nicely I had driven, old relatives, and the weather. I couldn't find a way into the conversation and wondered if he was doing that on purpose. Leaving my mother alone to do the dishes, I went back to my room and opened the notebook. Referring to a magazine article that gave the dimensions of the ideal face, I documented my measurements in a section of the notebook called RECORDS AND LISTS. I was sitting cross-legged on the floor, with a hand mirror on my lap, measuring the distance between my eyes, when he knocked on the door.

"Hi," he said, standing in the doorway. I didn't know whether to invite him in or not. I wasn't allowed to have boys in my room, but he was a man, and besides that he was my uncle. "So this is where you live," he said, looking around. My room was decorated to look the way I imagined a film director's penthouse in New York City might look. The walls were painted a stark white; the floor was bare except for a director's chair and a small glass table holding a telephone and a radio. Along one wall shelves were crammed with books and manila folders holding the scripts for films I had created, arranged in order of their ratings. "Where do you sleep?"

"I have a mattress rolled up in the closet." I decided not to invite him in because he might ask about the notebook on the floor.

"If you get lonely, come downstairs; I'm just reading. Adela has gone to bed."

I waited until he had gone, shut and locked the door, put some lip gloss on, then wiped it off, then went downstairs. He sat in my father's chair, and I sat on the couch with a pillow covering my legs, because they spread when I sat down and made me look fatter than I was in reality. He spoke in a low, easy voice, glancing at my eyes while he talked. He told me his theory on the various planes of existence. Animals and rednecks live on the first plane, average people on the second, and people like us on the third.

"How can you tell that I'm on the third plane?" I asked.

"Very rarely in my life have I met another person I felt could understand me. Maybe I'm just shy, but I don't feel comfortable around many people. With you, there was an immediate connection. I feel like I could tell you anything, and you would understand."

I widened my eyes some and gave him my priestess stare.

"When I do the radio show, I am Dr. Foxx. It's not just a joke." He lit a cigarette for me and one for himself. "You're the first person I've ever said that to."

Rule Number Forty-six was: *Stay on the third plane. Do not let shallow people drag you down to their level.*

Every night that week, after my mother went to bed, I sat in the den talking to Carl. Each morning when I woke up I felt years older. He moved to the couch, under the lamp. We kept the rest of the lights off in the room, because the light hurt his eyes (light-colored eyes are more sensitive to light, he said). I told him anything that came into my head, and he listened, asking a question here and there, letting me pause to form my answers. I imagined that this is what it would be like to be married.

"Do you think I'm too young?" I asked him one night.

"Too young for what?"

"To be living on the third plane."

"You strike me as quite sophisticated."

"I'm pretty juvenile, actually." I was wearing a pair of cutoff army shorts, and my feet were bare, each toenail painted a different color. I wanted to undo the ponytail in my hair, but I thought that would be too obvious, so I just leaned back against the couch to hide it.

One night I brushed my hair out of the ponytail and put on a long black skirt with my sweatshirt. I put on eye shadow and root beer–flavored lip gloss. Before going downstairs, I practiced my facial expressions in the mirror.

"I like your dress," he said, looking up from his psychology textbook.

I sat down on the other end of the couch and didn't know where to look. It wasn't a dress; it was a skirt. I pushed my hair behind my ears, trying to think of a way to change the subject. Obviously, he thought that I had gotten dressed up for him.

"You took your ponytail out," he commented, still looking at me.

"It was just getting on my nerves."

"Oh. I liked it."

"Would you like a cocktail?" I regretted that immediately, because I didn't know how to get him a cocktail if he did want one.

"If you're having one, that would be nice. That is, if Adela doesn't mind."

"Adela is asleep." I had just started calling my mother by her first name, and it felt strange on my tongue.

I went through the house in my sock feet, without turning on any lights. When I got to the kitchen I stepped gingerly over the floorboard that creaked and propped the refrigerator door open with a grapefruit, for some light. There wasn't any alcohol in the house except for rum that Adela used in baking and kept in a cabinet over the stove. I climbed up on the counter, pausing to listen for footsteps, then slowly opened the cabinet door. I had my hand around the bottle when a cookie cutter clattered to the floor.

For what seemed like hours, I stayed crouched on the counter. My heart sounded as loud as the hum of the refrigerator. When my foot had gone to sleep, I took the bottle again and slid down to the floor. I was trembling all over and had to wait for a moment before I could steady the tray enough to carry the drinks back through the dark house.

"The bar is pretty dry," I said, setting the tray down on the coffee table, arranging myself beside him on the couch. "Do you like rum?"

"Sure." He sucked an olive off his toothpick. "Rum and Coke?"

"Diet Coke."

"Superb." As he lifted the drink, the ring on his finger shone bright gold in the lamplight. He put his arm across the back of the couch, so that if I leaned back my head would touch his hand. I imagined a day when I would be thin and brilliant and people would hesitate before they spoke to me.

He took his vials out, swallowed a pill from each, and then said something that shocked me. "I don't suppose you know why I take this medication. Last year after your father died, I went into therapy and discovered that I have a chemical imbalance. My brain simply doesn't produce enough endorphins, the chemicals that signal pleasure in the brain. Basically, my natural level of happiness is too low. The way I see it, God makes mistakes; we all come into this world flawed."

"What would happen if you stopped taking the pills?"

He laughed. "I wouldn't try that."

"You mean you can never be happy unless you take a pill every day of your life?"

"It's not that much trouble. As I said, I'm just correcting a natural mistake. There are so many unhappy people in the world, and they feel guilty about their unhappiness. I know now that it isn't always something you can control. I hope you don't mind me saying this, but sometimes I think you're very depressed. I'd like to help you."

The shadows in the room seemed to take on new shapes, making everything unfamiliar and frightening. What if Carl was crazy? What if I was crazy? I imagined us in a black and white film—a young girl with sunken cheeks and great dark eyes was slowly going insane. This appealed to me. I let a few minutes pass and then said, "I've considered suicide." For a moment I saw the reflection of my face distorted in his glasses; my eyes were black holes, my mouth blown out and lopsided.

Then the lights snapped on, one after another. Adela stood in the doorway, clutching her bathrobe around her. Her face was hard and white with anger.

"What are you doing in here with the lights off?"

"There's a lamp on," I said, blinking in the light.

"What are you doing," she repeated, looking at Carl.

"We were just talking." He lit a cigarette.

"In this house we talk with the lights on. It's four o'clock in the morning." He tried to say something, but she cut him off.

Later he told me, "Adela was once considered a great beauty, but when she is angry she looks like a witch."

The night before he left I told Adela that we were going to see *Invasion of the Body Snatchers*. I filed my toenails and put on so much baby powder that it came off on my clothes in large white circles; I had to take everything off and beat it clean again. I wore Musk and a cherry-flavored lip gloss.

"So," I said, driving along with the headlights on high beam, "what do you want to do?"

"I thought we were going to a movie."

"We could go to a movie, or we could go somewhere else."

We went to the Starlight Lounge at the Quality Court. At the door, when the policeman asked me for identification, I fumbled in my purse pretending to look for it. In the car Carl had given me a Seconal, and I felt strong in the powers of persuasion. I was sending vibrations to the policeman, putting messages inside his mind: *She's twenty-one if she's a day. Don't annoy these nice people.*

"She's my niece," Carl said. "She's just going to have a Coke." I took his elbow as we walked across the lounge. In the bar it was dark and cool and quiet. A few businessmen scattered about the small round tables watched us walk by. At the bar two waitresses in halter tops flirted with the bartender.

"How's your headache?" Carl asked, pulling a chair out for me, pushing it under while I sat down.

"Fine. Thanks for the Seconal. What is it again?"

"Barbiturate." He looked nervously around the room and back at me. It had an evil sound, like something long and thin, moving along with thousands of legs in slow synchronization, something with poison in its mouth, but it felt cool and silky inside of me.

A waitress in a purple halter stood by our table with her hand on her hip. Her mouth was painted purple, and she wore purple eye shadow. Around her neck hung a silver cross. Her perfume was so strong I could taste it, and I hoped that Carl wouldn't get it mixed up with mine.

"I'll have a rum diet Coke highball," he said, "with olives, of course, plenty of olives."

"That's cute." She leaned closer to him so that her breasts knocked up against each other in the halter. I considered sticking my leg out to trip her when she walked by. He changed his order to a Cutty Sark on the rocks, and I had a virgin strawberry daiquiri that arrived with a tiny blue paper umbrella.

"You're beautiful," he said.

"So are you." I wasn't embarrassed at all. He was wearing a

sport shirt, slacks, and Hush Puppies. Anybody looking at him would think he was just another businessman, somebody with a wife and kids who rode a lawn mower every Saturday. Nobody would guess that he was Dr. Foxx.

I felt my face stretching into a grin and didn't even try to cover my braces.

"What?"

"I was thinking that if you took our brains out they'd look alike," I said. "They'd be the same shape or something."

"Or two shapes that connected." He took a long drink and whispered, "Do you think people are staring at us?" His eyes were light and silvery behind his glasses, like blind eyes.

The other people in the lounge seemed like fish moving in an aquarium, watching us through the glass. When I looked back at him my vision blurred, and I saw the people moving inside of his glasses, the businessmen in their sport shirts, the waitresses with their faces painted into single expressions, weaving into each other.

"I wonder if we look like a couple," he said. "If they think that."

"We're exactly alike."

"We have the same blood, you know. The problem I foresee . . ." he paused, because this was a joke between us, and I laughed, waiting for him to continue, "the problem is the offspring." In the joke we got married and had a monster baby, an insane little creature, with two fingers on each hand and a long tail. "We have to name the beast," he said in his Foxx voice. We finally named him Cutty Sark Seconal.

"Adela wouldn't approve," I said.

Leaning forward across the table he picked up his hand like it were a telephone. "Adela? This is Carl. Fine, just fine. How are you? I've got some news, actually. Your daughter and I have decided to get married." He covered his phone hand with the other hand to whisper, "She's not pleased," and then raised the phone hand back to his mouth. "Yes, mam, that's what I said. We'd like to have the reception at the club and all."

I put my hand to my cheek and spoke into my palm like a telephone. "Hello," I said, "this is Rickie."

"Excuse me, Adela; I've got someone on the line." He turned his shoulder away from me and spoke into his hand. "Foxx here, the little man inside your telephone."

"Do you know me?" Across the room the waitress and the bartender whispered to each other and watched us. I looked down at the blue umbrella in my empty glass. "This is Rickie. Is this Uncle Carl?"

"Foxx here," he said, into his hand. I put my hands flat on the table and stared at the side of his face.

"It's me," I said. "It's just me. Stop it."

In the morning after he left I broke Rule Number One and cried.

4.

He gave me a number where I could call after midnight, for free.

"Foxx here, the little man inside your telephone," he answered. His voice came through as clearly as it had on the radio show, but now he was talking to just me. I called almost every night, in the dark, so my mother wouldn't see a light under my door if she woke up. My hand glowed green from the light of the dial.

We told each other what we were wearing, so we could see each other, and he described his apartment to me until I could envision myself there talking to him. It was a basement apartment, like a cave, he said, illuminated with the blinking colored lots of radios and stereos and recording devices, and I saw it in my mind like the Bat Cave. Sometimes he taped our phone conversations and played them back to himself when he missed me. I opened a new section in my notebook called CARL.

One night when we had talked for four hours and were running out of things to say, he began to list the contents of his bathroom cabinet. He kept makeup. "Just Grecian formula, and sometimes a bronzer for men. On the rarest occasion, I use a touch of eye shadow." I didn't know if he was joking or not. "If women can wear it why can't men?" he asked.

From his textbooks he read me long descriptions of psychiatric illness, and we continually diagnosed each other and everyone in the family. Then we would mix all the illnesses together to create a personality for Cutty Sark Seconal.

"We are thoroughinbreds," he liked to say.

Not since I had dug tunnels to China did I feel so close to another person. We lived in the dark, in imaginary rooms, without bodies. Only a thin wire, hundred of miles long, connected us by our voices, which flew from our mouths faster than the speed of sound. I told him about my notebook, and sometimes I even read some of it to him.

"Do you have a boyfriend?" he asked.

I wouldn't say.

"If you did have a boyfriend I think I'd be jealous." We talked until three or four o'clock in the morning. I slept in my desk at school, longing to lie down on the floor. My grades dropped sharply, and Adela was convinced that I was using drugs. One day when Carl sent me a package in the mail, she opened it. It was a sketch of him when he was twenty-four.

"I thought he was sending you drugs," she said. "I'm sorry."

"I wish he would. I wish he'd send me a plane ticket. I can't stand living here with you anymore! How dare you open my mail!"

When she cried I tried to put my arms around her, but she wouldn't let me. She didn't let people comfort her. She went on making the green bean and mushroom casserole, slamming the cabinet doors, her face wet and crumpled-looking. She had a job now, and she was always tired.

"I love you," I said.

"Words! All you have are words."

"Why don't you like him?"

"I didn't say I didn't like him. Carl has a lot of problems. He's a bad influence on you. I want this business between the two of you to stop."

"What business. He's my friend. He's my uncle. He's Dad's brother."

"You should make some friends your own age. You ought to have a boyfriend."

"I don't want a boyfriend, thank you."

"Why do you call him on the telephone at all hours of the night? Answer me that." She stopped stirring and looked at me through sad red eyes.

"Why do you spy on your own daughter? Answer me that."

She put the casserole in the oven, slammed the door, and left the kitchen.

I framed his sketch and hung it on my wall. I sent him a photograph of myself when I was first born, which was taken in the year that he was twenty-four.

"Adela thinks you're a bad influence on me," I told him, sardonically, and he was indignant.

"I have great esteem for you," he said. "You are not a child, although she refuses to recognize that. You make your own decisions. How have I been a bad influence on you?"

5.

My day narrowed down to that hour when I picked up the phone, when there was nothing of me in the world but a glowing green hand holding our voices.

"We will never lose our connection," he said. "Even when you get married, this connection won't be broken."

I wrote the word LOVE in the notebook. It was terrible to write it, but I had to. Then when it happened I was not prepared for it. He said it so softly that I didn't hear the first time.

"I love you," he repeated, still whispering.

It was what we always said before we hung up, but this was different. He didn't say goodbye.

"Rickie, there is something I have to tell you. I don't know how you'll take this." I heard the flick of his lighter and the long draw of his breath. "I'm afraid sometimes that you put me on a pedestal."

"You think that I worship you?"

"That's a little strong. It's just that I don't think you see me as a man."

"I didn't think you were Jesus," I said, but it didn't come out right.

"Maybe I shouldn't say this."

"I hate it when people do that! If you promise to say something, then say it." I didn't hear what he said, his voice was so low. "What?"

"I love you. I love you like a man loves a woman. I want to hold you. I want to kiss you." There was a long pause—I watched the glowing dial move around the clock. "Oh God, I said it." My hand shook. I set the phone down for a moment, and then picked it back up.

"Hello," I said. "May I speak to Dr. Foxx, please?"

"Foxx here. Little man inside your telephone."

"Dr. Foxx, I'd like to report to our listeners that a monster has been sighted."

"Just a minute, please. Let me get a pencil and jot this down. Facts only, mam."

"I don't know what to say."

"You don't have to say anything if you don't feel like it. We'll never mention it again. It won't make any difference in our relationship."

"It's just that I never thought about us as having bodies before."

"We'll take it slowly." After he hung up I looked up vulva in the dictionary.

Now sometimes when I called him I hung up before I finished dialing and had to start over again. Everything was the same as before except that after about an hour we lowered our voices.

"What are you wearing?" he asked. "What would you like me to do to you?" Once at a Christmas dance I had put my tongue in a boy's mouth; it tasted like spit. Afterward whenever I saw him I looked away.

It was a gray November day, growing dark early in the afternoon, and I was sitting in the den with the TV on, when I broke Rule Number One for the second time. Tears streamed down my face; no noise came out. When Adela got home from work she dropped her pocketbook and knelt down on the floor, putting her arms around me.

"Hush," she said, although I wasn't making a sound. The smell of her perfume, and the softness of her cheek, wet now with my tears, made something squeeze so tight inside of me that I was afraid I'd talk. "Were you lonely?" she said, digging through her pocketbook for a Kleenex. She found one with her red mouth print on it and wiped my face. "I'm sorry I wasn't here when you came home from school. I'll try to leave work earlier from now on."

"I was just watching a sad movie. I wasn't really crying." She held me tight, smoothing back my hair with her cool hand.

For a week I didn't call him, and then one night I got up my courage.

"Your voice sounds hard," he said. "Is something the matter?"

"You're my uncle. This is incest. It's illegal."

He hung up.

I redialed for an hour, getting his answering machine: "Hello, this is Dr. Foxx, the little man inside your radio. I'm sorry I cannot come to the phone right now. If you'll . . ." An hour later there was a new message. "Hello, this is Carl. I'm sorry I cannot come to the phone right now . . ." I dialed the number for three and a half hours without stopping, leaving a message every time. At 4:30 A.M. he picked up the phone. He sounded like he had been asleep.

"You hung up on me," I said.

"We were cut off. I don't think my phone's working."

"You said you loved me. Can't you even talk to me now?"

He spoke slowly and carefully, in a doctor's voice. "Rickie, you know that I care about you very much. I'm worried about you. Your phone call tonight . . . well . . . it was a shock."

"You started it. You weren't shocked then."

"You're upset."

"How can you talk like this. You were my best friend in the whole world, and then you said—"

"What did I say, Rickie?"

"You said that you wanted to make love to me."

"I never said that. You are confused."

"How can you lie to me? I wrote it all down. I have all the dates and everything right here in my notebook. Do you want me to read it to you?"

He hung up again, and I called back continuously until five-fifteen.

"It's very late," he said. "And I'm very tired."

"Don't hang up on me again."

"I told you, the phone is out of order."

"Do you love me?"

"I love you as a friend." He cleared his throat.

"I wrote everything down."

"You had a paranoid delusion."

"Liar!"

"If you are upset, then we can talk about it another time."

"I'm not upset." I took a deep breath, and then lit my last cigarette as he began to talk about a psychological experiment, something he was doing for his doctoral thesis: a paper discussing the reactions of a girl seduced by her uncle. He wasn't making sense anymore.

"I guess I just didn't realize you'd take it so seriously," he said in his regular Carl voice, and I hung up.

I took his picture off the wall, covered it with a towel, and broke the glass into tiny pieces with a paperweight. Then I tore the sketch up and watched the tiny chips of paper whorl down the toilet. The notebook went like that too. Then I felt like I had ripped myself to pieces and was scattered over the world, all along the telephone wires and down in the drainpipes. For the rest of the night I sat in the window waiting for the sun to rise, trying to come up with a new rule.

David Foster Wallace

David Foster Wallace was born in 1962 in New York, grew up in Illinois, was educated at Amherst College and the University of Arizona at Tucson, is the author of a novel, *The Broom of the System* (Viking/Avon), and a collection of stories of which the following piece is the title (Norton/Avon), and, with Mark Costello (the lawyer, not the writer), of a nonfiction book about rap music and racial issues, *Signifying Rappers* (Ecco Press), is working on something long for Little, Brown that looks like it will NOT be in by the contracted 1/1/94 deadline, has never before been late with anything, anywhere, ever, and is not in a good space about this at all, and is currently teaching English, for reasons connected less with salary than with health insurance, at Illinois State University at Bloomington-Normal, Illinois.

PERSONAL TIDBIT W/R/T "GIRL WITH CURIOUS HAIR": a close female acquaintance severed all connections with DFW shortly after the story was written and (in an ill-considered move) shown to her, claiming that anyone who could write such a thing was clearly a very troubled young man indeed, a conclusion DFW did and still does deny.

GIRL WITH CURIOUS HAIR

For William F. Buckley
and Norman O. Brown

Gimlet dreamed that if she did not see a concert last night she would become a type of liquid, therefore my friends Mr. Wonderful, Big, Gimlet and I went to see Keith Jarrett play a piano concert at the Irvine Concert Hall in Irvine last night. It was such a good concert! Keith Jarrett is a Negro who plays the piano. I very much enjoy seeing Negroes perform in all areas of the performing arts. I feel they are a talented and delightful race of performers, who are often very entertaining. I especially enjoy watching Negroes perform from a distance, for close up they frequently smell unpleasant. Mr. Wonderful unfortunately also smells unpleasant, but he is a good fellow and a sport and he laughs when I state that I dislike his odor, and is careful to remain at a distance from me or else position himself downwind. I wear English Leather cologne which keeps me smelling very attractive at all times. English Leather is the men's cologne with the television commercial in which a very beautiful and sexy woman who can play billiards better than a professional makes the assertion that all her men wear English Leather or they wear nothing at all. I find this woman very alluring and sexually exciting. I have the English Leather cologne commercial taped on my new Toshiba VCR and I enjoy reclining in my horsehair recliner and masturbating while the commercial plays repeatedly on my VCR. Gimlet has observed me masturbating while I watch the English Leather cologne commercial and she agrees that the woman is very alluring and states that she would like to lick the woman's vagina for her. Gimlet is a bisexual who is keen as anything on oral sex.

We had to stand in the dumb line for a long time at the Irvine Concert Hall in order to see Keith Jarrett in concert because we were late in arriving and did not beat the rush. We were late in arriving because Big had to stop off to sell LSD to two people in Pasadena and to two women in Brea, and even in the long line to see Keith Jarrett he sold some LSD to two fellows, Grope and Cheese, who had driven by motorcycle all the way up to Irvine to be his LSD customers. Big is a skillful punkrocker musician who also makes LSD in his room in my friends' house, and sells it. I like to beat the rush for lines and do not prefer being late, but Gimlet fellated me instantly the instant she and Big and Mr. Wonderful picked me up in their used milk truck at my new home in Altadena, and I had an orgasm on Highway 210, and it felt very good, so Gimlet made me not mind being late in arriving or paying for the tickets, which were very expensive, even to see a Negro.

Grope and Cheese instantaneously placed the LSD they'd purchased on their tongues and decided to stay and go to the Keith Jarrett concert with us after Gimlet offered to make me pay for their tickets. Gimlet introduced me to Grope and Cheese, who were of roughly high school age.

Gimlet introduced me to Grope and Cheese; she said Grope, Cheese: Sick Puppy. And she introduced Grope and Cheese to me, as well. My name is Sick Puppy even though my name is really not. All my good friends are punkrockers and rarely have names except names like Tit and Cheese and Gimlet. Gimlet's real name is Sandy Imblum and she is from Deming, New Mexico. Cheese asked Gimlet if he could touch the tip of her hair and she invited him to sit on a picket fence instead, causing me to react with laughter.

Cheese looked very immature for a true blue punkrocker and was unfortunately not attractive. He was bald-headed but displayed whiskers of hair here and there and he wore spectacles which were pink and had a thin neck but he seemed like a good egg, but Grope did not like my new suit which I had purchased in Rodeo's on Rodeo Drive or my Top-Siders or my tie from my prep school which had Westminster Military Academy on it and an American flag as well. He stated that I did not seem like a fine fellow or a good egg and that my clothes were unattractive. He also disliked the smell of my English Leather cologne.

Grope's utterances peeved Gimlet and she told Mr. Wonderful to harm Grope, therefore Mr. Wonderful kicked Grope in the midsection with his heavy black boots, for Contra combat in Central America, with studs in the toes. Grope became in extreme pain and was forced to sit on the curb smack dab in the middle of the line to see Keith Jarrett, holding his kicked midsection. Gimlet placed fingers in each of Grope's nose's nostrils and asked him to apologize to me or she would try to pull the nose from amid Grope's features. Pain and unpleasantness are very unpleasant for people with LSD on their tongue, and Grope apologized instantaneously without even having to look at me.

I informed Grope that his apology was totally accepted and that he seemed like an A-OK sort of person to me, and I shook Grope's hand to let him know that Sick Puppy was no spoilsport, and Big helped him up and let him lean on him while I paid the face behind the window of the Irvine Concert Hall for six tickets to see Keith Jarrett, which cost one hundred and twenty dollars. Grope told Big that his LSD was numero uno while we all entered the balmy and comfortable and tastefully decorated interior lobby of the Irvine Concert Hall. Gimlet whispered to my ear that in return for paying for the tickets to see Keith Jarrett and keeping her from liquidating, she would attempt to keep my erect penis in her mouth for several minutes without having an orgasm, and that she would let me burn her with several matches on the backs of her legs, as well, and this made me very happy, and Gimlet and I placed our tongues in each other's mouths while all our friends formed a circle around us and indicated their vocal approval. The other crowds coming to see Keith Jarrett's concert were in approval of our bunch's happy go luckiness and gave us a generous amount of room and privacy in the Concert Hall's spacious lobby.

Mr. Wonderful and Big and Gimlet had all taken a large amount of Big's LSD, which is a special kind he manufactures for concerts and is free of amphetamines which might make a fellow fidget, and Grope and Cheese had taken LSD also, therefore they were all under the influence of LSD, which made them super amounts of fun to be with. I had not taken any LSD because LSD and other controlled substances unfortunately do not affect me or my state of normal consciousness. I cannot become high from ingesting drugs, and all my friends who are punkrockers find this very fascinating and a lot of fun. I was a very popular and outgoing peer in prep school and college and business school and law school but could not become affected by controlled substances in these environments either. My friends the punkrockers like me to buy very large amounts of drugs and take them and not become high while they are all affected. Last month for my birthday they made me place over two paper squares of Big's LSD on my tongue and then we all went joyriding in the new sports car I received from my mother for my birthday. It is a Porsche with six forward gears and two reverses and a leather interior. And turbo-charged! Gimlet and Big placed drugs on their tongues also and we went driving like greased lightning down the Pacific Coast Highway in reverse until a policeman pulled us over and I was forced to give him a gift of a thousand dollars not to incarcerate Gimlet when she determined that his revolver was in reality a radioactive chemical waste product and attempted to pull it out of his holster and throw it at a palm tree in order to kill it. The officer was a fine and gentlemanly man, however, and was very happy to receive a cash gift of a thousand dollars. We went away in a forward gear and Big began to laugh at Gimlet for temporarily believing that she could kill a service revolver by throwing it at a palm tree, and he laughed so heartily that he wet his pants and could have damaged some of the leather interior of my new Porsche, and I have to admit that I got peeved, and gave Big the cold shoulder, but Gimlet let me burn one of Big's nipples with my gold lighter at a rest stop, so I became happy and felt that Big was a fine individual once more.

Last night we arrived at our row of six seats in the Irvine Concert Hall and sat in our seats. My new friend Grope sat down far away from me next to Big, and Mr. Wonderful sat beside Big also. I sat between Cheese and Gimlet who sat at the end of our row of six seats. Far down on stage in the Irvine Concert Hall was a piano with a bench. The woman seated behind Gimlet tapped me on the padded shoulder of my new sportcoat and complained that Gimlet's hair was creating problems for her vision of the piano and bench on the stage. Gimlet told the woman to Fuck You, but good old Cheese was concerned at the situation and politely traded to Gimlet's outside seat so as to solve the vision problems of the woman, who was coughing at what Gimlet said. Cheese was a shrimp and he had very little hair to ascend from his head into the air so he was a good fellow to sit behind. Gimlet only has hair at the center of her round head, and it is very skill-fully sculptured into the shape of a giant and erect male penis, otherwise she is bald like Cheese. The penis of her hair is very large and tumescent, however, and can introduce problems in low spaces or for those people behind her who wish to see what she can see. Her friend and confidante Tit sculptures Gimlet's hair and provides her with special hair-care products from her career as a hairstylist which makes Gimlet's hair sculpture rigid and real-istic at all times. I have my hair maintained at Julio's Unisex Fash-ion Cut Center in West Hollywood, with an attractive part on the right side of my hair and a feathering technique on the sides so that my ears, which are extremely well shaped and attractive, show at all times. I saw the fine hairstyle I have in *Gentleman's Quarterly* and clipped the picture to show Julio my hairstyle. Mr. Wonderful has a mohawk which last night was a very light shade of violet, but which on many occasions is orange, as well. Big's hair is extremely long and thick and black and covers his head and shoulders and chest and back, including his face. Big has a plastic facemask for vision which he has had woven into his hair at eye level, utilizing the skill of Tit. The hair in the vicinity of what is probably Big's mouth often tends to be unattractive because food passes through this area when he dines. I do not remember how Grope wore his hair.

Cheese leaned across me and told Gimlet she was a real trouper for trading seats so the coughing woman could enjoy the performance, because Keith Jarrett was an outstanding Negro performer whom everyone should get to see for their own musical good, and he asked me to agree. I was happy to agree with Cheese and calm down Gimlet so she would not be a pain in the neck, and Cheese was indeed correct when the Negro Keith Jarrett ap-peared on stage in slacks and shoes and a velour shirt which hung loose because it was too large for him, and sat on his bench at his piano. Like many Negroes, Keith Jarrett had an afro of hair; from where our six seats were located in the Irvine Concert Hall all I could see of Keith Jarrett was the back of him and his hair's afro while he played.

But he played awfully well! I told Gimlet I thought this performer was swell for a performer who was not a punkrocker like Gimlet and Big and Mr. Wonderful, who together comprise an excellent and skillful punkrock band known far and wide as Mighty Sphincter, and Gimlet who was very affected from the LSD at this juncture looked at me as if there was something extremely interesting behind me. She licked my cheek with her tongue for over thirty seconds but soon stopped and directed my attention to a small and young blond girl in a lower row, and stated that the girl's hair was a fascinating and curious thing to observe. She stared at the small girl below us with great intensity while Keith Jarrett played some of his concert.

As my friends and I listened to Keith Jarrett play the piano in the Irvine Concert Hall last night I was thinking what a super bunch of guys and gals my friends were and how glad I was that I had gotten to be friends with such fine and fun persons! They are very unique and different from my past friends whom I had growing up in Alexandria, Virginia, and attending fine schools and universities such as the Westminster Military Academy, Brown University, the Wharton School of Business at the University of Pennsylvania, and the Law School at the University of Yale. All my past friends have real names and wear clothes similar to mine, and are very attractive and skillful and often fun but never the barrel of monkeys which my new friends in the Los Angeles area are! I met all my new punkrocker friends at a party which occurred shortly after I arrived here in the Los Angeles area for my new job which pays me over a hundred thousand dollars per year.

At the party in Los Angeles for the Los Angeles Young Republicans I was there with Ms. Paisley Campbell-Greet, a fine gal whom I was trying to convince to fellate me and subsequently let me burn her, and I was talking and quipping for several hours with her and several Young Republicans when several punkrockers in leather and metal clothing, who were at political odds with the Young Republicans on many social issues, spontaneously showed up out of nowhere and gate crashed and began to eat the expensive refreshments the Young Republicans' Ladies Auxiliary had prepared, and to take drugs and break objects. The host of the party received a finger in his eye when he complained to the largest punkrockers, who were Big and Big's chums Death and Boltpin, that they should be more sporting and well-bred fellows.

And slightly after this time of the finger in the eye at the party I became embroiled in a fracas with a Young Democrat at the party who had gone to law school in Berkeley, California (why did they even let him in is what I want to know!?!). Paisley Campbell-Greet knew this fellow and we were all chatting in an amiable manner when I innocently and proudly broached the subject of my father and my brother and my brother's recent promotion and responsibility and honor.

Cheese leaned toward my body and made the assertion that the Negro Keith Jarrett was such a skillful and pleasurable musician because his jazz music performance was in reality *improvisational,* that Keith Jarrett was in reality composing his performance as he performed it. Gimlet began to cry because of this and because of the small girl's curious hair and I lent her one of my silk handkerchiefs which complements the color and design of several of my wardrobe ensembles.

At the Young Republican get-together I stated that my family on my maternal side owns a company which manufactures high quality pharmaceutical products, while my family on my paternal side is true blue military aristocracy. My father is one of the highest-ranking individuals in the United States Marine Corps, and he and my brother and I are related to the finest fighting general the American nation has had since Ulysses S. Grant. My brother is thirty-four and is now a Lieutenant Colonel in the United States Marine Corps and has the honor of serving as the carrier of the Black Box of nuclear codes for the President of the United States.

At the outset my brother was merely the night officer on this duty and merely sat at attention in a chair with the Black Box attached to his wrist outside the private bedroom of the nation's President at night, but now he has proven such a fine carrier of nuclear codes that he is the day officer on this duty, therefore he can be frequently seen on television and in all types of media, standing at attention at all times closer than ten feet to the President, carrying the Black Box of nuclear codes which are important to the balance of power of our country.

The Young Democrat who had sneaked into the party became off the wall about my statements about my brother the day officer for the codes and he began to be awfully impolite and to speak loudly and to gesture democratically in the air with his arms in his corduroy sportcoat, then one time he poked me in the chest with his finger. Paisley Campbell-Greet stated that he was drunk as well as passionate about the issues of our nation's defensive policies but being poked in the chest really gets my goat and I took my gold lighter and set the Democrat from Berkeley Law School's beard on fire. He got super upset and began running here and there and hitting at his beard with his hand, and Paisley was really ticked as well, however I was happy that I had set his beard on fire with my gold lighter.

And how I met my new punkrocker friends and became Sick Puppy is Gimlet and her friend Tit had been bobbing for lemon slices in the Young Republicans' punch bowl from Tiffany's and the attorney whose beard I had lit was on fire in the region of his head, and he pushed them aside from the punch bowl to extinguish his head in liquid. Gimlet got angry at him for this action and attempted to hold his head under the surface of the punch so he would be deprived of oxygen. Paisley Campbell-Greet attempted to pull Gimlet off the Democratic attorney and this got under Tit's skin so she tore Paisley's expensive taffeta dress down the front, so that the appearance of Paisley Campbell-Greet's breasts was demonstrated to many people at the party. It made me happy that Gimlet had tried to hurt the burning attorney, and I began to predict that Paisley Campbell-Greet would refuse to fellate me to get even for igniting her friend from Berkeley, plus her breasts turned out to be extremely small and pointy, so I laughed heartily at the exposed sight of Paisley's cocktail gown and greeted Gimlet and complimented her penis of hair and told her I was happy that she had tried to Pecos the attorney who had poked me because my brother carried the Black Box of nuclear codes for the President of the United States. And when Gimlet and her clique of Tit and Death and Boltpin and Big and Mr. Wonderful learned that my brother carried the nuclear codes for our nation's President and that it made me happy to ignite attorneys who get my goat, they caucused and decided I was the most outstanding and fine Young Republican in the history of the planet earth, and they spirited me away from the Republican cocktail party in their black secondhand milk truck with Druidic symbols painted skillfully on the paint before the police whom Paisley and the lit attorney called could come and make trouble for me that could lose me my job that pays me a great deal of money.

That night Gimlet and Tit fellated me, and Boltpin did as well. Gimlet and Tit made me happy but Boltpin did not, therefore I am not a bisexual. Gimlet allowed me to burn her slightly and I felt that she was an outstanding person. Big acquired a puppy from the alley behind their house in East Los Angeles and he soaked it with gasoline and they allowed me to set it on fire in the basement studio of their rented home, and we all stood back to give it room as it ran around the room several times.

At the Irvine Concert Hall last night Grope nursed his midsection and began to opine that Keith Jarrett was firing forms of electricity at him from the outer regions of his Negro Afro, and he became a nervous Nellie. Gimlet no longer cried but did become even more interested and fascinated with the blond and curled hair of the young child sitting with an older man in a very attractive sportcoat two rows of concert seats below our six seats. Gimlet stated that the girl's curious hair represented radioactive chemical waste product anti-immolation mojo and that if Gimlet could cut it off and place it in her vagina beneath the porch of her stepfather's house in Deming, New Mexico, she could be burned and burned and never feel pain or discomfort. She was crying and beating at fictitious flames, and subsequently tried to rise and run pell-mell over concert seats down to the hair of the girl, but Mr. Wonderful held Gimlet back and offered her his assurances that he would attempt to get her some of the curious hair at an intermission, and placed something in Gimlet's mouth courtesy of Big.

Next to me at the end of our row of concert seats Cheese became very interested in me as a person and began to talk to me as we listened to Keith Jarrett improvise his performance right on the spot on his bench. Cheese stated that while it was evident that I was a swell individual he wondered how I had come to become friends with my punkrocker friends in Los Angeles, Big and Gimlet and Mr. Wonderful, since I did not look like them nor did I dress like them or have a distinctive punkrocker hairstyle, nor was I poor or disaffected or nihilistic. Cheese and I began a deep conversation which was very fascinating and I told him several facts about myself which he found interesting and compelling. We talked in depth while Mr. Wonderful restrained Gimlet and Big restrained the nervous Grope, quietly so as to be able to hear the very good melodies our entertaining Negro performer was putting forth at all times.

I informed Cheese that my punkrocker friends and I were thick as thieves and that although I could not dress like them for reasons of my job and family traditions I admired my friends' fashion sense like all get out. Since Gimlet knows that my excellent job and well-to-do family are what provide me with lots of capital at all times, she is not unhappy that I cannot dress in leather and metal or shave my head or sculpture my hair like a true blue punkrocker. My job is very fascinating and pleasurable and I have had it for less than a year. At the law firm where I am an Associate I am a corporate liability troubleshooter. Sometimes the products certain manufacturers manufacture have bugs and defects in them which might injure a consumer, and when a consumer gets a wild hair about being injured and attempts to litigate against one of my firm's clients, I am called in to troubleshoot. This often happens with such products as children's toys and power tools. I am an extremely effective corporate liability troubleshooter because I enjoy a challenge very much and enjoy jumping in there with the old Corps spirit and licking the competition! I am especially pleased and challenged in my career when it really happens that a manufacturer's product has a bug and has injured a consumer, because then it is even more challenging to try to convince a jury or a jurist that what really happened didn't really happen and the manufacturer's product did not injure the consumer. It is more challenging still when the consumer is right there at the proceedings and is injured, for a jury tends often to feel sorry for an injured person, especially if the person is a racial minority and has swarms of small children, as racial minorities when they appear in court tend to. But although I have already had many corporate liability cases to troubleshoot I have only failed to bring home the bacon once or twice, because I enjoy a good competition in which I am part of the process, and also because people naturally like me out of instinct, because of my appearance. The average layman would be surprised to know how much juries are impressed by appearances. I am fortunately an entirely handsome devil and appear even younger than twenty-nine. I look like a clean-cut youth, a boy next door, and a good egg, and my mother stated at one time that I have the face of a heaven's angel. I have the eyes of an attractive marsupial, and I have baby-soft and white skin, and a fair complexion. I do not even have to shave, and I have finely styled hair without any of dandruff's unsightly itching or flaking. I keep my hair perfectly groomed, neat, and short at all times. I have exceptionally attractive ears.

I explained to Cheese that dressing in an accepted manner and looking a lot like an angel helps me in my career and that Gimlet comprehended this fact. My career pays me over a hundred thousand dollars per annum, and my mother also sends me checks from her personal wealth, so I have a great deal of liquidity on hand, which makes Gimlet and Big and Mr. Wonderful a very happy bunch of punkrockers.

Before I got angry at Cheese I liked him a lot. Unlike Gimlet and Grope, LSD-taking made Cheese a quite happy-go-lucky fellow last night at Keith Jarrett's concert. He did not see false events or get fidgety, but instead merely recounted that the paper on his tongue made it possible for him to discern the Negro Keith Jarrett's music with many different of his five senses. He could hear it, but see and smell and taste the music, as well. Cheese stated that some of the music smelled like old velvet in a trunk in an attic, or like vitamins, or medicine, or morning. He asserted that he could see Keith Jarrett's improvisational compositions as well. He gamely tried to describe in his own terms what a sunset looks like through fire, apricot and blue, and through smoke, plum and black. He said sometimes the music resembled weak light behind ice. I became happy merely listening to the sensual recountings of Cheese, and when Gimlet placed her hand on my penis in my gabardine slacks and claimed that there were secret worms and snakes in the small blond child's curious hair which were incessantly moving and spelling out the names of Gimlet's family of Imblums in Deming, New Mexico, I gave her a big buss.

Cheese knew a great deal about many other genres of music besides punkrock. He felt that Keith Jarrett was a very talented Negro performer. He stated that only a genius could have a seat on his bench before thousands of distant spectators and begin to play any old melodies which were floating around inside his head with its Afro. Cheese posited that for Keith Jarrett there are billions of these ditties, that he plays, and subsequently marveled to me that Keith Jarrett not only played the little tunes with skill but

also joined them together in unique and interesting ways, im-
provisationally, so that each of his piano concerts was different
from all the others. The manner in which the little melodies were
linked was arranged by Keith Jarrett's subconscious, stated
Cheese, thus his concerts were linear, Keith Jarrett's piano performance was a line instead of a composed and round circle. The line
was like a little life story of the Negro's special experiences and
feelings. I informed Cheese that I did not know that Negroes had
subconsciousnesses but enjoyed the sound of the music a great
deal, and Cheese frowned. Gimlet began to moan in a way that got
me very sexually excited and Gimlet did not even tell the coughing
woman behind Cheese to Fuck You after the woman behind
Cheese requested that we all please keep our voices subdued so
that everyone in the audience in the Irvine Concert Hall could
enjoy the concert, but Cheese was frowning yet and he informed
the woman that he would stomp her husband if she did not get out
of our face so she zipped her lip and I held Gimlet's hand and put
one of her fingers with white nail polish that tastes like vanilla,
which I enjoy, inside my mouth.

The small girl with the yellow hair Gimlet felt was chemical
and occult appeared to be drowsing and leaning against the shoulder of the older man's finely tailored sportcoat. I admired the
sportcoat and wished that it belonged to me instead of the man. I
wanted the man to turn around in his concert seat so that I could
see who owned the sportcoat and I began to decide whether to
throw a penny at the back of the fellow's head to induce him to
turn around.

However besides being a fine all around bald punkrocker with
pink glasses Cheese could also be intelligent and clever. He was
extremely interested in yours truly as a person, and without me
even noticing the fact Cheese took us from discussing musical
genres and Keith Jarrett's Negro experiences and emotions to no
music and my white experiences and emotions. Cheese betrayed
that he was anxious to learn why I had such satisfactory relations

with my punkrocker friends. He said he wished to understand a Sick Puppy like me. He began to look very serious on his LSD trip but he became funny in a way which I found entertaining and engaging. He divulged his position that punkrockers were children born into a very tiny space, with no windows, plus walls all around them made of concrete and metal, often despoiled with graffiti, and that as adults they were trying to cut their way out of the walls. They were attempting to move quickly along the very thin edge of something and accomplished this feat by failing to care if they fell over the edge or not. Cheese stated that my punkrocker clique all felt as if they had nothing and would always have nothing therefore they made the nothing into everything. However Cheese stated that I was a Sick Puppy who already had everything, thus he wished to inquire as to why I traded my big everything for a big nothing. Cheese was being curious and amusing from his seat on the edge, but he persisted in looking at the side of my fair face, and had his hand on the sleeve of my new sportcoat, which I did not like, for his fingernails were unclean. He asked me why I was Sick Puppy.

I proposed to Cheese that he was a fine fellow and that I was enjoying having an in-depth conversation with him a lot and that I admired his earring. His earring was composed of bone. At these statements Cheese became a grump once more and I told him to turn that frown upside down.

Gimlet observed my penny in my hand while I was gazing at the back of the older man's head, and she read me like a book. She requested into my ear that I throw my penny at the girl with the curious hair so that the girl would be hurt and turn around in her seat and Gimlet would utilize the opportunity to observe the face of the girl with the curious hair. She said she predicted the girl's face would be the face of an absolute giant, with planets rotating in the sockets of her eyes, and that her breath would smell like apples. She stated that the curious hair when removed from the child and placed in Gimlet's LSD-influenced vagina would alter Gimlet from a Sandy Imblum to an area of fire with arms and legs and vagina of proper heat. Cheese politely asked Gimlet whether she would care to take some tablets of Vitamin B_{12} in order to tone down the strength of her dosage of her controlled substance, however Gimlet had stopped being aware of Cheese. She placed her hand in the vicinity of my gabardine penis and thereupon stated that when she was full of curious active hair and fire she would pay a little visit to my father at his office in the United States Marine Corps and throw herself into his warrior's arms and commit the sexual act with him and when he had his orgasm he would catch on fire from Gimlet and immolate while she cut open his warrior's throat and allowed me to bathe in his blood. Gimlet's a first-rate gal but I have to admit that these statements got under my skin, Gimlet talking about my father and the sexual act in public in the Irvine Concert Hall. Cheese hypothesized that Gimlet was having an unpleasant LSD experience and advised Mr. Wonderful to keep his well-developed arm around her for various persons' protection, and Big told Cheese to zip the old lip and mind his own business.

I was royally peeved at Gimlet and as the back of Keith Jarrett's Afro head began to move in a side-to-side fashion and as his music became louder and more like punkrock, I crossed my arms and began breathing through the nostrils of my nose with anger at Gimlet. Subsequently I got her in a stare-down and stared at her with anger. Gimlet's black pupils in her eyes became so large that they obscured her eyes' color and she began to become frightened of yours truly and to cry, which made me a small amount happier. Cheese put his unclean hand on my new sportcoat's sleeve once more and I turned to him with my arms previously crossed and must have appeared extremely ticked off at him, as well, for putting his hand on my sleeve, for his immature eyes as well became extremely wide and purple behind his pink glasses and he felt at the whiskers on his head and stated quietly that we had to step into the interior lobby of the Concert Hall and have a chat with each other for a moment, and wait for the other kids to join us in the lobby in a moment at the hour's intermission. I was mad and on the horns of a dilemma about whether I wanted to throw my penny at the girl with the hair's head or burn Cheese with my lighter in the lobby, and I decided to burn Cheese and I trailed him up the stairs of the aisle and into the pleasant and cool lobby of the Irvine Concert Hall. Gimlet asked me Sick Puppy where are you going? but I gave her the cold shoulder.

Except when we entered the lobby I failed to want to burn Cheese because it would not have been any fun because when we entered the lobby Cheese spontaneously sat down on a pleasant bench owned by the Concert Hall in his leather pants and black combat boots and leather shirt with amounts of chain and ammunition strapped across his poorly developed chest and back and bald head with bristles and whiskers and began to cry, so that tears of Cheese's began to run out from underneath his rose-colored spectacles. Cheese began to look as young as he truly was, which was a minor. I knew that Big's LSD on the tongue was having an effect upon good old Cheese and that, unlike me, his consciousness became affected by controlled substances.

While crying, Cheese stated that he did not understand me and that I frightened him. I claimed that that was a riot of amusement: a punkrocker with ammunition such as Cheese being frightened of a dapper and handsome civilian like Sick Puppy. I said no harm no foul and offered to ask Gimlet to fellate him very skillfully, however Cheese ignored my offer and took the hand I proffered in friendship and with his poorly maintained hand pulled me down on the attractive bench beside him. It was difficult to hear Keith Jarrett from the lobby.

Cheese restated that he was unable to conceptualize a Sick Puppy such as myself, and stated that he also did not understand the happiness that was exuded by me at virtually all moments. It took him time to verbally grope for the word happy. Do you know what I mean, he inquired. There is something about you that is so totally happy, Sick Puppy. I patiently explained to Cheese once more about my great amount of income and clothing and fine home entertainment products, however Cheese shook his predominantly bald head and claimed that he meant a different word by the word happy which he had groped for. I wish to know why you are so *happy,* he said. After he kept asking me why I was happy he asked me if I loved Gimlet. I put the arm of my new sportcoat around Cheese's leather shoulders and informed him that Gimlet was aces in my book, and that on many occasions I was made happy by Gimlet because she fellated me and gave me pleasurable orgasms, and allowed me to burn parts of her body. Tears ceased to crawl from behind Cheese's pink lenses but he persisted in looking and staring at me in a fashion that made me want to hurt him until I hypothesized that he had entered a type of substance-induced hypnosis in which a person often stares at objects as if they were too large to comprehend, often for a long time. I did not know if I should leave Cheese in the lobby in a state of hypnosis but I wanted to hear Keith Jarrett play music, therefore I forgot Cheese and went away from him to the public drinking fountain and then to the doors of the auditorium. However before I could enter the doors of the auditorium I heard Cheese's voice call and I remembered Cheese once more and he no longer blindly stared like a bunny in my headlights when I arrived back at his bench and did not even have to look or stare transfixed at me in order to say that if I would tell him what was the nature of the happiness I exuded at all times he would allow me to burn him a little and also allow me to burn his fiancée, who was part Negro.

I stated to Cheese that he had made me an offer I couldn't refuse but that, however, his question stymied yours truly because I had already patiently explained to him that there were myriads of times and occasions when things made me happy. The fact of the matter is that there have only been a few things that historically have ever made me unhappy and gotten me down in the dumps. Exemplum gratia, one thing was the time in college at

Brown University when I went to proudly enlist in the United States Marine Corps R.O.T.C. program to continue to follow in the footsteps of my father and brother who serve with honor in the military and the Recruiting Colonel made us take a dumb personality test and I flunked and later when I went back to politely complain they gave me another dumb test and said I flunked it, as well, and then made me speak to a doctor who came in the R.O.T.C. office and then the Recruiting Colonel for Brown University called my father who was busy with important work in Washington, D.C., and my father was super peeved at the whole incident. The Colonel repeatedly addressed my father as Sir, and apologized for interrupting his work, however I never got to enlist in any R.O.T.C. programs for officer training at Brown University or elsewhere. And exemplum gratia, another thing was the occasion in Alexandria, Virginia, when I was eight and my sister was ten and my brother who now carries the nuclear codes for the President was at Westminster Military Academy and my sister and myself were in my brother's room playing in his desk and we came upon magazines in low drawers and the magazines, which were erotic, were full of men and women committing sexual acts and we read the magazines and witnessed pictures of men placing their penises in holes between the women's legs and the men and the women looking very happy and I took my sister's underpants off and my underpants off as well and placed my penis which was very excited from the magazines into a hole my sister and I found between her legs, which was her vagina, but having me place my penis in her vagina failed to make my sister happy and my father entered the room when she called him and saw us committing a sexual act and he took me down into his workshop by our playroom in our home's basement and burned my penis with his gold lighter from the United States Corps and stated that if I ever touched his little girl again he would burn my penis off with his gold lighter and I had to go to a doctor and obtain ointment for my burned penis, and was unhappy and down in the dumps.

If it were not a sign of ill breeding to discuss private family matters in public as my parents taught me as a child I would have filled Cheese in on examples of times I was historically unhappy and state to him as well that in my book Gimlet is aces and frequently makes me happy by fellating me and letting me burn her, for these are the only two events which make me become happy in matters of the birds and the bees. Unfortunately, even though I am one handsome dude and desirable on the part of many girls throughout my school and life, my penis declines to become erect when they want to commit the sexual act, and will only be erect if they fellate me, and if they fellate me I wish to burn them with matches or my lighter very much and most women dislike this event and are unhappy when burned and thus are chicken to fellate me and only wish to commit the sexual act.

However Gimlet is not chicken and she will. Furthermore Gimlet knows that what would make me the happiest corporate liability troubleshooter in the history of the planet earth would be to kill my father and that I will kill my father and bathe in his blood as soon as I can do it without maybe getting caught or found guilty at it, maybe when he is retired and my mother is weak, and Gimlet promises to help me and to kill her stepfather as well and she fellates me and lets me burn her sometimes.

I conversed with Cheese and my voice sounded slowly thick to my ears because recalling historical events from the past frequently affects my state of normal consciousness in the manner controlled substances affect other persons, and influences me. I stated to Cheese that I could not regrettably answer his question, yet I would give him a cash gift of a thousand dollars in return for Cheese making his Negro fiancée bathe thoroughly and then fellate me and then allow me to burn her with matches on the backs of her legs.

Cheese glanced at yours truly in a semihypnotized fashion for a long period, and I became confident that he was going to agree to accept the gift and that we would consummate a deal, however at this time Keith Jarrett's jazz piano concert had its hour's intermission and persons began to enter the lobby of the Irvine Concert Hall. The persons were moving slowly and my heart in my chest was beating slowly. The people were exiting the auditorium doors and conversing, utilitizing motions which were in slower motion even than the NFL Highlights Show, a show which frequently shows the commercial in which the beautiful and sexy woman playing billiards asserts that all her men wear English Leather cologne or they wear nothing at all. My state of normal consciousness became historically affected even further as Cheese persisted in staring at me and people in the lobby proceeded to mill and purchase refreshments and drink from the public drinking fountain and enter the restroom facilities extremely slowly, and the air in the Irvine Concert Hall became similar to lit ice, and Cheese's voice as he began to decline my initial offer of a deal came from distances, and his pink glasses began to have the appearance of two dull sunrises through ice.

From the attractive bench in the slow lobby I began to attempt to see if Gimlet and Big and Mr. Wonderful and Grope were coming out to help me persuade old Cheese to accept my offer of a gift, yet I instead found myself noting with extreme interest the slow running of the older and distinguished gray-haired and athletic man in the sportcoat. The sportcoat had appeared to be the real McCoy from above his back in the Irvine Concert Hall, however now in the lobby it appeared to have unattractive narrow lapels and also nonEuropean tailoring, which are fashion features I dislike. The man was running with amusing slowness, carrying the young girl with the curious hair, and was being pursued through the slow and crowded lobby by Mr. Wonderful and Gimlet, who had left Grope and Big in the dust in their pursuit of the man and the girl with the curious hair. The mouths of my friends Mr. Wonderful and Gimlet were open wide in a laughing and excited manner and Mr. Wonderful had something metal and bright in his hand and Gimlet's hair's penis sculpture was becoming disordered at the tip and her eyes continued to be all dark black pupil rather than white and color and pupil and she was running slowly in her leather and plastic and reaching out with her hand for the curious hair of the girl with the curious hair who was asleep in the protective arms of the distinguished older man running slowly past me in narrow lapels, and when I saw the beautiful and pale face of the sleeping girl over the bouncing shoulder of the running man the face slowly made me extremely joyful and excited, and as Gimlet and Mr. Wonderful slowly caught the man by the rear portion of his unattractive sportcoat near the front of the lobby of the Irvine Concert Hall and as Gimlet's hands with vanilla nails and Mr. Wonderful's bright object were almost in her curious hair the girl with the hair seemed to awaken in the older man's arms and she gazed incessantly and directly at yours truly, sitting at attention on Cheese's bench and removing Cheese's hand and unsightly nails from the wrist of the sleeve of my sportcoat, and I slowly assumed a happy and comforting and reassuring expression at the young blond girl and rose to my feet from the bench as Gimlet's hands became even slower yet and were moving in the girl's radiant hair and Mr. Wonderful was doing something with the bright thing to the man who was the girl's father. And here's what I did.

Tamara Jeffries

"*Inscrutable* is one word I've heard used to describe me. Quiet, more often. It's true: I don't talk a lot or loudly. If you can't tell what's going on inside my head by looking at me, read my work. Almost everything I've written so far has been, at least in some small way, autobiographical—even when I write about someone totally different from me. I'm in there. But then, I believe that we're all in each other. I believe in One."

Tamara Jeffries, twenty-nine, was born in Danville, Virginia; she lives and writes in Atlanta. Her first published short story, "Little Anderson," won the *Essence* 1991 short story contest and sparked her fiction-writing aspirations. Her fiction has also appeared in *In the Tradition: An Anthology of Young Black Writers* and *Catalyst* magazine.
  She is currently working on a collection of short fiction under the working title *Aboriginal Translations,* as well as a novel called *Praline and Savage.* She has written two children's books, is adapting one of her stories for the stage, and is writing spoken-word pieces to be recorded with music for what she calls an "urban funk opera." All very slowly.

BLACK TEA

Da . . .

Dad-dy.

Daaaddy.

I calling you. I talking to you now. I been talking to her—to the Mama—but she just keep crying. I want her to stop crying. Crying and telling me to go. I want her to stop drinking that tea.

I want to come be with y'all. That *my* spot in the place between you. You the Daddy. She the Mama. I the chile. And I want to come now.

———

I tole her. Come in her dreams and tole her. *"See, Mama? Mama. Here I am."* That's what I say. (In her dream I look just like you. But her nose.) And she wake up, kinda smile. But not long. Because in real life I not there. I not there yet.

Every time the moon get big, that seed fall. I tell her: *That my seed. That me, Mama. I don't want to fall. Don't let me fall.* She just get mad and sometimes cry and sometimes fuss and always drink that tea and pretend she don't hear me. But she hear.

She trying to keep me away, this time. Last time, I didn't ask first. I just came and got up in there. It warm in there. (You know it warm in there.)

And when the moon got big that time, nothing come down. She got scared. I could tell by her heart-sound. She talk to me and talk to God. But we ain't listen. (I don't know what God doing. I was sleep.)

But something wrong. I feel it. Then it was all noise and voices I don't like. And then that big light and the big wind and . . . they trying to get me. I was scared, Daddy. That *my* place. Nobody 'posed to be in there but me. Me and you and mama's heart-sound. But they come in there. She let them come in there. I try to hold on, Daddy. I try to hold, but everything all loud and too bright and upside down. She scream. I scream, too, but nobody hear.

After, she say she sorry. She say she sorry. She say she sorry. I understand. I go. She send her heart-sound with me to be my friend. Both us make her too sad, she say.

———

I go for a long time and don't worry Mama. Now I want to come back. I creep back real soft and whisper in her ear: *Mama.*

She talk back to me sometime. But she don't have nothing nice to say. "Go tell *him.* Go worry *him* to death." Say too many children running round without no daddy and she ain't raising no chile by herself. Say you don't know how to be 'sponsibility (some big word she say).

"He won't do nothing but leave. I'll look up one day and he'll be gone. Then what?" That's what she say. Then she press her lips. She don't say no more 'cause she 'member she talking to me and I not there. I not there *yet.*

I tell her you gone stay. I tell her you make a way best you can. I tell her, Daddy, but she won't listen. She don't hear me when I say you gon' love us. You gon' take care. I say ev'ything be alright this time. She don't listen to me and when she do, she just cry and go get some that tea. (Daddy, I don't like that tea.)

She just scared. You and me, we got her. We lay our ear near her heart and hear mm-hmm, mm-hmm. But she don't hear the yes, yes, yes, yes, yes, yes, yes.

You tell her, Daddy. You tell her everything be okay. Put your finger on her mouth real soft when she be fussing. Kiss her so she smile, 'stead of press her lips together. Tell her *you* see me in a dream, too. Look just like you. But her nose. Mm-hmm.

And make her some different tea.

Charles Oldham

"I grew up in Florida, the dirty little appendix of America, where all the doomed dreamers, sociopaths, and people on the run eventually seem to end up. Something about the combination of corruption, hubris, and cheesy hucksterism makes for a fairly potent fuel-air ratio of characters and story material. In any case, it has a lot to do with the way I see the country as a whole.

"I'm a recent graduate of the Iowa Writers Workshop, and live in Iowa City with my wife and dog. We can't wait to get back home."

LONGSTREET'S STEARMAN

From below, the airplane is the merest dark cross against the pale afternoon sky, the distant noise of the engine carrying faintly on the breeze. It spirals slowly upward, encircling the sprawl of farmers' fields and loblolly hammocks, the town with the bank and sidewalk shops, the combination fire and police station, the garage, the tavern, and the new fast-food franchise. Other aircraft pass over—tiny silver arrowheads of airliners on their way to Atlanta or Jacksonville, or a crop duster rising suddenly from a tree line—but this one is known by shape and sound, the characteristic geometry of its movements, the clockwork of the afternoon appearances in the vast Georgia sky above a little town on the coastal plain. Anyone would know it is Longstreet's airplane, and that he will be up until dusk.

Patrick Longstreet looks out past the capital "N" of the port wing strut and the cat's cradle of bracing wires to the sinking sun, the wind whipping past his face and carrying the steady racket of the engine, a clattering, rhythmic thrum. He props the stick between his knees and zips his jacket higher against the wind, checking the straps of his seat belt and parachute to make sure he hasn't unhooked anything. The old hands at the airstrip have given him much grief over the parachute, which he once told them was for "eventualities," letting the word hang in the air between them until they cut their eyes away. He had decided he would rather be known as an eccentric than as the banker's son or the banker to be. But he doesn't really know why he wears it, other than pure love of equipment. The more gear he has, the less he feels like the banker-trainee, and he is free to imagine himself as the famed test pilot doing high Mach stick and throttle work, rocketing alone through the wild blue while the astronauts flick switches in their tiny capsules like trained monkeys, Ground Control watching their every move.

He thrusts his head out full into the slipstream, opening his mouth to let the wind blast into his lungs.

"They can *have* those goddamn spaceships!" he screams over the engine noise.

The land is a broad plain curving away on all sides into a thin haze, and Patrick turns above the red dirt scars in the cutbanks, the dark irregular islands of trees among the fields and pastures, row upon row of corn, tobacco, rice, peanuts, potatoes and sorghum and millet, the clumps of black Angus clustered around stock ponds, the roofs of farmhouses, barns, chicken sheds, and warehouses, the silver sheen of swamp through cypress, the sunken white rowboat in the little lake to the west, the rusted shell of an old car seen through trees by the highway, and the gridwork of the town like a squared-off splotch of paint. He knows it all by heart, as well as any of the farmers know the dips and rises of their fields. The wind roars through the ear flaps of his old leather helmet and everything scrolls out beneath the bright yellow fabric of the lower wing. He tries to think of cartography—the scale and beauty of things and all the landmarks of a hometown warehousing previously unremembered failure.

But instead he sees the huge plat map on his father's office wall, his own aerial photographs overlaid in spots, the grand and secret plans for the fields and woods, balance sheets and equity, loan payments and acreage, resale value and agricultural prices. His father's world of the future. And in all of the photographs from the wide-angle lens of the camera, a bit of the landing gear of the Stearman appears, the bare tires vague smudges at one edge, a reminder of his complicity and own bleak bargain with the world. The Stearman buckets in a thermal like some invisible pothole and he moves the stick slightly to level the wings. He keeps the nose pointing above the horizon and continues climbing, the landscape moving more slowly as he gains altitude. He settles himself more comfortably in the seat for the long climb and thinks about gravity, imagining an elastic cord connecting him to the ground.

Trapped. Lately he's been having the same daydream, tossing it back and forth, trying to forget it, expanding on the particulars until he scares himself. He dreams of popping open the belts, rolling inverted and dropping out of the cockpit, shrinking to a dot like Wile E. Coyote dropping into a canyon. The plane would right itself and fly on until the fuel ran out somewhere over South Carolina, and make a perfect landing in the middle of a VFW picnic, scattering geezers in all directions. He imagines them regathering slowly, running mottled hands over the bright paintwork, gazing into the empty cockpit, stealing glances at each other in a silence complete but for the musical tinkling of the engine as it cools. Back home the mystery would never be solved. Robert Stack would bring a camera crew to town, and locals drinking at the tavern would argue theories, the most popular being that he was snatched from the cockpit by space aliens. Billy Reese would tell about the time he jack-lit a bigfoot from his truck, and old Mr. Carlson would start in on cattle mutilations and the depredations of the U.S. Army Corps of Engineers.

Patrick makes a quick scan for flocks of birds or airplanes on collision courses, trying not to think about old Mr. Carlson and his two sons and their financial situation, which he knows down to the last dollar. He remembers the sons as great linebackers during his high school days, but unlike their father, they are apparently incompetent farmers. He knows Carlson himself only as a storehouse of conspiracy theories and as a fishing addict who left the running of the farm to his sons so that he could retire to his custom-built bass pond.

This morning Patrick's father had paced around the table at a board meeting, considering out loud ways to acquire some of the old man's land. "Boys," his father said, "I been studying some figures here on old Carlson and he's got equity up the yin-yang, but considering what he'll get for the crop, what he owes us for the pond, and those . . . cash flow problems of his, I think it's time to piss on the fire and call in the dogs. Old boy's got seven hundred twelve acres and that front thirty out by the highway is a jewel without price." He indicated a grease-penciled area on a large photograph taped to the wall, and Patrick stared at the vague shadows of his airplane's tires, hanging over the land like black clouds.

He dips a wing to catch a glimpse of Carlson's property and sees him sitting in a johnboat in the middle of the pond, waving crazily. Probably thinks I'm scaring the fish, Patrick thinks. Wonder how he'll feel when the Wal-Mart goes in. The boat is tiny and the wavelets of the pond are like the crenellations of curdled cream. He waggles his wings, wondering how many bass are in the pond. A hundred? Two hundred? How many old lunkers cruising around like U-boats while he waits with his rod and his old sportsman's patience. He'll catch every one of them assuming his heart holds up.

He looks out through the shining disk of the propeller and watches a couple of drops of oil smack into the front windscreen, flattening out in the propwash. He catches himself humming in a monotone with the engine as the plane bobs like a cork in the thermals. This is what airplanes should sound like, he thinks. Airplanes today sound like bugs or vacuum cleaners. He wonders if his father knew he'd be back eventually, or if he had him on all the time, giving him plenty of line and reeling in slowly so that he never felt the hook.

"Ah, nature," his father said. Patrick was twelve and they stood out on the eleventh green, his father's golfing partner beating the bushes for a lost ball. "When I was a boy this was the big empty, Patrick. There was nothing to do and nowhere to go. Now we've got this course; we've got a bowling alley." Patrick handed a fresh beer to his father. This was his job, driving the cart, caddying for his father, and cracking beers for the buddies. He had heard this one before, and it was worse than the usual speeches about the mystery of the one-iron or sand traps as a test of character. He would rather be hanging around at the airstrip, or home building another model airplane, or even reading or watching Tarzan. Anything.

"Someday by God we'll have chain restaurants and a shopping mall, and I'll finance it all." He put his arm around Patrick's shoulders. "Someday," he said, gesturing with his beer can, "this'll all be yours." Patrick looked dubiously at the skinny pines lining the fairway. Not me, he thought. He was going to become a legend.

Patrick nudges the throttle for a little more power, and stares down at the clouds, in echelon of various heights. The ground merely shrinks away and loses detail, but the clouds give an almost dizzying proof of altitude. He no longer carries maps, with their outlines of hazards, tower frequencies, military operations areas, airways, flight levels, and restricted zones. All those invisible lines in the sky. Despite the maps, Patrick almost never sees another airplane.

The sky stretches off into incredible blue infinity in all directions. He remembers his long cross-country flights during college, a place rich sons and daughters of the South attended on failing to make the cut for the Ivy League. Patrick had arrived with dreams of doing something spectacular with his life, but remembers college chiefly as a series of abortive relationships with well-groomed coeds, fraternal binges, scholastic panic, and hunting expeditions involving huge expenditures on alcohol and ammunition, most of the latter going straight up into the air.

When his friends were drunk they had a mode of behavior Patrick came to think of as feudal, and he had not missed the fact that they were golfers, every one. He had gotten his pilot's license before he had been old enough to drive a car, and now he went back to it, taking cross-country flights on all the golfing weekends he skipped, knowing no hole in one could equal the feeling of stretching the kinks out of his body some cool morning in another town, his rented Cessna shaking itself like a wet dog as the prop spun down to a stop. Even so, things weren't turning out as he had planned.

He looks up to see clouds like cathedrals towering miles above him, one man in a tiny airplane. He has never failed to be surprised by the simplicity of this matter of scale. The ground, he thinks, gets smaller, and so do I. People vanish up here. Earhart and Glenn Miller, Nungesser and Coli over the Atlantic, the French ace Guynemer into a cloud bank, thousands in the wars. Probably mistakes. A series of small mistakes, a couple of unfortunate coincidences, and no one will ever know what happened. The huge sky just swallows up the little specks, and they disappear forever.

There is an almost imperceptible shudder and Patrick advances the throttle and lowers the nose slightly, shallowing out his climb. He watches the sun glancing off the bright fabric of the lower wing, and listens for the changing tone of wind through the bracing wires, hearing the music of their vibration with incredible clarity. He judges his speed from the sound and then looks at his airspeed indicator; smiling to himself because he's guessed it exactly. He climbs much more slowly now in the thinning air.

In particular he remembers waking up from a blackout, his feet tangled in the sheets and a girlfriend parading around the room naked, holding a tumbler of champagne in one hand and gathering clothes with the other. The glitter of jewelry against her sleek skin took his breath away and he sat up on his elbows, trying to back-track through the evening.

His tongue was a dry, swollen thing and his nose was blocked solid. She was moving with frightening purpose and Patrick felt he might be in love.

"Fill me in," he croaked. She regarded him from across the room, sighting along the lip of the glass. It appeared as if she were about to make a toast.

"You're a nice guy, compared to some of your pals," she said, "but you're not going to make it. You're just a boy with ideas and a safety net."

Patrick tried to work up some anger but could only smile bleakly at her. He thought he knew what she meant, exactly.

Down below the shadows lengthen and creep slowly along the ground, but he is awash in sunlight, having to squint through the goggles each time his turns take him into the sun. This, he thinks, is what all the photographs are missing, something alive and moving instead of all those still gray images. The engine falters and his heart leaps up into his throat for a split second before it catches again. He checks the fuel gauge hanging from the upper wing and watches the instruments suspiciously, snapping his finger against the glass to free any sticking needles.

He daydreams, contemplating a blistering low-level run to Atlanta to find a companion. "Climb into my antique flying machine and return with me to my little cow town," he sees himself saying to a stunning blonde. They are in evening clothes and his goggles dangle from his hand.

At work the tellers are all church bake-sale types who criticize his poor eating habits and tell him to get more sleep. He finds anonymous memos in his "In" box with names and phone numbers of eligible local bachelorettes, and there is the occasional whispered intercom call—"Come and take a look at window three, Mr. Longstreet. That's Mary Ellen Heureux. Daddy owns the feed store? She's just back from Auburn and about as cute as a button, although that skirt's a little too short for my tastes." They tell him, over and over, he's the spitting image of his father.

The Stearman has always been a little heavy on the controls, and now Patrick is grateful for it, the plane yawing only slightly as he unbuckles his belts and stands on the rudder pedals to remove his parachute. He unbuckles the chest and leg straps, and pulls one arm at a time from the harness, like removing a coat, the other hand always on the stick, aware that nothing is holding him in the airplane now. When it is off he stands in the cockpit, his mouth dry and his legs trembling and weak, and pushes the parachute against the windblast into the empty cockpit in front of him. "I've got your safety net right here," he says to the wind. He drops back down into his seat, breathing heavily, and buckles himself back in. "No parachute," he murmurs. No parachute. It is the title of a book he read as a boy, about World War I fliers in their Camels or SE 5s, Fokkers or Albatri, fragile, inflammable machines, made of wood and wire and doped fabric; going up on dawn patrols and fearing the "flamer," where the choice was between burning or jumping to one's death. But still there was a code, a chivalry in place, breaking off combat when an opponent's guns jammed or his engine seized. One true thing. He remembers it struck him as being enormously romantic.

After college, Patrick quit bartending jobs he had found for himself and jobs in banking his father had gotten him through connections. He balked at the banking jobs, but his father reminded him of college costs, and Patrick felt guilty about his worthless degree and lack of career. His father was getting old, and Patrick assumed he had stared oblivion in the face and seen in his son the chances of a dynasty.

Patrick's very last decampment was from a working internship at an Atlanta bank, and he had landed in Key West with the sense that he was going to have to cinch down everything that was flapping loose or lose himself completely. He took a room and spent his days wandering the island, the end of the line and asylum for so many over the years. He was unfazed by the cheesy T-shirt stands, luxury hotels, and hordes of tourists. He thought he recognized an undercurrent that ignored all but the essentials—that a half hour's walk in any direction brought one up against the gulf, and that there was only one road in or out. It was the essence of limited options.

One night at the shrimper's bar Patrick met an ex-Navy pilot who flew tourists around the islands and said he might need a little help once the season started. The next morning he took Patrick up for a check flight, and Patrick badgered him until he agreed to talk to the owner. Patrick flew home coach on the last of his money to pick up some clothes and his logbook, his heart full of wild hopes.

He arrived midway through one of his parents' cocktail parties, hung over and wearing the clothes he had slept in.

The local gentry were arrayed around the room in various low-slung postures, several conversations going at once over loud clarinet music from the stereo. When Patrick came in the conversation dropped to a murmur and his father turned from making a drink at the bar. He looked steadily at his son.

"Whatta you say, sport?"

Patrick took his sunglasses off. "I want to move to Key West and live on a boat," he said to everyone. This was hilarious. His father doubled over and careened around the room spilling bourbon. Patrick turned his back to them, sensing he had said something disastrous. Maybe a little drink, he thought. On the second orbit his father straightened up and threw an elbow to the back of Patrick's head that made his ears ring and propelled him halfway down the hallway to his room. He glanced back and saw his father one step behind, drink in hand. He kept moving. There was a crash of breaking glass from the living room and a man's voice sang out "Drink Patrol!" Patrick found the light switch and saw that his father was already leaning in the doorway, rolling the cold glass along his forehead.

"Christ Almighty," he said softly. "That must've been your mother's decanter. For the next year I'll be hearing about how it was a family heirloom and about four hundred years old, and about how Jeb Stuart once drank from it."

Patrick stood and waited for something else but his father stood silently in the doorway and gazed around the room as if seeing it for the first time. Wash up, Patrick thought, your credibility is shot. He took off his shirt, heading for the bathroom.

"Got a call from George Cowley, up in Atlanta," his father said, bringing him up short. "Said you called in a couple Fridays ago to say you weren't gonna be in, to find another boy. Said you told him you were in Key West and looking for a boat." Patrick's mind raced. He thought of how asinine his plan would sound and realized for the first time what little chance it had of working out. He realized he was squeezing the soiled shirt in his fist and tossed it into a corner of the bathroom floor.

"Guy down there, flies tourists around the islands at thirty bucks a shot. Got this old Waco, beautiful, deep blue Imron paint job, except he doesn't have the cowling on, which is too bad 'cause the Waco has this beautiful cowling, you know, little blisters for the cylinder heads and all." He said this as he walked into the bathroom. His father was absolutely silent. Patrick ran the sink and watched it fill with water. "Anyway," he went on, his voice echoing strangely off the tiles, "he needs a second pilot for the tourist season, like three days a week. I figured I'd do that awhile, live on an old boat to save money, fix it up and sell it to buy an amphibian. Then I could fly people over to the Tortugas, or maybe even Cuba; Cuba could open up anytime with the wall coming down and Castro smoking those big mambos year after year." When he reached for a towel his father was in the doorway, pinching the bridge of his nose between his fingers, his head bowed.

"Boy," he said with ultimate weariness, "you're retarded. What's worse, you're expensive." Patrick looked at his father with something like admiration. "How many jobs is this, since you graduated?" Patrick nearly started counting on his fingers and caught himself. He looked at his puffy, sunburned face in the mirror and saw a young wino. "Known George since college," his father said. "Had a drive on him . . . boy could drive a dead cat three hundred yards. Kind of embarrassing, Patrick, George knowing more than me about what my own son was up to." He finished his drink and set it on the edge of the sink with a subdued clink of ice cubes.

"This last deal of yours is the screwiest one yet. I figured something better from you, Patrick. All that money for flying lessons and you gonna start up Conch Airways." He rubbed his eyes with the heels of his hands. "Well, we're just gonna have to set things right," he said. "I've got a deal for you and I want you to think about it real seriously." He peered at Patrick until he nodded. Patrick actually felt relief course through him. The bill had been presented. His father picked up the glass. His mother's voice called from the living room.

"I guess we'll leave it till tomorrow," his father said. "I'm gonna go clean up the goddamned antebellum whiskey jug."

The needle on the altimeter barely creeps around the dial. The plane climbs laboriously and Patrick has to fight to keep it from shuddering into a stall. The air is much colder here and he wishes for a scarf, thinking he can actually feel the air getting thinner. He wills himself to be lighter and whispers to the airplane. I love your airplane smell and your honesty. I love your sturdy legs and taut fabric skin, the beautiful spruce in your wings, your cables and tubes and wires, and your wonderful reciprocating heart with its sweet voice of unending tiny explosions.

———

"Let's get this straight," Patrick said, standing in the sand trap. "I get the Stearman, a house, and a salary." His father nodded and pulled a sand wedge from his own bag, rubbing at some dirt on the clubhead.

"And in return you do my aerial surveying, fly clients around anytime I say, and start training at the bank, from the bottom up. Here, son, use mine," he said, handing the club to Patrick. "We'll have to get you some new clubs."

"That's the deal," Patrick said. He took a swing and a spray of dirt shot into the air, the ball untouched.

"It's the best one you're gonna get, which I think you know," his father said evenly. "You want to get under it more."

"I want the title outright, and I want the bank to cover fuel, insurance, and repairs."

"Done. You're not just going for the ball here, you want to lift the sand under it."

"And, Dad. Don't try to make me play this stupid game again."

He has flown snap rolls and Cuban eights, Immelmanns and outside loops, hammerhead stalls, barrel rolls, and tailspins, giggling as he felt gravity rearrange his organs. Other times he has lost all orientation with the ground and sky, the airplane juddering viciously through another revolution, and felt a flash of terror and shame, stupid, the horizon spinning madly in the corner of his eye, reborn when he figured a way out. He never doubted he would come up with a way out.

The plane wallows in the thin air somewhere above twenty thousand feet, on the edge of falling out of the sky. The engine roars at full power, the gauges warning that it will soon turn itself to junk. Patrick feels as if everything is standing still, balanced on the point of a needle. He thinks: So this is it. I'll find myself a little wife, settle down, come home to a hundred twenty channels on the satellite dish, buy gadgets, soup up the bass boat, drink expensive liquor, and have as much fun as possible before I get old and die. Work up to a multi-engine rating so I can fly anything around in circles. Go on vacations to exotic places where I'll never be able to live. Build a bomb shelter in the backyard. Watch my teeth fall out one by one.

One wing drops sickeningly and he bangs the stick against its stop in the opposite direction—Jesus, Jesus, Jesus, Jesus—until the controls finally bite and he is level again. Spots swim before his eyes and the altimeter is too blurry to read. He gulps air and remembers something from long ago about oxygen starvation. He tries again to read the altimeter but now he can't find it on the instrument panel. "What a swindle," he murmurs. He knows there is a point where the machine will go no higher, an absolute ceiling he cannot push through, but he believes he hasn't reached that point yet. He thinks of the weight of the aerial camera dragging him down and wishes for a way to jettison it. He bangs his fist on the edge of the cockpit in frustration and lowers the nose.

In the Keys he looked out over the side of the Waco and saw the iridescent water, turquoise and purple and pale green like colors from a child's paint box, like flowers, an impressionist painting of a lush, abandoned garden, the islands only small, broken flag-stones on an overgrown path. Warm wind blasted tears from his eyes and he hung over the side like a child.

He thought it was much too beautiful for a place where all the roads ran out. He thought it was much, much more than anyone deserved.

Patrick eases the throttle back and drops through the darkening sky. He notices a car's headlights cutting north along the highway, and the airstrip's flashing beacon ahead and far below. Lights start to appear in the tiny houses, barely visible in the twilight, and he imagines the pale blue glow of hundreds of televisions pouring through open windows into the night that is gathering near the ground. He pulls the throttle back to an idle, the engine backfiring and burbling quietly, and he listens to the wind whistling musically through the wires as he descends, keeping an eye on the beacon and thinking, with some desperation, of the moment the wheels will cheep against the runway, a perfect three-point landing.

5-18-93

Dear Michael Wexler :

Thank you for contacting in regards to <u>Voices</u>
<u>of the Xiled</u> . Enclosed you will find "Raping Gilligan,"
"<u>Zeitgeist</u> : The Movie," "Toonage," and "This
Sporting Life." Please consider any of these
fictions for publication in the anthology.
I am indeed a card carrying member of the
Xiled generation and although I have an M.F.A.
in Creative Writing, I feel like I have been
wandering through this combustible wasteland
without a Rand McNally road atlas since high school.
Therefore, I welcome the thoughts/ideas of an
anthology dealing with the 18-32 age group.
Thank you for your time.

S.A.S.E. enclosed

Dean Albarelli

Dean Albarelli grew up in Burlington, Vermont, and has lived in Ireland, Virginia, Iowa, and New York City. He now lives in Provincetown, Massachusetts, at the tip of Cape Cod, where he's worked as a lobsterman and directs the Provincetown Fiction Workshop. His short stories have appeared in *20 Under 30: Best Stories by America's New Young Writers* (Scribner's), *The Hudson Review* (where he's been a frequent contributor), *The Southern Review, The Quarterly,* and elsewhere. With his brother, playwright H. P. Albarelli, Jr., he recently coauthored a one-act play published in a special issue of *Witness* featuring American humor.

"Winterlude" was originally published in *Storm* (London) and in *Witness.*

WINTERLUDE

Hampson was in one hell of a foul funk: just "laid off" at the paper; a note in the morning mail saying his rent would soon increase; and this afternoon, for some reason, light bulbs blowing out in the kitchen and bathroom of his tiny apartment. By the time he found a parking space at the shopping center, off beside the enormous snowbanks, his car had begun drawing attention with its tubercular sputter, a blue-black cloud pluming from the exhaust pipe. There were days, and this was one of them, when he could almost believe things had been better before Alicen left. Not that she'd "left" precisely—in fact he'd told her to go, wouldn't have it any other way—but "left" was how he tended to think of it now.

He pulled the parking brake and felt in his shirt pocket for the very last floater, washing it down with a handful of snow from the roof of his car. For several months now he'd been relying each day on the little melt-in-your-mind masseuse, though he didn't like thinking it was a habit. Still, he liked even less the few times he'd been flat out of pills and presidents these last few months; better by far the groggy release of chemistry than the stupid spates of spleen and self-pity he stumbled into without it.

He'd just turned up Aisle 4 in search of light bulbs when he glimpsed it, but only momentarily, so he had to wonder if he'd seen correctly. The girl—she was college age, wearing a heavy gray wool coat—stood close to the display shelves in the kitchenware section. She seemed to have slipped something, something shiny, a fancy winged corkscrew maybe, into one of the big pockets at the side of her coat. Seeing Hampson, she began twisting one of the coat's black buttons in her free hand. He pretended not to have noticed, occupying himself with the light bulbs he'd located. The girl began humming to herself, touching at several items on the shelves before moving off to another part of the store.

When he got to the Express Lane she was standing in line two lanes away. He could see her purchases at the end of the black conveyor belt—a box of tampons, a tin of Planters cashews, and a bottle of liquid wash detergent. He tried to discern evidence of anything in her pocket, but the coat was big and bulky and the pocket looked normal.

The cashier swept up Hampson's items and smiled, a bottled blonde with rather unattractive dark roots showing close to her scalp. She poked her painted nails at the register, and his light bulbs totaled $3.37; Hampson dug into his jeans and found he had three ones, a quarter, and several pennies. Reluctantly, he wrote a check, his forearm casually hiding a full page of unbalanced transactions. He knew there were at least forty dollars left in the account, but that was all until his severance pay was processed. And then what? He hadn't been quite so poor since college. That was one thing you could say for marriage anyway—Alicen's passbook had always had four-digit numbers in the balance column.

He handed the woman his check.

"Do you have some ID?" she asked.

He produced a laminated state press pass—coat and tie photo —and a long-outdated ID from the university he'd attended in the East.

"Do you have a Sale Days Courtesy Card?"

"No. I've got a driver's license. A local library card . . ." Alicen had never left the apartment without several credit cards in her wallet, but Hampson was too disorganized to ever be responsible for such a thing.

Blonde-on-Black took his flimsy, dog-eared driver's license, a thick square of unlaminated paper perforated down the middle, and inspected it. "This is a driver's license?"

"Yes, it's from Vermont. They don't use photographs. It's valid, though. I mean, my check's not going to bounce."

"I'm sorry, if you don't have a Courtesy Card, you at least need a local driver's license." She shrugged sympathetically. "There are a lot of transients in this town."

Transients, he thought, do I already look so unemployed? Funny word to issue from the peroxided head now staring at him. "Jesus," he said, "how do I get a Courtesy Card?" The man behind him was shifting his weight and sighing.

The cashier reached beneath the counter and pulled out a letter-sized form with questions in fine print on front and back. "You just fill this out and bring it to the manager's office, over on the plat—"

"Oh, fuck, forget it," he said. He stuffed the checkbook into his coat pocket. "You're not gonna take this check?"

"I'm sorry, I can't."

He crumpled the check and glanced at the light bulbs. "You're a very accommodating woman, you know? And by the way, you should give your hair the treatment again real soon." He walked off thinking *stupid what are you saying Jesus contain yourself.*

When he stepped outside the college girl was about twenty yards away, shoulders hunched, walking quickly to her car. He hoped she *had* ripped something off. Just what the place deserved.

And then, still full of an angry rush of adrenaline, he had an idea.

The girl was heading for a little red Saab parked beside one of the enormous r-shaped light posts. The floater hadn't quite kicked in yet; his knees felt briefly the way they had in high school, the first time he'd set his skis into the track of the fifty-meter jump. He picked up his pace. "Uh, excuse me, miss."

She turned quickly, wide-eyed with surprise, half slipping on the snow-dusted ice.

"Sorry, didn't mean to startle you," Hampson said. He paused. He was being too polite.

"Yes? What is it?" the girl said.

"David Forbison, store security. Uh, I think you might have left the store with something unpaid for?"

She furrowed her brow and shook her head, slowly stepping backwards. "No, everything's right here in the sack. I have the receipt."

She was too nervous; he was convinced now he'd seen her take something. "Well, I believe I'm right, ma'am, and we ought to check it out." He glanced around to make sure no one overheard them. "Would you please come back into the store with me?" he said, guessing this would quickly establish his credibility.

"No, I won't. I haven't done anything." She seemed short of breath. A rather fetching young fraulein, genuine yellow hair, rosy round cheeks.

"Well, would you at least reveal the contents of your pockets for me?"

"The contents of my pockets are none of your fucking business. It's getting cold out here—please leave me alone."

"Ma'am, I think you must realize I'm empowered to arrest you. I'm trying to keep this from being any more awkward for you than it needs to be. Now, if you could just reveal the contents of your pockets for me, we could have this all over with."

"What do you think I—you can't just . . ."

But her eyes were beginning to well up now. A man carrying a large shopping bag and a new yellow broom glanced at them as he walked by. The girl waited until he'd passed to speak. "Look, don't arrest me. Please. I did take the corkscrew. But this store *owes* me money. I bought a colander here last month that got all rusty the first week I had it. I mean, this place owed me that much at least."

"You could have returned it. We have a very reasonable re-fund policy."

"They'd never have taken it back," she said, brushing her cheek with a mittened hand.

"Anyway," he said, "that's not the point now."

"Do you have to arrest me?" Her voice cracked. "Can't you just take it back in with you?"

"That's not really possible. Look. I'll tell you what." He glanced back toward the store. "You look pretty cold, could we talk in your car for a minute?"

She looked newly concerned now, but after a moment said, "I guess," without taking her eyes off him. She got in and unlocked the passenger door, leaving her own door slighty ajar. The car had an expensive cassette deck, and there were half a dozen tapes spread out across the dashboard. The girl settled her hands in her lap, her glance not quite meeting his.

"What's your name?" he asked pleasantly.

"Betsy," she said.

"Betsy what?"

"Betsy Dance."

"Is that really your name?"

"Yes! Honestly."

"It's a nice name." He'd scrunched around in the seat so that he was facing her profile. He noticed now that her nose must have once been broken, a minor angular flaw amid the gentle curves of her face. "You seem like a nice girl, Betsy. Probably go to the university, right?"

"Uh-huh," she said. "I do."

"Probably never done this kind of thing before." Maybe she had, maybe she hadn't. People loved it when you discerned fine qualities in their faces. "Am I right?"

She turned slightly. "No, you're right. I never . . . I've never . . ." She shook her head.

"Okay," he said. He paused. He was glad he'd let the short scruff of beard grow recently; he still felt vaguely disguised beneath it, his awareness of the whiskers somehow making it easier to adopt this paternal moron tone, when he was probably only seven or eight years older than she.

"I'm not real eager to get you into trouble, Betsy. But I've got a job to do. I mean"—he snuffed hard, a little nuance of character for the role—"I'm hired to do a specific kind of work here, and, you know, it's not always pleasant, but I do it." He paused again, uncertain now whether he could really go all the way with this. "So. I've got this . . . 'obligation' to my employer. And then I've got the problem of commissions."

"Commissions?"

"Right. See, the security staff gets a flat salary here, but we also work on commission. Which means if I apprehend a shoplifter and then let him go—or let her go—I'm letting money flow right out of my own pockets. See?"

"Yeah, I see." She pulled at the tasseled end of her wool scarf. "How much do you get for busting someone? I mean, apprehending."

"Well, it varies. It goes up each time. Me, I've got a pretty good record. I've stopped nine shoplifters just since the first of the year, so my bonuses are increasing, see?" The floater had settled in. He was having to work hard now to keep from indulging the ignoramus accent that kept trying to creep into this ludicrous delivery.

"Well," she ventured, "maybe I could help you out a little and you could overlook it? I mean, with all due respect. Not a bribe or anything, but just . . . you know?"

"Well, that's a possibility, Betsy." He caught himself staring at a hole in the leg of her jeans, where the soft blonde hairs of her knee showed through.

"If I give you ten bucks, can we forget it, please?"

He maintained an even expression and settled his gaze on her until she let out a nervous and slightly impatient sigh. "Betsy, you don't already have a criminal record, do you?"

"No, of course not!" She blushed deeply.

"Because the boys inside there ain't the type to slap your wrist and send you home." He sighed and peered back toward the store windows as if checking for someone. Betsy Dance glanced back that way, too, her eyes widening with anxiety.

"I mean, maybe I'm wrong," he said, "but I figured it'd be worth a little more than ten dollars to you not to catch a criminal record." He lifted an old Dylan tape from the dashboard and examined it, then slid it into the cassette deck. "Not to have a cruiser come take you downtown, where you'll get your pretty little fingers all covered with ink."

The tape wasn't playing; her pretty little fingers stuck a key into the ignition, and suddenly Dylan was crooning, *Winterlude, winterlude, my little apple . . .*

"You hear what I'm saying?" Hampson asked. "You really want your name in the Day in Court column, where all your professors can read it over their morning coffee? I mean, Betsy, think about it: *ten bucks?*"

"Well, how much do you want?" Her left hand edged toward the door handle.

Good question—how much *did* he want? The Saab, her Italian shoes, her general demeanor spelled sugar daddy, which meant this little prank might just be good for, what, a hundred? Solid chunk of the next rent check. "I just want it to be worth my while, Betsy, to do you a favor when I'm putting my job on the line. I mean, I could get my ass canned for letting you go."

"All right, all right, look. I'll give you . . . seventy-five dollars. If that's not enough you can go ahead and bust me."

"That sounds about right." He nodded.

She drew her upper lip over her teeth and removed her wallet from her shoulder bag. "I've got a ten . . . and a couple of ones here," she said, her fingers shaking slightly as she sorted through the black leather wallet. "Can I write you a check for the rest?"

"A check," he said, considering. "Sure, just give me the ten and make out a check for sixty-five."

Her hand continued to shake as she quickly completed the check. She asked him his name and didn't seem to notice that he was now Chris Hampson and not David Forbison. She tore the check out and handed it to him. He glanced it over, folded it in half with the crisp new ten, and slid them into his coat pocket.

"Oh, I almost forgot," Betsy said, reaching into her own coat pocket. Hampson heard a solid *clink* and saw a flash of metal in her fingers. He braced against the door thinking *Jesus, she's got a weapon,* but it was only the shiny silver corkscrew, which she held out to him.

He stared at it, then pushed it back to her, his fingers registering the cold pink skin on the back of her hand. "You keep it, Betsy. We'll call it compensation for the rusty colander." He unlatched the door and a fragile pencil length of snow fell from the edge of the roof onto his shoulder. "Be good now," and he was out of the car and walking across the parking lot. His knees were shaking, and a perverse triumphant laugh strained to burst from his lungs.

Three weeks later, his savings dwindled, living on Kraft macaroni and cheese, Hampson had picked up part-time hours at a bookstore on Dubuque Street. He still dropped floaters at home most days, and had noticed that sometimes now, if he went for a day or more without, a certain anxiousness descended on him and an activity as simple as aiming toothpaste onto his toothbrush would cause his hand to shake. He'd also had the runs on and off for a week, though maybe it was just the lousy diet.

He'd been half tempted to phone his mother and ask for a

small loan—two or three hundred bucks—but it was easier to avoid communicating with her. She had received the news of his impending divorce as if he'd announced his membership in a satanic cult. And with his father and older brother recently sentenced for a billing scam in their fuel oil delivery business—yet another of the new year's glad tidings—he doubted she had extra cash on hand.

Besides, he'd just met a young med school student specializing in pharmacology, a white-robed rube who hadn't yet figured out the street value of floaters. Doing business with young Dr. Discount might just allow him to maintain his frequent-flyer status. If he could continue economizing—cheap pills, a few dollars a day for food, gradually selling his books and records off—the job at the bookstore might just see him through.

Wednesday evening he was working the register near the front window when he happened to notice Betsy Dance, in her oversized coat, stroll into the bar across the street. It wasn't quite closing time yet, but he began ushering the few remaining customers out of the store. In ten minutes he'd locked up and was pushing into the smoky dimness of the Prairie Dog, its customers an odd mixture of local working class folk and the cheerful, shallow, well-fed, and ill-informed undergrads he'd come to detest. Betsy Dance was sitting at the bar alone. She had a Coke in front of her and was writing on a sheet of paper. Hampson settled unnoticed on the stool beside her and spoke quietly: "Your check bounced."

Still writing, Betsy Dance turned slowly, a look of mild curiosity on her face until their eyes met and she recognized him. She started suddenly, knocking her drink over on the polished surface of the bar. A young bartender rushed over with a cloth. "Never get hired that way," he told her with a wink.

Hampson squeezed a quick smile at him, but sat waiting until the guy had finished wiping the wood dry and moved off.

Betsy Dance glanced behind her and swallowed, then turned

back to Hampson. "I'm sorry," she said quietly. "I didn't think it would do that."

"I think you did," Hampson said. "I think you tried to screw me, Betsy. Think you tried to corkscrew me." Immediately, and almost involuntarily, he had adopted the persona of his store detective.

"Look," she said, "not here, please?" She began jotting a number on the slip of paper and Hampson started to say, "Oh no, Betsy, you're not gonna—" but she ignored him and called to the bartender. "Excuse me? I've got to run—could you please give this to Zack for me? And tell him I *can* manage Thur"—she glanced at Hampson—"Thursdays, it's no problem."

She grabbed her gray coat from the stool beside her, glanced briefly at Hampson with a disdainful scowl, and headed for the door, Hampson close behind.

A group of frat boys came jostling through the door as Betsy Dance stepped outside, four of them carelessly and unwittingly blocking Hampson's path. When he got to the sidewalk she was already thirty yards away, sprinting toward Iowa Avenue, coat clutched against her side, left arm pumping madly.

"Jesus!" he said, and he took off after her, wondering, as his stomach began rumbling with hunger, just what he planned to do if he caught her.

She stopped in the middle of the street to let several cars pass, glancing behind her once, and then tore in front of a bus, making a beeline for a cluster of university buildings. Hampson dodged an elderly couple and heard the man swear at him as Betsy Dance sprinted up the walk that led to the Scientific Research Center.

He was out of breath and feeling wild by the time he reached the heavy glass doors of the building. Two or three students sat smoking in the lobby, warming themselves on the narrow bank of radiators that lined the bare brick wall. The place had an early evening emptiness about it: dim lighting, the distant whirring of a janitor's heavy waxing machine. He walked straight ahead into the huge lecture theater, but it was empty. Unless she was behind the lab table. He jogged down the carpeted steps: not there. Back out to the lobby, where there were restrooms down the hall and to the right. He felt a little dizzy now, his short sidewalk sprint a good deal more exercise than he'd had in the month or so since he'd begun eating so frugally. He knocked on the door marked WOMEN, got no response, and stepped in. Nothing. Pushed the stall doors open, one-two-three, to be sure she wasn't trying any movie tricks. On the way out he caught a glimpse of his red and sweaty face in the mirrors. What the hell was he doing? He was angry now, though he knew it made little sense. When his bank statement had arrived three days ago and he'd learned her check had not been covered—meaning the check he'd sent his landlord was about to bounce—he'd been furious, shouting obscenities and kicking a hole in the kitchen wall.

Now he walked quickly down the wide corridor to the big corner classroom on the left. And past it to a staircase. A trace of wet footprints there. And likewise on the second-floor landing. Department of Biology. A maze of corridors and offices. Come out, come out, wherever you are. There. A noise. Down there in the gloom, the sounds of someone sniffling. Louder now. A light switch on the wall. No, keep it dark.

Distinctly now, he heard the rapid panting breath of a girl in tears. And, as he walked nearer, pathetic as all hell, the moaned word "Ple-ease." Followed by "Sto-o-op." Which he did. Over-whelmed by a sudden discomfort of self-disgust.

"Betsy, what do you think I am, anyway?" he pleaded, surprising himself with the sudden surrender of his goon persona.

She was huddled into a corner at the end of the corridor. "I don't know," she said, whimpering. "Can't you just stop? Please. I can give you the money. I mean it."

"Betsy, I don't even want the money. Look, I'm just gonna come down there and talk to you."

"No, please, leave me alo-oh-oan," she said. The pathetic vibrato of wet fear in her voice somehow summoned for him his older sister, the night his father had stunned all of them and taken his belt to her in the kitchen.

"I will, I'll leave you alone, but I'm going to talk to you first."

She stopped whimpering, but she was still cowering against the wall, sniffling and breathing in jerky heaves.

"Betsy, look, you're making too much of this. I'm not even a security guard really. I was just pulling your leg that day." She was edging into the corner as he drew near. "I thought you looked like a nice girl and I wanted to meet you," he said, almost believing now that it was so. "It was the only way I could think of."

"Yeah, right," she whined skeptically.

"I mean it," he said, "I just got a little . . . carried away."

He was only a few feet away from her now, feeling awkwardly threatening as he peered down on her in the dim corridor. "Can I sit? Do you mind if I sit?"

She moved her head slightly to one side and back, indicating No, but now he wasn't sure to which question. He sat.

Her coat was on the floor beside her; she hugged her arms to her chest, shivering.

"Why don't you put your coat on. Here," he said, and he draped it over the front of her and around her shoulders. "Come on, take it easy," he said. "I'm not what you think, okay?"

"Well, I'm not what *you* think."

"How do you know what I think?"

His question hung there and she shrugged slightly, causing the coat to slip down off her shoulders. He moved closer to replace it and she huddled into its warmth. He glanced at her hand on the floor, a jade and silver ring on one of her slender pink fingers; after a moment he took her hand and held it. She tensed briefly, but didn't withdraw it, and he began rubbing her fingers warm.

"Give me the other," he said after a minute, and he reached beneath her coat for her right hand.

"No. Stop."

"Why?"

"Because. I don't know you."

"Come on, Betsy, don't get so Emily Post on me all of a sudden."

"I'd just like to go home," she said. "Can I go now?"

He gestured to the empty corridor.

She clutched her coat and started to get up, but as she leaned forward to raise herself, her face almost deliberately near his it seemed, he met her mouth with his lips, causing her to rear back and bump her head against the wall. He started to apologize, but she was kissing him back now, an aggressive and toothy mouth-merging which for a moment he half construed as a bizarre sort of attack: her mouth mashing his lips, her slightly imperfect front teeth clicking and grinding the enamel of his own incisors, she finally unleashed a warm dart of a tongue, simultaneously reaching behind her head and rubbing her bruised blonde scalp.

He was kneading her breast through her sweater—through two sweaters, really: a black turtleneck and, beneath it, a thin cashmere crewneck with a price tag or designer's card still affixed—he was doing this when she whispered suddenly, "I have a key."

"What?"

"I have a key. To this office." She gestured her chin at the door behind him.

It had been more than five months since he'd slept with a woman, that is, since Alicen's farewell fuck. He hadn't much thought about sex since then, but suddenly his need was so fervently urgent he was ready to lie naked on cold linoleum, on a goddamn metal desktop if she was fussy, this Betsy. But this was an office with tenure: an old and well-preserved Persian rug; several large and handsomely framed Currier and Ives prints; and, against the windows, a black leather sofa. There was even a quartz space heater.

Betsy Dance stood watching him silently, speaking only to answer that the office belonged to someone she'd worked for. She pulled the two sweaters off all at once, revealing her marvelously pert little pointed breasts, smooth pink nipples that hardened before his eyes in the cold. Over the next thirty minutes she was oddly silent, save for her high-pitched song of orgasm, a throaty three-note theme that quickly brought Hampson to a squirming shudder of his own. At one point, he thought, she had begun to say the name Stewart, or at least "Stew," though maybe it was just "It's too . . ." Too what? Good? Big? Not likely. No, it was probably "Stew." Which was okay, he guessed, since the whole time he held her heaving pink and white body, there was one red word that rang out in his own head: Alicen.

All in all, a most unusual February afternoon.

But lying alone in his own miserable bed that night, his fingers absently kneading the dried residue of sex from his pubic hairs, it was not the girl's reticence or purloined cashmere, nor even her little conical breasts or distinctive come music that Hampson found himself dwelling on. The thought that held him now was why, since she had that key, had she not let herself into the office before he'd found her?

Afterward, as he was driving her home, he'd asked her about herself. She was from Northfield, Minnesota, she allowed, a bio major, parents divorced, one older brother. Northfield, Hampson said, isn't that where Jesse James nearly bought it? She nodded, silent and vaguely moody now, and a moment later he thought he saw her dab a single tear from the edge of her nose. He considered making a joke about her belated concern for the James gang, but thought better of it.

When he let her off, neither of them said anything about calling or seeing the other again. And though he often thought fondly, in the days that followed, of their odd tryst on the black sofa, he was just as glad now that he'd made no last-minute plans or promises.

Instead, Betsy Dance called him. About a week later. At the

bookstore. She was very sorry to bother him, but she thought he might be willing to help her. Could he? She sounded nervous.

"Well, yeah, if I can," Hampson said. "What's the problem?"

"I'm at the police station. They won't release me unless I post bail."

He let go a short, stunned laugh. "What'd you do?"

"I'd rather talk about it later, but can you help me?"

Hampson turned away from Perrin, the store owner, who was chatting with a customer nearby. Whispering now, he asked, "Were you shoplifting?"

"Sort of."

He blew an exasperated bit of static into the mouthpiece. "That other time wasn't the first, was it?"

"No," she said quietly. "It wasn't. That's why they're being tough now."

He was silent.

"But, Chris?"

"Yeah?"

"In the office that night? That was a first."

"Bullshit," he said, and Perrin turned around with his brow furrowed.

"It's not . . . bullshit," she said. "And I do need your help."

"Isn't there anyone else you can call? What about your family? I mean, your old man gave you a Saab to come to school with, he's not about to stiff you bail money."

"The car's my neighbor's and she's out of town." Her voice was trembling. "My father lives in California—I've been trying to reach him all day. Please, Chris, don't make me spend the night here. I need two hundred and fifty dollars. I've got a waitressing job at the Prairie Dog—I'll be able to pay you back. I can give you a hundred as soon as I get home."

"What about your mother?"

"She's a—away. Somewhere. I don't know."

"Betsy, I'd like to help you, but I don't even *have* that much—in the bank or anywhere else."

"Please, Chris. Don't say no."

"Betsy, look, just keep trying your father. Anyway, you must have friends here . . ."

"I don't *know* anybody at this goddamn school."

"Betsy, I want to help you," he said, "but I honestly can't. Really, I'm sorry. Look, I have to get back to work here." He hung the phone up gently.

When his shift ended, he got Perrin to advance him his next check and walked over to the police station. A young officer led her out to the booking desk and she said a simple "Thank you, Chris," looking calm and self-possessed and even rather prim. But when they got outside she hid her face in his parka and began sobbing. He stopped and stood patting her back but she said, "No, let's get out of here," and he led her to his car.

Twenty minutes later they were in the kitchen of her apartment. Betsy had stopped crying and sat with both hands wrapped around a mug of tea. Neither of them had spoken for several minutes.

"Betsy, why do you need to do that shit, anyway?"

"Don't," she said. "I'll go get the money right now. Just don't do this to me." She got up and headed for the bedroom.

He wanted to say the money could wait, but in fact it couldn't. Even if she gave him a hundred now, he was still down by fifteen Hamiltons. And getting thinner by the day on a new stringency diet of Ramen soup (five packages for 99¢).

While she rummaged through drawers in the bedroom, he quietly pulled open the fridge: a bowl of tuna fish salad with diced pickles that would do very nicely. Plus a little square of lasagna with some honest-to-God meat in it. He eased the refrigerator closed and sat waiting for her.

She brought out a stack of tens, fives, and ones—her waitressing money, apparently—and counted out a hundred and fifteen dollars. "There—I owe you a hundred and thirty-five now."

Hampson nodded and slid the money to the edge of the table. "I thank you," he said.

She sat down and glanced at him, picking at a button on her blouse. "I really do appreciate it."

"No problem. About the balance, though . . ."

"Well, I could write you a check if you want." Behind the damp trace of tears an ironic imp gleamed, tugging slightly at one corner of her mouth.

Hampson watched her for a moment and then removed her hand from its nervous picking. "You're a funny girl."

"Funny ha-ha?"

"Funny peculiar, too."

"Well, well."

"You wouldn't happen to have any lasagna just lying around?"

Her Mickey Mouse alarm clock said eight-fifteen. They'd been dozing for over an hour. He traced his thumb along the goose bumps of her upper arm, felt himself getting hard again as her wrist grazed his still sensitive penis. There was a child's bright watercolor on the wall, a large matted piece with a green girl and a blue man sitting beneath a large and limbless brown tree. There were also several family photographs—pictures of her father and brother anyway.

"How come there are no pictures of your mother here?"

She shrugged.

"Why?"

"I don't know. We don't really get along."

"Why is that?"

"My mother . . . is just . . . a bitch," she said.

"Wow, never knew anyone with a bitchy mother before."

She allowed a small smile. "Now you do."

Over the next few weeks a routine of sorts ensued, including, on weekends, makeshift meals and gin binges in Betsy's apartment (weekdays she seemed to get by on popcorn); regular bouts of daytime sex (a strictly nocturnal activity with Alicen); and occasionally helping Betsy with a writing assignment ("Degradation and Revenge in *The Scarlet Letter"*). She never visited his own apartment, and only rarely urged him to spend the night at hers.

He was still doing floaters most days, but convinced himself his need was less urgent now. Betsy didn't know about the pills; the few times she'd asked if he was high, he claimed he'd been drinking. He figured she was troubled enough without another dubious habit. Still, his sailing solo had less to do with altruism than anxiety over maintaining his modest stash.

Most weeknights Betsy worked at the Prairie Dog. Alone in his own apartment, Hampson would lie in bed reading a book borrowed from work, or take to the medicine cabinet and levitate. Their relationship seemed somehow tentative, but there were nights when he lay in bed feeling a sad and almost sentimental longing to visit her, even in the collegiate chaos of the bar, though he knew that doing so would only be a disappointment.

Early one evening in the first week of March, he was working the register at the front of the bookstore when Alicen walked in with one of her old comrades from the law school. His heart drummed up and his face went hot. He hadn't seen or spoken with her in at least two months. She was living in Des Moines now, working for some slime bag law firm that handled farm foreclosings. She claimed she was planning to take her knowledge to the other side eventually, but it sounded like rationalization to him.

"Chris!" she said in apparent surprise. Her dark straight hair was cut short now, with a subtle, unbraided rat's tail in back—no doubt a daring bohemian touch among the pinstripers at the firm. "You're still here."

"Well, yeah."

"I just mean, I thought when you got, when you left the paper you were . . . I don't know," she dropped her voice discreetly, "I thought you didn't like it out here."

"I don't."

"I know. I mean, I figured you'd left town by now."

He shrugged. "I need some cash first."

"Oh. I wish I could help you," she said.

He rolled his eyes.

Sonia, the comrade, touched Alicen on the arm and said, "I'll let you two talk, I've got to look for something."

Alicen nodded and stepped closer to the register. "Don't be nasty with me, okay?"

"I'm not being nasty."

"Is it really just cash that's holding you back?"

Hampson studied her face. Did she know about Betsy? He doubted it. Doubted she'd care. "What do you mean?"

"I just mean, I don't know, up-and-coming young journalist, *Register* nominates you for a Pulitzer, so now you're a bookstore clerk?"

"The *Register* also fired me."

"So? I heard they bent over backwards to keep you on. You could have told them you were going through a divorce. What are they supposed to do when you hardly turn anything in for over a month?"

"Where'd you hear that?"

"I saw Roger what's-his-name at a party in Des Moines. He also said you'd been overdoing it with Percodan or something."

"Roger. The guy's a Christian Scientist, he thinks taking Tylenol's like sucking Satan."

"He wasn't talking about Tylenol," she said, her eyes suddenly zeroing in on his, gauging, he guessed, his pupils.

"Get lost," he told her, his eyes squinting disdain.

"All I'm saying is, other papers don't know they let you go. Send your clips around. Show them the series on the farm crisis. I know it's been a bad time, but come on. It's not as though you don't have options."

"What are you getting at—you're ashamed to have a former husband who works in a bookstore?"

"Give me a break. I just hope you're not letting a couple of . . . adventitious setbacks ruin you."

"Is that what they call it in the legal world—an 'adventitious setback'? That must be what the scarlet A stands for. I always wondered about that."

"Don't be a jerk, cut it out."

"Fuck you."

"Jesus, Chris, you're such a prick. I'm trying to help you. Anyway, I thought what's-his-name at the *Tribune* said they might have something up there."

Hampson shrugged.

"Did you go up there and talk to him?"

He shook his head and glanced toward the door. Betsy had just come in and stood about ten feet away, scanning the magazine rack, uncertain whether she should approach him just now. "Hi," he said, summoning a lackluster smile, and she jumped her eyebrows, lifting a single mittened hand.

Alicen turned and took Betsy in. She caught Sonia's eye at the back of the store and motioned to her. Sighing, she turned to Hampson again and leaned closer. "Get it in gear, Christopher," she said quietly. "Life's not just going to wait for you, you know." She buttoned her expensive coat and glanced again at Betsy. "Life's not, but she is, I gather." Betsy, he noticed, was keeping a covert eye on Alicen.

He didn't answer, just met her eyes evenly until she shrugged and said, "I give up. Goodbye, Christopher."

"See ya," he said flatly.

It was in fact a far more civil encounter than he might have expected—particularly on his part. But then, why parade his hurt any more than he already had? He'd swallowed enough pride just consenting to that awful and silent final fuck the night she'd left. Two minutes of a strange tumescence packed as much with rage as with lust, and then, before either of them had even approached a climax, he had suddenly gone soft, his limp penis shrinking from

Alicen as if in distaste. The more he'd tried to stay hard, the more clearly he saw the scene he'd happened upon a week earlier: Alicen, black hair wild on their living-room floor, receiving the bare-assed thrusts of David Forbison, her fellow editor at the *Law Review*.

Betsy wandered over to the counter now. "Was that your wife?" she asked quietly. He was a little surprised she'd stood guard there by the magazine rack; for all the nights she'd nestled close in recent weeks, he still detected a certain indifference in her affection that he expected to preclude anything like jealousy.

Which was fine with Hampson. In three years he'd thrashed his way through enough of the conjugal jungle to do him in for a lifetime. Why suffer another safari when you could always visit the zoo? Nonetheless, he knew that cash and lassitude were no longer first on the list of things keeping him here. There was also this Betsy. Betsy Banditti. Betsy of the Five-Finger Discount. That night when he'd asked her about her mother, when he'd found her so reticent, had seemed to establish a set of ground rules to which he was more than willing to adapt. Rule Number One being: *Don't ask.* There were benefits to such reticence. Privacy is dignity, after all, and Hampson—betrayed by his wife, fired by his editor, his father and brother serving five years each—Hampson simply didn't want to be asked.

But walking home with Betsy after his shift had ended, she did just that. "She stuck you, didn't she?" Betsy said.

"What?"

"Her. Your wife. She hurt you, right?"

"When?" he said, annoyed now.

"I don't know. Sometime. It's obvious."

"I guess."

"You don't have to tell me about it." She paused. "Just tell me this: Do you feel sometimes like you'd like to get even with her?"

He slowed and watched her face for a moment. In the cold like this, the two points of skin where her nose had once been broken showed up whiter than the rest of her snowy complexion. "I don't even think about her." He shrugged. "Why?"

"I don't know. I just wondered."

"Okay, Betsy, you show me yours and I'll show you mine."

"What do you mean?"

"Hey, let's be candid, okay? Somebody stuck you, too, right? I mean, you're asking me don't I sometimes want to get even. There's somebody *you* want to get even with, isn't there?"

"Maybe," she said.

"So . . . ?"

"You said you'd show me yours first," she said.

"Forget it, Betsy, I don't even want to play."

"But I'd really like to know," she said. "I care about you, Chris, I'd like to know what happened." He glanced at her. Maybe there was more affection there than he'd realized. "Really," she said.

He blew a purse of air and shook his head, scuffing at a chunk of snow. "I told you I used to work for the newspaper."

"Uh-huh. You told me you were a store security guard, too."

"I covered eastern Iowa for the *Register*. You can look it up if you want. Anyway, I was supposed to cover a very angry farm rally in Decorah one afternoon. But about eight miles from town I came on this accident. Big tractor-trailer loaded down with new Buicks, lost half its load in the middle of Route 80."

Betsy shook her head slightly. "I'm not sure you understand what I was asking about."

He turned and fixed her with an icy glare. "I'm getting to it, Betsy, just hold your fuckin' ponies."

"Sorry." She touched his arm in apology.

"The *real* accident was the three-car pile-up behind all the Buicks. Which I arrived at about a minute after the whole thing happened. Not a cop or ambulance in sight yet. I get out and in the first car I stop at there's this old lady with a wig half hanging off her head. The car radio's going, she's mumbling to herself, and when I open the door I see her forearm's barely attached at the elbow. Let me know if I'm boring you, Betsy, because I'd just as soon drop it."

"No, tell me."

He dipped his chin into the collar of his coat. "The husband was already gone. And her arm might as well have been. I put a tourniquet on her and she was basically gonna be all right. But when she realized about him, she started tearing her hair out. I mean literally, her real hair. With her one good arm. So I hold her down and wait till the emergency crew arrives.

"And shit, the last thing I wanted to do then was drive to a fucking farm rally in Decorah, write up my little five-hundred-word piece on it. So I turned around. Thinking about this woman and her husband, and I remember, I thought, God, I hope Alicen's home. I felt this real . . . a real intense devotion, like I'd never felt before. Made all the little fights we'd been having look like nothing, you know? Who cares about that shit, people can die. It was a real wake-up call." He paused. "Yeah. Like wake up, ass-hole. Because she was home all right. She was home, and she wasn't alone. So. Is that the part you were waiting for? There you go. 'The Good Samaritan,' for modern day viewers."

"That's awful," Betsy said. She slipped her arm around him.

They stopped at the edge of a driveway as a car backed out, then continued in silence for a minute.

"Tell me about Stewart," he said finally.

Her head jerked, fully alert.

"It is about Stewart, isn't it?"

Betsy stopped. "How do you know that?"

"You said it once . . . in your sleep."

"Oh . . ." She toyed with the zipper of her parka. "You're not going to like this, but you know that office we were in that time?"

"That's Stewart's?"

"Not exactly, it belongs to the professor he worked with. Stewart was getting a Ph.D. Or still is, I guess. We'd go up to Northfield now and then, to spend the weekend at my mother's house." Her voice became deliberate as she kept it from veering into emotion. "She and I were going through a, uh, well, we had more or less of a truce since I'd left for school. Before then we used to fight a lot. Real screaming scenes. And worse. That's why my nose is so ugly."

"She broke your nose? I mean, it's not ugly at all, but she broke it?"

"She clobbered me with a bag of carrots when I was twelve, and it never got set right. I think 'cause she was afraid I'd tell the doctor. Before that I was actually kind of pretty."

"Betsy, you're very pretty, it's barely even noticeable. Was that typical, though?"

"Well, it was the only time she broke my nose. But things were getting a little better the last few years. Plus she seemed to like Stewart. Which was new. In high school she'd always hated my boyfriends. She either made fun of them or wouldn't talk to them." She shrugged. "And . . ." She drew the word out slowly, as though she would stop. "Stewart was giving a paper in Chicago one weekend, so my roommate and I—I had a roommate then— we decided to go to Northfield together. I needed some things, and I thought," she jerked her shoulders, "I thought I'd surprise my mother. And when we got there, Stewart's car was in the drive- way, so I figured the seminar had been canceled, that he came right up there to see me. Except he hadn't even known we were going. Anyway . . . Anyway, *you* can imagine the rest of it."

Hampson waited. "What?"

"What do you think?"

"You mean he and your mother . . . ?"

"The two of them. In the shower together," she said, her voice cracking slightly.

"Jesus." He saw her eyes glaze over. "How old is your mother?"

"Forty-three. But she looks about thirty."

Hampson shook his head.

"The point is," she said, swallowing unshed tears, "we ought to get even. Don't you think?"

"Get even," he said hollowly. That was the point? The point, he would have thought, was that given such similar experiences, maybe there was some odd logic in the crazy crossing of their paths.

"Well, why not?" Betsy said.

He turned and studied her face. Her complexion was wonderfully ruddy now, the evening chill and the quick burst of emotion combining to heighten her elfin Nordic features.

"I know she hurt you, Chris, and I could help you get her back. I mean, not get her back of course, but get back at her. Or at the guy if you want. But if I do, you'll help me too, won't you?"

He licked the inside of his mouth, thinking. So she wanted to get even. Was that such a base instinct? *Nemo me impune lacessit.* Nobody fucks *me* over and gets away with it. Nobody fucks my mother and gets away with it, either. So why should David Forbison screw Alicen with impunity?

Vengeance; it was simple logic really, the oldest logic on earth: Eat from that tree and I'll fix *your* wagon—and your little serpent too.

"What is it you want to do exactly?" he said.

About a week later Betsy was getting dressed for the second shift at the Prairie Dog while Hampson sat gloomy, drinking gin and tonics on the easy chair in her bedroom. "I put a full tank of gas in your car," she said, pulling a pair of wool tights on over her underwear.

He nodded, feeling his pocket for the two unfamiliar house keys she'd given him.

Betsy tugged the waistband of the thick black tights high on her belly, halfway to her bra. "That way you won't have to stop up there." She snatched a denim skirt from the closet and stepped into it. "It'll be better if nobody sees you afterward. Don't you think?"

"Mmm."

"Don't be so glum, Christopher. It's not a murder, for Christ's sake. Plastic surgeons do it all the time." She walked to the dresser and as she passed him mimed a slow blow to his nose—"Pow!"— but he didn't respond. "And remember," she said, "don't get hung up over the cash and jewelry and stuff. If you get it, great, but that's just, you know, the cover."

"I've got it, Betsy, okay? I've got it."

"Sor-*ree,*" she said.

He sipped at his drink and added gin from the bottle on the floor beside him, glancing at her Mickey Mouse alarm. A month ago he'd considered the clock pathetically tacky, but now he found it rather touching. What a fucking sap. Always thinking a woman might be the missing piece of the puzzle forming his half-assed picture of happiness. Only to find each time that his jigsawed vision of joy was missing much more than he'd guessed. "You're sure we're gonna be business as usual after this?" he asked.

Betsy turned from the closet. "Of course! Why not?"

"I don't know, I mean, suppose you resent me for it? Christ, Betsy, she's your fucking mother."

"That's just biology," she said. "Is that what's bothering you?" She came and stroked his cheek.

He shook his head once, then shrugged, poking a finger at the wedge of lime in his drink and holding it beneath the surface. "Tell me some more bad shit about her," he said.

It was snowing outside of Northfield. A Jeep had gone off the road near the interstate exit, but it didn't look like much; a state trooper was already on the scene laying chains. Not that Hampson would stop anyway. No dodges, he was going through with this thing. He'd nearly said no the day before, but Betsy was bent on it now. Besides, cash in the kitchen freezer, jewelry in the bedroom —if all went as planned he could bag the bookstore job and score enough floaters to lie back and levitate until spring. Then maybe get his amputated ambition out of hock. Make a down payment on some incentive.

In any case, he was ready now to kick some ass. Deviate some septum. Whatever. That perfect patrician nose upon which, according to Betsy, her mother had always prided herself. Bango. Say bye-bye. Just let me at that nose and we can call it a night. Then again, better hope she resists a little or it might look pretty suspicious: *Thief ignores valuables; hammers homeowner's nose.* Even some hick Northfield cop might trace the motive there. Not that any old Sherlock could ever fathom the mind of Betsy Dance.

He switched his high beams on and took another swig from the Thermos of gin and tonic. By now it had cut through the blissy passivity of his pills, nudging him into the anger this evening would hinge on. So: remember to feel for it—cartilage caving in on the knuckles. That's how it was with Charlebois on the playground all those years ago: felt it *and* heard it. A right satisfying sensation too. This, though? How satisfying could this be? Still, if it made Betsy happy. A strange girl, but also a girl he was beginning to love, he realized. Be a pity to spare the rod and spoil the relationship.

Which brought him back to the more troubling aspect of this little errand. Not the criminal violence of it, but the fact that the whole thing confirmed Stewart—Stewart whatever-his-name, Stewart the Ph.D.—the whole thing confirmed old Stew as the guy Betsy couldn't get over, the ugly tattoo on her heart. But then, this might be what it took to banish the bastard. And what's a little humble pie to a man who's found his wife humping her brains out on the living-room floor?

Dakota Street wasn't hard to find. A pleasant neighborhood of upper-middle income homes, turn-of-the-century places with spacious yards and wide driveways. The type of people who took notice, no doubt, of a rusty and unfamiliar out-of-state car parked on the street. For which reason Hampson continued on for several blocks, down the hill to a condo unit with a half-filled parking lot. He was shivering now—the cold in part, but little anxiety quakes as well. He cut the engine and got out, stood beside the car pissing a gin and tonic valentine into the snow. Oh, the things we do for love. Then stuffed the ski mask into his coat pocket and hoofed it back up the hill.

Dakota Street. Except for the solitary scrape of a distant driveway being shoveled, the neighborhood was quiet. A good chance she'd yell, scream, whatever. Neighbors . . . ? Just get the goddamn door closed.

217 was the number he wanted, but as he neared 207 he slowed, realized the sporadic shoveling was just ahead. So let's just take it across the street here, collar turned up against the cold. Let these nice tall pine trees obscure us, that's the ticket. Should have been over here anyway. Don't let that G and T buzz make us careless now. So: addresses ascending by twos means 209, 11, 13, 15 . . . shit. Betsy, what am I walking into here? You said she motherfucking lived alone! What's this guy doing out in her drive —whoops, no, strike that, all systems go here. Little M/F confusion there, Houston. Back to full throttle. Slight of figure, long of hair, yellow of boots—definitely an F. As in Fractured.

Her back was to him as she shoveled, Hampson making his way from tree to tree until she was only thirty yards away. His heart was doing a mad percussion number now, but his breath had lodged somewhere between mouth and lungs, unmoving.

Across the street Jenna Dance stopped and unzipped her parka, leaning on the shovel. A good sign: only one light on in the handsome brick house. Maybe best to follow right in behind her when she finishes.

She pulled her white knit hat off now and ran her hand through her hair—hair as blond as Betsy's. He could only see her in profile, but she didn't look especially malevolent; be easier if the bitch had fangs. Never mind that, though, keep the venom flowing. It's going to happen.

He dropped to his knees as she approached the last section of unshoveled driveway near the street. Almost alarming how much she looked like Betsy. Prettier, though. A more perfect face. At least for the moment.

A car rolled around the corner and Hampson lay down on the sidewalk, hidden by the snow piled high on either side. When he stood again she'd finished the driveway and was walking into the garage. He pulled the keys from his pocket. Soon as she starts closing that garage door. Get in there and wait for her. Get her while she's winded.

But she came back out carrying a small sack. Salt? Clomping through the snow to the largest maple tree in her front yard. Not salt. Birdseed. Filling a goddamn feeder. Wonderful, I'm here to mug St. Francis of the frozen fucking north. Only forget it, lady, I'm not the least bit touched. So you're a bird lover, big deal. Hitler and his generals used to weep over Shakespeare, it didn't make them human. Just get in the house so we can dance this number.

But she wouldn't. She zipped her coat back up and sat on the top porch step, her breath drifting off in vapors. By now he had to piss again, finally indulging himself in a quiet steamy leak into the snow, kneeling this time for minimum noise.

For five, ten, it had to be fifteen minutes she sat there looking meditative, depressed maybe, chin cradled in her mittened hands. Eventually she leaned down and scooped a handful of snow from the top of the shrubbery, holding it to her face and nibbling from it.

Don't do this, he thought, just cool it with the sensitive shit. Feeding the birds, nibbling snow, you're still a bitch.

But either the gin was wearing off or he'd pissed the last of his venom into the snow, because goddamn it, he had some second thoughts now. And yet how simple, to land one nose-breaking blow, rifle her jewelry box, her secret cash stash. He thought of Betsy, in bed the night before, hovering over him for hours on her knees. Melting into her sheets, her mouth, he'd said to himself, yes, I'll do it for this girl, a crazy criminal thing, but she's been wronged and I'll do it.

And yet. And yet. Better to break Alicen's goddamn nose. That was the face he'd gladly do damage to. What happened here, though, in that house across the street, it wasn't his life.

He stepped out from behind the tree and she started suddenly —her hands dropped stiffly to her lap. He watched her and spat into the street, locked eyes with her as she rose and walked hurriedly into the garage. In a second the automatic door kicked into action, slowly creaking closed. Bitch.

He stepped into the street and picked up a slender, palm-length piece of curbing cement that had been scraped loose by a snowplow. It had the vaguest shape of a trumpet, though it arched and sailed through her big front window rendering the precise chiming notes of a percussionist's triangle.

He got back to Iowa City just before midnight, and when he saw the police cruiser outside Betsy's apartment he panicked briefly, thinking, in a quick burst of paranoia, that someone had seen his plates in Northfield. Then he noticed a small crowd gathered in the driveway, students mainly, each holding a big plastic cup of beer, and he relaxed. Another neighborhood party out of control. Goddamn weekend began Thursday nights now in these college towns. When did they study? Books? Ideas? Social justice? Their idea was to just be social. Most of the little pricks were voting Republican now, which was fitting, since their main aim in life was having a grand old Party.

An officer blocked the door to the back stairs of the house, refusing to let Hampson in, though he claimed he lived there, refusing even to hint at what had happened. Betsy would be at work for another hour, but he was worried now; hers was the only apartment accessible by the back stairs.

No one in the crowd seemed to know what had happened

except that an ambulance had recently come and left. He was about to try a second assault on the stairway when he noticed Reed—"Lieutenant Loose Lips" to knowing reporters—swaggering Reed who succumbed to glottal gab at the merest hint of newsprint.

"Reed!"

He was getting into a cruiser parked across the street, but turned and smiled. "Hamster. Looking pretty scruffy these days."

"What's going on?"

Reed shook his head. "Sorry, Crisco, still in the middle of something here. Catch me tomorrow—I'll give you some quotables."

"Strictly off the record, man. What is it? Off the record, Reed, just two guys talking."

Reed glanced around. "Love quarrel, looks like." He smiled and waggled his tongue in a perverse manner. "Vicious stuff. Girl who lives upstairs, waitress, runs into an old beau on the job. They start flirting, she brings him home, they do the nasty and they're lying in bed. Thirsty now, right? Girl gets up to open a bottle of wine. Comes back and stabs him in the vitals with a corkscrew."

"Jesus! Betsy? She stabbed him in the—heart?"

"You know that chick? Not the heart, man, the *vitals:* bitch skewered his poor dick. But hey—who knows?—maybe he was a lousy lay. Come too fast, could be your last. Ha!" He released a taut man's belly laugh and mock-punched Hampson's shoulder. "I *know* you'd love to quote me on that one." He opened his car door and got in, slammed the door and rolled the window down.

Hampson was reeling now, dizzy, wanted only to go sit on the curb.

"So. Let it be a lesson to you, Crisco."

"What?" he mumbled vaguely.

"What?" Reed imitated. "Fucking-A, man, you're just no good without a notebook, are you." Then, peering closer, "Jesus, you don't look good, guy."

Hampson nodded, his mouth hanging open dumb, mumbled some inarticulate sound as he crossed the street.

Reed tore off with his cherry top flashing, snow spraying from behind his tires.

The crowd, mainly college boys in shirtsleeves, had begun to disperse, heading back across the street to the party still in session there.

"Hey, guys, check this," someone called, and everyone drifted back to the driveway. Sitting on the curb Hampson turned to see two cops escorting Betsy out the door and down the icy driveway to the cruiser waiting there. She wore her parka and mittens, but he could see her hands were cuffed in front of her. Her mouth was bruised and swollen on one side. He started to stand and she saw him, her eyes came alive suddenly. "Chris!" she called, and the beer-guzzling college boys turned to look at him. But before she could say anything more, an older officer set his hand on her head and ducked her into the back seat.

He stumbled into his own apartment ready to crash, the gin and the drive finally taking their toll, though his chest still surged with a sick anxiety. He went to the medicine cabinet and popped a floater, kicked off his boots and got under the covers fully dressed, but soon the phone began ringing. For a solid minute he listened to it. Ten minutes later the same thing. Her one call. A short time later it rang again. When it stopped he got up and removed the receiver, went back to bed, then got up again and unplugged the jack, stood wrapping the cord around the disembodied phone. He found a cardboard box and set the phone in it. Dropped papers from his desk into the box as well. Then walked to the closet and swept his clothes from the rack. Lifted his suitcase to the bed, opened it, and emptied each of his drawers into its gaping mouth. The big bottom drawer, a disaster of chipped veneer, he carried to the next room, filling it with his few kitchen wares and a stack of books.

He got back into bed then and slept for four hours, rose at six o'clock and stripped the covers. In the medicine cabinet there was a small vial with a half dozen more floaters in it. Brushing his teeth he eyed the brown container, then twisted the plastic lid off and poured the remaining pills into his hand. Dropped them into the toilet. Pissed and flushed.

By ten o'clock he was forty miles outside of Chicago. He passed the exit for Aurora and about a quarter mile later came upon an attractive redheaded girl in tight jeans and a green down parka, holding a hand-lettered sign that read EVANSTON. His foot came off the pedal and his hand felt slowly for the direction signal as he studied her. Their eyes met. A tall soft-looking girl, with a pierced nose apparently. Sort of a gangly hip innocent. He held the direction stick without moving it. His foot dropped back to the pedal and pressed. The girl, an amber world of possibilities, receded in his rearview mirror.

"Hoof it," he whispered.

Jennifer Egan

Jennifer Egan was born in Chicago and moved to San Francisco in 1969, when she was six. Having experienced the sixties mostly through stolen glimpses from the family car or while being pulled briskly by her mother past groups of hippies, she spent her teenage years longing for an era she'd missed. It is that longing—for something absent, or lost, some more "real" existence than our own—which Egan finds particularly characteristic of her generation. Oz's Emerald City seems the archetypal object of such longing—both the glitter it throws off from a distance and its essential emptiness at close range. Image culture—advertising, fashion, movies, TV—provides, Egan feels, the glittering facets of our Emerald City, a place that forever slips out of range just at the moment when we feel we've reached it.

EMERALD CITY

Rory knew before he came to New York what sort of life he would have. He'd read about it. He saw the apartment, small but high-ceilinged, a tall, sooty window with a fire escape twisting past a chemical-pink sky. Nights in frantic clubs, mornings hunched over coffee in the East Village, warming his hands on the cup, black slacks, black turtleneck, pointed black boots. He'd intended to snort cocaine, but by the time he arrived that was out. He drank instead.

He was a photographer's assistant, loading cameras all day, holding up light meters, waving Polaroids until they were dry enough to tear open. As he watched the models move he sometimes worried he was still too California. What could you do with sandy blond hair, cut it off? Short hair was on the wane, at least for men. So there it hung, golden, straight as paper, reminiscent of beaches he'd never seen, being from Chicago (in Chicago there was the lake, but that didn't count). His other option was to gain or lose some weight, but the starved look had lost its appeal—any suggestion of illness was to be avoided. Beefy was the way to go; not fat, just a classic paunch above the belt. But no matter how much Rory ate, he stayed exactly the same. He took up smoking instead, although it burned his throat.

Rory stubbed out his cigarette and checked to make sure the lights were off in the darkroom. He was always the last to leave; his boss, Vesuvi, would hand him the camera as soon as the last shot was done and swan out through the sea of film containers, plastic cups and discarded sheets of backdrop paper. Vesuvi was one of those people who always had somewhere to go. He was blessed with a marvelous paunch, which Rory tried not to admire too openly. He didn't want Vesuvi to get the wrong idea.

Rory turned out the lights, locked up the studio and headed down to the street. Twilight was his favorite hour—metal gates sliding down over storefronts, newspapers whirling into the sky, an aura of potential and abandonment. This was the way he'd expected New York to look, and he was thrilled when the city complied.

He took the subway uptown to visit Stacey, a failing model whom he adored against all reason. Stacey—when girls with names like Zane and Anushka and Brid regularly slipped him their phone numbers during shoots. Stacey refused to change her name; "If I make it," she said, "they'll be happy to call me whatever." She never acknowledged that she was failing, though it was obvious. Rory longed to bring it up, to talk it over with her, but he was afraid.

Stacey lay on her bed, shoes still on. A diet Coke was on the table beside her. She weighed herself each morning, and when she was under one hundred twenty she allowed herself a real Coke that day.

"What happened at *Bazaar?*" Rory asked, perching on the edge of the bed. Stacey sat up and smoothed her hair.

"The usual," she said. "I'm too commercial." She shrugged, but Rory could see she was troubled.

"And that was nothing," Stacey said. "On my next go-see the guy kept looking at me and flipping back and forth through my book, and of course I'm thinking fantastic, he's going to hire me. So you know what he finally says? I'm not ugly enough. He says, 'Beauty today is ugly beauty. Look at those girls, they're monsters. They're gorgeous, mythical monsters. If a girl isn't ugly I won't use her.' "

She turned to Rory. He saw tears in her eyes and felt helpless. "What a bastard," he said.

To his surprise, she began to laugh. She lay back on the bed and let the laughter shake her. "I mean here I am," she said, "killing myself to stay thin, hot-oiling my hair, getting my nails done, and after all that the guy says I'm not ugly enough."

"It's crazy," Rory said, watching Stacey uneasily. "He's out of his mind."

She sat up and rubbed her eyes. She looked slaphappy, the way she looked sometimes after a second gin and tonic. Eight months ago she had bought her own ticket to New York from Cincinnati, after a year's meticulous planning. And this was just the beginning; she hoped to ride the wave of her success around the world: Paris, Tokyo, London, Bangkok. The shelves of her tiny apartment were cluttered with maps and travel books, and whenever she met a foreigner—it made no difference from where—she would meticulously copy his address into a small leatherbound book, convinced that it wouldn't be long before she was everywhere. She was the sort of girl for whom nothing happened by accident, and it pained Rory to watch her struggle when all day in Vesuvi's studio he saw girls whose lives were accident upon accident, from their discovery in whatever shopping mall or hot-dog stand to the startling, gaudy error of their faces.

"Rory," Stacey said. "Look at me a minute."

He turned obediently. She was so close, he could smell the

warm, milky lotion she used on her face. "Do you ever wish I was uglier?" she said.

"God no," Rory said, pulling away to see if she were joking. "What a question, Stace."

"Come on. You do this all day long." She moved close to him again, and Rory found himself looking at the tiny pores on either side of her nose. He tried to think of the studio and the girls there, but when he concentrated on Stacey they disappeared, and when he thought of the studio he couldn't see Stacey anymore. It was a world she didn't belong to; this was why Rory loved her and also why she would fail. Watching Stacey's tense, expectant face Rory felt a dreadful power; it would take so little to crush her.

"Never mind," she said when he didn't answer. "I don't want to know."

She stood and crossed the room, then leaned over and pressed her palms to the floor. She had been a gymnast in high school and was still remarkably limber. The limberness delighted Rory in a way that almost ashamed him—in bed she would sit up, legs straight in front of her, then lean over and rest her cheek againt her shins. Casually, as if it were nothing! Rory didn't dare tell her how this thrilled him; if she were aware of it, then it wouldn't be the same.

Stacey stood up, flushed and peaceful again. "Let's get out of here," she said.

Her apartment was right off Columbus, a street Rory prided himself on hating, but which nevertheless mesmerized him. He and Stacey walked arm in arm, peering into the windows of restaurants as eagerly as diners peered out of them. It was as if they had all been told some friend might pass this way tonight, and were keeping their eyes peeled.

"Where should we go?" Stacey asked.

Rory cracked his knuckles one by one. He often felt a moment of panic when asked this question, as if there were some right answer he didn't know. Where was everyone else? Occasionally he

...ense that they had been exactly where he ...e, but had just left. The worst part was, he ...vere. The closest he came was in knowing ...know; his roommate Charles, a food stylist ...llops, and of course Vesuvi. Vesuvi was his

...owntown, enjoying the last warm days of au-...seediness of Seventh Avenue. They passed in-...patches of old cobblestone were exposed be-...tar, relics of another New York Rory dimly ...m novels: carriages and top hats, reputations and insults.

"Rory," Stacey said, "do you feel more something, now that you're successful?"

Rory turned to her in surprise. "Who says I'm successful?"

"But you are!"

"I'm no one. I'm Vesuvi's assistant."

Stacey seemed shocked. "That's not no one," she said.

Rory grinned. It was a funny conversation. "Yeah?" he said. "Then who is it?"

Stacey pondered this for a moment. Suddenly she laughed—the same helpless way she had laughed on the bed, as if the world were funny by accident. Still laughing, she said, "Vesuvi's assistant."

At Stacey's suggestion they took a cab to a Tribeca bistro where Vesuvi often went. It was probably expensive, but Rory had just been paid—what the hell, he'd buy Stacey dinner. Maybe he would even call his roommate Charles and see if he was back from LA, where he'd been styling all week for Sara Lee. Rory didn't envy Charles his job, although he made good money; sometimes he was up half the night, using tweezers to paste sesame seeds on to hamburger buns or mixing and coloring the salty dough which looked more like ice cream in pictures than real ice cream did.

Rory had been horrified to learn that in breakfast cereal shots it was standard to use Elmer's glue instead of milk. "It's whiter," Charles explained. "Also it pours more slowly and doesn't soak the flakes." Rory had found this disturbing in a way he still didn't quite understand.

Inside the restaurant Rory spotted Vesuvi himself at a large round table in the back. Or rather, Vesuvi spotted him, and called out with a heartiness which could only mean he was bored with his present company. With a grand sweep of his arm he beckoned them over.

The waiters pulled up chairs and Rory and Stacey sat down. Stacey ordered a gin and tonic. Rory could see she was nervous— the girls at the table were faces you saw around a lot: redheaded Daphne, Inge with her guppy-face, others whose names he'd forgotten. What distressed him was seeing Anushka, a moody teenager whose journey from some dour Ukrainian town to the height of New York fashion seemed to have happened in an afternoon. Once she had lingered at the studio while Rory cleaned up after work, humming a Fine Young Cannibals song and flipping aimlessly through his copy of *The Great Gatsby.* "My father is a professor," she told him. "He teaches this book." "In Russian?" Rory had asked incredulously. Anushka laughed. "Sure," she said, curling the word in her accent. "Why not?"

Outside the studio, they had hovered uncertainly in the dusk. Rory was supposed to meet Stacey, but felt awkward saying so to Anushka. Instead he'd blundered forward and hailed a cab, leaving Anushka standing on the curb, then paid the driver three blocks later and taken the subway to Stacey's. He'd arrived shaking, mystified by his own idiotic behavior. Anushka had frightened him ever since; last week, while he was loading Vesuvi's camera, she had casually reported the numerical value of her IQ and then subjected him to a humiliating quiz on the Great Books. "Have you read much Dostoyevski?" she'd called up the rickety ladder where Rory was grappling with a light. *"The Brothers Karamazov?*

No? What about *War and Peace?"* When Rory called back down that *War and Peace* was by Tolstoy, Anushka had colored deeply, stalked back onto the set and not spoken to him again. Rory felt terrible; he'd never read a word of *War and Peace.* He had even considered confessing this to Anushka after the shoot, as she grumpily gathered her things. But what the hell, he'd decided, let her think he was brilliant.

Amid the models sprawled Vesuvi; sphinxlike, olive-skinned, his close-cropped beard peppered with gray though his wild curly hair showed no sign of it. He was short, and wore high-heeled boots which Rory found spectacular. Vesuvi was a man of few words, yet he often gave the impression of being on the verge of speech. Conversation would proceed around him tentatively, ready to be swept aside at any moment by whatever Vesuvi might say. Rory watched him adoringly over the glass of bourbon he'd ordered (but loathed), unable to believe he was sitting with Vesuvi after all the times he had watched him glide away in cabs, feeling as if everything that mattered in the world were disappearing with him. Yet Rory wasn't entirely happy; everyone at the table was watching him, especially Anushka, and he felt that in return for being included, he was expected to do something crazy.

He glanced at the next table, where conversation seemed more lively. It was a group of downtown types, the men like deposed medieval kings in their bobbed haircuts and gigantic silver medallions. During his first month in New York Rory had gone out with a girl like the ones at the table—Dave, she'd called herself. She wore nothing but black: bulky sweaters, short loose skirts, woolen tights and round-toed combat boots. The thrill of the relationship for Rory had lain mostly in watching Dave undress—there was something tremendous in the sight of her slender white form emerging from all of that darkness. Once she'd finished undressing, Rory had often wished she would put part of the outfit back on, or, better yet, dress completely again and start over. But he'd never had the courage to ask.

"You look familiar," Vesuvi said, eyes on Stacey. "Did I use you for something?"

"Once," she said. "Four and a half months ago."

"Right, I remember now. It was that . . ." He waved a languid hand, which meant he had no idea.

"For *Elle*," Stacey said. "Bow ties." It had been her best job, and she was crushed when the pictures the magazine printed had left out her head. To use them in her book would look desperate, her agent said, so she kept them pasted to her bathroom mirror. Rory looked at them while he was shaving.

Vesuvi sat back, satisfied. The question of whether or not he had worked with a girl always troubled him, Rory had noticed, as if the world were divided between girls he had shot and girls he hadn't, and not knowing which side a girl was on caused a cosmic instability.

"You worked for *Elle?*" Anushka said.

"Once," Stacey said.

"So far," Rory added.

Anushka glanced at him and then at Stacey, with the same startled look she'd had when Rory left her on the curb. He felt guilty all over again.

"Have you worked for them too?" Stacey asked. Anushka nodded absently.

"You're on the next cover, aren't you?" someone said.

Rory felt Stacey move in her chair. "Yes," Anushka said dully. Then she seemed to take heart, as if she were hearing this news for the first time. "Yes," she said, grinning suddenly, "I got the next cover."

She lit a cigarette and smoked; exotic, dragon-like, black hair tumbling past her shoulders. For a moment all of them watched her, and against his will even Rory was moved by a face so familiar from pictures. Never mind what you thought of Anushka; she was that woman—you recognized her. There was an odd pleasure in this, like finding something you'd been looking for.

"When do you leave for Tokyo?" Anushka asked Inge.

"Next week," Inge said. "Have you been?"

"Two years ago," Anushka said, straining for the weary drawl of an expert. "Wait until you fly to Osaka at 7 A.M. and the Japanese businessmen are coughing out their lungs into the airport garbage cans. They smoke like fiends," she concluded, wagging her cigarette between two fingers. Rory listened miserably; Stacey was barely surviving in New York and here was Anushka, who not only had been to Japan but had the luxury of complaining about it. He rattled the ice in his glass and impatiently cleared his throat.

Anushka glanced at him and turned serious. "Still," she said, "the culture of Japan is fascinating."

"The culture?" Inge said.

"You know, the museums and things. The theater."

Vesuvi, who had seemed on the verge of sleep, roused himself and turned to Anushka. "You, inside a museum?" he said. "That I don't see."

The girl looked startled.

"You must have gone there on location," he said.

"I did not! I just went. You don't know everything about me."

Vesuvi shrugged and sat back in his chair, his lazy eyes filled with amusement. Anushka blushed to the neck; the pink tinge seemed at odds with her extravagant face. Helplessly she turned to Stacey. "Have you been to Japan?" she asked.

"I wish."

"What about Milan?"

"No," Stacey said, and Rory noticed with surprise that her drink was almost gone. Normally one cocktail would last Stacey an entire night, her sips were so tiny.

"Paris?"

Stacey slowly shook her head. Rory noticed a change in Anushka's face as she sensed her advantage. The others were quiet. Vesuvi sat forward, looking from Anushka to Stacey as if they were posing for him.

"You've never worked in Paris? I thought everyone had worked in Paris."

"I've never been to Paris," Stacey said.

"London? Munich?" Anushka turned to the other girls, confirming her surprise. Though she didn't glance at Rory, he sensed that all this was meant for him, and felt a strange, guilty collusion with her. He saw Stacey's hand shake as she lifted her glass, and was overcome with sudden and absolute hatred for Anushka—he had never hated anyone this way. He stared at her, the gush of hair, the bruised-looking mouth; she was ugly, like the man had said today. Ugly and beautiful. Confused, Rory looked away.

"Well," Anushka said, "where have you been?"

Stacey didn't answer at first. She looked double-jointed in her chair, heaped like a marionette.

"I've been to New York," she said.

There was a beat of silence. "New York," Anushka said.

Vesuvi started to laugh. He had a loud, explosive laugh which startled Rory at first. He had never heard it before.

"New York," Vesuvi cried. "That's priceless."

Stacey smiled. She seemed as surprised as everyone else.

Vesuvi rocked forward in his chair, boots pounding the floor. "I love it," he said. "New York. What a perfect comeback." Anushka just stared at him.

It began to seem very funny, all of a sudden.

A chuckle passed through the group like a current. Rory found himself laughing without knowing why; it was enough for him that Vesuvi had a reason. His boss gazed at Stacey in the soft-eyed way he looked at models when a shoot was going well. "It's a hell of a place, New York," he said. "No?"

"The best," Stacey said.

"She's never been anywhere else," Anushka protested. "How would she know?"

"Oh, she knows," Rory said. He felt reckless, dizzy with the urge to make Anushka angry. "You don't get it, do you?" he taunted.

"There's nothing to get," she replied. But she was starting to look uncertain.

Vesuvi dabbed with a napkin at his heavy-lidded eyes. "Next time you go to New York," he told Stacey, "take me with you."

This was too much for Anushka. "Goddammit," she cried, jumping to her feet. "We're all in New York. This is New York. Have you gone completely crazy?"

But laughter had seized the table, and Anushka's protests only made it worse. She stood helplessly while everyone laughed, and Rory hooted all the louder to keep her in her place.

"That's it," she said. "I'm getting out of here."

"Go back to Japan," Rory cried. He had trouble catching his breath.

Anushka fixed her eyes on him. Her makeup made them look burned at the rims, and the irises were a bright, clear green. He thought she might do something crazy—he'd heard she once punctured an ex-boyfriend's upper lip by hurling a fork at him. He stopped laughing and gripped the table's edge, poised for sudden movement. To his astonishment, the charred-looking eyes filled with tears. "Rory, you're full of shit," she said.

She yanked her bag from under the table and hoisted it onto her shoulder. Her long hair stuck to her wet cheeks as she struggled to free her jacket from the chair. Rory thought of his high school lunchroom; girls stalking out mad, clattering trays, their long, skinny legs wobbling above high-heeled shoes. He felt a pang of nostalgia. She was just a kid, Anushka; she was younger than he was.

"Hey," Vesuvi said, standing and putting his arms round her. "Hey, we were just having a joke."

"To hell with your joke." She turned her face away so that no one could see her crying.

Vesuvi stroked her back. "Hey now," he said.

Chastened, the group sat in guilty silence. Stacey and Rory traded a look and stood up. No one protested as they slid their jackets on, but when Rory opened his wallet to pay for their drinks, Vesuvi winced and waved it away. Anushka still clung to him, her face buried in his neck.

Vesuvi spoke to Stacey in a lowered voice. "I've got something coming up you'd be perfect for," he said. "Who are you with again?"

Stacey told him the name of her agency, barely able to contain her delight. Rory listened unhappily; Vesuvi said this all the time to girls and forgot the next minute. It was just a pleasant salutation.

They left the restaurant and headed toward the East Village. Rory longed to reach for Stacey's hand, but she seemed far away from him now, lost in her thoughts. Outside a market, a boy perched on a stool cutting the heads off beans. A barber swept thick tufts of dark hair into one corner of his shop. From an overhead window came music, and Rory craned his neck to catch a glimpse of someone's arm, a lighted cigarette. The familiarity of it all was sweet and painful to him. He searched the dark shopfronts for something, some final thing at the core of everything else but he found just his own reflection and Stacey's. Their eyes met in the glass, then flicked away. And it struck him that this was New York, a place that glittered from a distance even when you'd reached it.

They climbed the four flights of steps to Rory's apartment. A slit of light shone under the door, which meant Charles was back. They found him standing at the kitchen table, wiping a slab of red meat with a paper towel. He had a blowtorch plugged into the wall, and a dismantled smoke alarm lay at his feet.

"You poor thing," Stacey said, kissing him on the cheek. "You never stop working."

Charles's mouth was like a cat's, small and upturned at the ends. It made him seem happy even when he wasn't. "Meat is my weak point," he said. "I've got a job tomorrow doing steak."

He was prematurely balding, and Rory felt painful envy for the look of hardship and triumph this gave him. Lately he'd searched his own hairline for signs of recession, but the blond surfer's mane seemed even more prolific. Most cruel of all, it was Charles who'd been born and raised in Santa Cruz.

"Here goes," Charles said, firing up the blowtorch. They watched as he moved the flame slowly over the meat, back and forth as if he were mowing a lawn. Its surface turned a pale gray. When the entire side was done he turned the steak over and lightly cooked its other side.

"Ugh," said Stacey. "It's still completely raw."

"Wait," Charles said.

He held a long metal spit to the flame until it glowed red. Then he pressed the spit to the meat. There was a hiss, a smell of cooking, and when he lifted the spit, a long black stripe branded the steak. He heated the spit several more times and pressed it to the meat at parallel intervals. Soon it was indistinguishable from a medium-rare steak straight off the grill. Rory felt an irrational surge of appetite, a longing to eat the meat in spite of knowing it was raw and cold.

Stacey opened the refrigerator. Rory always kept a supply of Cokes for her in there; diet, of course, but also some regulars in case she had earned one that day and not yet rewarded herself. To his surprise, she pulled out a can of regular now.

"What the hell," she said. "I mean really, what difference does it make?"

Rory stared at her. She had never said anything like this before. "What about Vesuvi?" he asked, ashamed of himself for saying it.

"Vesuvi won't hire me. You know it perfectly well."

She was smiling at him, and Rory felt as if she had peered into the lying depths of his soul. "Vesuvi doesn't know shit," he said, but it sounded lame even to himself.

Stacey slid open the window and climbed onto the fire escape. The sky was a strange sulfurous yellow, beautiful even though it seemed unrelated to nature. The shabby tree behind Rory's building was empty of leaves, and made a pattern of cracked glass against the sky. Stacey drank her Coke in tiny, careful sips. Rory stood helplessly inside the window. He needed to say something to her, he knew that, but he didn't know what it should be.

He shook a cigarette from his packet and placed it in his mouth. Charles was working on a second steak. "By the way," Charles said, pointing with his chin at a spot near Rory's head. "I baked us a cake—a real one."

Rory turned in surprise and lifted a plate from above the refrigerator. It was a tall, elegant cake with giant dollops of whipped cream along its edges. "Charles," Rory said, confused, "haven't you been doing this all week?"

"Yeah," Charles said, "but always for strangers. And never to eat."

He bent over the steak, his blowtorch hissing on the damp meat. He looked embarrassed, as if his preference for real cakes were a weakness he rarely confided. Rory felt shamed by Charles's honesty—he'd told the truth, not caring how it sounded.

Rory climbed out of the window and sat beside Stacey. The bars of the fire escape felt cold through his jeans. Stacey held her Coke in one hand and took Rory's hand in the other. They looked at the yellow sky and held hands tightly, as if something were about to happen. Rory's heart beat quickly.

"So maybe it doesn't work," he said. "The modeling. Maybe that just won't happen."

He searched her face for some sign of surprise, but there was none. She watched him calmly, and for the first time Rory felt that Stacey was older than him, that her mind contained things he knew nothing of. She stood up and handed her Coke to Rory. Then she leaned down, grasped the railing of the fire escape and straightened into a handstand. Rory held his breath, watching in frightened amazement as the slender wand of her body swayed against the yellow sky. She had no trouble balancing, and hovered there for what seemed a long time before finally bending at the waist, lowering her feet and standing straight again.

"If it doesn't work," she said, "then I'll see the world some other way."

She took Rory's face in her hands and kissed him on the mouth—hard, with the fierce, tender urgency of someone about to board a train. Then she turned and looked at the sky. Rory stared at her, oddly frightened to think that she would do it, she would find some way. He pictured Stacey in a distant place, looking back on him, on this world of theirs as if it were a bright, glittering dream she had once believed in.

"Take me with you," he said.

Christopher Taggi

"I remember a family car trip I had taken a long time ago. It was summer, and we were driving north through the Carolinas and Virginia. There was a stretch of road where the only thing to see was sunbaked fields. The same thing over again for hundreds of miles. It played tricks on you. You were moving, but going nowhere; you spent the whole day living one moment but not *really* living it. You didn't feel the hot swath of tar, or the roadside weeds, or the dry trickle of the breeze. You were closed off. '95' grew from that one image of that one piece of road.

"I'm a recent graduate of Cornell University, where I majored in history. To Alessandra, thanks for reading all my stuff, and for your encouragement. To my mom and dad, most of all, thank you. I could not have done this without all the help you've given me, all that you've taught me."

95

They had left the kudzu and the tin shacks behind them. Hank couldn't remember where the malevolent green had stopped and the endless fields of wheat had begun. The day blended away on either horizon.

"Come with me," he had asked her, on her front porch where she sat stroking her sundress and sipping lemonade. "This is your last chance."

She had stared across into the sunlight before speaking in considered tones. "Where?"

"North maybe. Someplace."

Without hurry, she had packed a single, deliberate suitcase and let him place it in the trunk of his car.

Since then, they had driven mostly in silence, watching the scenery and letting the air conditioner blow back their cool hair. Outside, the sun smothered the scorched parchment fields with gauzy heat, leaving the air silent and still. The highway stretched out to nothing, wandering through the reeds like a tenuous argument, feeble and making little progress. To pass the time, Hank would fix a spot on the horizon and watch it until his car narrowed the distance and finally sped past. Most of the time, he'd only catch the glint of a road sign, but sometimes he'd see a house or a grain silo. As he drove by these, he'd glance out the window to see if anybody really lived out here in the middle of nowhere. The seams of the highway bumped under the tires, hypnotic, ticking away the afternoon like a dream.

"Where are we going," Annie said, not really asking.

Hank frowned and kept looking ahead, his light brown hair falling in wisps across his forehead. He drove with one hand atop the wheel, and the other resting on his knee, probing a hole in his jeans. Preoccupied, he stared solemnly into the limitless fields. After several minutes, she turned to watch the road.

Away in the distance, he observed a tiny speck maturing into something interesting, possibly a house or a barn. As a child, he had played this watching game on long road trips with his parents. It seemed they had always been moving, never staying in one place for too long. His dad would pack all their belongings into the car in less than an hour, working slowly while Hank sat in the driver's seat dangling his feet and pretending with the wheel. Off to some vague destination they would travel, talking of opportunities and jobs, maybe a new house and good friends. Sometimes his dad would let him sit on his lap and steer, but mostly Hank sat in the thin space between his parents, eyeing the road.

By now, the shape had resolved itself into a billboard. LUCKY LEO'S FIREWORK EMPORIUM, it boomed in explosive neon colors. LARGEST SUPPLY OF FIREWORKS IN ALL OF DIXIE! FREE PARKING and DELICIOUS RESTAURANT. 20 MI. On the horizon, a dot materialized and Hank supposed it was another billboard.

Reminded by the sign, he asked, "Would you like to eat?"

"That would be nice," she said.

Sometimes Hank and his parents would stop for food, pulling off the road to park with the tractor-trailers, to sit in a lonely booth with a foil-wrapped dinner. The diners were never busy: only a few tired people sat scattered beneath the yellow lights. The clank of metal pots drifted from the kitchen in a lonely, midnight-sounding way. Without much effort, Hank could imagine the rest of the world sleeping while he sipped Coke through plastic straws, listening to Roy Orbison croon over the PA. He ate hamburgers, the kind he only ate on car trips, with the flat bun and sweet ketchup pressed thin around the meat. Their novelty was delicious. On these occasions, his dad would only have a cup of ice water, claiming he disliked the greasy food. He said, "No sense in buying something you don't feel like eating." Hank wanted to ask if they were poor, but he kept silent.

"Opportunity, that's what everybody needs," his father said. He acted the same way whenever he quit a job: talking resolutely, moving from here to there, touching things absently. His eyes clouded with the nowhere stare, and a hardness in his throat approached but didn't quite touch anger. Hank could hear it, lubricating his father's restlessness. "Opportunity. It makes people rich, makes people famous. All you have to do is go out there and find it. And you can find it anywhere . . . this is a land of opportunities."

He watched the next billboard zoom past. LUCKY LEO'S 10 MI. FIREWORKS, FOOD and FREE PARKING. LARGEST IN DIXIE! The highway thumped.

"How do we know when to stop driving?" Annie asked.

Hank shrugged, staring off in front of the car. "I suppose when we get tired. We'll know."

She turned back to look out the window at the passing wheat, or the white line along the side of the highway. She had an incredible capacity to stare. "We're not going back?"

"No," he said, after a while. From the corner of his eye, he thought he saw her smile, a momentary flex of the muscles in her neck, but he wasn't sure. He never knew what she was thinking. Her words touched him like rain, cool and pleasant, trickling down his ears and over his lips. She lived in the future, all promise, and evaporated to a misty shadow as minutes ticked past, slippery like a fading dream. He remembered their meeting, the white of her shoulders and the lilt of her voice. Hank had said something and she had laughed. She had kissed him easily, on her porch, where the mosquitoes circled the burning light. And when he opened his eyes, his fingers were in the small of her back, pulling her toward him. After that, they saw each other frequently, driving off into the quiet heat to places he could no longer remember.

Once, they had found an old quarry, pitted craters in silver rock. Annie disregarded the trespassing signs, and he followed her into the gorge, placing his feet carefully among the loose stones. Far down, shade cooled the air, and a small lake sat still and green. He couldn't tell how deep it was, but it looked nice for swimming. Slowly, Hank stripped down to his underwear, watching Annie undress, feeling the gritty rock under his toes. He dove long and shallow; Annie followed him in, splashing. They pulled lazy strokes and listened to their echoes reflect off the crevice walls. Hank moved closer, reaching for Annie's hand, and she brushed against him, slippery, hot. When they kissed, he could feel the water in her mouth, cool and tasteless.

"I know how much you like me," she said, lying on the rock, the water beaded on her skin.

Hank watched her and smiled, unable to find a response.

Now, with his foot touching the accelerator, he thought about leaving her. Coolly at first, then in roundabout ways. The more he tried to stop, the harder it became. He would drive to the restaurant, and they would sit for some time, talking. Hank would excuse himself to the bathroom and smile once over his shoulder. Easy, the road would slide under his car, ka-thicking, and perhaps the radio would play just loud enough to let him hear the swift wind picking at the windows. He would wear sunglasses, and no emotion would show on his face. And somewhere behind him, Annie would look at her watch, wondering what could be taking so long. Hank wondered if she would cry, and how hard. He wondered what she would think, and what she would hope for when her phone rang. Somehow, this notion touched him more than any kisses. And then he thought about his dream.

He noticed her staring at him, and felt as if he contemplated an act of violence. She had been watching, but she couldn't have known. Hank smiled anyway.

He had thought these things before, but in the end, he never gave in to the highway. Early, before sunrise, he would call her and say, "Take the day off, come with me." He would drive to her house and she would cross the dew-soaked lawn, leaving mint-colored footprints in the thick grass.

Hank had been watching the low building for several minutes, and by the time he could make out the LUCKY LEO'S sign, he had already noticed that there were no cars. The place looked empty, or closed. But as he eased the car off the highway, he could see that the largest supply of fireworks in all of Dixie must have gone off simultaneously a long time ago. Only the charred, outer brick shell of the building remained. The roof had fallen in, and through the broken windows, they could see the blackened heap of wood and tar paper that had been Lucky Leo's.

He pulled the car around to the side of the building and turned off the engine. "I suppose we're not going to eat," Annie said.

"Let's look around anyway."

All that remained of the front door was a rectangular hole in the wall, outlined by the sooty shadow of flames. Glass crunched as their footsteps churned up plumes of dust. Above the door, a blackened sign read L   LEO'   FIR   OR S. Faintly, the smell of just-struck matches drifted on the air, sulfurous, and sunlight poured in between the remaining beams of the ceiling, lighting the charred walls. Not much remained. Twisted metal scattered the shelves of a display refrigerator, the corpses of burst soda cans. Pieces of steel shelves poked through heaps of fallen tar paper and masonry, and a melted cash register had oozed like lava along the countertop.

Hank picked his way over the wreckage, heading for another doorway across the room. Stumbling forward, he could see the remnants of fallen lighting fixtures beneath the heap. Annie followed several yards behind him. Through the portal, he could see tables and chairs.

"I think we found the restaurant," Annie said. "Cajun today."

They dusted off an aluminum table and sat. Already, sweat beaded on his upper lip, tasting salty. Although the restaurant shaded them from the sun, it wasn't much cooler: the heat seemed to flow from every direction, not just from the sky. He would blast the air conditioner when they got back to the car, and he imagined how the coolness would feel on his face. From the table and through a crumbled wall, they could see the highway. Cars whispered by every few minutes.

They sat in silence until she spoke. "So what were you thinking about before?"

He said, "Oh, some dream I keep having," like it was nothing at all, and he smiled to prove it. But he wanted her to press him so he could tell.

"Tell me about it."

He smiled at her, the confused smile he surrendered whenever he didn't know what to say. Letting his gaze slip away, he watched the highway over her shoulder. It shimmered with the heat.

"It bothers you," she said.

He took a deep breath, like he used to before the priest in confession, thinking OK, *this is the last one, I tell on this breath.* "Hm. It's strange." He felt like stopping but went on anyway. "Do you ever get those dreams where you've finally found something that you've lost?"

"Not really," she said.

He stared into the rippling sunlight for a moment. "Well, this one is really strange. Sometimes, at night, I dream that it's Saturday and I'm cleaning my room. The sun is coming through the window, and it's morning sun, very yellow. Which is kinda strange because my room doesn't get sun until the evening. But I'm there going through my closet anyway, putting clothes back in their place. Then, I go to my bed and bend to reach this shirt that is underneath. But when I get there and actually see what is under my bed, there are all these socks."

"Socks?"

"Yeah, but not just my regular socks. These are all the socks that I have ever lost, *ever*. You know, sometimes you'll do some wash, and a sock will just disappear . . . You'll leave it in the machine or something. So, under my bed are all my lost socks. Dark ones with the odor-eater toe, and some whites with those colored bands at the top, like the ones I used to wear playing basketball. All folded and sitting in a neat pile, just as if they had been there all along, only I had forgotten where they were. I was excited."

Now his voice slowed as he considered his words. "You know how Christmas is extra-special for a kid? Well, when I wake up it feels like Christmastime, but better. Like I've gotten everything I wanted, but it's also *more* than that . . . it's like finding out for certain that God exists and everything will be alright. But when I look under my bed, there is nothing there. Just some dust. And I feel disappointed. And then, after a minute, I'll see the same bed I've been sleeping in, and I'll see the same view out the window. My clothes from yesterday will be in a pile on the floor and the room is dark. And I can't believe it was all a dream, because it felt so *real*. So I try to remember where I could have put those socks, just to make sure. But I know I never really found them. I know it was only a dream. The thought of putting on more of my clothes and going to work disgusts me.

"I realize that nothing is different, that nothing good or special or wonderful has happened to me. And I feel empty. Just empty."

Annie looked down at the blackened table without saying a word, considering, letting the silence fill the gap between them. Hank watched her and stroked the top of her hand with his thumb. Talking was easier now that he had started. "My parents," he said, "never stayed too long in one place. They were always looking for better work, for a better life. Looking to be happy, I guess. You know, they'd see a picture in the newspaper some- where, or in a magazine that told how good life was in this or that city, or in some part of the country. And before long, we'd pack up all our stuff in the car and take off for the promised land. But we'd never stay there all that long, either. We were always getting up and going, trying to find something that was better than what we had."

With his eyes, he followed a passing car on the highway. Annie watched him cautiously. She said, "You aren't happy."

"Sometimes I am. Mostly, I guess I just feel like I can't be really happy. Just missing something important."

She drew her hand away. "You don't love me."

"I don't know." He paused but could not meet her eyes. "Sometimes I like you, and maybe I think I might even love you a little. And sometimes I hate you. I look over at you and try to imagine what leaving you would be like. I'd just stop coming one day, and you would be worried, and maybe you would cry. Think- ing about you crying makes me feel bad, but I still think about doing it. I don't know whether I'd feel good or bad. Or anything at all."

Hank could see the knotting motion of her hands. There was a question he had to ask. "Do you love me?"

She considered for perhaps a minute and then turned away. "No."

When Annie walked back to the car, Hank let her go by her- self. Alone, he stared down the long highway. Perhaps he owed her some shred of emotion; he thought he should feel angry, or sad, or relieved, if only to prove the contact between them. But he felt none of those things, and it seemed pointless to try. She would not leave him, and what he needed was down the road.

When Hank found her sitting with the air conditioning running and her eyes red, he asked, "If you like, I will take you home."

"No," she said, "let's keep going."

He raced the engine and pulled away, leaving the charred remains behind them.

Nicole Cooley

"'The Photograph Album' was the last story I wrote as a student at the Iowa Writers Workshop, a story in which I felt free to break all the 'rules' of writing I had learned. What I love about writing fiction now is that sense of freedom from narrative and linguistic constraint. I want to write fiction that explores the possibilities of language, that uses the language of poetry. My work has appeared in *The North American Review, Iowa Review,* and *Poetry,* among other magazines. I live in Atlanta and am working on a novel entitled *Judy Garland, Ginger Love.*"

THE PHOTOGRAPH ALBUM

The girl is sleeping. She is ten, maybe twelve. A line of elephants is carved into the wooden headboard of her bed, their trunks lined up. The wallpaper is patterned with circus figures: lions, three-legged horses, a woman swinging on a trapeze.

The man stands over her bed with his camera, steps closer, adjusts the flashgun.

The shutter clicks. The flash is an explosion of light. The girl wakes up. She begins to cry.

Why begin with this? Is this a story that could start anywhere?

"Once upon a time, in the city of _____, there lived . . ."

No—the story starts with what was saved. A single clue, what my father left behind when he disappeared, a box of photographs. No family scenes, no birthday parties on the beach, no portraits from school. The pictures are all the same: the child sleeping. No photographs of my father. But he was there. The camera always in his hands.

———

Three months ago, my father left Sarasota, the city where he was born and had lived all his life.

Why would a man leave a house where he lived entirely alone?

Why would a man leave when he had nothing to escape from?

For six weeks, the Florida State Police conducted a search for him. They dragged the lagoons. Their searchlights trailed the edges of the marshes. The policeman stood on the porch, tapping his pencil against his clipboard, saying, We've come up with nothing. We want to question people who might have known him. Didn't your father have any friends? He wanted a picture to show around the neighborhood and looked at me suspiciously, eyeing the camera hung on a strap around my neck. No pictures? No pictures at all?

The search was given up soon after. The police had no leads. The policeman with the pencil: There is no reason to keep this case open.

The case was filed in a cabinet in the 37th Precinct downtown, my father's entire story as it's known, three neatly typed pages.

The search is not over.

The story does not end here.

I open my investigation into my father's life.

Early Saturday morning when I am nine, lying in bed in the room I share with my grandmother, Nana. Someone has thrown the curtains open; sunlight scatters on my circus dolls on the bookshelf, on the lady sword swallower figurines my father has given me. I hate the lady sword swallowers. Dressed like ballerinas, they lift their swords high in the air and smile tiny, evil smiles.

The door to the room bangs open. My father walks over to my bed, wearing a dark suit and tie, dressed for work. My father never enters my room; I know something is wrong. I am afraid that I have slept for longer than a single night, that I have slept for days and now it is a school morning again. My father's face is pale. His mouth is trembling.

"Read this." He throws a newspaper on the bed. "The bottom of the page."

I find it, under "News from Siesta Key": "Woman, thirty-five, loses control of car on the Sarasota Bay Bridge. Bridge police believe that death occurred upon impact with the bridge side rails. Divers have recovered the front door of the car. The woman's identity has not yet been released, pending the notification of relatives." Beside the article is a blurry picture, taken in the dark, of the middle section of the bridge, its rails knocked out. Cars are stalled in a long line beside the empty space.

"Your mother is dead." My father's voice is flat. Then, louder, "Are you listening, Ellen? Your mother is dead."

I do not look up from the newspaper page. I read the paragraph again. I stare past my father to the window, thinking, *Red curtains, the curtains in this room are red, you see red if you look straight into the sun.*

"Get dressed." My father pulls the blanket from the bed. I yank my nightgown over my knees. "Go help your grandmother."

I hold the newspaper closer to my face. There are two policemen in the photograph, pointing to the air above the dark water where my mother's car has been.

The story could start with New Orleans, where I was living when the landlord of my father's rented cottage called me. The production company was in the middle of editing a documentary on silent films. The part of the documentary I'd been hired to research, the five minutes devoted to "Women of the Silent Era," had been cut in favor of a segment on Charlie Chaplin's childhood. "Their faces are interesting," the director said, studying the photos I'd collected of Louise Brooks, Lillian Gish, and Pola Negri. He shrugged. "We need somebody to do research on Chaplin's half brother. You can help with that."

The company was under contract to keep paying me until the documentary was done, so I took some reels of film, locked myself in one of the screening rooms, and watched one after another, all the films the director did not plan to include: *The Temptress, Love 'Em and Leave 'Em, Our Dancing Daughters* . . .

Until the landlord called. "Is this Mr. Goodman's daughter? You'd better come home."

After the Florida police gave up the search, I moved into my father's cottage on a Siesta Key. I had never been in his house before, but I knew he'd return there if he came back to Sarasota.

I stood on the front steps. I was scared. I rang the doorbell though I knew the house was vacant, then fitted the key into the lock. I took a deep breath and walked inside.

The walls were clean, white stucco. No paintings or posters. Dressers and tables free of clutter. I looked for open books, cups left unwashed in the sink, notes he scrawled to himself. I would have settled for anything, a piece of paper with *Pick up milk* written on it, an old magazine. There was nothing to offer any clue of his daily life.

I photographed each empty room four times, one shot from each corner.

I found the shoebox full of photographs under his bed. The girl in the pictures was ten, twelve, fifteen years old. I arranged the black and white squares on the floor in a line. Do the photographs arrange themselves into a story?

It is not much of a story, but he would not want the story told.

Her father's shadow appears at the end of the bed. He wears a white suit, leans closer. No sound. She holds herself still, waiting for the light.

In New Orleans, one scene repeated, one shot, carefully, expertly composed.

I stood at the screen door of my house, in the center of the frame. Late in the evening or maybe morning. The man on the other side of the door, on the porch, was not visible, but he was there. I stood in the doorway, the belt of my robe pulled tight, my hands in my pockets. The man was leaving. I wanted him to leave. I had photographed him and now I had no use for him. Then was the part where I told him goodbye.

He was not visible. I didn't see him. Instead, I was seeing myself as he saw me—

Did the man think, She is pretty, she is ugly, she has an ordinary face? Her expression was blank. He couldn't read her.

This was how she wanted it. She had to keep anyone in her new life from knowing her.

The man left and the scene changed. I closed the door, went back inside my house.

There are facts about my father and there are lies. Facts: He works at the Sarasota Visitors' Bureau downtown. I visit him there once, with my mother. I am young. He has an office at the back of the building, full of cabinets. He shows the office to us, pointing out the stacks of papers and the blue-lined graphs. My mother leans against the wall, her hat tilted over her face. (Her face is shadowed. I can't see her face.)

She sighs. "Tell her how what you do all day is something nobody gives a damn about."

My father ignores her. He turns back to me, opening the top drawer of his desk to show me a protractor, a transparent ruler, a set of colored pens. He holds the pens gently, lifts the maps up by their edges, as if they are delicate. He handles everything with care.

Another fact: My father wanted to work for the circus, which stopped spending winters in Sarasota around the time that I was born. The site was turned into a museum. My father had told me that my grandfather had a job with Ringling Brothers. He cleaned cages in the animal barn. I know this, but my father created another version of the story in which his grandfather ran the circus from the center ring.

One of the lies: We pretend that my mother has simply left. We pretend she takes her coat from the hall closet one evening and shuts the door of the house behind her.

Nana is always in my room now, in her bed. The room smells of talcum powder and unwashed sheets. I try to make her take her medicine. Nana used to open her mouth like an obedient child as my mother slid the spoon in. For me, she clenches her teeth and turns her face away. She won't come to the table, so I bring her meals to her on a tray.

Sometimes, I wake up in the night and hear her crying. I cover my head with a pillow to drown out the sound.

The truth: I could never write the story of my mother. A week after her death, she is gone from every place in the house. He takes her clothes from the closet, he gives away her wedding china, he throws her bottles and jars on the bathroom shelf into the trash. One day, it occurs to me where I can find her, in the photograph album under Nana's bed. I look for the album; the album is gone. I go into the sun room where my father sits reading the newspaper. "Where is the picture album?"

He points without looking up. "Where it's always been."

I know this is a lie. I find the book on the wicker table in the sun room. The first page, where her baby picture had been, is blank. Yellow glue stains dot the page. I turn. I remember some of the pictures on the next page—my mother at eleven on a painted pony, in her high school uniform, a plaid skirt. The page is empty. Except for the wedding photograph from which my mother's face has been removed. Neatly, a perfect oval missing from the center of the picture. Her white dress remains, her hands still hold a fluted glass. I flip quickly through the rest of the book; every-where, my mother's face has been cut out.

"Put that down." My father crosses the room in long strides and snatches the book from my hands. "Your mother did it," he says quietly. "You shouldn't look at that. I didn't want you to see that. Things are different now, Ellen, and I want you to forget about that time."

I know my father wanted me to see the album. He left it out, knowing it was only a matter of time until I saw it. The next day, it disappears.

I know something else too, something I do not want to remem-ber. Last year, I came home from school and found my mother in the kitchen. It was too early for her to be cooking dinner. She was hiding something in her lap. Scraps of paper littered the table. There was a glass of transparent liquid at her side and a glass of ice. "Get out," she said when she saw me. "Don't you dare come in here."

I haven't been back to Florida in ten years, since I left for college. That was the last time I saw my father.

One afternoon I forced myself to leave his house and take the bus out to the Ringling Estate. The parking lot was full of cars and campers. I walked through the grounds where everything was in bloom—oleanders, crotons, date palms. Everything was too bright —as if the landscape had been filmed in technicolor. Electric or-ange flowers, leaves the color red it made you nervous to look at, all under a gleaming blue sky.

I followed the path to the circus's old winter quarters by the bay, where the performers and animals lived when the circus trains returned home after summers on the road. The show trains were repaired and repainted during the winter and in the spring the circus would leave again. The animal barn was full of tourists, but wire cages still lined the walls, where once there were dwarf mules and polar bears, kangaroos and pygmy elephants. A woman wearing a badge that said "Circus Museum Docent" pointed out the practice rings where rehearsals had been held each day. The crowd of visitors nodded and smiled.

I was a visitor. I hid my camera inside my jacket.

Next to the Bengal tiger cage, I found a family that had drifted away from the tour. A father and his two children, a boy and a girl. The father was arranging his children with the empty cage as a backdrop. He moved them into place, then stepped back to take a picture, when he noticed me, standing nearby and watching.

"Would you mind taking a picture of us?" he asked. "The camera is real easy to use. Just stand back over there and press the red button. I'll show you how to do it."

I had not spoken to anyone for days. If I started speaking, I sensed that I would not be able to stop. I would talk and talk to his man till he began to back away, frightened, leading his children out of the museum, shielding them from me, I would be left standing alone, telling my story to myself.

There was so much to say that I did not say anything. I took the instamatic camera from his hands. The children posed against the tiger cage. They seemed to be used to posing; they had probably posed hundreds of times for their father on that vacation. I wondered where the children's mother was. Dead or disappeared, I thought. The father rested his arm on his daughter's shoulder, gently, protectively.

I knew photographs do not tell the whole story. I snapped the picture. At night, at home, the father could have been doing anything to that girl.

Another scene my father would not want to remember—once, shortly before he brings home his camera, I take a picture of him. With a Brownie camera given as a favor at a birthday party. I sneak into the sun room, creep up behind his chair, then jump out and press the button.

My father rises from his chair, his face dark red. "Give me that." He reaches for me.

I hide it behind my back. In one quick movement, he wrenches it from my hands, twisting my arm hard. He takes the camera outside and throws it in the trash.

In New Orleans, she liked to photograph the men while they were asleep. She waited until their eyes closed, until their breathing became slow and even, until she was sure that it was safe to get out of bed. She slipped on her robe and took one of her cameras from the kitchen. She hid the cameras there, in the cupboards with her cereal boxes and soup cans.

She stood at the edge of the bed with the camera, holding her breath, as quiet as she could be. This was the moment she waited for as soon as she asked the men to come home with her.

She didn't want the photographs themselves. She wanted the moment, the split second where she held the camera in her hands and turned it on them. Recording their faces meant nothing to her. She never developed any of that film. What would she have done with those photographs? Men from the companies she worked for, men she met in the park or on the street. They meant nothing to her. She had no desire to save any of them.

My father wants me to have the set of circus dolls he collected during his childhood. The first one, a snake charmer, was given to me when I was born.

The others follow. When I turn seven, I am given the entire collection. My father brings three shoeboxes into my room and opens each one, lifting the figures from the tissue paper, laying the dolls out in a line on the floor. "Look, Ellen." My father names each figure for me. Here is the bareback rider, the wire-walker, the bear that rides a bicycle. I touch the ringmaster doll—he wears a red coat and a top hat.

And the other, more frightening figures: the albino family, the Siamese twins with their two mouths frozen in a smile. "Go on. Take them. They're yours now." My father pressed Tom Thumb into my hand. He closes my fingers into a fist. "I want you to have them."

My mother appears in the doorway of the room. "Why on earth would she want a bunch of stupid, old-fashioned toys?"

The truth is, I don't want them. I want ordinary toys like other children have, balls and tops and dolls with smooth, golden hair. My father's toys scare me. The albino family stares up at me with mean, pink eyes.

The first camera I bought for myself in college was a Minolta 35mm. It came in a small blue box with an instruction booklet: *"A MINOLTA 35MM makes it easy to capture the world around you. Or express the world within you. It feels comfortable in your hands. Your fingers fall into place naturally. Everything works so smoothly that the camera becomes part of you. You are the camera and the camera is you."*

Nana lies in her bed, her face turned toward the wall. My father stands over her. "Get up now, Mother," he says. "This can't go on." I sit on my bed, twisting the hem of the blanket. "You two are impossible." My father turns and leaves the room.

Nana is whispering, then her voice grows louder and I see that she is talking to me. She says, "He was a bad baby. He refused to let me feed him. He wouldn't suck. I had to feed him with a teaspoon and pinch his nose shut so he would open up his mouth." I cover her shoulder with a sheet. "A bad baby," she says again.

I don't know what else to do. I don't want to leave my room and face my father. I go over to the circus dolls on the shelf. The figures make a family: the trapeze artist mother, the lion tamer father. The children are human cannonballs and clowns. "Are you listening?" Nana says from the other side of the room.

As soon as the girl blinks the light from her eyes, her father is gone. Across the room, in the other bed, Nana doesn't stir. The flashgun never wakes her. The girl will lie awake till morning, counting the hours off on the clock beside her bed. She draws her knees up to her chest, making herself small.

Florida winters. Days of rain. Soaking rains that fall for most of the day and when the rain stops at night, the air is more humid than before, the air is heavy, filled with water. The drainage ditches clog with leaves, the palms bending under the force of the wind.

Sometimes the street floods and becomes a river. Branches and porch furniture float away. Laughing and calling to each other, children row boats up and down the street. I watch from the window. My father does not allow me to go outside during the day because I am supposed to stay in and take care of Nana, but Nana will not let me touch her and pretends to be asleep when I approach the bed. Her eyelids flutter and I know that she is faking.

Two rats swim by the front steps. A boy in a rubber boat drops his cap and lets it float away into the waves. I am exhausted. When I rub my eyes, the skin burns.

It is the middle of February, and I have already missed fifteen days of fifth grade this quarter. "You have to watch your grandmother," my father says. "Some things are more important than school."

Each night, he comes home with another circus figure for me. These are made of cheap plastic, unlike his childhood toys. The collection on my bookshelf grows: zebras, tigers, polar bears. I never touch them now.

In New Orleans, at the end of the afternoon, before I punched out my time card, I turned off the projector and took an elevator to the storeroom in the basement of the building, an enormous room with a cement floor where the props for our documentary were kept. Painted posters advertising the early days of Universal Studios ("Universal Moving Pictures Are Mightier Than Pen or

Sword"), kinetoscopes, metal dollies that were once used to run the cameras on.

There, I found a box of cards: *"Photos of Moving Picture Players—All True Likenesses."* I sat on the cold floor and looked through the box. Everyone was there. I held Douglas Fairbanks up to the light. He looked like my father, his hair slicked back and smooth, his lips parted in a small, sad smile. I hid the postcard at the bottom of the box.

On the box top was printed, *"Do not fail to get a set of these pictures for your postcard album, for the walls of your bedroom, or to mail to your friends."*

My father comes back from the dead or the bay or the sky or from whatever town he lives in now. He sits across from me. We face each other, but he does not look at me.

His cigarette burns down to a long ash. His face is tired. His hands shake as the shutter clicks again and again. One picture after another. He does not look at me. He does not look through the lens.

I cannot capture his attention. The light flashes on the floor. I do not appear in any of these photographs.

My mother's car lies at the bottom of Sarasota Bay. I can see it—the car sinks slowly into the sand. The fenders rust. Mollusk shells cover the metal. Fish swim in and out of the car through the missing door—eels, carp, angel fish with glittering yellow fins.

At the bottom of the bay there is no light. The bottom of the bay is a dark and silent museum. I want to go down there. I used to think that I could live down there. It would be quiet, calm.

I would be safe. I would sit in my mother's car and close my eyes. I would be alone. This would be a place where I could sleep.

The first production company I interviewed with in New Orleans after college was making a film about the circus. The director studied my résumé. "You're from Sarasota?" He moved his chair closer to mine. "You must know about the circus then."

"A little." I did not want to be asked questions about my life.

"We need a research assistant to travel back there and collect footage of acts from the archives."

"I would prefer to work here," I told him.

"Well, that's a shame, because we could use you as a resource." The director touched the tips of his fingers together, a pose that I could tell was designed to make me believe he was thinking, appraising my situation. "You must still have family there, right?"

"My parents are dead." It sounded like a lie as soon as I said it.

"I'm so sorry." The director rolled his chair away from me, back behind his desk. He stacked some folders into a neat pile. "We have a position open to do research in the office."

"Could I help with filming? I've had experience," I said.

The director didn't look at me. He pretended to be very busy arranging his pens in a line on his desk. "We leave the camera work to our permanent crew. You'll have plenty of time to work with cameras."

My first job was to sit in the film library and read through old copies of *The National Vaudeville Artists' Annual,* looking for information on certain performers. I had been assigned the Fire King and the Human Hairpin. I collected facts about Ivan Chabert, the Fire King: He drank boiling oil and burned the shirt off his back in his act. There were pictures of him standing on lighted candles. The Hairpin could extend his height up to twelve inches. During his act, he would ask the largest man in the audience for his coat and then expand his chest to such a size that the coat would no longer fit him, and then, a few minutes later, he would make himself so small that he could wear the jacket of a child.

I imagined my father swallowing fire. A look of terror crossed his face as he lowered the flaming sword into his mouth. I made him grow larger, smaller. He was a little boy. I turned the camera on him, flashed the light in his face, watched him cry.

His pictures are never taken during the day. In daylight, the camera disappears. The girl does not know where it is kept.

She tries to stay up all night, sitting in the kitchen with her schoolbooks spread open on the table. It is hard for her to keep up in school; he hardly ever lets her go. She colors maps for Geography, practices long division.

After several hours at the table, she will be unable to stay awake any longer. She rests her head on her stack of books. She'll wake to her father's strong arms carrying her to bed, knowing that, once again, she's failed.

I never left the cottage without my camera, hidden in my jacket, but I never photographed anything outside of the house. I liked knowing I had the camera with me; hung from the leather strap around my neck, it banged against my ribs as I walked. The pressure of the camera against my body kept me safe. At night, I set it on my father's bedside table where I could see the outline of the black box in the dark.

When I moved to New Orleans, the other research assistant on the circus project, a man about my age, told me to buy a gun. "This city is more dangerous than you think," he said. "You don't know what it's like here. Aren't you from some little town in Florida?"

I didn't answer. There didn't seem to be any point in telling him that Sarasota was not a little town. I let him think he knew more than me. I let him think he knew about me. Still, I wanted him to know I could protect myself. I wanted him to know that I did not need anyone.

I carried my camera everywhere in Sarasota. It was my secret. I walked downtown, studying the composition of the street, the old alongside the new: art galleries with walls made entirely of glass, curio shops, bright palm trees and stone benches set along the side of each street.

I stood in front of the Sarasota Visitors' Bureau. The Bureau had been moved to a tall, modern building, all chrome and glass and glittering in the sun. I stared up at the new building until the glare of light hurt my eyes. I would not find anything about my father there.

I try to take the story back into the past:

Fifty years ago, the circus trains roll home for the winter, my great-grandfather takes my father out to watch the trains arrive. My father sits on the trunk of his grandfather's car and watches the scene unfold before him.

The clowns are men with tired faces, carrying their own costume trunks. The skin on the camels' backs is rubbed bare and pink. The elephants stumble down the ramp as they are led from the train. The midget family looks like a group of fat children.

I couldn't take the story beyond that. What was my father thinking? I could see him, sitting on the car, holding his grandfather's hand, but I could not read the expression that flickers across his face.

Inventing my father's life revealed nothing.

The policeman with the pencil: There is no reason to keep this case open.

I studied the photographs of my father's empty rooms, held each one up to my face. What did I expect to find?

I dream of living in a museum. Not an actual museum—not the Circus Museum or the Florida Museum of Natural History. Both are too crowded, full of schoolchildren on field trips, and too neatly arranged, whole worlds under glass in perfect order—faded costumes, fossils of exotic extinct birds, everything labeled and explained.

Instead, I imagine disorder, a world where there are no rules, no routines, where no one breaks into your sleep each night. I could be alone in this dark, safe place. I would walk through the rooms and look at everything—jumbled boxes, bottles, empty picture frames—and no one, no one, would be looking at me.

She tries to talk to Nana about the photographs.

Sitting on the edge of Nana's bed, she rests her hand on the old woman's arm. For once, Nana lets the girl touch her. Emotion rises up in the girl, fills her throat. She loves her grandmother. Her grandmother will listen to her. Her grandmother will save her.

Do you ever hear noises at night? she asks.

Nana's face is turned toward the wall. Noises? What noises?

Do you hear someone—she can't say it, "my father"—in this room when you are asleep?

How could I hear anything if I'm asleep?

I mean, someone, he comes in here at night and—

Who? What are you talking about? Nana pulls the sheet over her shoulders.

He has this camera—

What camera? There's no camera in this house. You're imagining things.

But he's here, the girl says, her voice rising. She can't help it. She has to make her grandmother understand. He comes in here and takes these pictures—

I don't have any idea what you're talking about. Nana rolls over in bed and looks at the girl. What's wrong with you? Don't you know this is how it started with your mother? She had terrible dreams.

It's not my mother, the girl begins, then gives up. No one will believe her.

Could she be dreaming all the photographs? Could she dream the same dream every night?

What is wrong with you? Nana studies the girl's face. You better tell your father that you have bad dreams.

When I returned to the Sarasota police station, no one remembered me. The case had already been forgotten. I couldn't blame anyone for forgetting. There were terrible crimes to solve, triple murders, hit-and-run accidents, boats of illegal drugs. My father's absence had not affected anyone. As far as the policeman knew, he had harmed no one. He had simply left.

In my jacket pocket, I had the folded page of the Classified Section with the ad: "Photographer wanted in the 37th Precinct police station. Professional experience required." In the waiting room, the man behind the bulletproof glass window directed me down a long, brightly lit hall.

"I have to warn you," the policeman said during my interview. "This job can be gruesome."

I nodded. I needed a job. I was almost out of money. That morning I had received a letter from the production company in New Orleans. The silent movie film was done. They enclosed my final check.

"You'll be photographing evidence for the crime lab," the policeman continued. "I have to tell you, there haven't been any other applications for this job, and we need someone right away. We'll hire you. I'll take you to the lab now to do some test shots."

I followed the policeman down the hall. I knew that accepting the job meant I'd stay in Florida. Was I still expecting my father to come back?

The policeman introduced me to a man in a white lab coat who nodded briefly at me and returned to studying a slide under an enormous microscope.

The objects I was to photograph were wrapped in plastic and labeled with white cards. I was given a zoom lens. The policeman laid the evidence out on a long, low table.

The first pictures I took—a child's shoe, a leather wallet, a woman's ripped silk blouse with a dark stain along the sleeve. I swallowed hard and tried to keep my hands steady as I photographed the blouse. I knew that I was not supposed to be thinking about where these things came from. I was not supposed to be imagining the owners of these objects. What had happened to the woman who wore the blouse? My throat tightened.

I looked through the lens and tried to tell myself that I was somewhere else. I tried to tell myself that I was already gone. The camera was there. I could disappear.

The girl imagines herself a high wire artist. She walks the wire on the tips of her shoes like a ballerina, using a parasol for balance, high above the center ring.

She cannot look down. Below her, her father holds the camera, waiting. There is no net to catch her when she falls.

Why did my father take the photographs? I could make up answers. He lost my mother and he did not want to lose me. Her image had disappeared. Did he think that he could keep me?

I want to believe this, but it's one of his lies.

The Minolta: "It's hard to tell where you leave off and the camera begins."

My mother's car lies at the bottom of the bay.

The man stands over the bed with his camera.

The policeman with the pencil: We've come up with nothing.

In New Orleans, I stand over the men with my camera.

I sat on the floor in my father's house and laid the photographs out around me turned facedown like playing cards. I took the scissors and started with the first row of white squares.

Turn the picture over quickly. Study it for a minute. Cut.

In the first row, I removed all of the girl's faces. I cut out her hands. The row that followed was arms and legs, then the torso, the waist, the stomach, the tops of her thighs. I gathered up all the pieces and made a pile in my lap. Then I began. I made new pictures. I took the camera from my father's hands. With a roll of tape, I reconstructed all the scenes. This time around, the girl could grow smaller, larger. Her face could disappear. An arm extending from her hair. A bent leg where her throat would be. Her closed eyes cut out and taped to her chest. She was headless. She was nothing but an open mouth.

When I finished, I taped my pictures onto the pages of a spiral notebook. My notebook. My story. The story I wanted to be told.

My father brings home the camera on the first anniversary of my mother's death.

I know I will have to live through this day again and again. For years. I picture calendars, years of calendars, each marked with a black X on the month of January. If I cut the square that marks this day out of the calendars, it will be worse—the day signified by an empty space.

My father is pretending this day is the same as any other. In the morning, he goes off to work, leaving me to take care of my grandmother. Nana locks me out of the room. When I try the door, the knob won't turn.

In the sun room, I wait for him to come home because I have decided to talk to him. I want to know what happened on the bridge—did she drive off the side? Was it an accident? Fear tightens in my chest. I try to breathe slowly. He comes home late, with a paper bag under his arm.

"Hi, Daddy." The word sounds unfamiliar, strange. I never call my father that. I am trying to make this day different.

"Ellen." He nods in my direction and turns to hang his coat in the closet.

"What's that?"

"This," he says, sitting down beside me on the couch, "is something I was given today. The Records department didn't need it anymore. Look." He lifts a black camera from the bag. "I brought it home to show you."

The tightness in my chest lifts and disappears. My father wants to show me something; there is something he wants me to see. When I reach for the camera, he jerks away and stands up from the couch.

"Don't touch it. I don't want it broken."

I fold my hands in my lap. My face feels hot. My father bends over the camera, fidgeting with a silver crank on the side. I tell myself, *now*.

"What did she do that night on the bridge?" I try to hold my hands steady in my lap.

My father points the camera at the floor.

"What did she do on the bridge?"

My father turns the camera toward the ceiling.

"What did she do on the bridge?" My voice shakes.

He aims the camera at a chair, at the wicker table, the window, the wall.

"Daddy," I try again.

It must be that word that does it. He looks at me. "Ellen, stop badgering me. Where's Nana? I ask you to do nothing around here but watch your grandmother and you can't even do that. I can't trust you to do anything." He shakes his head. "I don't ever want to find you playing with this camera. This is not a toy. This is mine. Do you hear me? This is mine."

I look down at my hands. "Ellen, you're not listening to me. Jesus Christ." He sounds disgusted. "It's late and you should be in bed. I don't want to see you for the rest of the evening." He leaves the room, taking the camera with him.

I sit alone in the sun room for a long time. My father does not come back. That night, he wakes me for the first time.

––––––

After the flash, I see white, white. When my vision clears, I see him slipping out the door of the room, away from me.

Why don't I scream? Why don't I call out his name?

I will not leave here. I will never leave home again. I will live in my father's house. I will stand in the doorway of the house, hidden in shadow, the camera in my hands. If my father comes back, I will catch him as he reenters his life.

He is surprised to see me; his face is frightened. I will take one picture after another of my father on the steps. I will arrange these photographs into a story.

I will block the doorway. I will not let my father back into his house.

Here I am in the doorway—I can see it. I raise my hands to take the first photograph.

May 1, 1993

Dear Mr. Wexler:

Enclosed you'll find the requested one-paragraph bio and four stories for submission to the "X-ile" project...or at least the four that I found most likely to pertain to the subject matter without whanging *completely* off into deep space. So, first:

> CHRIS HUDAK. Born in San Francisco. Always thought he knew more than his parents & teachers----turns out he was right. Wanderer. Trek fan. Longhair. Cyberpunk. Heavily influenced by Dennis Etchison. Hasn't done jack *shit* in the way of academics, and anyway aren't you tired of reading bios with phrases like "got his MBA and went on to be martyred in the reign of etc, etc..."? Thinks Kerouac & that whole crowd couldn't write for sour fish poop. Wants to party with Stephen King & Don Henley. Likes Disneyland a lot. Spends lotsa time in planes, trains & scuzzy clubs, usually with a PowerBook and a large container of something alcoholic. Went to Japan once. Almost perpetually in trouble. Worships Wile E. Coyote. Skinny. Muscular. Eats a lot.

Admittedly, these aren't the usual "Whinin'-'bout-My-Generation" slacker/twentysomething/Gen-X'er vignettes, but a little....stranger. These are stories from the dark side of an already somewhat depressing genre: Two of them are about that creepy, almost supernatural sense that one's life has stopped in some kind of static, inescapable limbo or hell [*"Static"/"The Down Side of Three"*] ; one is a look at the nature of the choices one makes...and will make...and has *always* made [*"The Number You Have Reached"*]; and the other is a ghost story, of sorts—about the lingering ghost of a time gone by, a "GenGeist," if you will [*"Side One (6:30)"*].

All stories—unpublished in anything worth mentioning—are on file at the Library of Congress (if you care, which you probably don't, and who could blame you?). *Anyway;* hope you like them. Keep in touch.

Chris Hudak

San Francisco, CA

Elizabeth Tippens

"I had a bad cold at the time I wrote this story, which accounts for some feeling of delirium on my part as I wrote it, and possibly for certain aspects of the character's state of mind, and perhaps even for the rhythms in the story. This story presented itself to me almost fully formed. Receiving a story as I *received* this one can never be counted on as part of my writing process. This one was a gift.

"Other stories of mine have appeared in *Cosmopolitan* and *Mademoiselle;* nonfiction in *Playboy, Rolling Stone, YM,* and *Desperately Seeking Madonna,* a Dell anthology of works on Madonna."

BACK FROM THE WORLD

He has decided never to get over her.

He wears his broken heart with a perverse kind of pride, like a medal from a war, a badge of obstinance he pins to himself each day as he goes about his job, and what you would call his life.

It is also a point of reference.

There are flying rats and loping dinosaurs, prostitutes and army men, and birds, always birds, endless pages of small, inky drawings. Sandy's basement room in his parents' house is full of them. And poetry. There is his poetry, which cascades in his mind all day as he performs the tasks of his maintenance job for the small town he grew up in.

He has turned thirty and thirty-one and now thirty-two, and, he feels, has made the transition from troubled youth to local eccentric. He knows his lack of ambition makes people embarrassed. People no longer ask about college or his plans. He has been to the army, to Germany. He has been to the Peace Corps, too. And he has been to New York City, to Columbia University to study ornithology, the science of birds, though everybody knows the real reason he went up there was to be with *her*. He has escaped to all the places a young man can escape to, and he is back again, an expeditionist who failed to make a claim. Back from the world.

There is much to be maintained in this town. More than half of its two hundred acres are parks and woods. It is a national historic landmark, a one-time Methodist campsite whose oddly shaped houses were once summer tents. Now these cottages, expanded over time, added on to in funny bits and pieces, are a gingerbread mix of styles: Victorian, Gothic revival, and pure ramshackle. Every so often *The Washington Post* does an article on the town, always calling it "Virginia's anachronism" and "quaint" "a town within a forest" or "a town ignoring time."

He drives the town tractor, mowing its many fields of grass. Summer is almost here. It is the clover making the grass smell so sweet. People wave and he waves back, as though his life, fractured and unwhole, is at least settled for now into this ruined pattern, like an eyesore, someone's architectural mistake that the whole town must simply live with after the bickering dies down.

Today he must cut the dead branches from the large oak tree on Main Street, across from the house where *she* grew up. Grew up so gracefully, he must note.

Her name is Faith. Faith Banning. And as the whole town knows, she is the love of his life, and always was. If only he could have been a scientist like his brother, working for a foundation or a university, he might have been able to keep her, for to his amazement, after years of adolescent longing, he had, as an adult, been able to track her down more or less between boyfriends, and to attract her with his passionate lovemaking and his devotion. With his tenderness. Passionate, devoted lovers were all but extinct in New York City, she said. Tenderness an anachronism. Imagine, she sighed, while he buried his head between her legs. How rare.

But the poetry came back, and he sat in their tiny studio apartment taking it down like dictation while he should have been in class or writing papers or thinking about graduation and getting a real job with the Audubon Society or the Museum of Natural History. How he had let her down. You're nothing but a pothead, she had said. And it was not the remark itself that wounded him so, because, yeah, he'd smoked some dope, but the bitterness with which she said it, and the fact that he had caused a woman to be bitter.

He cuts the dead branches into smaller pieces with an ax, using an old stump as a chopping block. He notes some geese as they fly overhead. Canada goose, *Branta canadensis,* Audubon plate no. 32. Force of habit. Migrating is a stupid thing to begin with and he notices geese aren't doing it much anymore.

He chops wood into the afternoon, amazed at how quickly the hours pass. Work is work. Work is one foot in front of the other, one labor, one task at a time, and though he does not look forward to it, neither does he fear it. It is his connection to the physical realm, anchoring him to a day-to-day life in which a picnic table must be painted in time for a holiday, leaves must be raked because it is fall, grass must be mowed because it is summer.

A girl named Chatsworth, Cat, speeds by on her bicycle. She waves and he waves. This Cat girl exercises like a demon, racing around town on her ten-speed bike. He'd heard she was anorexic, but she really isn't looking all that skinny anymore. He wonders if she craves food. Is she excited by it, or disgusted? Or is she over it now, her adolescent fling with self-starvation, with death. Is she normal again? Is she hungry?

The words "statutory rape" run through his mind, although he has no idea if so old-fashioned sounding a law even exists in Virginia. Cat is still in high school he believes, and he has never before been attracted to someone who is still in high school. Well, not since he was still in high school, that is. It's absurd, his attraction to the girl. She isn't pretty. What would he and the Cat girl have in common besides the town itself, which because of its anachronism status is the source of endless chauvinism and snobbery among its residents?

For these past two years, since coming back from the world, his lovers have all been women older than himself, some married to husbands he waves to as they drive off to work in the morning, some divorced, and one widowed by a suicide. And there was one who would allow him to enter her only from behind. I can't face you, she'd said, I can't face myself.

Sandy is not without his vanity and he has been pleased to please these women, to provide them with their fantasy of the sweaty, shirtless groundskeeper, to take the time their husbands wouldn't take, to suck their clean pink toes, one by one. But Cat has made him aware of his age, of the premature gray hair that runs in his family. He is getting fat—cheap, starchy food and too much beer—though he still runs his five to eight miles a day.

No, he will not pursue an anorexic high school girl. Her youth and the possibility that her condition makes her vulnerable in love would make him feel like a creep, and so far he is not a creep, and would like to keep it that way.

The days pass and he finds himself aware of the time of day. The Cat girl gets out of school at three o'clock in the afternoon. She is home by three-thirty; on her bike by three forty-five. He waves and she waves. That is all.

How he wishes it were a mirage, the documentary film crew that follows him about the town. But for once this particular irritating vision is quite real. These not-for-profit do-gooders have been given a grant to do a film about the town for public television, and they are up early most mornings, following him in their pickup truck, recording the sound of his tractor with a microphone.

"Hey, how's it going?" yells a guy with a beard.

But he will not speak. He will allow others to speak for him. Tell his tale. The boy who grew up in this town but could never quite make his way in the world outside it. Keeper of the grounds.

The one and only employee of the town. He will let others charac-
terize him. Perhaps they will think he is mute. An anachronistic
local eccentric, he. A birdwatcher. Or perhaps he will speak a
poem and they will have all the faded gentility they need, and will
pack up and go.

"I say, man, how's it going? Have you lived in the town for
long?"

Sandy guns the tractor's motor and speeds ahead. An old
crank. A young, old crank.

He makes it to the lake, where, for now anyway, he has managed to ditch the film crew. He dismounts his tractor, which he
can't help thinking of as "trusty," and goes to unlock the shed
where the algae net is kept. Summer is nearly here, and the lake
must be readied for tireless suntanned children and their mothers
bearing beach towels and sandwiches. He stands on the dock with
a net and tries to fish the thin film of algae out of the water.

The lake is man-made, and was dug out from a natural spring
about seventy-five years ago. It won't clean itself. It is his job to
clean it, and he is thankful for the labor it takes.

He knows the shoreline of this lake, its curve, where the land
will swell or dip beneath his next step, as well as he knows anything. The shoreline of this lake, he thinks, my area of expertise,
the only thing I really know.

Perhaps his net will come upon the snapping turtle, which is
really more than one snapping turtle, maybe as many as five or six,
and "it" has never, as he has always heard people say, grabbed on
to someone's foot and refused to let go. But he knows how a
legend can persist, despite the truth.

He hears the splattering sound of tires treading over gravel
and looks up to see the Cat girl peddling down the path, coming
toward him at top speed.

"Just warning you," she calls out, "the film crew is coming."

Sandy drops his net and runs for the tractor. He hops on and
drives behind a thick wall of cattails. He turns off the engine,

climbs down from the tractor, leans against the wheel, and waits. The Cat girl reappears through the long reeds, pushing her bicycle through the marsh.

"What is the big whoop over small towns?" she asks, leaning her bicycle up against the tractor. "Mention small towns and everybody goes ape shit, whipping out the checkbooks. What do they think they're going to find here, family values? What about the seedy underbelly? How about some grant money for the seedy underbelly? I personally object to the way NEA grant money is being handled by the fascists."

Ape shit? Fascists? Underbellies? Sandy has never really heard the Cat girl speak. Until this moment behind the cattails she has been not much more than another kid growing up in this town, a kid his sister or Faith probably baby-sat for. He watches as she pushes her short brown hair away from her eyes and loosens the blue bandanna she has twisted around her neck.

"Do you think they want to come over to my house and watch my mother hover over me while I choke down solid food?"

She is quite astonishing, he decides. With freckles. Her feet and hands are very large. She wears silver hoops in her ears and a thin, knotted band of leather around her ankle.

He makes a gesture with his fingers toward her lips.

"Shhh," he murmurs.

He hears the film crew coming with their cameras and their microphones and their wobbly silver reflecting sphere which they hold up to capture the light. *They* of the khaki shorts are coming down the path, huffing and puffing on foot because he has locked the outer gate against their vehicle.

He and Cat are quiet enough so that he is privy to the lovely sound of her breathing. He dares to look at her face, and she dares, daring girl, to look back. Her eyes are a deep brown and far apart, and there is something uneven about them, something defiant in their lack of uniformity, as though her face itself issues forth a challenge to symmetry, to the order of things.

"You remind me of a comic book character called She-Rah, He-Man's twin sister," he whispers. "As I recall, She-Rah could breathe underwater."

"Special powers huh?" she says, narrowing her eyes.

"I'd say so," he says, still whispering.

"I like that," she says, "I'm a feminist."

"Ah," he says, "a feminist."

"Yes," she says, "and that is why I cannot get along with high school boys. They think I'm a lesbian."

"Is that so?" he says, mightily intrigued.

"They are so immature," she whispers.

"Lowest form of life in the cosmos," he says. "Take it from one who knows."

Voices can be heard beyond the cattails, and he and Cat are both quiet a moment listening for the film crew. They are out there, wondering, no doubt, what has happened to their prey.

"Let me ask you this," she says in a hushed voice. "Why do you stay here when you're not stuck here to rot like I am, when you can go anywhere?"

"You don't look rotten," he says.

"The rot is on the inside," she says.

"I know what you mean," he says. "How old are you, any-way?"

"Oh please," she says. "How old are you?"

"Want to see something?" he asks her.

He parts a row of cattails. Behind the tall reeds black and yellow spiders the size of silver dollars have their webs spinning everywhere, like shiny, loosely woven lace, shivering and sparkling in the sun.

"Jesus," she says.

"May I call you?" he asks.

"Of course not," she says. "I'll meet you somewhere."

———

Sandy can hardly subject a lover of his to a basement room filled with dank artifacts and collected bottles from the woods, musty stacks of books, and scattered pages of poetry and drawings.

He has been entrusted with the key to the McKibbys' house, which he is watching for its owners while they are in England for a year of academic fellowship. He sits nervously on the McKibbys' double bed, the double bed of those naive and guileless McKibbys who have no idea that their house will be used for illicit sex, for a rendezvous with a teenaged recovering anorexic who refuses to disclose her chronological age. He is wondering exactly how to go about seducing a high school girl when he hears her barging noisily up the stairs. She appears in the doorway, her ten-speed bike hoisted above her shoulder.

"I can't leave it outside," she says, "someone might see it."

"Of course," he says. He rises quickly to take the bike off her hands, but she beats him to it, setting the thing down and leaning it gently against an antique bureau.

Cat stands there for a moment looking too girlish in her bike shorts and sneakers, her short brown hair cropped off in a blunt haircut. He stands there, too, awkwardly, he knows, unsure of what to do next. He would like to kiss the supple nape of her long neck.

"If you're wondering if I'm a virgin, I'm not," she says.

"Oh, okay," he says, nodding his head. Why hadn't he been wondering about it? She could have been a virgin. Creep, perv, statutory rapist, he thinks.

She moves toward him and he touches her soft brown hair. Don't go through with it, he tells himself, but she is in his arms now. He cups her small chin in his hand and kisses her more deeply than he had meant to, and than he had imagined he would. As he leads her toward the McKibbys' double bed he notices how easy it is to cross over the lines you have drawn for yourself, how very easy, like falling, like slow motion. Once you have done it.

———

Later in the evening he sits at his desk in his musty basement cell and records the poetry which came to him during the day. His parents, retired teachers, spend most of their time now at their cabin in the Blue Ridge Mountains. But still, he confines himself to his cave in the basement, where the dark and the damp will occasionally attract a miraculous little frog, or an interesting species of spider.

The geese find their way into a poem, flying oddly, syncopated, outside their usual V formation. Circling, he finds the geese of his poem are circling for a landing. And Cat, whose smell is still on him. An image of her long swan's neck comes to him and forms itself nicely into couplets. But he doesn't jot this one down. Just lets it flow. He thinks of her eyes, brown and uneven, which inspire no poetry at all, but glare and squint with their realist's view of the world.

He remembers when he finally showed Faith a handful of the many poems inspired by her, years' worth. You're making me up, she told him. This isn't me. I'm not Venus. But by then she was annoyed with him. By then he'd made her weary. Her acting career was going nowhere, she said. She was recording pornographic voice-overs, which, she said, were destroying enough of her brain cells to notice. Sandy found the phone sex sexy in the corny, obvious kind of way that makes men hot, and that women are contemptuous of. But all of it made Faith scowl.

Now she is on a soap opera. He's heard. He can watch her every day at noon if he chooses to. He's heard that she has a small but recurring role and that her character has some kind of ill-defined drug problem. He's heard she looks prettier on TV. He chooses not to watch. The whole town watches him not watch.

He runs.

Parts of the town which border the woods are pitch-black at night. You can look into those woods and see nothing, an inky pool of endless black. The drop-off point. The end of the world.

Sticks and gravel crunch beneath his feet. Once in those woods he found a doll with blood on its mouth, hanging from a tree by a noose. The thought makes him run a little faster. It is two miles to the high school where he used to run cross-country, where he now circles the track in eerie night light, ghosts everywhere as always, and it is two miles back into the town.

He takes a turn onto Main Street. Everywhere there are reminders and now it is Faith's parents' house. Lately he has begun to remember, though dimly, something of the house's former owners, before the fire, something of a time before the Bannings bought and remodeled it, something of a time before, in his mind, there were flames, then ashes and rubble from which *she* emerged.

At least he is not the village idiot, he thinks, passing Derreck Wells on Main Street. He had played with Derreck Wells every day in fifth and sixth grade. In junior high they walked to school together in the next town over, day in, day out. But Derreck Wells had some kind of psychotic break in high school and is now the village idiot, a bulging-eyed crazy man who enters people's unlocked houses and stands in their living rooms.

"Hey," he says to Derreck Wells. Derreck is standing beneath a streetlight drinking beer. He is also the town drunk, begging embarrassed neighbors for the beer money his own parents refuse him. Most people are afraid of Derreck Wells, the poor son of a bitch. You couldn't see the signs of what was to come. They'd played together with plastic army men every day for two years. Every day. *For two years.*

"Hey, man, got any money?" His eyes are bloodshot. Popping out of their sockets.

"Here, brother," Sandy says, handing Derreck the couple of bills he has stashed in his sock, money he can't really afford to be giving away. What had they talked about on the way to school?

Cat is gifted, and because she is gifted she has been given a grant by the Commonwealth of Virginia to spend the summer writing a paper on the literary topic of her choice, which she has decided will be the popular misuse of the term "Lolita."

"Nabokov doesn't mean for us to take Humbert Humbert's judgments at face value," she tells Sandy. "Lolita is a male projection. In the patriarchy men invent female sexuality to alleviate their own anxiety," she says.

"I hate when that happens," he says, frowning.

He swears he sees a hint of a smile begin to form on her lips, and he decides it is important to make the Cat girl laugh. Yes, making Cat laugh is now his goal, the only goal that he can think of. They have made love and now he lies with her, naked on the McKibbys' double bed, the double bed of those naive and guileless McKibbys.

"Lolita is not a seductress," Cat says. "She's just a girl having sex with a man."

"Like you?" he asks. He rubs her flat white stomach. She is freckled on her long, well-muscled arms and legs, but her stomach, hidden by her serious swimmer's tank suit, remains as white as a china plate. Not like Faith, whose smooth stomach was always as berry brown as the rest of her skin in summer.

"I want to know about New York," Cat says, sitting up in bed. "I want information."

"The elevators smell like human urine," he says.

"Gross," she says. "Is that all?"

"No," he says, "they've got pigeons."

Cat rises from the McKibbys' double bed and dresses. She is not at all curvaceous, but is angular here and there, and not what he's used to. But she is natural in her nakedness, un-shy and unashamed. Sandy watches as she pulls on her black bicycle shorts, the jogging bra which flattens her breasts, and her thick white socks. He likes watching her dress, always for action, for speed, for endurance. He does feel moved though, despite the armature of her athletic wear, to offer her something, advice, something worldly she can arm herself with.

"Don't lose your anger at the world," he tells her.

"You sound like some old fart," she says, tying up her running shoes.

"I don't care," he says. "Fight the power, honey."

"Honey?" she says.

He kisses her goodbye and she leaves, now that darkness has completely fallen, first, separately, so that no one passing by will suspect.

The morning is wet from the spring rain, but the sun is trying to burn through and will succeed by late morning. He thought he heard a screech owl late last night. *Otis asio.* Audubon plate no. 30. He thinks it may be nesting in the rafters of the town garage. He lets the emergency brake off of the tractor and rolls silently out of the garage so as not to disturb the nest.

Will he grow old here? Has he returned for good?

I can't love you, she said when she kicked him out. Where is your life going? You scare me, she said. And, pothead.

There is a fence to be mended on the very edge of town, on the border that separates the town from a field of corn they do not own. No one can find him here as he nails new wood onto old wood. Work. One task at a time. His savior.

He walks into the cornfield. It is not well cared for and he has no idea who owns it, but it has always been here, beckoning to be disappeared into.

He imagines Faith with her sunglasses on. And why not? She is just a mortal woman after all, who gets a headache from the sun. I'm not some goddess, she said, handing him back his poems. You don't really see who I am. It was flattering at first, she said, but now . . .

He'd wanted to paint the walls of her apartment, each one a different pastel color. But by then the walls were closing in on her. Making them pretty would not dissuade those walls of hers. Those walls knew their course.

He is lying on his back in somebody's cornfield, looking at clouds. He makes a black crow sighting. *Corvus brachyrynchos.* Audubon plate no. 4. Hardly worth noting—he is, after all, lying in a fucking cornfield.

Her body is no longer his, even to dream about. Tan in summer, soft, a birthmark like a coffee stain on her left hip. Ah, the prominence of her pubic bone. *I have always loved your pubic bone, at least since I've been aware of your pubic bone, which is since Paleolithic man first made art, drawing stags which drifted eternally across a river, on the cave walls at Lascaux.*

He feels a satisfying sense of suffering, fresh as renewal, rushing in to fill him up. It is there, and without it he'd be lost. Who would he be without it? Just a man with no ambition who knows how to operate a leaf-blowing attachment. A village idiot.

He is lying in the McKibbys' master bedroom, naked on the pale blue bedspread of their double bed, waiting for Cat. He has left the back door open and she will slip inside and join him when she is done eating dinner with her parents, who, she has told him, supervise her every forkful of food.

He thinks of Faith. At first when they made love it was like incest. It had been so long, a whole life of desiring her, of watching her rub Coppertone on her bare arms and legs, a taboo. And there was the alarming fact that his brother Carey had fucked her, taken her virginity, right here in the McKibbys' house while they were away at the Maryland shore, and bragged about it, hatefully, until Sandy had come at him with a baseball bat, ready to bash his brother's brains in. But *he* and Faith had skipped the adolescent fumbling, which he was glad of. Your brother is a terrible lover, she'd told him. It was over in five seconds. She'd only known him, Sandy, as a man who knew what he was doing. How strange to hold her actual face in his hands. After all that time. Most men die before they hold their dream. His dream. And she had dreamed of spending her life with *him.* It is enough.

He hears the downstairs door open and footsteps entering the house. He doesn't move from his spot on the McKibbys' double bed. She knows he is up here, waiting, the breeze from a half-opened window blowing across his naked body. His uncensored thoughts of Faith have given him an erection which he will rudely use to make love to another woman, though he wonders if perhaps he wasn't aroused by some unsettling combination of the two of them.

A tall dark figure appears at the bedroom door. He gasps, a sudden intake of his own breath, startled, then scared. His erection disappears. A pair of bloodshot, crazy eyes stare at him, survey his nakedness with dumb fascination.

"Derreck," he says, softly, gently, "it's me, man, Sandy." He reaches for his clothes, slowly. "I'm taking a little nap, man. Just resting up here. But now we both have to go. It's not our house, okay?"

Sandy pulls on his jeans and T-shirt.

"I wanted to ask you about the army. You think I'm too burnt out to join the army?"

"No, man, the army'd be good for you." Sandy pulls on his work boots and ties them hurriedly. "Let's go outside and talk about it."

"I need money for beer," Derreck says. "I'm starting to shake." He holds out his hand. Instinctively, Sandy grabs hold of Derreck Wells's trembling hand to steady it. He has the skin of an old man. There are people Sandy does not know living in Derreck Wells's face. There is a large smudge of dirt on his chin.

Sandy turns Derreck Wells slowly by his bony shoulder and steers him down the stairs and out of the house, locking the door behind him, taking the key with him so Derreck won't see where he keeps it hidden in the mouth of the drainpipe by the kitchen window. He ushers the shuffling Derreck Wells down Main Street to his parents' house, slowly, getting him there bit by bit.

"Did you see any action? In the war?" asks Derreck.

"No, man, I was in Germany, in peacetime, jacking off."

Derreck wants to know about the military alphabet.

Sandy tells him, "A is alpha, B is bravo, C is Charlie, D is delta, E is eco . . ."

"E is eco," says Derreck Wells, slowly, and with great effort, "I think I could learn this."

Cat speeds by on her bike, a furious, fast-moving girl. What must they look like to her, the two of them at twilight, making their way down Main Street with such labor, like old, old men. Sandy aches a moment for Derreck as he coaxes him down the street. He aches for Derreck Wells and his lost youth and potential, for youth and potential itself. For his own.

Cat shoots him a look as she whizzes by, a shrug of a look to acknowledge their failed rendezvous. Though it has only just begun, he wonders how long this can last with Cat. She will go to college. When? Next year? As soon as the fall perhaps?

"Derreck," he says, finally depositing Derreck Wells on his own front steps, "you take care of yourself now, man." He gives Derreck a small military salute.

"You were my friend," says Derreck Wells. It seems like a moment of clarity, of pristine remembrance, clear-eyed and sane. But it passes in a flash, like a glint of sunlight through the trees.

Running is the thing to stave off the edginess; otherwise he fears he will drink hard or fuck a dangerous woman, someone diseased or knife-wielding and insane. Or worse, he will simply smother gently in a narcotic cloud of marijuana. So he runs the two miles to the high school, circles the track, and runs the two miles back into town. He runs to beat the storm, for the heavens are full of their seasonal threats of rain. Thunder rolls in. Lightning lights up the sky in a sudden flash. His legs turn to knots. His lungs ache with every step.

He kicks off into a wide-open field across the street from the Bannings' house. The rain is on its way and he turns in a few dizzying circles.

The storm breaks. The rain pours. And there is no more lightning in the sky.

He slows and stops to catch his breath after the sprint. He looks up at Faith's bedroom window which is surrounded by the hemlock trees she used to climb down, sneaking out at night to meet his brother, or his brother's best friend, or even Derreck Wells before the psychotic break.

Now, looking up at her bedroom window, where he has found himself so many times before, he waits for a vision, an hallucination of something up there. A figure. Someone dancing. A girl with her long arms outstretched, spinning, spinning. A knowledge that he can still conjure her.

Lightning strikes nearby. The air sizzles. A tree across the park becomes singed. Lightning really does strike people, doesn't it? He is standing in an open field waiting for a ghost while lightning strikes close enough to smell. He is going crazy like Derreck Wells. He is in danger of going crazy like Derreck Wells.

He flees, running straight for Cat, running straight to her house where he is sure she is in her bedroom, reading Nabokov's letters and *The Annotated Lolita* beneath her covers. She is in there, he is sure. She is gifted, a gift. Not a ghost. Not a figment. Cat.

Of course he cannot go inside. But he watches the rain drench the geraniums her mother has planted in clay pots near the porch, and he is reassured enough to keep from weeping.

In the light of morning shameful memories dissipate or become clouds, harmless, fluffy, and good-natured.

He drives down Main Street in the brilliant light of day to face the Banning house and its wraparound porch. Faith stood there on that porch as a five-year-old girl and asked him to punch her in the stomach. She wanted to feel what it was like to be punched in the stomach. He didn't want to do it, to hit a girl, but she begged and it was not in him to refuse her anything, even then. The blow stunned them both, and then she went running for her mother, wailing, *Sandy punched me.* He was banished and in trouble. Hitting a girl. Perhaps that is where it all began.

It is a Sunday in May and some of the old gang who still live nearby assemble in the park for a muddy game of tackle football. The pickup teams need filling out and sullen teenagers whose hell on earth it is to be trapped in uncool, quaint surroundings—not a mall in sight—have been persuaded to join it. Even Derreck Wells ambles out of his parents' house, crosses Main Street, and plops down in the muddy grass to watch. Sandy, too, has been coaxed into joining the game, and as he breathes hard, inhaling the wet earth, he is pleased by the smell of spring mud which is caked on his elbows and his knees.

He goes out long, fumbles, and swears loudly. He bends forward to catch his breath and looks up to see, here, in broad daylight, an unexpected figure coming toward him. It is Faith coming across the park with her towheaded little niece, her sister's child, who is dressed for church in white patent leather shoes. Faith waves and encourages the little girl to wave. Sandy cannot recall the little girl's name. Or his own. Or anything else at all.

"Hey," some of the guys say.

"Hi," she says, looking right at him. She is wearing sunglasses. Why could he not be spared the sunglasses, the black sweater, and the cowboy boots, spared the walk, the look, the fingernails painted red, spared the celebrity of it all; spared the greeting, the long, drawn-out Hiii?

Hi? That is it? He'd given her his poetry. He'd jerked off his whole life thinking of her. Now he could be anybody.

He burns, feeling his face aflame with emotions too many to comprehend. Lust, regret, hate. His heart thuds madly in his ears. Is she looking at him? Is he expected to say something? Is she speaking? Is he deaf? He nods an awkward greeting and backs away from her, tossing the football to one of the younger members of the pickup team, a boy to whom Faith Banning means nothing at all.

He fully expects that the next time he sees Faith she will be in some picturesque part of town being earnestly interviewed by the documentary film crew. How they will love one another. How they will gravitate toward one another for warmth, for life itself. How they will make each other glow. But that is not what happens. Faith startles him, peering around the garage door, her head back-lit by the early morning light. She has sought him out, intruded, and brought with her too much light for his eyes. He has the eyes of a hostage, a prisoner, he thinks.

"What are you doing down here?" he says. He is sitting on a pile of milk crates drinking coffee from a Thermos.

"I thought you might be down here," she says, taking one cautious step inside the garage door and removing her sunglasses. He looks into her face and feels, disconcertingly, as though he were looking into a mirror.

"Shhh," he tells her, pointing to the rafters, "there is an owl's nest in here."

"With baby owls?" she asks.

"Not yet," he says. He screws the lid back on his Thermos.

"I'm getting married," she whispers. "I wanted to tell you that."

He looks at her, trying to absorb the information. He has been expecting some kind of news like this. He has felt it gathering, rustling in the trees. It has been coming, announcing itself on the screech of the owl, and now that it is here before him, he feels a strange kind of relief.

"The wedding will be here in the town, in the little park," she says.

"I repaired the gazebo," he finds himself telling her. "I've re-placed all of the original floorboards."

"It looks beautiful," she says. "Will you come?" she asks.

He does not know what to say to the real Faith Banning who stands before him in the flesh, perhaps he never has. He sees tiny lines around her eyes that did not used to be there, tiny lines that are not visible on her TV show where she is painted for war and kindly lit. (Okay, so he watched. Once.) But the strong morning light is merciless, and her face, naked and pale and more than two years older, will not cooperate with his memory. She lives, she breathes, she marries. She will not stand frozen like a statue where he left her.

"I hope you'll consider coming," she says, slipping her sunglasses on. "Good luck," she says, backing out of the town garage, "I mean that."

Good luck. He means to turn his wit upon those words, to let them tumble around in his brain, losing meaning with every turn until he has mocked them to death and pummeled them into nothing. But Faith leaves and strangely her words rest rather peacefully in the atmosphere. He stares at the garage's threshold where she stood moments ago and wonders only when the owl's eggs will hatch. That is what he thinks of, all he wonders about.

Together he and Cat climb the stairs to the McKibbys' bedroom. He waits for her now in the kitchen, since the incident with Derreck Wells.

They take a shower together in the bathroom off of the McKibbys' master bedroom, and then lie naked and damp on the blue bedspread. He has grown to love the way her collarbone juts out.

"I locked the door," he says. "Maybe we can keep Derreck from materializing on us, like the sneaky doppelgänger he is."

"They should have the film crew interview Derreck Wells," she says. "A day in the life of Derreck Wells." A joke at Derreck's expense, but not unfunny, he thinks, not unlike the remarks his brother and his friends used to make as they all tried to comprehend Derreck Wells, their old friend, one of them, now the village idiot, now another of the town's anachronisms in this, the age of enlightenment and psychopharmacology.

"Now there is the seedy underbelly for you," she says. "So why don't they take their grant money and go film that?"

"Your subversive ideas always arouse me so," he says, kissing her ear. She has three earring holes in her left ear. Three pale silver earrings.

"Are you going to tell me to fight the power now?"

"No," he says, "are you going to tell me how we live in a fascist state? Because if you are, I don't mind a bit."

"As a matter of fact, I'm not. Are you going to give me more excruciating details about birds?"

"Oh yes," he says. He enjoys his role as boring bird enthusiast. "You know," he says, propping himself up on his elbow, "geese aren't migrating much anymore. They say that the actual longitudinal distance of migration is shortening."

"Why?" she asks, rolling her couldn't-care-less eyes elaborately. He longs to tickle her, but to tickle is the cheat.

"For reasons as yet unknown," he says. He loves her dark serious eyebrows.

"What exactly is a doppelgänger?" she says, propping herself up too. Curious, serious girl.

He pauses to recall for her the exact definition. In Germany he became a collector of foreign words for which the English language has no equivalent, like *zeitgeist* and *weltschmerz. Poltergeist?*

"Well?" she says, impatiently.

"Since you ask," he tells her, "a doppelgänger is a ghostly double that haunts its fleshly counterpart."

Cat smirks and says, "I hate when that happens."

He watches her eyes search his face to see if he has gotten his own joke. She laughs. He has inadvertently caused her to laugh. And her laughter flutters against him, reminding him of a kiss on the eyelid.

"Get it?" she says. "Get it?"

He closes his eyes and reaches inside himself for Faith. But she will not rush in as she always does. She cannot be conjured to fill the vastness inside him, the endless black of the woods at night. He is just there inside it, alone and terrified with not one poem running through his mind. He is released and he knows it. Come back. Who will he be without his broken heart?

He opens his eyes to Cat, her face there before him expected and unexpected. *There,* as present and real as the work he does each day. He clasps her hand, which he holds for a long time, while night begins to fall outside the McKibbys' house. He thinks of the dogwood trees he must plant tomorrow. And there is the porch of the Women's Club to repair because it is late spring now and nearly time for their annual rummage sale.

And everywhere there are more dead branches to clear away.

Tim Hensley

From those who brought you "McSlacker: The Thermos" and "Gerontology X: The Incontinence Brief" shambles author Tim Hensley. He's still home with parents. He's still a meek prig. He wrote this story in a "creative writing" class. He's currently employed as a part-time temporary. You, Dear Proofreader, have truly rejected "The Man" in consumption. O fractious Doubleday—
"The Proofreader" was initially published in *Asylum*.

THE PROOFREADER

"The stock is smashed repeatedly by type and travels along a back conveyor belt under heating ducts which bake the inc dry. An employee inspects the product and discards imperfections. The rest fall into a cardboard box and are then placed in a different cardboard box," the overweight woman siad.

She took a look at his application and offered him a rope of black licorice form a plastic tub on her desk. He was applying for the position of proofreader of wedding invitations. He wanted a part-time job while he went to school.

"Your previous experince was as a boxboy at Alpha Beta?" the overwight woman asked.

For the interview Brian wore a shirt with buttons and smiled but could not stop himself from noticing that the womans strapless top was too tight and it looked as if she had four breasts.

"Yeah. It was only a summer job, but I did become familiar with working around a conveyor belt," Brain replied.

He tugged at the rubbery strand as they talked.

———

The overweight woman adinistered a test in which he was to find as many mistakes as he could within a time limit. He passed.

The job secured, Brian weft the room and went into another room where the exit was. There he noticed a girl dressed in black typing at a computer terminal. Brian thought she was cute. She wore a red wristwatch, was tall and then, and had nostrils that looked like commas. Her fingers moved over the keys like a threatened spider. Brian wanted to speak to her but saw she was busy staring intently at what she was typing. He wished he was a sentence.

Brian got a parking ticket while being interviewed. The officer indicated his error with a blue pen.

Brian was nineteen years old and an english major at the local university. He found out about the proffreading job by looking on the schools job bored. He knew that when he received his degree, with his name on it, mechanically reproduced by a factory much like the one he was now employed at, he would have a true sign of his knowledge, and that then he could go out into the real world and find a real job.

In Brians room the carpeting had not been replaced since he was a child. It had a repeating pattern of squares, each filled with a cartoon character. These characters werre suffocated by a bed, crushed by a desk, and impaled by chair legs. When Brian entered he stepped on Mary Worths head. That night he dreamed he was inthe carpet. He could not leave it, only crawl into different boxes.

Brian was single and his many attempts at finding a girlfriend had failed. After waking up, he thouhgt of a solution to this problem. He decided that couples employ each other and that meeting someone was like a job interview. He decided not to wear his eyeglasses or flared pants. Perhaps he could echo yesterdays success! With the girl in black! He would try to make a good impression and would lie about his experience.

He turned on his TV. A beautiful woman was inside. She was on a game show called "Wheel of Fortune." She stood neXt to a row of boxes and when they lit up she spun them to reveal letters. These eventually formed a sentence. Contestants won prizes if they could guess the sentece before it was formed.

Signet Thermography was located on a street of intdustrial buildings that ended in a cul-de-sac. Each building on the street was required by law to display a sympol of four different colored squares with numbers in them to indicated hazard levels. At Cignet, for instance, there was a machine which manufactured matchbooks imprinted with the names of couples that could burst into flames unless carefully attended.

On his first day at work, Brian was given a rubber stamp with the letter "R" on it and a blue pen.

"The work comes in batches pinched by clothes pins. You indicate all errors with the blue pen using a system of symbols. Then you stamp this box on the customers copy with the "R" to show that you have read it," L said.

There were two other proofreaders at Signet and they also had rubber stamps with characters on them: L and B. L was an overwight man. When he walked his thighs rubbed together making a zipper sound. He spent most of the da$ exhanging gossip with B about wich employee was sleeping with which. B's love of gossip was driven by a fear that she might be in it. She smoked cigarettes and the matches that lit them came from the matchbook machines badly printed couples. Both L and B were married.

———

During the coffee break, L said to R, "So Brian, I bet you're a real stud with the ladies, eh?"

"Frank, you're terrible! Don't tease him," said B.

"You think i'm terrible?"

"You got it, honey."

"Well give me some penicillin so I can get rid of it."

"Ha-ha. What a card. We need to get rid of you."

Then B asked R if he had a girlfriend.

"Uh-uh."

"Well, you're young. I'm sure there are lots of girls just dying for a handsome young man like you."

"Uh, thanks. Who's that girl in black?"

"Ah Brian," said L, "think she's a hot number, huh? Her names Alison, she's a typesetter."

After break, the proofreaders resumed stamping with a three letter alphabet from which no words were formed.

R inspected hundreds of people deeply in love looking for errors. He, himself, was not allowed to make errors. He read in elegant script:

In this world of uncertainty and confusion, we too have found each other.

We request the honour of your presents.

We will be untied on June thirteenth.

At two o'clock noon.

The marriage will be consummated in the old house in memory of our deceased father.

Reception in rear of Our Lady of Sacred Heat.

R glanced at each word. Each word went through his eyes. Then each word traveled along a conveyor belt into a cardboard box. After a few hours, the words could only be understood as a string of letters in the correct order. His eyes began to water from hunching under the flourescent lamp above his desk.

———

"Sunlight isn't blue and doesn't flicker, while flourescemt light is and does," the optometrist later explained. "This causes eyestrain. Thsi eyestrain can be stopped by having your glasses tinted pink, Brian."

At the end of one of the batches, R found a note that read:
Dearest,
If you saw, say, a mailbox or a clothesline while walking down the street you would read it as if it were an invitation. But what is the grammar that forms the thoughts that describe the malebox, clothesline? I must see you. And you will proofread this invitation. But it's really in a foreign language. When you look at my face you will see acme or a beautiful nose. How? I am in love with you. Pleawe meet me in the bar of the fast lanes bowling alley at eight tonight.
Your secret admirrer
R did not completely understand the note but was excited. He capped his pen. He thought of Alisons lips covered with red ink, each kiss a reproduction of her lips.

R took a time card pith "Gerber, Brian" typed on it and placed it inside a slot where it was perforated.

As Brian left work, a couple entered the House of CArds StaionEry Shop and chose an invitation from Signet's "Momento Mary" line. Couples used Signet Thermograp, a company with over two hundred employees, to create an image or object using language. This became a sign of their love.

By having his face phtographed and laminated, Brian became twenty-one.

———

Then he went to Sears to buy a blazer for his date. He stood on a conveyor belt which took him up to the Mens clothes department. He tried on coats in front of a mirror which split him into three. Each coat was not a coat but a lifestyle of coat wearing. Each Brian appraised himself and looked for faults. None of the coats fit trian that well. He bought one and the sales clerk desensitized it so it would not set off an alarm.

On his way out, Brian passed a line of toy children that came with birth certificates.

Patrons of the fast lanes bowling alley stepped on a rubber carpet to come inside.

At 8:04 Brian entered the bar. He toook a slow look around. It was dark. There was a jukebox and a row of stools. The jukebox played a love song that was interrupted by strikes. AFter he had made sure that Alison was not there he sat next to Foy, the overweight woman who had interviewed him.

"Hello Brian, aren't you a little young to be in here?" she asked. She wore a black drss and bowling shoes. Brian noticed that her eyebrows and eyelashes were not real.

"Well, I'm . . ."

He began to feel hot in his coat.

". . . Listen Foy, i'm a little confused. Did you send me a note to meet you here?"

She looked at the ice cubes in her glass.

"You better kepp this a secret. I'm married. If you tell anyone I'll fire yoiu. That note was meant for Frank. I forgot it was in a batch of work you might see."

Brian looked at his right foot.

"Oh, I won't tell, cross my heart."

———

Brians shoes were put into a compartment. Then he wsa given different shoes with numbers on them. He was also given a score sheet with a row of squares on it. In each square was a smaller square.

10 thrust his fingers and thub into the sockets and orifice of a bowling ball. He rolled the ball toward the pins. Kluunk! It came back on a conveyor belt.

The next day at work R learned that Alison had been fired. He sat at his desk and stamped. His spinal cord began to slouch into a question mark.

[Editor's note: When this story first ran, a number of readers failed to appreciate the obvious typographical subtext, ironically remarking on the "irony of such bad proofreading of a story entitled 'Proof-reader.'"]

Abraham Rodriguez, Jr.

Abraham Rodriguez, Jr., is a Puerto Rican-American who spends much of his time hanging out with kids in the same South Bronx neighborhood where he grew up. He brings his writing to them for critique, and their responses affirm that his stories are indeed mirror images of their own lives and the environment in which they live. "My writing has become more realistic and human through knowing these kids. Unfortunately, more involvement means more hurt. Some of my friends have been killed and it hurts me very much."

Rodriguez began writing when he was ten years old after his father, a poet, bought him his first typewriter. He dropped out of high school at sixteen because he was unchallenged and "tired of seeing the heroin addicts hanging out in the hallways." He continued writing and began writing songs and playing guitar. He earned his high school equivalency and attended City College of New York for four years, during which time he won first prize in the Goodman Fund Short Story Awards two years in a row.

Rodriguez has become a more disciplined writer in the past few years and continues to write songs and play guitar in his punk rock band, Urgent Fury. However, in order to pay rent and eat, he takes odd jobs for two or three months, then lives off his savings for as long as possible. "I have stock jobbed, mail clerked, messengered, washed, cleaned, served, delivered, pressed, stamped, and baked. But, being broke is such an important part of being a writer."

It was good fucken shit, not that second-rate stuff. It was really good shit, the kind you pay a lot for, so I stared at Smiley for a while cause I got real curious bout whea the money came from.

"What," he said, lookin at me while he rolled anotha joint.

"Whea you get the money, macho?" I axed him, an he started backin up into the riot gate we were standin in front of.

"Aw, c'mon, don't start."

"Me start?" I yelled, real loud, cause I knew it bugged him whenever I did that on the street an everyone knew our problems. "I'm not startin nothin, I juss wanna know whea you got the money, whachu been husslin."

"It wasn't no hussle, *muñeca,* juss chill out."

"Yeah, yeah, I heard that before, man. If the fucken cops come snoopin around the house for yuh ass again, Smiley man, thass it, we're through. I don't wanna fucken hassle with that no more."

"Shut up an, like, smoke."

I'm serious, Smiley got some real special shit, don't taste like tree bark. We smoked an hung out for a while, then Smiley went to the Super to see bout maybe gettin some work, cause usually Smiley could get somethin to do, like plumbin or puttin up a ceilin someplace, an then we could have money for rent. The goddamn food stamps ran out. Now we're in some serious shit. I din't know before, but when I went upstairs with my friend Sara, I saw the empty book. I'll tell you somethin else we ain't got: food. I checked the frigerator an the bastid's empty, even the light bulb quit on us. It smells all mildewy in thea, an thea's some green shit growin in the egg tray. Clusters of dead roaches float in some dingy water at the bottom. Thea's a half-empty box of Sugar Pops. Dinner.

Check it out, Smiley don't really care bout food anyway. When we first moved in together, he knew I couldn't cook for shit, but he said fuck it, cause he wanted his favorite piece of ass with him. (Thass my sentimental Smiley!) Thea's no housecleanin either cause thea ain't much of a house, juss a two-room apartment on the fifth floor that came complete with a mattress. (We washed it off first.) We got a small black-and-white TV, a love seat that smells funny an has a paint can for a fourth leg, an a old bureau we grabbed off the street that came with its very own roaches. (For free! Whea else but in America?) Thass all our furniture. We got a gray exercise mat we use like a dinin area on the floor, so when people come to eat they gotta sit on the floor like chinks or those hindoos.

Sara hung out with me for a while until we finished the last joint. She has a radio. It's really her man's, but she carries it around anyway. She played it while we sat by the windows, cause it was spring an the breeze was cool an fresh. Sara is kinda dark, but she's Rican, with long hair. She's gotten a little fat, but then she had a baby bout two weeks ago.

"Whea's the baby anyway?" I axed, thinkin bout that little dark bundle I saw wrapped tightly in blue at Lincoln Hospital when she had it an I went to visit.

"It's around," she said tiredly, not wantin to talk bout it.

"Whea around?"

"I think Madgie's with him outside the bakery. Or maybe I leff him by the liquor store. I dunno." She shrugged like thea was a bug on her shoulder.

"Man, you gotta cut that shit out," I said, without too much conviction. "Yuh a motha now," I added, feelin it was the right thing to say an shit. "You gotta be responsible an take care of your baby."

"I know," she said loud, forehead all pruned up. "I know that! What, chu think I don't know? You think I treat my baby mean? He hangs out with me alla time! Alla time, dammit, he's thea, remindin me!" She lay back on our dinin mat. "Shit. Tell me I don't care bout my kid. I bet if you had a kid, you do better?"

I din't say nothin cause I knew she was all crotchety bout that kid. This always happens with her, so, like always, I juss let her blow all her steam out. You could tell it was botherin her. Her man (not the one with the radio, he's the new man), the father of the kid, at first seemed hip to the idea of a boy, but then he got real pissed off. One night, they were outside the liquor store an it was bout midnight. They were both drinkin, an they got in a fight. He wanted to know what right she had to fuck up his life. All he knows how to do is drink an stan around, he ain't got time for no babies, so what she come with this shit now for? She threw a half-empty bottle of Smirnoff at him, which really upset some of the otha winos nearby cause it was such a waste of good drinkin stuff. She got all teary an stood out in the middle of the street with the baby carriage.

"Fuck you!" she screamed, all hoarse. "I don't give a fuck!" An swoosh, a car passed bout three inches from the baby carriage.

"I hope you get kill, bitch!" he screamed back.

A big bus appeared, one of those new air condition ones from Japan that look like bullets. It started honkin. She swung the baby carriage at it. Thass when I stepped in. I had been waitin for Smiley an saw the whole thing. I dragged her off the street to her house whea I fixed her a drink. (Her apartment, by the way, is worse than ours. At least ours has a ceilin over the bathroom.) The baby was cryin like somebody stepped on it.

"Put this over his face an he'll shut up," she said, handin me a blanket. "It always works."

I took him into the bathroom, the only otha room in that dump thass private, an I shut the door on him so his cryin sounded far-off an echoey.

"I'm so fucked up!" she wailed. "I lost my man, an here I am stuck with that . . . that . . . ohhhh, fuck that bastid! Mothafucka, iss all his fault! To hell with him! Who needs him? You think I need him to bring up the baby? I'll bring it up all on my own, who needs him? That prick. He better gimme money, ain't no way he's gonna walk out on me an not gimme money, I don't care if we ain't married, he still has to gimme money, that bastid . . ."

"If you don't stop screamin, the baby ain't never gonna shut up an sleep," I said.

Her eyes got all wild. "Din't I tell you," she screamed, "to put a blanket over it? Put a blanket over the baby's head an it'll shut up!"

So much for the memory. She was lyin on the dinin mat like a corpse, her eyes cuttin holes in the ceilin. Everything was quiet now. When the joint finished, she tuned the radio to some house music.

"So whachu name the baby?" I axed, now that she had calmed down.

"Baby," she said. "It's called Baby."

I grimaced. "Thass stupid."

"Fuck you, juss whachu know bout babies?"

Okay: I know that I got leff in a carriage in the hot sun when I was a baby, my older brotha told me. He said my motha got drunk an forgot whea I was, an I hadda go to the hospital. I remember when I was three, my motha was with this man. She got drunk an put a hankie over my eyes so I couldn't see, then the two of them spun me around an around. They sped off in his Camaro, strandin me on Randall's Island for a long time. I got lost an walked around an cried a river, until cops saw me an took my hands an told me stories. They showed up in the Camaro an felt all embarrassed. A big Irish cop with a thick mustache got real mad. He noticed they were both stoned an gave them tickets. When we got home, my motha beat the livin shit outta me. "It was juss a game," she howled. "You din't have to go fuck it up."

"I don't know," I said to Sara. "I'm juss fucked up." I got up, away from her. I din't wanna talk bout babies no more. I went to my favorite drawer in the bureau an got my stuff. Sara watched. She liked to watch me shoot up, though she never did H cause she said she din't wanna die. She juss liked to watch an ax stupid questions like if it was school an I was her tutor. I took out my kit but let it lie for a while cause I was still buzzin from the joint.

I hate it when people say I'm a junkie an shit cause it's really not true. I know I got it all under control, an plus I know I can stop anytime I want. (I did once, for three whole days, an then since I knew I could take it or leave it, I took it, cause I mean, what else is thea? Why shouldn't I feel sweet?) Some Hispanos been axin me whea I picked up such a habit, cause around 149th thea ain't no sixteen-year-old girls on H. The fack is, I used to hang out in the village with this funky guy named Matt who used to do crazy shit like steal cars for a day juss to ride around. I met him through a friend in junior high. Me and him used to hang out a lot in that park with the big white arch thing whea he used to deal H to all the junkies who hung thea. I axed him what it was like to take H, cause I seen him sniffin it, an he gimme a book to read: *Christiane F.* I read like four pages an said enough of this shit, I hate books.

He got mad an said I should learn somethin, but I wouldn't go near it again, so he said fuck it. I should learn the hard way then. He shot me full of H. I first felt like I was gonna throw up on him, my stomach was dribblin around an my head felt like it was separatin from my body. I got real nervous until Matt told me to relax an not be uptight, an then I started feelin real good. The next day he shot me up again an made a joke bout that bein my last free sample. When that freeze hit me, I was on cloud nine, ten, eleven. I was free of everythin that bugged my head out, like my motha, who was out fucken like a dog in heat, or my bad grades in school, or my older brotha, who one day disappeared without even a fucken poof leavin only a pair of Pro Keds on the kitchen table as a goodbye. Nah. I wasn't thinkin bout nothin at all, juss gettin more sweet H an takin more trips into that sweet nothin land.

I hadda keep shootin after that. One time I bought some real bad shit from some guy I din't know, a fucken Latin dude, an it was awful. I felt like if bugs were crawlin all over an I couldn't stop scratchin. That was the only time I ever got fucked up. That was a year ago that I turned on, I mean, an since then, I haven't gotten the sunken face or the bags under the eyes or the circles neither. I look great. In fack, guys keep axin me out all the time, but I got Smiley, so I say nah. I'd only be like my motha if I said yeah.

Smiley's two years older than me. He's tall an sleek, with a sorta beard that feels nice. He smokes pot like a stove. He dropped out of high school to work in a car shop on Bruckner Boulevard. He lived in whass now our place with two otha dudes cause his father hated him an his motha din't really care bout nothin much. His father used to beat her around like a Ping-Pong. Smiley got sick of it, so one day, durin one of his father's drunken freak-outs, Smiley took a kitchen knife an stabbed him. Yeah, Smiley stuck him, an they threw him in Riker's Island for six months. I think thass one of the most heroic things I ever heard of in my life, which is why I really love him, cause he's so sweet an courageous. He met me one day cause one of his roomies, a thin kid with a bushy head an a face used to stompins, brought him to school to hang out, an he met me in the cafeteria. We started seein each otha an got it on. Six months ago, he kicked out his roomies for bein slobs, an he axed me to move in. You betcha ass I did. I leff my nympho bottle-sucking motha on Cypress Avenue with her roomful of men doin rotatin shifts. She din't miss me.

For a little while, thea were fluffy clouds an flowers an what they call "romance" on TV. I should end that whole story with one a those happy-ever-after things like in all great lit, but thea's always trouble. Last summer, the cops busted him twice cause he lost his job an started doin some husslin. Once they caught him with stolen goods, the otha time he got fingered in a muggin. I tried to get him to stop, but then he has to get his smoke, an I need my H; I get real cranky without it.

My buzz faded out, so I lit my juice an shot up quick, cause Sara was gettin loud. (She always does when she gets high, always sayin the stupidest shit as loud as she can.) I juss floated away an only came back to the room years later when she mentioned Diana.

Check it out, Diana is this sixteen-year-old girl who's really preggoes, like out to here. I don't know how many fucken months gone by. She's younga lookin than I am an has a real pretty complexion, like an Ivory girl, skin dark an smooth, eyes bright, tiny red lips that pout, a nice narrow waist. The first time I seen her, when she moved in with her motha an sister, I said, this one won't last. She din't. She got fucked fast enough by this guy everybody knows, named Freddie, who thinks he's all bad an acts like a beat boy. Now she's real big, an he's nowhere in sight.

"I know her motha," Sara was sayin, walkin around real fast. "I talk to her alla time, you know, she like, talks to me, knows I'm a motha too. She's a real slick lady, no shit. Works in Lerner's, that store? The one on Third Avenue, no shit, she sells dresses." She laughed hysterically for some fucken reason. I told you, she gets this way when she's on smoke.

"An like, she's a real decent, upstandin woman, she don't be hangin out with all these scums an shit heads. She got it all together. She really care bout her two girls, which is why issa shame bout Diana. An Marissa be fourteen nex month. Hope it don't happen to her!"

Yeah, Marissa, fourteen, wears black boots an skintight pants an waist cords an glossy lipstick an two huge plastic heart earrings. She's next. Nah, I don't think it's good for a growin girl to have a motha who works at Lerner's.

"Though I seen her yesterday, she was wearin a miniskirt with those . . . those wild panny hoses an shit with the designs on them? Shit, man. Her motha dresses her real good. She's really a motha, you know." She leaned real close to me. "She's tryin to get Diana to get a abortion."

"It's too late," I said, knowin Diana was too far gone for one.

"Yeah, but she knows somebody who'll still do it, an cheap too. I told you, girl, I talk to her, she confide in me an shit! I tole her it was the right thing to do. Babies can be the death, man. I tole her I shoulda aborted mines. You know? I axed her if she wanted my baby, but she said nah."

I started laughin. That was really wild!

"I'm serious, *muñeca,* I really meant it, cause I know she's a good motha."

"An she said no?"

"Yeah."

"You really give yuh baby away to somebody if they take him?"

"Sure, why not?" she said, gettin up, as if I insulted her or somethin. "She can bring it up good. Give it a good home, an toys, an money, an shit." She wasn't facin me. "I don't wanna talk bout this no more."

"Okay," I said, feelin like I did somethin wrong. "You want some Sugar Pops?" I brought the box over from the fridge an dug deep into it, poppin the stuff into my mouth.

"Nah, I gotta go," she said, an poof, a kiss on the cheek an she was out the door, with the fucken radio too.

Talkin to Sara bout babies made me feel funny inside. It's like, I don't know, I think I could be a great motha sometimes, but then I think maybe I'm too fucked up to even take care of myself, an I don't know enough bout things an life, an maybe I'll juss fuck up the kid. Those otha times, when I think I could really swing it an be a good motha are kinda painful cause it gets like an itch, an it makes me wanna swell up right away. I guess cause I was thinkin bout it so much, an cause I was high on H, when Smiley came in late at night, I axed him bout babies.

"What about um?" he axed back, rollin a joint as he sat on our dinin mat.

"Do you ever think of havin one? One for us?" The thought made me all crazy. I hugged him, like I had a billion tiny worms dancin in my veins. He pushed me away, got real serious.

"You not pregnint," he said, angry. "You pregnint?"

"No, Smiley, I—"

"You better not get fucken pregnint, or I'm out the fucken door. You see that door?" he yelled, pointin to it. "I be out of it if you get pregnint. I ain't supportin no fucken baby. Thass that. No way. Be bad enough supportin me an you." He got up, lickin his joint shut. "You got enough H?" he axed before he went into the "bedroom."

"Yeah," I said, feeling like somethin got taken out. He saw my spression an kinda felt bad, so he came over an kissed me an picked me up like some baby an planted me in bed an kissed me again. "Now, we don't want no babies, okay?"

"Okay," I said.

An then we fucked.

The next night, I was sittin on the stoop with Diana. It wasn't like I planned it or nothin, it's juss Smiley wasn't home, an I decided to wait for him outside. I had been in the fucken apartment all day long, throwin up, mostly. Maybe it was the smoke an the H? I told Millie bout it, an she laughed an said, "Uh-oh," but the bitch vanished before I could get the story out of her.

Anyway, I was gonna hang out for a while an went downstairs. Thass when I heard cryin, soft cryin an sniffin. I looked down the hallway an saw somebody down by the otha stairwell that goes to the otha side of the buildin. It was juss the top of a head behind the handrail whea everybody puts their garbage. I walked right over, cause I'm a curious bitch, an saw it was Diana in a cute blue maternity thing that said BABY an had a arrow pointin to her belly. She heard me sneakin up an got all self-conscious. We weren't really close or nothin, juss talked once or twice, so I started yappin a whole lot, first bout the smell of the hallway, then garbage. I told her my top ten worst insects list (she cracked up), an then finally I got to ax. "So how come yuh down here cryin?"

Diana kinda sighed an rearranged her long hair with a toss of her head. She wiped at her face clumsily. "My motha an I had anotha fight about the baby."

"She still wancha get rid of it?"

"Yeah. She knows I'm seven months," her voice cracked, "but she don't care. She says she's gonna do whass bess for me if she gotta break the law to do it, an she says she'll drag me down if I don't want to. I juss wasn't inna mood for all that shit tonight, so I juss ducked out."

"What bout your man, whea's he?" I tried soundin like a therapist I saw on TV.

"I don't know. Freddie went away. I ain't seen him in six months." She started to cry again, an I gave her a big hug. She was tremblin a little, juss like Sara's baby when I first picked it up from its crib two weeks ago an it looked like a tiny red prune. We walked out to the stoop an sat thea for a while.

"You think your motha's gonna come down an getchu?" I axed.

"I don't know. She'll send Marissa. She expected me to sit thea an hear anotha sermon about what I gotta do, but I'm not gonna, I'm not gonna kill my baby," she said firmly, her voice gettin louder, "because it's mines, an Freddie's, an someday he'll come back, an even if he doesn't, so what? The baby is . . . a produck of our love for each otha, a part of us, you know? Thea's a part of me in that baby, an if I let her kill it, she'll be killin somethin of mines! I feel it, you know? It moves around in thea. It does bumps an grinds an shit! It's juss waitin to be born. I'm not gonna let her murder my baby!" she yelled, clenching her fists as if she was gonna punch me.

"Don't get so worked up," I said, tryin to calm her down.

"Worked up? Don't get so worked up? You ack like this is somethin trivial, like buyin *lechuga o tomate!* It's not, you know. It's a baby. An it's mines, dammit, mines!"

"An how you gonna bring it up?" I axed, already gettin too involved, but somethin happens to me when I get yelled at. "If you have it, you gonna stay witcha motha?"

"No way. I know a friend who lives near Melrose. She's gettin it ready. In a week, I can go live with her."

"So what? How you gonna bring it up? How you gonna feed it? You got money for that, or is yuh friend also a fucken bank?"

"She's gonna help me til I get on my feet," she said slowly, as if she was tryin to remember lines from a play.

"Yeah? An how you gonna get on yuh feet? You leff school?"

"I'm goin back."

"Takin the baby witcha?"

"Stop it."

"You'll need money for a baby-sitter. Whea's it gonna—"

"Freddie'll help," she said angrily.

"He's halfway to Bermuda by now." I knew that was cruel, but juss who the fuck she think she is yellin at me like that when I try an help?

"Fuck you!" she yelled. "Yuh juss like my motha!"

Thass when Marissa appeared in the doorway, wearin a polka-dot miniskirt with wooden sandals that clacked real loud.

"Ma says to come up," she said, a finger in her mouth.

"I'm not goin up thea. You tell . . ." The words froze in her mouth, cause juss as she turned to tell Marissa off, she spotted her motha coming down the hall.

"I'm not comin witcha!" Diana screamed, jumpin off the stoop an tryin to run away. This was when her motha put on some speed an grabbed her, pullin her to the stoop again.

"Let her go!" I yelled, tryin to untangle them, but I got an elbow in the face real hard from one of them. They both collapsed on the sidewalk, Diana yellin "I hate'chu!" an throwin punches like a demon. Millie, the daughter of the guy who owns the bodega next door, started yellin for the cops. Diana's motha was hittin back now, an hard, up on her feet while Diana rolled on the ground from the punches, getting soaked from a dribblin hydrant she slid under. Her motha started pullin on her real fierce while screamin bout respect. I thought she'd hurt her or somethin, so I lunged, pullin her away.

"Leave her alone!" I cried.

"Leave her alone?" her motha roared back in my face, her eyes real big. "Leave her alone? With you? She's my daughter! Do you hear? She's my daughter, not yours! My baby! An she's not endin up like you!" Her voice was hoarse, her arms flyin around like pinwheels as she gestured wildly at the crowd (which always forms at the first sign of a free show). "Buncha junkies an shits, you gonna save my daughter from me? I'm savin her from dirt like you!" She grabbed Diana again and started draggin her. "Less see you stop me, *carajo!*" She had completely flipped, her eyes bulgin, her hair a mess, her red blouse all torn up. She kept draggin Diana even though she screamed an swung out at her, her otha arm gettin scratched up from scrapin against the sidewalk. Two guys from the bodega came out an pulled her motha off, because Diana was movin funny, holdin her stomach.

"Oh God!!" she cried, louder than anythin I ever heard in my life. She wriggled an folded into a ball, clutchin her stomach. I bent over her, tryin to unfold her, me an Millie both tried, but we couldn't. When she looked up at me, her face looked horrible, all cracked inside.

"Oh shit, get an ambulance!" I yelled, at nobody an everybody, while Marissa stood frozen to the spot, by the stoop, starin blankly as if watchin TV, absently pullin up on her designer panty hose.

It was a week after that that Sara gave away her baby. She got rid of it somehow, I don't fucken know how, I juss kept seein her without it so I axed her one day, an she juss got this real idiot grin on her face like when she's stoned, an she said, "It's gone," an then she walked away from me with her blarin box, over to her new man by the liquor store, with the gleamin pint of brandy. I juss ran home to my H after that, I juss couldn't deal with it.

I don't know, I don't read much, don't watch news, don't care bout how many got fried in Nicaragua or wherever, but sometimes I get this feelin, an it's not bout politics, cause that guy Matt, who turned me on to H, was a real militant black motha who was always sayin the system hadda be overthrowed, an I think he's still sayin that from his sewer hole somewhere.

I don't got a head for that shit, you know? But this feelin I get. I look out my window an see it all crawlin by, see it all scribbled on Sara's face, stamped on Diana's torn maternity suit. I remember her motha's words, an they all seemed to hit me somewhere. Shit, I even feel it now when I look in the mirror an see the circles under my eyes an the marks on my fucked-up arms: we're in some real serious shit here. It's no place for babies. Not even a good place for dogs.

I guess I can't pretend I'm alive anymore. Diana's baby was lucky; it died in the incubator. On my seventeenth birthday, I dreamed I was in that incubator, chokin. Smiley woke me up with a cupcake that had a candle on it, yellow flame dancin nervous, like it might go out any second. He remembered.

Smiley noticed I changed a little, cause I wasn't so happy anymore. I juss wanted to take my H an cruise on my run an not botha. He even got mad cause I din't wanna fuck so much no more. I din't tell him I was pregnint, not even after four weeks passed.

I saw Diana on a corner, in shorts an Pro Keds, all smiles, cause she was high, her eyes lookin like eight balls.

"Lissen," she said. "I was wonderin if like maybe you could do me a favor and shit? Can you like turn me on to some Horse? I really wanna try it, an Sara said you'd turn me on. Whacha say, yeah?"

Somethin inside me popped. I'm not normally a violent person, but like a reflex an shit, I smacked her right in the face, hard. She fell back about three feet against a riot gate that rattled.

"Whachu do that for?" she yelled, blood burstin over her teeth from a busted lip. She was breathin heavy, like some tough butch. I juss stared at her, then went upstairs to my H. I felt bad for her motha. I felt like maybe her motha shoulda beat her up more. I wished my motha woulda cared that much for me. A good motha in life is a break, an nobody with a good break like that got a right to go lookin for H.

"Man, you out already?" Smiley said one night in surprise, going through my kit. "I thoughtchu had a week's worth."

Smiley din't know thea was a tiny baby inside of me, but I knew it. I also knew thea was a part of me in that baby, an a part of him, an zero plus zero equals zero. So I din't say nothin.

I got a abortion.

Charles D'Ambrosio

Charles D'Ambrosio was raised in Seattle, but he's lived in Chicago, Hoboken, Paris, New York, Iowa City, Madison (Wis.), and Hoquiam (Wash). Currently he is living in Los Angeles and looking for somewhere better. Meanwhile, he is completing a collection of stories to be published by Little, Brown and Company.

"Her Real Name" was initially published in *The Paris Review*.

1.

The girl's scalp looked as though it had been singed by fire—strands of thatchy red hair snaked away from her face, then settled against her skin, pasted there by sweat and sunscreen and the blown grit and dust of travel. For a while her thin hair had remained as light and clean as the down of a newborn chick, but it was getting hotter as they drove west, heading into a summer-long drought that scorched the landscape, that withered the grass and melted the black tar between expansion joints in the road and bloated like balloons the bodies of raccoon and deer and dog and made everything on the highway ahead ripple like a mirage through waves of rising heat. Since leaving Fargo, it had been too hot to wear the wig, and it now lay on the seat between them, still holding within its webbing the shape of her head. Next to it, a bag of orange candy—smiles, she called them—spilled across the vinyl. Sugar crystals ran into the dirty stitching and stuck to her thigh. Gum wrappers and greasy white bags littered the floor, and on the dash, amid a flotsam of plastic cups, pennies, and matchbooks, a bumper sticker curled in the heat. "Expect a Miracle," it read. The man and the girl had been living in his car for the past month. Neither of them had bathed in days.

The girl cradled a black Bible in her lap, the leather covers as worn and ragged as old tennis shoes. The inner leaf contained a family tree dating back to 1827, names tightly scrawled in black against yellowing parchment, a genealogy as ponderous as those kept in Genesis, the book of the generations of Adam. The list of ancestors on the inner leaf was meaningless ancient history to the man, whose name was Jones, but the girl said her family had carried that same Bible with them wherever they went, for one hundred and fifty years, and that she wanted it with her, too. "That's me," the girl had said, showing Jones her name, the newest of all, penned in generous loops of Bic-blue. She'd written it in herself along the margin of the page. *b. 1960–*. The girl read different passages aloud as they drove, invoking a mix of epic beauty and bad memories, of Exodus and the leather belt her stepfather used to beat her when she broke a commandment—one of the original ten, or one of his additions. Jones wasn't sure what faith she placed in the austere Christianity of her forefathers, but reading aloud seemed to cast a spell over her. She had a beautiful church-trained voice that lifted each verse into a soothing melody, a song whose tune of succor rose and fell somewhere beyond the harsh demands of faith. Only minutes before she'd read herself to sleep with a passage from Jeremiah.

Now, as if she felt Jones staring, the girl stirred.

"You were looking at me," she said. "You were thinking something."

Her face was shapeless, soft, and pale as warm putty.

"I could feel it," she said. "Where are we?"

They hadn't gone more than a mile since she'd dozed off. She reached for the candy on the seat.

"You hungry? You want a smile, Jones?"

"No, none for me," Jones said.

"A Life Saver?" She held the unraveled package out.

"Nothing, thanks."

"Me eating candy, and my teeth falling out." The girl licked the sugar off a smile, and asked, "How far to Las Vegas?"

Jones jammed a tape in the eight-track. He was driving a 1967 Belvedere he'd bought for seven hundred dollars cash in Newport News, and it had come with a bulky eight-track, like an atavistic organ, bolted beneath the glove box. He'd found two tapes in the trunk, and now, after fifteen thousand miles, he was fairly sick of both Tom Jones and Steppenwolf. But he preferred the low-fidelity noise of either tape to the sound of himself lying.

"Why don't you come with me, little girl," he sang along, in a high, mocking falsetto, "on a Magic Carpet ride."

"How far?" the girl asked.

Jones adjusted his grip on the steering wheel. "Another day, maybe."

She seemed to fall asleep again, her dry-lidded eyes shut like a lizard's, her parched flaking lips parted, her frail body given over to the car's gentle rocking. Jones turned his attention back to the road, a hypnotic black line snaking through waves of yellow grass. It seemed to Jones that they'd been traveling through eastern Montana forever, that the same two or three trees, the same two or three farmhouses and grain silos, were rushing past like scenery in an old movie, only suggesting movement. Endless fields, afire in the bright sun, were occasionally broken by stands of dark cottonwood, or the gutted chassis of a rusting car. Collapsing barns leaned over in the grass, giving into the hot wind and the insistent flatness, as if passively accepting the laws of a world whose only landmark, as far as Jones could see, was the level horizon.

"He's out there," the girl said. "I can feel him out there when I close my eyes. He knows where we are."

"I doubt that very much," Jones said.

The girl struggled to turn, gripping the headrest; she looked through the rear window at the warp of the road as it narrowed to a pinprick on the pale edge of the world they'd left behind; it was out of the vanishing point that her stepfather would come.

"I expect he'll be caught up soon," she said. "He's got a sense. One time he predicted an earthquake."

"It's a big country," Jones said. "We could've gone a million other ways."

"But we didn't. We went this way."

"Maybe if you think real hard about Florida that'll foul up his superduper predicting equipment."

"Prayer," the girl said. "He prays. Nothing fancy. We're like Jonah sneaking on that boat in Tarshish; they found him out."

The girl closed her eyes; she splashed water on her face and chest.

"It's so hot," she said. "Tell me some more about the Eskimos."

"I'm running out of things to say about Eskimos," Jones said. "I only read that one book."

"Say old stuff, I don't care."

He searched his memory for what he remembered of Rasmussen, the Nordic Viking.

"Nothing's wasted," Jones said. "They use everything. The Inuit can make a sled out of a slain dog. They kill the dog and skin it, then cut the hide into two strips."

"I'm burning alive," the girl said.

"They roll up the hide and freeze the strips in water to make the runners. Then they join the runners together with the dog's rib bones." Jones nibbled the corner of an orange smile. "One minute the dog's pulling the sled, the next minute he is the sled." He saw that the girl was asleep. "That's irony," he said, and then repeated the word. "Irony." It sounded weak, inadequate; it described nothing; he drove silently on. Out through the windshield he saw a landscape too wide for the eye to measure—the crushing breadth of the burnt fields and the thin black thread of road vanishing into a vast blue sky as if the clouds massed on the horizon were distant cities and they were going to them.

She'd been working the pumps and the register at a crossroads station in southern Illinois, a rail-thin girl with stiff red hair the color of rust, worried, chipped nails, and green eyes without luster. She wore gray coveralls that ballooned over her body like a clown's outfit, the long legs and sleeves rolled into thick cuffs. "I've never seen the ocean," she'd said, pointing to the remains of a peeling bumper sticker on Jones's car. ". . . be sailing," it read. She stood on the pump island while Jones filled his tank. The hooded blue lights above them pulsed in sync to the hovering sound of cicadas and both were a comforting close presence in the black land spreading out around the station. Jones wanted to tell the girl to look around her, right now: this flat patch of nothing was as good as an ocean. Instead, making conversation, Jones said, "I just got out of the Navy."

"You from around here?" she asked.

"Nope," Jones said.

He topped off his tank and reached into the car where he kept his money clipped to the sunvisor.

"I knew that," she said. "I seen your plates."

Jones handed her a twenty from his roll of muster pay. The money represented for him his final six months in the Navy, half a year in which he hadn't once set foot on land. Tired of the sea, knowing he'd never make a career out of it, on his last tour Jones had refused the temptations of shore leave, hoping to hit land with enough of a stake to last him a year. Now, as he looked at the dwindling roll, he was torn between exhaustion and a renewed desire to move on before he went broke.

"Where in Virginia you from?"

"I'm not," Jones said. "I bought the car in Newport News. Those are just old plates."

"That's too bad," the girl said. "I like the name. Virginia. Don't you?"

"I guess it's not special to me one way or the other," Jones said.

The girl folded the twenty in half and ran her thin fingers back and forth over the crease. That she worked in a gas station in the middle of nowhere struck Jones as sexy, and now he looked at her closely, trying to decide whether or not he wanted to stop a night or two in Carbondale. Except for the strange texture and tint of her red hair, he thought she looked good, and the huge coveralls, rippling in the breeze, made her seem sweet and lost, somehow innocent and alone in a way that gave Jones the sudden confidence that he could pick her up without much trouble.

"You gonna break that?" Jones asked, nodding at the bill.

Her arm vanished entirely as she reached into the deep pocket of her coveralls and pulled out a roll of bills stained black with grease and oil. Jones took the change, then looked off, around the station. In the east a dome of light rose above Carbondale, a pale yellow pressing out against the night sky. The road running in front of the station was empty except for a spotlight that shone on a green dinosaur and a Sinclair sign that spun on a pole above it.

"Don't get scared, working out here?" he asked.

"Nah," she said. "Hardly anyone comes out this way, 'less they're like you, 'less they're going somewhere. Had a man from Vernal gas here the other night. That's in Utah."

"Still—"

"Some nights I wouldn't care if I got robbed."

Jones took his toilet kit—a plastic sack that contained a thin, curved bonelike bar of soap, a dull razor, and a balding toothbrush —out of the glove box. "You mind if I wash up?"

"Washroom's around back," she said. "By the propane tanks."

In the bathroom, he took off his T-shirt and washed himself with a wetted towel, watching his reflection in the mirror above the sink as though it were someone else, someone from his past. Gray eyes, a sharp sculpted jaw, ears that jutted absurdly from his close-cropped head: a Navy face. Six months of shipboard isolation had left him with little sense of himself outside of his duties as an officer. In that time, held in the chrysalis of his berth, he'd forgotten not only what he looked like, but what other people might see when they looked at him. Now he was a civilian. He decided to shave, lathering up with the bar of soap. The mustache came off in four or five painful strokes.

For a moment the warm breeze was bracing against his cleanly shaven face. He stood in the lot, a little stiff, at attention, and when the girl waved to him from the cashier's window, Jones saluted.

"See you later," he said.

"Okay," she said.

Jones drove away, stopping at a convenience store about a mile down the road. He grabbed two six-packs, a cheap Styrofoam cooler, and a bag of ice and wandered down the aisle where the toys were kept. He selected a pink gun that fired rubber suction darts. He returned to the station and parked his car in the shadow of the dinosaur. He waited. The girl sat in the glass booth behind a rack of road atlases, suddenly the sweetheart of every town he'd traveled through in the last few months. To be with someone who knew his name, to hear another voice would be enough for tonight. Jones twisted open a beer and loaded the dart gun. He licked the suction tip, took aim, and fired.

"Hey," the girl shouted.

"Wanna go somewhere?" Jones asked.

They'd crossed the Mississippi three weeks ago and driven north through Iowa, staying in motels and eating in diners, enjoying high times until his money began to run out. Then they started sleeping in the car, parked at rest stops or in empty lots, arms and legs braided together in the back seat of the Belvedere. One morning Jones had gone to a bake shop and bought a loaf of day-old sourdough bread for thirty-five cents. It was the cool blue hour before dawn, but already, as he crossed the parking lot, the sky was growing pale and the patches of tar were softening beneath his shoes and in the sultry air the last weak light of the street lamps threw off dull coronas of yellow and pink. Only one other car was parked in the empty lot, and its windows had been smashed out, a spray of glass scattered like seeds across the asphalt. As Jones approached the Belvedere, he saw the girl slowly lift the hair away from her head. It was as if he were witness to some miracle of revelation set in reverse, as if the rising sun and the new day had not bestowed but instead stripped the world of vision, exposed and left it bare. Her skull was blue, a hidden thing not meant for the light. Jones opened her door. She held the wig of curly red hair in her lap.

"Damn," he said. He paced off a small circle in the parking lot.

The girl combed her fingers calmly through the hair on her lap. She'd understood when she removed the wig that revealing herself to Jones would tip fate irrevocably. She felt that in this moment she would know Jones, and know him forever. She waited for Jones to spend his shock and anger, afraid that when he cooled down she might be on her way back to Carbondale, to the gas station and her stepfather and the church and the prayers for miraculous intercession. When Jones asked what was wrong with her, and she told him, he punted the loaf of sourdough across the empty lot.

"Why haven't you said anything?"

"What was I supposed to say, Jones?"

"The truth might've made a good start."

"Seems to me you've been having yourself a fine time without it," she said. "Hasn't been all that crucial so far."

"Jesus Christ."

"Besides, I wouldn't be here now if I'd told you. You'd have been long gone."

Jones denied it. "You don't know me from Adam," he said.

"Maybe not," she said. She set the wig on her head. "I'll keep it on if you think I'm ugly." The girl swung her legs out of the car and walked across the lot. She picked up the bread and brought it back. "These things drag out," she said.

She brushed pebbles and dirt and splinters of glass from the crust and then cracked the loaf in half.

"You didn't get any orange juice, did you?" she asked. "This old bread needs orange juice."

She reached inside and tore a hunk of clean white bread from the core and passed the loaf to Jones. He ate a piece and calmed down.

"Who knows how long I've got," she said.

When they headed out again that morning, going west seemed inevitable—driving into the sun was too much to bear, and having it at their backs in the quiet and vacant dawn gave them the feeling, however brief, that they could outrace it. It was 1977, it was August, it was the season when the rolling fields were feverish with sunflowers turning on withered stalks to reach the light, facing them in the east as they drove off at dawn, gazing after them in the west as the sun set and they searched the highway ahead for the softly glowing neon strip, for the revolving signs and lighted windows and the melancholy trickle of small-town traffic that would bloom brightly on the horizon and mean food and a place to stop for the night. If Jones wasn't too tired, he pushed on, preferring the solitude of night driving, when actual distances collapsed unseen and the car seemed to float unmoored through limitless space, the reassuring hum of tires rolling beneath him, the lights of towns hovering across the darkened land like constellations in a warm universe. By day, he stopped only when the girl wanted to see a natural wonder, a landmark, a point of historical interest. Early this morning they'd visited the valley of the Little Bighorn. Silence held sway over the sight, a silence that touched the history of a century ago and then reached beyond it, running back to the burnt ridges and bluffs and to a time when the flat golden plain in the west had not yet felt the weight of footprints. Jones watched the girl search among the huddled white markers, looking for the blackened stone where Custer fell. She'd climbed over the wrought-iron fence to stand beside the stone and a bull snake cooling in the shadow slithered off through the yellow grass. She seemed okay, not really sick, only a little odd and alien when she took off the wig. Now and then Jones would look at the girl and think, *You're dying,* but the unvarying heat hammered the days into a dull sameness, and driving induced a kind of amnesia, and for the most part Jones had shoved the idea out of his mind until this morning when they'd discussed their next move.

"We could drive to Nevada," she said. "Seems we're headed that direction, anyhow."

"Maybe," Jones said.

"It only takes an hour to get married," the girl said, "and they rent you the works. A veil, flowers. We'll gamble. I've never done that. Have you? Roulette—what do you think, Jones?"

"I said maybe."

"Jones," she said. "I'm not into maybe."

"I don't know," Jones said. "I haven't thought it out."

"What's to think?" the girl said. "You'd be a widower in no time."

Jones squeezed the girl's knee, knobby and hard like a foal's. "Jesus," he said.

"It's not a big commitment I'm asking for."

"Okay, all right," Jones said. "Don't get morbid."

Night fell and the highway rose into the mountains. With the Continental Divide coming up, Jones couldn't decide whether or not to wake the girl. She didn't like to miss a landmark or border or any attraction advertised on a billboard. They'd stopped for the Parade of Presidents, "America's Heritage in Wax," and to see alligators and prairie dogs and an ostrich and the bleached white bones of dinosaurs, and by now the back of the car was covered with bumper stickers and decals and the trunk was full of souvenirs she'd bought, snow-filled baubles, bolo ties, beaded Indian belts, engraved bracelets, pennants. Wall Drug, Mt. Rushmore, The Little Bighorn, and a bare rutted patch of dirt in the sweet-grass that, according to a bullet-riddled placard, was the Lewis and Clark Trail—she'd stocked up on hokey junk and sentimental trinkets and the stuff now commemorated a wandering path across state lines, over rivers, up mountains, into empty fields where battles had been fought and decided, and down the streets of dirty, forgotten towns where once, long ago, something important had happened.

Jones gave her a shake, and said, "Now all the rivers flow west."

"Jones?" She was disoriented, a child spooked on waking in unfamiliar surroundings. "I'm not feeling too good."

"You want to lie down?"

"I could use a beer," the girl said. "Something to kill this."

Jones eased the car over the breakdown line. The mountains cut a crown of darkness out of the night sky, and a row of telephone poles, silhouetted in the starlight, seemed like crosses planted along the highway. He arranged the back seat, shoving his duffel to the floor and unrolling the sleeping bag. The car shook as a semi passed, spraying a phalanx of gravel in its wake.

"Let's get there soon," the girl said.

"Get in back," Jones said.

"I'm praying," she said.

"That's good," he said. Jones ran his hand over the girl's head. Wispy strands of hair pulled loose and stuck to his palm. "We'll stop in the next town."

Back on the road, the wind dried his T-shirt and the sweat-soaked cotton turned stiff as cardboard. Beneath him the worn tires rolled over the warm asphalt like the murmur of a river. On the move once more, he felt only relief, a sense of his body freed from its strict place in time, drifting through the huddled blue lights of towns named after Indians and cavalrymen and battles, after blind expectations and the comforts of the known past, after the sustaining beliefs and fears of pioneers. Outlook, Savage,

Plentywood. Going west, names changed, became deposits of uto-
pian history, places named Hope and Endwell, Wisdom and Inde-
pendence and Loveland. Whenever the road signs flashed by, lu-
minous for an instant, Jones felt as though he were journeying
through a forgotten allegory.

The girl asked, "When do you think we'll be there?"

"We're not going to Las Vegas," Jones said. He had not known
his decision until he spoke and heard the words aloud.

"Why not?"

"I'm taking you to a hospital."

"They'll send me home," the girl said.

"They might."

"Dad'll say you abducted me."

"You know that's not the deal."

"Don't matter," the girl said. "He'll say you're working for
Satan and his demonic forces, even if you don't know it. He says
just about everybody is."

"Well, I'm not," Jones said.

"You might be without you knowing it," the girl said.

They were crossing the Bitterroot. Jones lost radio reception,
and so he listened to the girl's prayers, words coming to him in
fragments, Jesus and Savior and Amen, the music of her voice
carried away by the wind, choked off whenever she dry-heaved in
the seat behind him. Somewhere in western Idaho she fell asleep
and for the next few hours Jones listened to the car tires sing.
Outside Spokane, on an illuminated billboard set back in a wheat
field, a figure of Jesus walked on water, holding a staff. Jones
considered the odd concession to realism: a man walking on water
would hardly need to support himself with a crutch. The thought
was gone as soon as the billboard vanished behind him. No others
took its place. Bored, he searched the radio dial for voices, but for
long empty stretches pulled in nothing but the sizzle of static, a
strange surging cackle filling the car as if suddenly he'd lost contact with earth.

———

A red neon vacancy sign sputtered ambiguously, the *no* weakly charged and half-lit. Behind the motel and across the railroad tracks, the Columbia River snaked through Wenatchee, flowing wide and quiet, a serene blue vein dividing the town from the apple orchards. The low brown hills were splotched with squares of green, patches of garden carved out of burnt land, and beyond them to the west, rising up, etched into the blue sky, a snowcapped mountain range rimmed the horizon like teeth set in some huge jaw.

"We're here," Jones said.

"Where?"

"Wen-a-tchee," he said.

"Wena-tchee," he tried again.

"Just a place," he said, finally. "Let's get upstairs."

In their room, Jones set the girl on the bed. He spritzed the sheets with tapwater, cooling them, and opened the window. A hot breeze pushed the brown burlap curtains into the room. The gray, dusty leaves of an apple tree spread outside the window and beneath the tree the unnatural blue of a swimming pool shimmered without revealing any depth in the morning sun. A slight breeze rippled the water and an inflated lifesaver floated aimlessly across the surface.

The girl was kneeling at the foot of the bed, her hands folded and her head bowed in prayer. She was naked, her body a dull, white votary candle, the snuffed flame of her hair a dying red ember.

"Kneel here with me," she said.

"You go ahead," Jones said. He sat on the edge of the bed and pulled off his boots.

"It wouldn't hurt you," she said, "to get on your knees."

"We had this discussion before," he said.

"I believe it was a miracle," the girl said. She was referring to the remission of her cancer, the answered prayers. Her stepfather belonged to an evangelical sect that believed the literal rapture of

Judgment Day was near at hand. Several dates he'd predicted for the end of time had already come and gone. Two months ago, he'd taken her out of medical treatment, refusing science in favor of prayer. Her illness bloomed with metaphoric possibilities and large portents for the congregation of the Church of the Redeemer in Carbondale, and was used as a kind of augury, variously read as a sign of God's covenant, or as proof of Man's fallenness, his wickedness and sin. For a while she'd been in remission and news of her cure had brought a host of desperate seekers to the church.

At a display in South Dakota, against the evidence of bones before them, the girl had said dinosaurs didn't die sixty million years ago. "It was about ten thousand years ago," she had insisted. Her stepfather believed they'd been on the boat with Noah.

"Some big ass boat," Jones had said. Jones no longer had any interest in arguing. But he said, "And now that you're sick again, what's that?"

"It's what the Lord wants."

"There's no talking to you," Jones said.

"We're all just here to bear witness," she said.

"Have your prayers ever been answered?"

"The night you came by the station, I asked for that. I prayed and you came."

"I was hungry. I wanted a candy bar."

"That's what you think," the girl said. "But you don't know. You don't really know why you stopped or what the plan is or anything. Who made you hungry? Huh? Think about that." The rush of words seemed to exhaust her. She wrapped a corner of the sheet around her finger, and repeated, "Who made you hungry?"

"So you prayed for me and I came," Jones said. "Me, in particular? or just someone, anyone?" He stripped off his shirt, wadded it up, and wiped the sweat from his armpits. "Your illness doesn't mean anything. You're just sick, that's all."

Jones cranked the hot water and stayed in the shower, his first in days, until it scalded his skin a splotchy pink. Finished, he toweled off, standing over the girl. She was choking down cries.

"Why don't you take a shower?" Jones said.

"Maybe I should go back home."

"Maybe you should just stand out there on the road and let your old dad's radar find you." Then Jones said, "If that's what you want, I'll get you a bus ticket. You can be on your way tomorrow."

The girl shook her head. "It's no place to me," she said.

"The Eskimos don't have homes, either," Jones said. "They don't have a word for it. They can't even ask each other, hey, where do you live?"

2.

Dr. McKillop sat on an apple crate and pulled a flask from his coat pocket. The afternoon heat was bad but the harsh light was worse; he squinted uphill, vaguely wishing he were sober. It was too late, though, and with a sense of anticipation, of happy fatality, he drank and the sun-warmed scotch bit hard at the back of his throat. McKillop felt the alcoholic's secret pleasure at submitting to something greater than himself, a realignment with destiny: he took another drink. Swimming in the reflection of the silver flask, he noticed a young white man. He was tall and thin, his cheekbones sharp and high, and in the glare his deep eye sockets seemed empty, pools of cool blue shadow. When the man finally approached, McKillop offered him the flask.

"I was told in town I could find you here," Jones said.

McKillop nodded. "You must be desperate."

The doctor wiped dust and sweat from his neck with a sun-bleached bandanna. One of the day-pickers had fallen from a tree and broken his arm and McKillop had been called to reset it. He was no longer a doctor, not legally, not since six months ago when he'd been caught prescribing cocaine to himself. The probationary status of his medical license didn't matter to the migrants who worked the apple orchards and McKillop was glad for the work. It kept trouble at a distance.

"Let me guess," McKillop said. "You don't have any money? Or you're looking for pharmaceuticals?"

"The bartender at Yakima Suzie's gave me your name," Jones said.

"You can get drunk, you can smoke cigars and gamble in a bar. You can find plenty in a bar. I know I have." McKillop pressed a dry brown apple blossom between his fingers, then sniffed beneath his nails. "But a doctor, a doctor you probably shouldn't find in a bar." He looked up at Jones and said, "I've been defrocked."

"I'm not looking for a priest," Jones said. The doctor's stentorian voice and overblown statements were starting to annoy him. The doctor wore huaraches with tire-tread soles and his toes were caked with dirt and the long curled nails looked yellow and unhealthy. He knotted his long raggedy hair in a ponytail.

Jones remained silent while a flatbed full of migrants rumbled by, jouncing over a worn two-track of gray dust and chuckholes. The green of the garden, of the orchards he'd seen from the valley, was an illusion; the trail of rising dust blew through the trees and settled and bleached the branches and leaves bone-gray. A grasshopper spit brown juice on Jones's hand; he flicked it away and said, "I've got a girl in pain."

"Well, a girl in pain." McKillop capped his flask and wiped his forehead again. He spat in the dust, a dry glob rolling up thick and hard at his feet. He crushed it away with the rubber heel of his sandal. He looked up into the lattice of leaves, the sun filtering through; many of the apples with a western exposure were still green on the branch. McKillop stood and plucked one of the unripe apples and put it in his pocket. "For later," he said.

The room smelled like rotting mayonnaise. Her body glistened with a yellow liquid. She'd vomited on herself, on the pillows, on the floor. Face down, she clutched the sheets and tore them from the bed. She rolled over on her back, kicking the mattress and arching herself off the bed, lifting her body, twisting as though she were a wrestler attempting to escape a hold.

Jones pinned her arms against the bed while she bucked, trying to free herself. Her teeth were clenched, then she gasped, gulping for air. Her upper lip held a delicate dew of sweat in a mustache of faint blond hair. She made fists of her thin, skeletal hands, and then opened them, clawing Jones with her yellowed nails.

McKillop drew morphine from a glass vial and found a blue vein running in the girl's arm. A drop of blood beaded where the needle punctured her skin. McKillop dabbed the blood away with the bedsheet and pressed a Band-Aid over the spot.

The girl's body relaxed, as if she were suddenly without skeleton.

Windblown dust clouded the window. Jones slid it open along runners clogged with dirt and desiccated flies and looked down into the motel pool. Lit by underwater lights, it glowed like a jewel. A lawn chair lay on its side near the bottom, gently wavering in an invisible current.

"She needs a doctor," McKillop said.

"That's you," Jones said. "You're the doctor."

McKillop shook his head.

"Don't leave," the girl said. Only her index finger flickered, lifting slightly off the bed, as if all her struggle had been reduced to a tiny spasm.

"Wait outside," Jones said to the doctor.

When he'd gone, Jones turned on the television, a broken color set that bathed the room in a blue glow; he searched for a clear channel but the screen remained a sea of pulsing static behind which vague figures swam in surreal distortion, auras without source. He stripped the bed, and wetted a thin, rough towel with warm water and began to wipe the vomit off the girl's face, off her hard, shallow chest, off her stomach as it rose and fell with each breath. "Feels good," she said. Jones rinsed the towel and continued the ablution, working down her stick-thin legs and then turning her onto her stomach, massaging the tepid towel over her back and buttocks, along her thighs. The curtains fluttered, parting like wings and rising into the room. It was early, but the sun was setting in the valley, the brown rim of hills holding a halo of bright light, an emphatic, contoured seam of gold, and different sounds —the screeching of tires, the jangling of keys, a dog barking— began to carry clearly, sounds so ordinary and near they seemed to have a source, not within the room, not out in the world, but in memory.

When the girl sank into sleep, Jones slipped out into the hallway.

"Your wife?" McKillop asked.

"Just a girl I picked up."

"Jesus, man." With forced jocularity, the doctor slapped Jones on the back. "You know how to pick them."

Out on the street dusk settled, a moment of suspension. The sky was still deep blue with a weak edge of white draining away in the west. An Indian crouched on the curb outside the motel, his face brown and puckered like a windfall apple in autumn.

Jones and McKillop entered a bar next door.

"I'm taking her to a hospital," Jones said.

"There's precious little a hospital can do," the doctor said. "Let's have a drink here," he called out. "They'll start a morphine drip. It'll keep her euphoric until she dies."

"Then I'll send her home," Jones said. In the Navy he'd learned one thing, and for Jones it amounted to a philosophy: There was no real reason to go forward, but enormous penalties were paid by those who refused. He'd learned this lesson rubbing Brasso into his belt buckle and spit-shining his boots for inspections that never came. "I could leave right now," he said. "I could drive away."

"Why don't you," the doctor said. "Turn tail, that's what I'd do." He ordered boilermakers and drank his by dumping the shot of bourbon into the schooner of beer. He polished off his first drink and called for another round.

"Deep down," McKillop said, "I'm really shallow."

Jones said, "I had this feeling if I kept driving everything would be okay."

"The healing, recuperative powers of the West," the doctor said. "Teddy Roosevelt, and all that. The West was a necessary invention of the Civil War, a place of harmony and union. From the body politic to the body—"

Jones only half listened. He found himself resisting the doctor's glib reductions.

"I'd like to hit the road," McKillop was saying. The phrase had an antiquated sound. Even in the cool of the bar, McKillop was sweating. He pressed a fat finger down on a bread crumb, then flicked it away.

"You looked bad when you saw her," Jones said.

"I'll be alright," McKillop said. He downed his drink. "I'm feeling better now. You'll need help but I'm not your doctor."

McKillop bought a roll of quarters and made a few sloppy calls to friends in Seattle, waking them, demanding favors for the sake of old times, invoking old obligations, twice being told to fuck off, and finally getting through to an old resident friend at Mercy Hospital, who said he'd look at the girl if nothing else could be done.

"We'll take care of her," McKillop said to Jones. They walked down to the section of windowless warehouses and blank-faced cold storage buildings, walked along cobbled streets softly pearled with blue lamplight, apple crates stacked up twenty, thirty feet high against the brick. Beyond the train tracks, the Columbia flowed quietly; a path of cold moonlight stretched across the water like a bridge in a dream, the first step always there, at Jones's feet. Through crate slats Jones saw eyes staring, men slumped in the boxes for the night, out of the wind, behind a chinking of newspaper, cardboard, fluttering plastic. Jones stopped. A canvas awning above a loading dock snapped in the breeze like a doused jib sail.

"Don't you worry, Jonesie boy," the doctor said. "We'll get her squared away. Tomorrow, in Seattle." He reached into his bag and handed Jones a vial and a syringe. "If it gets too much, the pain, you know, give her this. Only half, four or five milligrams. You can do it, right? Just find a vein."

A fire burned on the banks of the river. A circle of light breathed out and the shadows of stone-still men danced hilariously. A woman walked through the grass outside the circle; her legs were shackled by her own pants, blue jeans dropped down around her ankles, stumbling, standing, stumbling, struggling. "I know what you want," she shouted back at the circle of men. "I know what you want." She fell, laughing hideously.

The doctor was clutching Jones's hand, squeezing and shaking it, and Jones got the idea that the doctor might never let go.

Outside the motel, the same wrecked Indian stood and approached Jones. His left cowboy boot was so worn down around the heel that the bare shoe tacks gave a sharp metallic click on the cement with each crippled step. He blinked, and thrust a hand at Jones.

"My eyes hurt when I open 'em," he said. "And they hurt when I close 'em. All night I don't know what to do. I keep opening and closing my eyes."

Jones reached into his pocket and pulled a rumpled dollar loose from his wad of muster pay.

"I swear," the Indian said. "Somebody's making my eyes go black."

Jones gave him the bone. He tried to see in the man the facial lines of an Eskimo, but his skin was weathered, the lines eroded.

"SoHappy," he said.

"Me too," Jones said.

"No," the Indian said, thumping his chest. "SoHappy. Johnny SoHappy, that's me. Fucking me."

He blinked and backed away, wandering off alone, shoe tacks roughly clawing the sidewalk.

The girl was awake, shrouded in white sheets, staring at the ceiling, her breathing shallow but regular. Jones lay in the bed beside her, suffering a mild case of the spins. The walls turned, soft and summery, like the last revolution of a carousel wobbling to a stop. He looked out the window. Under the moonlight each leaf of the apple tree was a spoonful of milk.

Jones felt the girl's dry, thin fingers wrap around his wrist, like a bird clutching at a perch.

"I love you," she whispered. Her voice was hoarse and frightening.

Jones shut his eyes against the spinning room. The spinning of the room crept beneath his closed lids, and Jones opened his eyes, to no effect. The room continued to spin.

"How about you, Jones? You could just say it, I wouldn't care if it wasn't the truth. Not anymore."

Jones pressed her hand lightly.

"Where are we, Jones?" she asked. "I mean, really. What's the name of this place?"

They were a long way from Carbondale, from the home he'd seen the night they left. An oak tree holding the collapsing remains of a childhood fort, a frayed rope with knotted footholds dangling from the hatch, a sprinkler turning slowly over the grass, a lounge chair beneath a sun shade, a paper plate weighted against the wind by an empty cocktail glass.

"I'm hot," she said.

Jones lifted her out of bed. She was hot, but she wasn't sweating. Against his fingers, her skin felt dry and powdery, friable, as if the next breeze might blow it all away, and he'd be left holding a skeleton. He wrapped her in a white sheet. She hooked her arms around his neck, and Jones carried her, airy as balsa, into the aqueous green light of the hallway and down the steps.

"Where we going?" she asked.

The surface of the pool shimmered, smooth as a turquoise stone. Jones unwrapped the sheet and let it fall. The girl was naked underneath.

"Hold on," Jones said.

He walked down the steps at the shallow end, the water washing up around his ankles, his knees, his waist, and then he gently lowered the girl until her back floated on the surface.

"Don't let go," she said, flinching as she touched water. In panic, she gasped for air.

"I won't," Jones said. "Just relax."

Her skin seemed to soak in water, drink it up like a dehydrated sponge, and she felt heavier, more substantial. Her arms and legs grew supple, rising and falling in rhythm to the water. He steered her around the shallow end.

"Except in songs on the radio," she said, "nobody's ever said they love me."

Her eyes were wide and vacant, staring up through the leaves of the apple tree, out past them into the night sky, the moon, the vault of stars.

"You think anybody's watching us?" the girl asked.

Jones looked up at the rows of darkened rooms surrounding the pool. Here and there a night-light glowed. Air conditioners droned.

"I doubt it," he said.

She let her arms spread wide and float on the surface as Jones eased her toward the edge of the pool. He lifted her out and set her down on the sheet. At the deep end of the pool, below the diving board, he saw the lounge chair, its yellow webbing and chrome arms shining in the beams of underwater light. He took a deep breath and dove in. The water was as warm as the air, easing the descent from one element to the next. Jones crept along the bottom until he found the chair. Pressure rang in his ears and a dizziness spread through him as he dragged it along the length of the pool. For a moment he wanted to stop, to stay on the bottom and let everything go black; he held himself until every cell in his blood screamed and the involuntary instincts of his body craving air drove him back up and he surfaced, his last breath exploding out of him. He set the chair against the apple tree.

They sat beneath the tree while Jones caught his breath. A hot wind dried their skin.

"I liked Little Bighorn the best," the girl said.

"It was okay." Jones watched a leaf float across the pool. "You really think he's looking for you?"

"I know he is," she said. "He's got all his buddies on the police force that are saved—you know, born again."

"You want to go back there?"

The girl was quiet, then she said, "Weekends, Dad and them hunt around under bridges by rivers, looking for graffiti with satanic messages. For devil worship you need the four elements. You need earth, wind, fire, and water. That's what he says. So they look by rivers, and maybe they see some graffiti, or they find an old chicken bone and they think they really got themselves something."

It seemed an answer, wired through biblical circuitry.

"Tomorrow you're going to a hospital," Jones said. "The doctor arranged it. Everything's set."

He carried the girl upstairs and placed her on the bed. In five weeks she'd gone from a girl he'd picked up in the heartland to an old woman, her body retreating from the world, shrunken and curled and lighter by the hour, it seemed. Her hair had never grown back, and the ulcerations from early chemo treatments had so weakened her gums that a tooth had come loose, falling out, leaving a black gap in a smile that should have been seductive to the young boys back in Carbondale. The whites of her eyes had turned scarlet red. Her limbs were skeletal, fleshless and starved. She'd said she was eighteen, but now she could have passed for eighty.

"You think I'll go to hell?"

"Probably."

"Jones—"

"Well, why do you talk like that?"

"I don't know." She clutched the sheet around her neck. "When I open my mouth these things just come out. They're the only words I have."

"One of my tours," Jones said, "we were on maneuvers in the Mediterranean." A boiler exploded, he said, and a man caught fire in a pool of burning oil. Crazed, aflame, engulfed, the man ran in erratic circles on the deck, a bright, whirling light in the darkness, shooting back and forth like an errant Roman candle, while other men chased him, half-afraid to tackle the man and catch fire themselves. Finally, beyond all hope, out of his mind, the man jumped over the deck railing, into the sea. "You could hear the flames whipping in the wind as he fell," Jones said. "Then he was gone. It was the sorriest thing I ever witnessed." Afterward, he'd helped extinguish the fire, and for doing his duty he'd been awarded a dime-sized decoration for heroism.

"Everywhere we go," she said, and there was a long pause as her breath gurgled up through lungs full of fluid, "there's never any air-conditioning."

Jones held her hand, a bone. He thought she coughed this time, but again she was only trying to breathe. Suddenly he did not want to be in bed beside her. But he couldn't move.

"The Eskimos live in ice huts," he said.

"Sounds nice right now."

"It's very cold," Jones continued.

"I wish we were going there."

The girl coughed, and then curled into a fetal ball. "It's like hot knives stabbing me from inside," she said.

Jones lifted himself from the bed. He turned on the bedside lamp and took the morphine and the syringe from his shirt pocket. "The first explorers thought Eskimos roamed from place to place because they were poor," he said. "They thought the Eskimos were bums." He ripped the cellophane wrapper from the syringe, and pushed the needle into the vial, slowly drawing the plunger back until half the clear liquid had been sucked into the barrel. "They were always on the move," he said. The girl bit into the pillow until her gums bled and left an imprint of her mouth on the case. Her body had an alertness, a tension that Jones sensed in the tortured angles she held her arms at, the faint weak flex of her atrophied muscles. She raised her head and opened her mouth wide, her startled red eyes searching the room as if to see where all the air had gone. "But when you think about it, you understand that it's efficient." Jones pushed the air bubbles out of the syringe until a drop of morphine beaded like dew at the tip of the needle. "Movement is the only way for them to survive in the cold. Even their morality is based on the cold, on movement." Jones now continued speaking only to dispel the silence and the lone sound of the girl's labored breathing. He unclenched her hand from the sheets and bent her arm back, flat against the bed. "They don't have police," he said, "and they don't have lawyers or judges. The worst punishment for an Eskimo is to be left behind, to be left in the cold." Inspecting her arm, he found the widest vein possible, and imagined it flowing all the way to her heart, and drove the needle in.

McKillop had taken the girl's purse and dumped the contents on the bed. He rummaged through it and found a blue gumball, safety pins, pennies, a shopping list, and several pamphlets from which he read. "Listen," he said. " 'For centuries lovers of God and of righteousness have been praying: Let your kingdom come. But what is that kingdom that Jesus Christ taught us to pray for? Use your Bible to learn the who, what, when, why, and where of the kingdom.' " He laughed. "Ironic, huh?"

"We don't know, do we?" Jones said.

"Oh, come on," the doctor said. He took up a scrap of notepaper. " 'Blush. Lipstick—Toffee, Ruby Red. Two pair white cotton socks. Call Carolyn.' "

"Stay out of her stuff," Jones said.

"I was looking for ID," he said. "What's her name?"

Jones thought for a moment, and then said, "It's better that you don't know."

"You didn't OD her, did you?"

"No," Jones said. Once last night he'd woken to the sound of the girl's voice, calling out. She spoke to someone who was not in the room, and began to pick invisible things out of the air. Watching her struggle with these phantoms had made Jones feel horribly alone. Delirious, she ended by singing the refrain of a hymn. He said to the doctor, "I thought about it though."

"You could tell the truth. It's rather unsavory, but it's always an option."

Jones looked at the doctor. "It's too late," he said.

"I've tried the truth myself, and it doesn't work that well anyway. Half the time, maybe, but no more. What good is that? The world's a broke-dick operation.

"The big question is," McKillop said, "who's going to care?"

"Her family," Jones said. "Born again Christians."

"I was raised a Catholic." McKillop pulled a silver chain from around his neck and showed Jones a tarnished cross. "It was my mother's religion. I don't believe, but it still spooks me."

"This is against the law."

"If you sent her home, there'd be questions."

"There'll be questions anyway," Jones said. "Her stepdad's a fanatic. He'll be looking for me. He believes in what he's doing, you know?"

"I vaguely remember believing—"

"Not everything has to do with you," Jones said. He felt the sadness of language, the solitude of it. The doctor had no faith beyond a system of small ironies; it was like trying to keep the rain off by calling to mind the memory of an umbrella.

The doctor had dispensed with the nicety of a flask, and now drank straight from the bottle.

"Never made it home last night," McKillop said.

"You look it," Jones said.

"I got lucky," McKillop said. "Sort of." He wiped his lips and said, "I wish I had a donut." He pulled the green apple from his pocket, buffing it on the lapel of his wrinkled jacket. He offered the bottle to Jones. Jones shook his head. "I'd watched this woman for a long time, desired her from afar, and then suddenly there I was, in bed with her, touching her, smelling her, tasting her. But I couldn't get it up."

"Maybe you should stop drinking."

"I like drinking."

"It's not practical," Jones said.

"Quitting's a drastic measure," McKillop said. He took a bite of the apple. "For a man who gets lucky as little as I do."

"I'll see you," Jones said.

3.

The peaks no longer appeared as teeth set in a jaw, but loomed large and then vanished as mountains, becoming sheered-off walls, slopes of crushed stone, of scree and talus, outcroppings of wind-stunted trees clinging to striated rock. Reaching the pass, the air was cooler, with patches of pure white snow surviving the intense summer heat in pockets of shadow. The odometer approached one hundred thousand for what Jones guessed was the second time in the Belvedere's life. He watched the numbers slowly circle around and return to zero. Briefly the ledger seemed balanced, wiped clean, and then the moment was gone. The numbers changed, and mile one was history.

By afternoon he had crossed the bridge at Deception Pass and driven south and caught a ferry to Port Townsend. He drove west

along 101 and then veered north, hugging the shoreline of the
Strait of Juan de Fuca, passing through Pysht and Sekiu, driving
until he hit Neah Bay and the Makah Reservation, when finally
there was no more road. It had remained hot all the way west and
now a wildfire burned across the crown of a mountain rising
against the western verge of the reservation. The sky turned yellow
under a pall of black smoke. Flecks of ash sifted like snow through
the air. White shacks lined either side of the street, staggering
forward on legs of leaning cinder block, and a few barefoot children played in the dirt yards, chasing dust devils. Several girls in
dresses as sheer and delicate as cobwebs stood shielding their eyes
and staring at the fire. Sunlight spread through the thin fabric,
skirts flickering in the wind, so that each of the young girls seemed
to be going up in flames.

Jones moved slowly through town, raising a trail of white dust,
which mingled with the black ash and settled over the children, the
shacks, a scattering of wrecked cars, and then along the foot of the
mountain he followed an eroded logging road until it too vanished. A yellow mobile home sat on a bluff and behind it, hidden
by a brake of wind-crippled cedar, was the ocean. Jones heard the
surf and caught the smell of rough-churned sea. A man in overalls
came out of the mobile home—to Jones, he looked like an Eskimo. Jones switched off the ignition. The car rocked dead, but for
a moment he felt the pressure of the entire country he'd crossed at
his back, the vibration of the road still working up through the
steering column, into his hands and along his arms, becoming an
ache in his shoulders, a numbness traveling down his spine. Then
the vibrations stopped and he felt his body settle into the present.

Jones got out of the car. The man hooked a thumb in his
breast pocket, the ghost habit of a smoker. Behind cracked lips,
his teeth were rotten. He watched a retrofit bomber sweep out
over the ocean, bank high and round and circle back over the hill,
spraying clouds of retardant. The chemicals fell away in a rust-red
curtain that closed over the line of fire.

"How'd it start?" Jones asked.

"Tiny bit of broken bottle will start a fire, sun hits it right." The man lit a cigarette. "Been a dry summer. They logged that hill off mostly, and don't nobody burn the slash. Where you headed?"

Jones said he was just driving.

"Used to be a love colony down there," the man said. He pointed vaguely toward the ocean. "You get the hippies coming back now and again, looking for the old path down. But the trails all growed over." The man ran his tongue over the black gum between missing front teeth. "I thought maybe you was one of them."

"No," Jones said. "Never been here before."

"You can park, you want," he said. "There's a game trail runs partways down."

"Thanks."

"You'll see the old Zellerbach mill."

He found the abandoned mill in ruins, a twisted heap of metal. He sat on a rusted flume and pulled a patch of burnt weeds from the foundation. With a stick he chipped at the hard, dry ground, and dug out three scoops of loose dirt, wrapping them in one of the girl's shirts. When he finished, he sat against a stump, counting the growth rings with his finger until near heartwood he'd numbered two hundred years.

A clamshell chime chattered like cold teeth beneath the awning of a bait shop. Inside the breakwater, boats pulled at their moorings. Jones walked up and down the docks of the marina until he found a Livingston slung by davits to the deck of a cabin cruiser. The windows of the cruiser were all dark, canvas had been stretched across the wheelhouse, and the home port stenciled across the stern was Akutan. He lowered the lifeboat into the water, pushed off, and let himself drift quietly away from the marina.

When he'd rowed out into the shipping lane, Jones pull-started the twenty-horse Evinrude, and followed a flashing red beacon out around the tip of Cape Flattery to the ocean. He kept just outside the line of breaking waves, hugging the shore, the boat tossed high enough at times along the crest of a swell to see a beach wracked with bone-gray driftwood. Jones pulled the motor and rode the surf until the hull scraped sand. He loaded the girl into the boat, up front for ballast.

He poled himself off the sand with the oar, and then rowed. Each incoming wave rejected his effort, angling the bow high and pushing the boat back in a froth of crushed white foam. Finally he managed to cradle the boat in the trough between breaking waves. The motor kicked out of the water with a high-rev whine, and Jones steered for open sea, heading due west. Beyond the edge of the shelf, the rough surface chop gave way to rolling swells and Jones knew he was in deep water. He'd forgotten how black a night at sea was, how even the coldest, dying star seemed near and bright in the dark. He became afraid, and drew the world in like a timid child, trembling with unreasonable fears—the terrible life below him, the girl's stepfather and his fanatic pursuit, his own fugitive life in flight from this moment. If it became history he would be judged and found guilty. Spindrift raked over the bow, splashing his face. The sea heaved in a sleepy rhythm. He crossed the black stern of a container ship at anchor, four or five stories of high wall, and when he throttled back to a dead drift he heard voices from the decktop, human voices speaking in a language he did not understand.

He ran another mile and cut the engine. The round world was seamless with the night sky, undivided, the horizon liquid and invisible except for a spray of stars that flashed like phosphorescence, rising out of the water. A cool breeze whispered over the surface. August was over. He'd piled the sleeping bag with beach rocks, and then he'd cleaned the car of evidence, collected the souvenirs, the trinkets, the orange smiles, the wig, and stuffed them down into the foot of the bag, knotting it shut with nylon rope. He'd taken the Bible, opened it to the genealogy, and scratched the month and year into the margins. Jones considered the possibility, as he rocked in the trough of a swell, that all this would one day break free from its deep hold in the sea, wash to the surface, the bumper stickers from Indian battles, the decals commemorating the footpaths and wagon trails of explorers and pioneers, the resting places of men and women who'd left their names to towns and maps. And then the girl herself, identified by her remains, a story told by teeth and bones, interpreted.

Jones looped a rope tether around the handle of his flashlight and tied the other end to the sleeping bag. He checked the beam, which shone solidly in the darkness, a wide swath of white light carved out of the air. He unpacked the soil he'd collected from the collapsed mill, and sprinkled it across the sleeping bag, spreading earth from head to foot. It seemed a paltry ritual—the dirt, the light—but he was determined to observe ceremony. With his tongue he licked away a coating of salt from the rim of his lips. His hands were growing cold and stiff. He hoisted the head end of the bag over the port side and then pivoted the girl's feet around until the whole bag pitched overboard. Jones held it up a final instant, clutching the flashlight, allowing the air bubbles to escape, and then let go. Down she swirled, a trail of light spinning through a sea that showed green in the weakening beam and then went dark. In silence Jones let himself drift until, borne away by the current, he could no longer know for certain where she'd gone down.

Back within the breakwater, Jones tied the lifeboat with a slack line to a wooden cleat. The mountain had vanished from view, swallowed by darkness, but a prevailing westerly had blown the wildfire across its crown, and a flare of red-yellow flame swept into the sky. An old Makah trudged up the road, dragging a stick through the dust, leaning on it when he stopped to watch the hieroglyphic write itself in fire on the edge of the reservation. Jones sat on the dock, dangling his legs. Flakes of feathery black ash drifted through the air and fanned lightly against his face. Spume crusted and stung his lips and he was thirsty. He listened to the rhythm of the water as it played an icy cool music in the cadenced clinking of ropes and pulleys and bell buoys. Out beyond the breakwater the red and green running lights of a sailboat appeared, straggling into port. The wind lifted the voices of the sailors and carried them across the water like a song. One of the sailors shouted, "There it is." He stood on the foredeck and pointed toward the banner of flames rising in the sky.

ACKNOWLEDGMENTS

The Editors gratefully acknowledge the following:

Richard Burgin, *Boulevard*
Peter Stine, *Witness*
Speer Morgan
Bill Berlin
Gerry Coles
Glimmer Train
Iowa Review
Grand Street
Ploughshares
Asylum
Alice Crozier
Chapter One Books and Cafe, Highland Park,
   New Jersey
Chris Vitriano
Bernie from Cafe Newz, New Brunswick, New Jersey
The White Rose System, Highland Park, New Jersey
Liz Malcolm
Rob Schwartz
The Hermetic
Kitchen Facers
Sarah Pinckney
Stacy Roth (and Collins too)
Ted Pryde
Peter Lugar
Topher Dawson
Sterling

Kim Eckhouse
Fiona Grant and Milkweed Editions
Bonnie Nadell
Richard Parks
Everyone we forgot to acknowledge . . .

Special thanks to:

Bob and The Ale N'Wich
Rob Crozier
Michael Kurtin
Sam Hodder
Whitney Terell
Chris Hudak

Extra special thanks to:

Our families
Warren Bratter
Warren Frazier
Bruce Tracy and Scott Moyers
Everyone who submitted to the collection . . .